SHADOW DISTANCE

GERALD VIZENOR

SHADOW DISTANCE

A Gerald Vizenor Reader

Wesleyan University Press

PUBLISHED BY UNIVERSITY PRESS OF NEW ENGLAND • HANOVER AND LONDON

ACKNOWLEDGMENTS

"Thank You, George Raft," "Measuring My Blood," "Haiku in the Attic," and "Avengers at Wounded Knee" are reprinted from *Interior Landscapes: Autobiographical Myths and Metaphors*. Copyright © 1990 by Gerald Vizenor. University of Minnesota Press. "Envoy to Haiku" was first published in the *Chicago Review*.

"Miigis Crowns" is reprinted from *The Heirs of Columbus*. Copyright © 1991 by Gerald Vizenor. Wesleyan University Press/University Press of New England. "Victoria Park" is reprinted from *Griever: An American Monkey King in China*. Copyright © 1987 by Gerald Vizenor. University of Minnesota Press. *Griever: An American Monkey King in China* was originally published by Illinois State University/Fiction Collective as the winner of its National Fiction Competition for 1986. "Terminal Creeds at Orion" is reprinted from *Bearheart*. Copyright © 1978 and 1990 by Gerald Vizenor. University of Minnesota Press. *Bearheart* was first published in a limited paperbound edition as *Darkness in Saint Louis Bearheart* by Truck Press in September 1978. "Shadows" is reprinted from *Dead Voices*. Copyright © 1992 by Gerald Vizenor. University of Oklahoma Press.

"Almost Browne" and "Ice Tricksters" are reprinted from *Landfill Meditation: Crossblood Stories*. Copyright © 1991 by Gerald Vizenor. Wesleyan University Press/University Press of New England. "Almost Browne" was selected by the PEN Syndicated Fiction Project for newspaper and radio distribution; "Ice Tricksters" was first published as "Almost a Whole Trickster" in *A Gathering of Flowers*, edited by Joyce Carol Thomas, Harper & Row. "Tulip Browne" is reprinted from *The Trickster of Liberty: Tribal Heirs to a Wild Baronage*. Copyright © 1988 by Gerald Vizenor. University of Minnesota Press. "Trickster Photography" was published in *Exposure*. "Separatists Behind the Blinds" is reprinted from *Wordarrows: Indians and Whites in the New Fur Trade*. Copyright © 1978 by the University of Minnesota. University of Minnesota Press.

"Double Others," "Casino Coups," and "Ishi Obscura" are reprinted from *Manifest Manners: Postindian Warriors of Survivance*. Copyright © 1994 by Gerald Vizenor. Wesleyan University Press/University Press of New England. "Ishi Obscura" was first published as "Ishi Bares His Chest" in *Partial Recall: Photographs of Native North America*, edited by Lucy Lippard, New Press. "Unnameable Postindians" was, in part, an essay

Acknowledgments continue on page 343.

Man and nature trade shadow and life. . . .

All writing invites to an anterior reading of the world which the word urges and which we pur- sue to the limits of faded memory. . . .

My truth in the book is my truth outside life. Thus my life grows around my books. . . .

You will die in the mirror.

Edmond Jabès, The Book of Questions

CONTENTS

ESSAYS

SCREENPLAY

INTRODUCTION

A. Robert Lee

. . . about Indian identity I have a revolutionary fervor. The hardest part of it is
I believe we're all invented as Indians. . . . So what I'm pursuing now in
much of my writing is this idea of the
invented Indian. The inventions have become disguises. Much of the power we
have is universal, generative in life itself
and specific to our consciousness here. In
my case there's even the balance of
white and Indian, French and Indian, so
the balance and contradiction is within
me genetically. . . . There's another idea I
have worked in the stories, about terminal creeds. . . . It occurs, obviously, in
written literature and totalitarian systems. It's a contradiction, again, to balance because it's out of balance if one is
in the terminal condition. This occurs in
invented Indians because we're invented
and we're invented from traditional stat-

ic standards and we are stuck in coins and words like artifacts. So we take up a belief and settle with it, stuck, static. Some upsetting is necessary.[1]

. . . mixedbloods loosen the seams in the shrouds of identities.[2]

. . . to try to come up with a single idealistic definition of tradition in tribal culture is terminal. Cultures are not static, human behavior is not static. We are not what anthropologists say we are and we must not live up to a definition. . . . We're very complex human beings, all of us, everywhere, but especially in America and especially among tribal groups and especially mixed-bloods. Mixed-bloods represent the actual physical union of the binary of tribal and Western. In my case it would be the premiere union between the French and the Anishinabeg or Chippewa. And I didn't have any choice in that, but I'm not a victim. I imagine myself in good humor and wish to live a responsible life, and so I'm not going to fall off the edge as some imperfect person just because I'm an accident in history.[3]

1. Neal Bowers and Charles L. P. Silet, "An Interview with Gerald Vizenor," *MELUS* 8, no. 1 (1981), pp. 45–47.

2. Gerald Vizenor, "Crows Written on The Poplars: Autocritical Autobiographies," in Brian Swann and Arnold Krupat (eds.), *I Tell You Now: Autobiographical Essays by Native American Writers* (Lincoln and London: University of Nebraska Press, 1987).

3. Laura Coltelli (ed.), *Winged Words: American Indian Writers Speak* (Lincoln and London: University of Nebraska Press, 1990), p. 172.

I

One of Native America's leading writer-contemporaries who considers "Indians" to be inventions? An enrolled member of White Earth Reservation, Minnesota, whose own crossblood Anishinaabe (or Chippewa / Ojibway) descent could not more have drawn him to past legacies of Native-white encounter yet whose best-known writing displays a wholly postmodern virtuosity? A Professor of Ethnic Studies at Berkeley while at the same time an adept in the oral and improvisatory, and so anything but academic, story-telling of the trickster? Even on first acquaintance, it would be hard to doubt the singularity, the bravura unpredictability, of Gerald Vizenor.

Such, at least, has been amply borne out in a lifetime's writing that is as dissident as it has been prolific. A more unremitting nay-sayer, for instance, to "the Indian" as Other, would be hard to come by. No stereotype has been sacrosanct. The gamut runs from Puritanism's "murderous wretches" to Rousseau's "Enfants du Paradis," from Twain's daemonic "half-breed" Injun Joe to Longfellow's anodyne Princess Minnehaha, from the dime-novel's "redskins" to the circus war-parties of Cody's Wild West shows.

A key symptomatic interest in this regard has been Edward S. Curtis's sepia photographic stills, "preserved metasavages," "consumable objects of the past," as Vizenor calls them in his essay "Socioacupuncture: Mythic Reversals and the Striptease in Four Scenes" (1987). For, no less than the ubiquitous Wooden Indian of coins, barbershops, and, most notoriously, museums (especially that which involved the "cultural striptease" of Ishi, California's last Yahi survivor), Curtis, too, he sees as having played his part in the overall "colonial roadshow." In *Manifest Manners* (1994), recent essays given over to "the myths of representations of Native Americans," Vizenor in consequence has positioned himself as postindian, an ongoing pursuer of all simulations that essentialize or ossify tribal people.

Of necessity, the great roll-call of "Indian" portraiture served up by Hollywood and TV has provided further grist to his mill. His own several film courses, at Berkeley and elsewhere, have regularly begun from D. W. Griffith's early one-reelers like *The Redman and the Child* (1908) or *The Squaw's Love Story* (1911) as instances of silent histrionic played out by white actors (in redface as against the blackface of *Birth of a Nation*?). Later stop-offs include technicolor spectaculars like the Jeff Chandler *Broken Arrow* (1950) or the Chuck Connors *Geronimo*

(1962), together with the marginally less stereotypical *Cheyenne Autumn* (1964), *A Man Called Horse* (1970), or *Little Big Man* (1970). Vizenor's own film, *Harold of Orange* (1983), full of trickster double-antics and consciously disruptive of plot-line and image, precisely seeks to undermine the beguilements of this all too effortlessly watchable screen faking of "The Indian."

In this respect he has been especially severe on a confection as influential as "The Lone Ranger," initially a 1930s radio and film serial before ABC's 1949–58 TV version with its Jay Silverheels update of James Fenimore Cooper's Chingachgook in the form of the ever compliant stage-Indian "Tonto." Latterly there has been added to the roster the box-office success *Dances With Wolves* (1990), with in its wake *Thunderheart* (1991), which probes the politics of mineral and land rights, and *Incident at Oglala* (1991), a documentary of the shoot-out between AIM (American Indian Movement—founded 1968) and the FBI that led to the subsequent trial and imprisonment of Leonard Peltier. *Wolves* remains vintage Hollywood to Vizenor, replete with captivity love interest and "Vanishing America" nostalgia and with all due allowance for Kevin Costner's patent good intent or even the use of subtitles for the Sioux language.

Sport, he again points out, contributes the still unashamed nomenclature of "The Atlanta Braves," "The Cleveland Indians," and "The Washington Redskins." New Age cults, equally, bring out his humor with their would-be shamanism and ersatz "Indian" crystals and other adapted paraphernalia. On another tack, he has been no less willing to take aim at Red Power chic, from the beads and feather symbolism of 1960s Hippyism to recent "media warrior" press conferences, and even the 1973 Wounded Knee confrontations, led, as he says in *Manifest Manners*, by "a union of urban crossbloods" and "two decades after the occupation of Wounded Knee . . . is more kitsch and tired simulation than menace."

Vizenor's interests, in sum, have turned time and again both to a lived, unmythicized Native America—centered inevitably in his own crossblood experience and in "the people named the Chippewa" as one of his "narrative histories" (1984, 1987) pointedly titles them—and to the subversion, the outfantasizing, of the monumental travesty involved in the single glyph "Indian." How could so unidimensional a trope, a word, ever have done service for all of Native America's heterogeneity, the tribal cultures of Plains or Pueblo, Coast or Woodland? Vizenor gives his own emphasis to the point in *Crossbloods: Bone Courts, Bingo, and Other Reports* (1990): "More than a million people, with hundreds of distinct tribal cultures, were simulated as Indians." Here, as elsewhere, the charge is laid against the reductionism at the core of the entire savagist "pan-Indian" myth—Demonic right through to Noble—whose latest twist he takes to be the Victim Syndrome.

For victimry not only again renders Native peoples "stuck, static," but at the same time defines "them" *only* by oppression (as can be said to have happened to the Jews in Germany or the Armenians in Turkey). Which is anything but to doubt his view of Native America as a history of brutalization and massacre, the overwhelming consequence of Euro-American phobia and will to domination. That, too, he believes has held across time and space: whether in New England, Virginia, the Great Plains, the Southwest and Pacific Northwest; or in the territories that, after "discovery," became British Canada and *La Nouvelle France*; or, through post-Columbian history, in the Caribbean and following Cortés's defeat of the Aztecs and the founding of *Nueva España* in 1521, in Mexico and each other hitherto "Indian" America intruded on by the further *encomienda* and religious colonization of Spain and Portugal.

A corollary, too, for him, has been the suggestion that somehow "Indians" have never accommodated, or never been able to accommodate, to modernity. Did they not once impede the Winning of the West, pose obstacles to the frontier and manifest destiny? Vexingly, the issue has been routinely linked with alcoholism, the update of an old association to do with "firewater." Nor, in his view, have matters been especially advanced by Michael Dorris's *The Broken Cord* (1990), however poignant the author's adoption of his son Adam and his account of Fetal Alcohol Syndrome (FAS). The stance of late assumed by Dorris and Louise Erdrich that women likely to give birth to FAS-affected offspring should be obliged to have abortions (or even be imprisoned) he argues has a double-strike against it. First, alcoholism becomes all too easily an "Indian" problem. Secondly, the kind of medical or judicial intervention envisaged involves an indefensible assault on human rights.

The temptation to regard "Indians" as object not subject, granted neither their own tragic wisdom nor their own reserves of self-sustaining identity and humor, has throughout, then, drawn his fire. Likewise, he has been always ready to contest (as in "The Tragic Wisdom of Salamanders") dehistoricized assumptions about "Mother Earth," or about "Indians" as merely some ready-made forward column of American environmentalism, or about tribal Creation and Vision systems as ever an unchanging cosmology of hoop, wheel, or circle. As might readily be assumed, anthropology with its "social scientific" taxonomies ranks especially low in his estimation, with Carl Jung or Joseph Campbell as proponents of archetype, all-one-under-the-mask versions of anima and totem, also among the villainy.

He has argued for the specificity not only of his own Anishinaabe, but of each tribal community. The range spans the populous Navajo to the sparse Pacific-Northwestern Kwakiutl, with in-between or along-side, the Sioux, Laguna-Pueblo, Hopi, Zuni, Apache, Osage, Chocktaw, Chickasaw, or Nez Perce, but, most of all, the "nation" of crossbloods like himself, the *métis* of French Canada, the *mestizos* of the Americas. These latter indeed "loosen the seams," or as he says with a well-seasoned eye to history as myth, "the shrouds," of identity, a shy at "terminal" interpretation of tribal, or for that matter, quite any other human complexity.

Vizenor himself, certainly, flouts any imagined rule of what it is to be an "Indian" author, from his early haiku, other poetry, and journalism, through his memorial histories and pictomyths of the Anishinaabe people, and into any or all of his essays, short stories, autobiography, film-making, and, to date, five novels. If indeed "we're all invented as Indians," then why not by one's own appointed flights of language and image ("wordarrows" in the title of the essay-and-story collection he published in 1978), re-invent the invention?

Yet as often as his work has gone against the grain, rarely has it not been served by his endemic comic tease. This irreverent, often priapic, gift for mockery derives, as if again by birthright, from trickster story-telling or myth. It has enabled his writing, as and when required, to break with, indeed to traduce, all linear cause-and-effect and to blur or elide the borders of fact and fiction, not to say create overlaps of material, in favor of his own new-found (in one sense his very old-found) "Indian" fabulation, "Indian" baroque.

Who, exactly, then, *is* Gerald Vizenor? Or, rather, who, exactly, does *Gerald Vizenor* think he is? To both questions he might say "indeed," but never "exactly," and especially to those who write about his work.

II

The opening, full-page, black-and-white photograph in *Interior Land-scapes: Autobiographical Myths and Metaphors* (1990), offers "Clement Vizenor and son Gerald, in Minneapolis, 1936." As an image of parent-child affection it looks replete. Smiling, open-shirted, a father in fedora holds his two-year-old in protective arms. The boy, bright-eyed, wrapped, although the "subject" of the camera, appears to be monitoring its very action. Behind them lie piled-up bricks and two stern, crumbling houses, one with a curtained window. The picture contains more than a few darkest hints of prophecy.

First, Clement William Vizenor, a "reservation-born mixedblood in dark clothes," a Chippewa house-painter and feckless ladies man, within a year would be found murdered with his throat cut in another Minneapolis street. Police left the death an "unsolved," a robbery perhaps or a jilted husband's revenge, at any rate another "Indian" who had got himself killed. Fatherless, his son would quickly be deposited with relatives, or fostered out, by his unavailing yet three-times-married mother, Laverne Lydia Peterson, herself the granddaughter of dispossessed Swedish immigrants. It was a passed-around young life and anything but well-served.

As *Interior Landscapes*, his aptly named "crossblood remembrance," gives every witness, Vizenor's life in these beginning years involved two related kinds of self-authoring. One was the literal, and understandably often bruising, hard-won survival into young manhood. The other, whose signs manifested themselves as early as third grade when his outward show was overwhelmingly one of withdrawal and silence, lay in the growing compulsion to act on, to write, the "tribal tricksters, benign demons, and woodland atomies of praise and pleasure, that arose in my imagination." The name Anishinaabe, as he explains in *Summer in the Spring* (1965, 1993), actually signifies "the people of the woodland" who "drew pictures of their dream songs, visions, stories and ideas on birchbark."

The trajectory that would take him from schooling in Minnesota to military service in Japan, from graduate student to community activist and staff writer for the *Minneapolis Tribune*, and from different American professorships to visiting scholar at Tianjin University, China, and that *Interior Landscapes* tells so compellingly, bears some repetition.

For the story of his times and places, journeys and weigh-stations, always weaves intricately into, and around, the other: namely the unfolding inner story of Gerald Vizenor, author. Herein indeed lie the "tribal tricksters" of his imagination. The upshot is that, as he now looks to pass his sixtieth year, he has achieved an encompassing if still less than sufficiently recognized—and celebrated—place in the literature not only of Native America but of America at large.

III

By suitably chance symmetry, Vizenor made his literary bow at the beginning of the 1960s. In March 1960, and in honor of Robert Vizenor, the son born to him and Judith Horns (they were married in 1959 and divorced in 1969), he produced *Born in the Wind*, ten pages of privately printed, intimate and celebratory, lyrics.

Two Wings the Butterfly: Haiku Poems in English followed in 1962, fifty-six haiku given over to the four seasons with ink paintings to complete a text-and-image whole. Haiku as a form has occupied him across three decades, in part a reflection of his interest in Anishinaabe pictomyth and, more immediately, in the Japanese language and the arts of calligraphy and silkscreen which he began to acquire during military service (he had been sent to Korea but, chance again, found himself required to disembark at Yokohama and then remain stationed in Japan). This elegantly bound verse pamphlet also has the engaging, and once more contrary, distinction of having been put together by The Printing Department of the Minnesota State Reformatory. Vizenor's life, and the art to which it gives rise, again had made the unusual into the usual.

In 1950, resentful at high school, denied a coherent family life by death and abandonment, and in spirit if not in reality a drop-out, the sixteen-year-old Vizenor lied about his age and entered the Minnesota National Guard. This, too, was the ex-boyscout who had been sent to camp on one-time Anishinaabe tribal grounds. In October 1952, when he turned eighteen, he enlisted in the Army, did his training at Fort Knox, Kentucky, and by spring 1953 found himself on the troopship that, en route to Korea, would deposit him in Japan (for a sample of Vizenor's capacity for comedy at his own expense, his "July 1950: The Masturbation Papers" in *Interior Landscapes* takes some bettering). He also turned down a possible place at Officer's Candidate School with the pleasingly ingenuous words, "Well, Sir, I just want to be with the men." A near Catch-22 run of typical happenstance followed, not least on account of having a name at the end of the alphabet.

One unlikely role gave way to another: clerk, for which he trained in typing at the Army's correspondence school; once in Japan tank commander in the 70th Tank Batallion (his fellow combatants, replacement personnel selected alphabetically like himself, were nearly all of Slavic background—names beginning with "v" or "w"); NCO trainee; soldier-student in several high school equivalency correspondence courses; theater jack-of-all-trades, director, and scriptwriter in an entertainment unit based near Camp Sendai; Army serviceman in civilian clothes whose love affair with Aiko Okada took him to Matsushima and other coastal venues; and, on discharge in August 1955, intending media specialist at the Capital Engineering Institute, Washington, D.C. Minneapolis, and White Earth beyond it, could not more have seemed a world behind.

Yet other twists lay to hand. Visiting with Army friends in New York City, he sat in on classes at NYU only to find himself, through 1955–56, and by a fudge of enrollment, a full-time student. But cash was short, and from 1956 to 1960, he transferred to the University of Minnesota, majoring in Child Development and Asian Area Studies. On graduation, he married, and became a social worker in the Minnesota State Reformatory, whose printing press he would put to his own use (a county welfare job that included parts of the Leech Lake Reservation was denied him because as an "Indian" he had relatives on the client file); and, from 1962 to 1964, he returned to the university for graduate studies in Library Science and, again, Asian Studies. The early Kennedy-Johnson years, with Civil Rights, The War on Poverty, Community Action Programs, and Headstart, implicated him in another turning-point. American "minority" status seemed destined for change, whether "Negro" as then was and "Black" as was soon to be, "Hispanic" as was and "Latino" as was soon to be, or "Indian" itself with its own pending change to "Native American."

First, he left the university, in part, ironically, because his own first serious "Indian" writing, a proposed graduate thesis on *The Progress*, the White Earth Reservation newspaper founded and edited by his own Beaulieu relatives, was not considered of "academic merit." He looks back on the decision as "institutional racism." Occasional journalistic pieces, however, had begun to find a home, the majority taken up with the plight of "urban Indians." The step into full-time activism followed readily enough.

From 1964 to 1968 he became a community organizer (which on more than a few occasions involved him in going against BIA policy decisions) and the hands-on, controversial director of The American Indian Employment Center in Minneapolis. Intentionally or not, he became notable enough to merit a visit from, and to become the frequent advisor of, then Senator Walter Mondale. But in the wake of this politics of "the street"—from welfare cases to tenancy problems, health or education referrals to counseling of every stripe—another politics, this time explicitly of "the word," was to do its beckoning.

The transfer from one to the other came about mostly through his report on the trial and (the later commuted) death sentence of Thomas James White Hawk. This South Dakota mixedblood Sioux, whom Vizenor has always believed suffers "cultural schizophrenia," obsessed him from the beginning. It led to "Thomas James White Hawk," an essay published in 1968, a specific case history that at the same time pointed to the far larger symptomology of the divided call on loyalties for most Native Americans. The White Hawk case together with that of Dane Michael White, a South Dakota tribal boy of thirteen who hanged himself in the Wilkin County Jail, Breckenridge, Minnesota, after being left mainly in isolation for six weeks for truancy, were to act as latest turning-points. They led him to become, from 1968 to 1970, a full-time reporter (Molly Ivins was a co-employee) for the *Minneapolis Tribune.*

His position at the *Tribune* also took different forms: general assignment staff writer initially, editorial writer with his own byline in 1974, and contributing editor from 1974 to 1976. He has had occasion to recall, and with not a little wryness, that his very first assignment was a piece arguing in the light of Robert Kennedy's assassination that America, even so, did not amount to a violent society ("'Violence' View Challenged" ran the headline). Not only, however, had the second Kennedy killing given him the opportunity of a career in journalism, a further irony offered itself in that RFK, as Chair of the Senate Subcommittee on Indian Education, had been spearheading an improvement in school and college opportunity for young Native Americans. Then, too, like other American newspapermen before him, most celebratedly Stephen Crane or Ernest Hemingway, he found that the regimen of matching word to experience edged him more and more toward the very literary vocation that would take him out of journalism.

Other markers showed themselves. One came out of his assignment in 1972 for a seven-part editorial series on AIM, which led not only to his journalism but to an array of pastiches based on the Wounded Knee events of 1973 and the whole ensuing Banks-Means-Bellecourt FBI and legal imbroglio. Another could be seen in his growing output of poetry, haiku as ever but also a range of other verse exhibiting its own tribal reference and metaphor.

Most tellingly, he had also been seized by the emergence of new and soon to be landmark Native-written texts, successors to the Thomas Wolfe, John Steinbeck, and Kahlil Gibran he had once found himself borrowing from the Camp Schimmelfennig Military Library in Japan, itself a name worthy of Vizenor's own best satiric devising. None, in this respect, more aroused his admiration or writerly sense of getting left behind than N. Scott Momaday's *House Made of Dawn* (1968).

Momaday, he saw, had fused Navajo, Pueblo, and Kiowa story-telling into a "modern" Native American portrait set in both immediate postwar Los Angeles and "Walatowa," a likely fictionalization of Jemez Pueblo. In Dee Brown's *Bury My Heart at Wounded Knee* (1970) Vizenor warmed to history that challenged "exceptionalist" self-congratulation and, whatever Brown's own personal origins, sought a Native American perspective.

Yet another kind of marker arose out of his return to the academy and to a formal context of books and scholarship. When Lake Forest College, Illinois, asked him in 1970 to undertake a year's teaching, paradox again played its part. For the first time ever he was asked to "memorialize" his life in a *Curriculum Vitae*. The graduate student of a few years earlier had become the professor. His sponsor wanted to employ him for his haiku rather than any social science or other skill. And, for a reporter who had already seen his share of the cutting-edge, he discovered himself not a little shocked, "distracted" he called it, at the campus drug scene.

Just as quickly, however, in 1970 he stepped into a Federal Deseg-regation Program in the Park Rapids School District, Minnesota; in 1971–72 became Director of Indian Studies at Bemidji State University, Minnesota; in 1973 was awarded a Bush Foundation Leadership grant and studied at Harvard, and, after his two-year stint as editorial writer for the *Tribune*, in 1976 accepted an appointment at Berkeley in Native American Studies, which he would alternate with teaching commitments at the University of Minnesota. In 1978 Minnesota made him their James J. Hill Professor. Vizenor's fellow Minnesotan novelist, Scott Fitzgerald, must have smiled down in amusement from his Jazz Heaven at a Chair so named: Hill, as railway magnate, serves as his ironic watchword in *The Great Gatsby* for one of the Gilded Age's most unregenerate robber barons.

Through his own Nodin Press ("nodin" means "wind" in Ani-shinaabe), which he sold after a year to the book distributor Norton Stillman, he published a series of handsomely bound and printed collections like *Seventeen Chirps* (1964), *Raising the Moon Vines* (1964), *Slight Abrasions: A Dialogue in Haiku* (1966), co-written with Jerome Downes, and *Empty Swings* (1967). Other small presses and publishers, among them Callimachus, Four Winds, New Rivers, and Crowell-Collier, would be involved in issuing his transcriptions of Anishinaabe tribal history, oral lore, and myth, notably *Escorts to White Earth, 1868–1968, 100 Years on a Reservation* (1968), *anishinabe adisokan: Tales of the People* (1970), the latter a revision of *Summer in the Spring* (1965, 1981, reissued 1993), *The Everlasting Sky: New Voices from the People Named the Chippewa* (1972), and *Tribal Scenes and Ceremonies* (1976), a volume made up of reprints of his journalism and magazine writing. In 1974, however, his interests drew him to the genre that would do most to establish his reputation. He began the first of his novels, a Pilgrim's Progress or dream-quest told in part as a book-within-a-book and in part as a satyricon, which initially he published in 1978 as *Darkness in Saint Louis Bearheart*, and then, in 1990, under the revised title of *Bearheart: The Heirship Chronicles*.

In June 1983, having two years earlier married Laura Hall, a Britisher of English and Chinese-Guyanese background who had been studying at Berkeley, he left Minnesota permanently. The call to yet other change had sounded. No small move, furthermore, was involved: Vizenor and Hall stepped at once west and east, to Tianjin University, and to a China still, if uncertainly, under Maoist political rules. In due course it would yield his second novel, *Griever: An American Monkey King in China* (1987), a satiric "tribal" fable that links Anishinaabe to Asian "mind-monkey" tricksterism and takes well-aimed shies at the shibboleths of both communism and capitalism, Chinese puritanism and American profligacy.

In Spring 1984, after an interlude writing in Las Cruces and Santa Fe, New Mexico, he returned to Berkeley, first half time and then full time, appointments he held for three years. In 1987 he then followed Highway 1 the seventy or so miles south to a senior professorship in literature at UC Santa Cruz, becoming Provost of Kresge College during 1989–90. Two years later, 1991–92, saw him in the David Burr Chair of Letters at the University of Oklahoma, Norman, before accepting his present full-time position, once more in Ethnic Studies, at Berkeley. His career, too, as leading Native American writer-professor has increasingly required that he play the inveterate conferee and panelist both in America and in different international forums, with a matching run of radio and TV spots. USIA lecture and reading tours have taken him in the last decade to Canada, Japan, Germany, Italy, and Holland, interspersed with research and other trips to Britain, Scandinavia, Tanzania, Guyana, and Hong Kong.

The writing from this latter decade has amounted to a near flood, to which should be added frequently anthologized pieces like the haiku included in Louis Untermeyer's *The Pursuit of Poetry* (1970), the adroitly reflexive memoir-essay "I Know What You Mean, Erdupps MacChurbb" in *Growing Up in Minnesota: Ten Writers Remember Their Childhoods* (1976), and "Bound Feet" and "Holosexual Clown," the two extracts selected by Ishmael Reed and his fellow editors in *The Before Columbus Foundation Fiction Anthology* (1992). *Matsushima: Pine Island* (1984), likely his most substantial "haiku dreamscapes" and again a sequence synchronized to nature's seasons, confirms the continuing hold of this most preferred of his verse forms. *Beaulieu and Vizenor Families: Genealogies* (1983) and *The People Named the Chippewa: Narrative Histories* (1984, 1987) maintain his abiding interest in, and deep inward respect for, "the shadow stories," "the stories in the blood," of his tribal origins.

Wordarrows: Indians and Whites in the New Fur Trade (1978) threads seventeen sketches of "the urban reservation" into a single seam. *Earthdivers: Tribal Narratives on Mixed Descent* (1981) mixes story and reportage to locate yet other contemporary tribal experiences of the city. *Crossbloods: Bone Courts, Bingo, and Other Reports* (1990) shows the local acuity of his newspaper-trained eye, whether for the issue of museum-held tribal "remains," reservation lottery, AIM militancy, or "Indian" nomenclature. *Landfill Meditation: Crossblood Stories* (1991) offers wordplay and spoof in just measure for his own brand of magic-realist tribal story-telling. *Manifest Manners* (1994), in turn, elides story into essay and vice versa to sustain his analysis of, and wholly unrepentant rebuke to, the collusions from whatever source that have been responsible for all spurious "Indianness."

Much of this work, too, had an alternative life, as it were, not just in newspapers like the *Minneapolis Tribune* or *Twin Citian* but in Italian, French, and German translations and in, to invoke the more prominent, literary journals like *World Literature Today*, *Fiction International*, *Caliban*, *Before Columbus Review*, *Wicazo Sa Review*, *Native American Literature*, and *Zyzzyva*. Given so unceasing a creativity, it does not surprise that he established the first Native American Literature Prize, while teaching at Santa Cruz, and in 1990 proposed, and then became the editor of, the University of Oklahoma Press's *American Indian Literature and Critical Studies Series*, acting in the process as mentor to a newer generation of Native-American writers like Kimberly Blaeser, Gordon Henry Jr., and Betty Louise Bell.

No sense of Vizenor, man or writer, however, could be complete without reference to *Interior Landscapes: Autobiographical Myths and Metaphors* (1990), quite his most inviting self-chronicle and deservedly winner of the PEN Oakland Josephine Miles Award. Like "Crows Written on the Poplars: Autocritical Autobiographies," a soliloquy on tribal history and the creative vocation that he contributed to Arnold Krupat's *I Tell You Now: Autobiographical Essays by Native American*

Writers (1987), it makes, too, a necessary context for his latest novels. These include the "comic discourse" of mixedblood fortunes in *The Trickster of Liberty: Tribal Heirs to a Wild Baronage* (1988), the teasing and about-face quincentennial "tribal story" of Columbus-as-Mayan in *The Heirs of Columbus* (1991), and the totemic parables of mixedblood encounter with urban society as elicited by the bear-woman Bagese in *Dead Voices* (1992).

Introducing *Narrative Chance: Postmodern Discourse on Native American Indian Literatures* (1989), an essay collection under his editorship given over to "translation and representation in tribal literature," Vizenor insists that "Native American Indian stories are told and heard in motion." The point could as readily apply not only to his own writing but to his own life. "Motion," or put another way "chance," can be said to have been his one constant. "Envoy to Haiku" offers a most exact summary. "Chance and the contradictions of tribal and national identities," it observes, "would become my sources of inspiration as a creative writer."

The Native America he sees himself obliged to confront, shaped by ancient footfalls yet ongoing and unfinished whether off or on reservations, endlessly various in tribal and crossblood nuance yet so often simulated as but the one "pan-Indian" phenomenon, has thus called from him efforts both of de-invention and invention. Across a rare show of styles and genres, he has given himself both to the reinscription of quite America's oldest narrative(s) and—in response to the ebbs of change and transformation and in Ezra Pound's lustrous phrase— to the resolve, the obligation, to "make it new."

IV

The selections of Vizenor's work that make up *Shadow Distance* are aimed to be at once "representative" and to confirm the vital alertness, the edge, of his powers of observance and fabulation. Such, to be sure, is anything but to diminish the substantiality of his sense of the world, the dense, lived historicity of the "Indianness" around which he has from the beginning woven image and story. Felipa Flowers, reservation *doyenne* and but one of the Jacobean plenty of a cast in *The Heirs of Columbus*, supplies a pointer. She is made to observe that "the world was united in clever tribal stories, imagination, memories." Something of this Vizenor credo, as it shows itself in the general contour of his writing, virtually invites emphasis.

Haiku, for all its objectivism, has been an especially intimate signature for Vizenor, and rarely more so than with regard to the natural order of landscape, birds, trees, animals, insects. The link, too, between haiku and Native American inheritance is made clear in "Envoy to Haiku." "Tribal dream songs and haiku," Vizenor notes, "are concentered in nature." In making his own haiku observe the play of senses as ceremony, he also aspires to emulate the spirituality of Matsuo Bashō, the classic master who (he can hardly forbear pointing out the contrast) happened to write "at the same time that my tribal ancestors encountered the colonists and their diseases."

Two Wings the Butterfly, his first collection, offers this exquisite drama:

> Long after the clouds
> Petals fell from slender stems:
> Clinging to the rain.

Seventeen Chirps likens the silhouette of human movement to that of a wading bird:

> We ran through the rye
> Like the crane conducts himself
> Across the lake.

Empty Swings contains its own dream vision of Clement Vizenor:

> With the moon
> My young father comes to mind
> Walking the clouds.

It little surprises that Vizenor should think that haiku "touched my imagination and brought me closer to a sense of tribal consciousness."

Matsushima: Pine Islands, whose Introduction invokes Bashō as emphasizing "commonplace experiences in haiku" and "the use of ordinary words in a serious manner," pursues these touchstones in a variety of ways. The most laconic cameo can find a place:

> fat green flies
> square dance across the grapefruit
> honor your partner

A Wallace Stevens orchestration of movement and sound like that of
"Sunday Morning" can readily be brought to mind:

> clothesline musical
> sheets dance with the wild wind
> thunderous applause

A simplest scene can remind of a tree full of sacred meaning and
association:

> cedar cones
> tumble in a mountain stream
> letters from home

Yet if a poem even more explicitly taken up with Anishinaabe legacy
were called for, reflecting Vizenor's overall sense of Native fortunes at
American hands, then "White Earth: Images and Agonies" surely hits
the mark. The contemplative irony is characteristic:

> late october sun
> breaks over the cottonwoods
>
> tricksters
> roam the rearview mirrors
> government sloughs
>
> colonial remembrance cards
> capture trees
> cultures close for the season
>
> beaded crucifixion
> double over in the reeds
>
> shamans at the centerfolds
> pave the roads
> publish their poems
>
> fiscal storms
> close the last survival school

animals at the treelines
send back the hats and rusted traps

touchwood at bad medicine

"Bad medicine," indeed, can be said to have done its work, America's effort to reduce its tribal cultures to the "colonial remembrance" of ruins and relics. Yet against every uncertainty, the landgrabs, the consumerism, the "fiscal storms," the bad hunting, Native America survives, and not least, as Vizenor indicates in a nice touch of reflexivity, through the "shamanism" of its presentday poets.

To this end, too, the four chapters from the twenty-nine that make up *Interior Landscapes* speak to his own "survivance," his own writing-in. "Thank you, George Raft" delivers a teasing genealogy, the "thirties screen star" as Laverne Lydia Peterson's fantasy of his good-time but darkly fated actual father. "Measuring My Blood" takes that genealogy back into Anishinaabe mythology, the contest of Naanabozho, the "compassionate trickster," with the Evil Gambler (the same life-death opposition appears in *Bearheart*), as a frame for the eventual "chance" murder in Minneapolis of Clement William Vizenor. "Haiku in the Attic" bespeaks the coming writer, the would-be tranquil poet and story-writer behind the then recent father, student, library assistant, European voyager, and hospital orderly. "Avengers at Wounded Knee," one of his several accounts of AIM at the Leech Lake Reservation and then Wounded Knee, underscores "political" Vizenor, his unwavering skepticism in the face both of intransigent state authority and of a "revolutionary tribal caravan."

Vizenor's fiction gives every ground to be called tribal-cum-postmodern, a radically self-aware and contemporary satiric trickster-ism that as easily invokes Jabès, Barthes, Lyotard, or Foucault as bear ceremonial, ghost dance, or dream-catcher. *Bearheart* with its "Cedarfair Circus . . . traveling to the fourth world" uses the *peregrinus* motif as a way of depicting—imagining—a futuristic America depleted in like measure of oil and spiritual balance. Each fantastical, motleyed pilgrim, from Proude Cedarfair himself to Benito Saint Plumero ("Bigfoot") with his phallic monster "President Jackson," or from Lilith Mae Farrier and her two canine lovers to Bishop Parasimo, wearer of "metamasks," or from the apostolic crows to the dogs Pure Gumption and Private Jones, embarks on a "magical flight" from the Mississippi headwaters to the sacred Chaco Canyon in search of a window into the tribal Fourth World. But to reach the harmony they seek, they must pass through, indeed at times ape and mirror, the reeling distortions of a world ruled by the Evil Gambler of Anishinaabe myth as "The Monarch of Unleaded Gasoline," cohorts like the "food fascists," "kitsch" AIM terrorists, and, above all, a mainstream hierarchy that seeks to preempt any culture or behavior out of synch with its own writ. Cedarfair's occasional resort to "panic holes" adds a further piquancy. "Terminal Creeds at Orion" so directs its surrealized, and deflationary, satire at hegemony, one-way political or cultural power systems.

Each of Vizenor's other novels yields a similar playfield, story-telling full of enciphered, if on occasion oblique, comic travesties and turns. *Griever: An American Monkey King in China* sets its hero, Griever de Hocus, the "mixedblood tribal trickster, a close relative to the old mind monkeys," to subvert through antics both terrestrial and aerial a Maoist China turned murderously against its own citizenry. "Victoria Park," with its portrait of a "revolutionary" world still full of colonial imprints and in which communists have become "shadow capitalists," gives the flavor of the novel's carnivalesque, its burgeoning textual fecundity (kept just the right side of overspill) itself the analogue of political liberation. *The Trickster of Liberty*, whose Tulip Browne with her "windmills" and "natural power" obsessions belongs to an iron-ically named "baronage" of mixedblood trickster-liberators, equally seeks to combat the "word holds" in which tribal people have been placed. Amid the forays he terms "socioacupuncture" against anthro-pology, against often mis-directed (and impossibly feuding) university departments of "Indian Studies," or against the "colonial necrophilia" of museums, the novel also offers the following working ethos: "The trick, in seven words, is to elude historicism, racial representations, and remain historical."

Casinos, "tribal remains," the Pocahontas legend, fellow Native authors like James Welch, Louise Erdrich, or Leslie Marmon Silko, the *métis* leader Louis Riel, again the fictional mixedblood Browne baron-age, and as title-figure and presiding spirit, the elusive Genoese "Co-lumbus" and his entrepreneurial and lazer-toting heir "Stone Colum-bus," all play their connecting roles in *The Heirs of Columbus*, quite one of Vizenor's most confidently imagined texts. "Miigis Crowns," a chapter whose mystery-story shadows the far larger historical mystery of the John Smith–John Rolfe–Pocahontas Anglo-American "founda-tion" myth, yet again reenacts, mimics, the enfolding of the one tribal story inside the other. To term *Heirs* a novel of "mixed means" would be to understate by half.

Dead Voices, however, deploys an altogether sparer idiom. Based on the seven-card chance game of wanaki, it acts as a cycle of spells or charms—in turn of stones, bears, fleas, squirrels, mantises, crows, beavers, and tricksters—each under the aegis of the Oakland bear-women Bagese and each passed on through the narrator Laundry. In their counter-voices, for which "Shadows" as the opening chapter acts as prologue, once again the dominant culture of the "wordies" is made subject to both an exorcism and a healing.

Vizenor's short stories share the same goal, not to say ingenuity. "Almost Browne," a tease on textual "Indians" under the guise of the "tribal blank book business"; "Ice Tricksters," a devious, witty send-up of consumer sculptures of "Indians"; and "Trickster Photographer," a take on Edward Curtis in the person of "Tune Browne," who creates his own countering (though equally fossilizing) portrait-album of "white senior citizens"—each rank as his variation on the fiction of fact. "Separatists Behind the Blinds," on the other hand, might be thought to do the reverse, the account of a proposed Communist Party–Urban Indian alliance (with the BIA in the wings) that mock-reportorially conjures political "fact" into literary "fiction."

Vizenor's essays exhibit the same well-managed ventriloquy. As literal or as full of combat and conviction as may be their point of departure, they can be playful (at times outright fictional as in parts of "The Tragic Wisdom of Salamanders" and "Reversal of Fortunes"), uninhibitedly invoke literary or other high theory, or circle around and across the "facts" as if unwilling to rest until all bases have been covered. Vizenor's art of the essay, in the Great Tradition of, say, Hazlitt or Baldwin, resides always in this identifying command of voice, in his case exacting, no respecter of piety, and ironic in a way that can tease even its own self-awareness.

"Double Others" and "Casino Coups," both from *Manifest Manners*, tackle, respectively, the distortions of "tribal identity" brought on by the historic "literature of dominance," and by the gains (the means to sovereign nationhood) and losses ("casino avarice with no moral traditions is a mean measure of tribal wisdom") that have come about in consequence of the 1988 Indian Gaming Regulatory Act. "Unnameable Postindians" equally looks two ways: at the "wannabe" phenomenon and mistranslation of tribal nomenclature and humor and, conversely, at "the *real* stories, the *real* names, nouns, and pronouns, heard in the *unnameable* cultures of tribal consciousness." "The Tragic Wisdom of

Salamanders" offers a "survivance meditation," a parable-essay on the burdens of, and antidotes to, "chemical civilization," while "Reversal of Fortunes," the Aristotelian echo in its title deliberate, both discusses, and becomes, another kind of "trickster discourse" on Vizenor's own imaginative "discovery" in his reportage and fiction (and in that of fellow teacher-writers like Louis Owens and Kimberly Blaeser) of contemporary Native America as "a postindian tribal nation."

"Crossbloods" ranges from reservation gaming to AIM business investment, from Anishinaabe and other tribal land claims to the incarceration of Thomas White Hawk, in supplying an anatomy, a wide-ranging if inevitably selective portrait, of crossbloods as "a postmodern tribal bloodline." "Sand Creek Survivors" links the massacre of nearly three hundred peaceably encamped Cheyennes by Colorado militia in 1864—and other massacres like those of the Blackfeet at Marias River or the Sioux at Wounded Knee—to the suicide and funeral of Dane Michael White in the 1970s, a latest massacre, albeit of one, yet also a latest instance of a survivor in "the memories of the tribal 'caretakers of the lands.'" In "The Shaman and Terminal Creeds" Vizenor explores a "case" of Anishinaabe/Ojibway spirituality as also borne down ambiguously through time, and in "Shadows at La Pointe," a similar past-to-present reference, the equally ambiguous carry-through implications for the tribal *métis* of the Fond du Lac treaty signed without their participation both by leaders of the Anishinaabe "woodland communities" and by John Quincy Adams.

"Ishi Obscura" holds a special place in the Vizenor oeuvre. "Ishi was never his name" offers but the opening strike in a deconstruction of the Yahi survivor as "simulation," the California "man of stone" and "racial photograph" made over into the "aboriginal" Last of the Vanishing Americans. Tables get turned exquisitely. Who is to be thought "the savage," Ishi or the mining prospectors who "found" him? Who constitutes "the other," the Yahi world or "the lonesome and melancholy civilization" that brought on its demise? Who, as it were, proved the subtler linguist, Ishi or Edward Sapir?

The essay does not shy, however, from contradictions that directly involve the essay writer himself. If Ishi acts as his own "Indian" forerunner at Berkeley, living out his days (at the well-meant behest of Alfred Kroeber) in the production of "Indian heritage" for the university's Museum of Anthropology, is there not a classic irony that Vizenor should have pursued few themes more tenaciously than the "invention of the Indian"? If Ishi "should be honored because he never learned to slow his stories down to be written and recorded," is it not

Vizenor as one of print's literary stalwarts who makes the point? Yet, however the play of affinity or contradiction between them is to be understood, one thing remains certain. Inside or outside the museum, both have won their own unique "tenure" in Native American culture.

V

Of necessity, and rightly, Gerald Vizenor belongs as a major player in "The Native American Renaissance," the preeminence of talent that runs diversely from D'Arcy McNickle (Cree/Salish) and N. Scott Momaday (Kiowa) to, among others, Leslie Marmon Silko (Laguna Pueblo), Louise Erdrich (Chippewa), James Welch (Blackfeet), Paula Gunn Allen (Laguna-Sioux), Linda Hogan (Chickasaw), Joy Harjo (Creek), Simon Ortiz (Acoma), and Wendy Rose (Hopi-Me-Wuk). In their writing-in of Native America, as in the parallel writing-in of African, Latino, and Asian America, ethnicity like gender finds new voice, a multicultural repossession of the word. Where once ethnicity might have been an assumption of margin, periphery, border, even silence, as against an agreed, and somehow unethnic, literary-historical mainstream, that simply no longer holds. Nor can rearguard nostalgia about a long-ago "agreed," or canonical, American culture make it so hold.

   In a BBC interview shortly before his death, James Baldwin was asked by the journalist Frank Delaney if he thought being black, gay, and raised in the Harlem of the Depression, had told against him as a writer. "No," he replied, "I think looking back that I had all the aces." For Gerald Vizenor, postindian crossblood, heterosexual, abandoned in the city, and who in *Interior Landscapes* remembers with considerable poignancy how a child actually mistook him for Baldwin at a literary reading given when the novelist was already ill of cancer, something of the same applies. *Shadow Distance: A Gerald Vizenor Reader* offers witness.

AUTOBIOGRAPHY

THANK YOU, GEORGE RAFT

George Raft was an inspiration to my mother and, in a sense, he was responsible for my conception. She saw the thirties screen star, a dark social hero with moral courage, in the spirited manner of my father, a newcomer from the White Earth Reservation.

"The first time I saw your father he looked like George Raft, not the gangster but the dancer. He was handsome and he had nerve," my mother told me. "The first thing he said to me was, 'I got lots of girls but I always like new ones.' He came by in a car with one of his friends. Nobody would talk like that now, but that's how we got together."

I was conceived on a cold night in a kerosene heated tenement near downtown Minneapolis. President Franklin Delano Roosevelt had been inaugurated the year before, at the depth of the Great Depression. He told the nation, "The only thing we have to fear is fear itself." My mother, and millions of other women stranded in cold rooms, heard the new president, listened to their new men, and were roused to remember the movies; elected politicians turned economies, but the bright lights in the depression came from the romantic and glamorous screen stars.

George Raft appeared in four movies that year: he danced with Carole Lombard in *Bolero*; as a paroled convict in *All of Me*, he and his lover leapt to their death from a hotel window; in *Limehouse Blues*, he played a mixedblood Chinese racketeer; and he portrayed a Mexican bullfighter in *The Trumpet Blows* and received some of the worst reviews of his career. My mother might have seen him in three movies the year before she met my father and became pregnant: Raft was a romantic detective in *The Midnight Club*; in *Pick-Up* he was a taxicab driver who gave a paroled women shelter in bad weather; and he was a nineties neighborhood gang leader in *The Bowery*. The Italian mixedblood actor and my father were swarthy, and they both wore fedoras. My father must have smiled on screen; he might have flipped a coin and overturned the depression in the winter tenement of my conception. My mother remembers the romantic dancers in the movies; that night she might have been Carole Lombard.

LaVerne Lydia Peterson, my mother, was seventeen years old, a white high school dropout. Lovey, as she was known to her best friends, was tall, thin, timid, and lonesome that winter. She was the eldest daughter of Lydia Kahl and Robert Peterson of Minneapolis. Her father was a bartender on the northside.

Clement William Vizenor, or Idee, a nickname and a tribute to his eyes, was twenty-four years old, a reservation-born mixedblood in dark clothes; he was a house painter and lived with his mother, two sisters, and four brothers. Everett, or Pants, the youngest, was seventeen, the same age as my mother. Idee, Lawrence, whose nickname was Tuffy, Jeek, and Bunny, who had been paroled from the reformatory, worked as painters for the same contractor. When they could not find work as mixedbloods, they presented themselves as Greeks; at last they were hired as Italians. They were told then that Indians did not live in houses and would not know how to paint one. Later, they corrected their identities; their employer was amused but not convinced.

My parents were married in the spring at Immanuel Lutheran Church. My father was a Roman Catholic and my mother was three months pregnant. I was born October 22, 1934, on a clear balanced morning at General Hospital in Minneapolis. LaVerne remembered the labor and pain of my birth under the sign of Libra that Monday. She was in the hospital for ten days. She said: "My feet tingled when I got up to leave, I could hardly walk. Funny how I can still remember that feeling." My first name was recorded on the certificate of birth, but my second and surname were not entered, for some reason, until eighteen years later. Adoption may have been a consideration, but no one would admit to that now.

George Raft was the inspiration of my conception; he gave his best performance that night, but he was not there for the burdens and heartache that came later. "Clement was a womanizer," my mother confessed to me. "I was out for a walk and there he was at a local bar between two women. Al Jolson was singing 'About a Quarter to Nine.' Whenever I hear that song I still think about what I saw then. I walked

home, sat outside, and cried. I wished someone loved me that much."
The song, which was a top hit on Your Hit Parade in 1935, ends with
these words: "The world is gonna be mine, this evening, about a
quarter to nine." My mother and father lived together for about a year.

My mother believed in the love that was promised by families, but
her father was an alcoholic and there were harsh memories at home.
"We waited in our winter clothes," she remembered, at night with her
brother and sister. When her father came home drunk and violent, she
said, "we would run out the other door to escape him." I heard these
stories, but he was never drunk around me. My mother said he loved
me. "He was tolerant in a way he was not with his own children."

Robert, my maternal grandfather, tended bar at the 305 Club, a
tavern on East Broadway. I was there several times with my grandfather; the bad breath, of course, but those patrons in the booths were
so generous to a child. They gave me their brightest coins, and peanuts
to feed the squirrels out back. I remember that tavern, the warm people
and rough boards on the porch, and the tame squirrels that ate from
my hand. Robert Peterson hated the world when he turned to alcohol,
but he cared for me. I might have been the one last courteous measure
of his mortality. A decade later, and a few months before his death, I
was able to care for him in a way that brought us both pleasure. Lydia,
my grandmother, had locked his clothes and other properties in a
trunk as punishment. I opened the trunk one afternoon, when the coast
was clear; he carried the clothes away in brown paper bags. I walked
two blocks with my grandfather and paid his last fare on the streetcar.
He pawned his rings and sold his clothes, but he never asked me for
money. Robert died a pauper in a transient hotel downtown, poisoned
with alcohol. Lydia never knew the trunk was empty when she gave it
to the Salvation Army.

LaVerne was insecure and sensitive to trickster stories. She did not
understand my grandmother, and she could not appreciate the critical
nature of tribal humor. "Alice Beaulieu kidded me about my skinny
legs," she told me, "and at that time I was very self-conscious." My
grandmother cared for me then; we lived in a tenement downtown. My
father painted houses by day with his brothers, and gambled at night;
he played poker and other games in backrooms at taverns and cocktail
clubs. Some relatives believe that my father gambled at clubs that were
owned by organized crime families. Was my father murdered for his
bad debts? My mother said that the detective who investigated the
crime told her to forget about the whole thing. "You're a young
women, better not look into this." LaVerne took his advice and never

said a word about the death of my father. She told me he had died in an accident. My mother had been taught to bear her wounds and burdens in silence. She was worried, curious, and bound to please; these common leads in the depression restrained her memories, a nuisance in the rush to decadence.

F. Scott Fitzgerald's *Tender Is the Night*, the popular novel of tragic hedonism, alcoholism, mental harm, and moral descent, was published in the year of my birth. Fitzgerald, the most gifted writer of his generation, was born in Saint Paul, about ten miles from our crossblood tenement, but he lived in a world removed by economic promises, a natural decadent paradise. The common social pleasures of his characters would have been felonies on the reservation. My uncles were convicted of crimes that would have been comedies of the heart at white parties on Summit Avenue and Crocus Hill.

LaVerne loved the music of the time; she matured in the depression. Some of her memories were tied to the sentimental phrases in popular songs. Alice, my grandmother, would remember the depression on the reservation, almost with humor. Her children and grandchildren lived with her, and her envies in a tenement were comic. My father, and his brothers, told better stories than the nabob novelists. The tribal tricksters in their stories were compassionate, crossbloods, and they liberated the mind.

MEASURING MY BLOOD

Alice Beaulieu, my grandmother, told me that my father was a tribal trickster with words and memories; a compassionate trickster who did not heed the sinister stories about stolen souls and the evil gambler. Clement William must have misremembered that tribal web of protection when he moved to the cities from the White Earth Reservation.

Nookomis, which means grandmother, warned her trickster grandson that the distant land he intended to visit, in search of his mother who had been stolen by a wind spirit, was infested with hideous humans, "evil spirits and the followers of those who eat human flesh." Naanabozho was the first tribal trickster on the earth. He was comic, a part of the natural world, a spiritual balance in a comic drama, and so he must continue in his stories. "No one who has ever been within their power has ever been known to return," she told her grandson. "First these evil spirits charm their victims by the sweetness of their songs, then they strangle and devour them. But your principle enemy will be the great gambler who has never been beaten in his game and who lives beyond the realm of darkness." The trickster did not heed the words of his grandmother.

Naanabozho paddled by canoe to the end of the woodland and took a path through the swamps and over high mountains and by deep chasms in the earth where he saw the hideous stare of a thousand gleaming eyes. He heard groans and hisses of countless fiends gloating over their many victims of sin and shame. The trickster knew that this was the place where the great gambler had abandoned the losers, the spirits of his victims who had lost the game.

The trickster raised the mat of scalps over the narrow entrance to the wiigiwaam. The evil gambler was inside, a curious being, a person who seemed almost round; he was smooth, white, and wicked.

"So, Naanabozho, you too have come to try your luck," said the great gambler. His voice was horrible, the sound of scorn and ridicule. Round and white, he shivered. "All those hands you see hanging around the wiigiwaam are the hands of your relatives who came to gamble. They thought as you are thinking, they played and lost their lives in the game. Remember, I demand that those who gamble with me and lose, give me their lives. I keep the scalps, the ears, and the hands of the losers; the rest of the body I give to my friends the wiindigoo, the flesh eaters, and the spirits I consign to the world of darkness. I have spoken, and now we will play the game."

Clement William Vizenor lost the game with the evil gambler and did not return from the cities. He was a house painter who told trickster stories, pursued women, and laughed most of his time on earth. He was murdered on a narrow street in downtown Minneapolis.

"Giant Hunted in Murder and Robbery Case," appeared as a headline on the front page of the *Minneapolis Journal*, June 30, 1936. The report continued: "Police sought a giant Negro today to compare his fingerprints with those of the rifled purse of Clement Vizenor, 26 years old, found slain yesterday with his head nearly cut off by an eight-inch throat slash.

"Vizenor, an interior decorator living at 320 Tenth Street South, had been beaten and killed in an alley. . . . He was the second member of his family to die under mysterious circumstances within a month. His brother, Truman Vizenor, 649 Seventeenth Avenue Northeast, was found in the Mississippi river June 1, after he had fallen from a railroad bridge and struck his head.

"Yesterday's slashing victim, who was part Indian, had been employed by John Hartung, a decorator. One pocket had been ripped out of the slain man's trousers. His purse lay empty beside him. Marks in the alley showed his body had been dragged several feet from the alley alongside a building."

The *Minneapolis Tribune* reported that the arrest of a "Negro in Chicago promised to give Minneapolis police a valuable clue to the murder of Clement Vizenor, 26-year-old half-breed Indian, who was stabbed to death in an alley near Washington avenue and Fourth street early June 27. Vizenor's slaying was unsolved." The murder was never solved, and no motive was ever established. Racial violence was indicated in most of the newspaper stories, but there was no evidence in the investigations that race was a factor in the murder. My father could have been a victim of organized crime. There was no evidence of a struggle; he had not been robbed; the police would not establish a motive for the crime. There were several unsolved homicides at that time in Minneapolis.

The picture of my father published in the newspaper was severed from a photograph that shows him holding me in his arms. This is the last photograph, taken a few weeks before his death, that shows us together. Clement wore a fedora and a suit coat; he has a wide smile. We are outside, there is a tenement in the background; closer, a heap of used bricks. I must remember that moment, my grandmother with the camera, our last pose together.

The *Minneapolis Tribune* reported later that the police had "arrested a half-breed Indian in a beer parlor near Seventh avenue south and Tenth street and are holding him without charge for questioning in connection with the slaying, early Sunday, of Clement Vizenor. . . . The man who, according to police, was drunk, was picked up after making statements that indicated he might know who Vizenor's assailant was. He is alleged to have claimed knowledge of who Vizenor's friends were, and of many of the murdered man's recent activities. . . . The murder was blamed by police upon any one of a growing number of drunken toughs roaming the Gateway district almost nightly, armed with knives and razors. The killing of Vizenor climaxes a series of violent assaults upon Gateway pedestrians in recent weeks by robbers who either slugged or slashed their victims."

In another report, the police "sought the husband of a former New York showgirl for questioning in connection with the knife murder of Clement Vizenor. . . . The man sought is believed to be the same who left with Vizenor from a cafe at 400 Tenth street south about five hours before the murder. Alice Finkenhagen, waitress at the Tenth street cafe, gave police a good description of the man who called Vizenor to come outside. Detectives partially identified the showgirl's husband as that man. Also they learned this man had resented Vizenor's attentions to his showgirl wife.

"Vizenor was called from the cafe at about 12:30 a.m. Sunday. Later he appeared at his home, then left again. His body was found at 5:30 a.m., his throat slashed, in an alley near Washington and Fifth avenues south. Police also were holding three half-breed Indians for questioning, in the case. Vizenor was a half-breed."

The report continues: "A former New York showgirl and her husband were released by Minneapolis police Thursday after questioning failed to implicate them as suspects in the knife murder. . . . Police learned that Vizenor's attentions to the showgirl had been resented by her husband. But that difference was amicably settled long ago, detectives found out."

The *Minneapolis Tribune* reported later that "Captain Paradeau said he was convinced Clement had been murdered but that robbery was not the motive. The slain youth was reported to have been mild tempered and not in the habit of picking fights. Police learned he had no debts, and, as far as they could ascertain, no enemies."

The Last Photograph

clement vizenor would be a spruce
on his wise return to the trees
corded on the reservation side
he overturned the line
colonial genealogies
white earth remembrance
removed to the cities at twenty three

my father lived on stories
over the rough rims on mason jars
danced with the wounded shaman
low over the stumps on the fourth of july

my father lied to be an indian
he laughed downtown
the trickster signature to the lights

clement honored tribal men at war
uniforms undone
shadows on the dark river
under the nicollet avenue bridge

tribal men burdened with civilization
epaulets adrift
ribbons and wooden limbs
return to the evangelists
charities on time

catholics on the western wire
threw their voices
treaties tied to catechisms
undone in the woodland

reservation heirs on the concrete
praise the birch
the last words of indian agents
undone at the bar

clement posed in a crowded tenement
the new immigrant
painted new houses pure white
outback in saint louis park

our rooms were leaded and cold
new tribal provenance
histories too wild in the brick
shoes too narrow

clement and women
measured my blood at night

my father
holds me in the last photograph
the new spruce
with a wide smile
half white
half immigrant
he took up the cities and lost at cards

Clement Vizenor was survived by his mother, Alice Beaulieu; his wife, LaVerne Peterson; three brothers, Joseph, Lawrence, and Everett; two sisters, Ruby and Lorraine; and his son, Gerald Robert Vizenor, one year and eight months old. When my father was murdered, I was living with my grandmother, aunts, and uncles in a tenement at 320 Tenth Street South in Minneapolis.

Twenty-five years later I met with Minneapolis police officials to review the records of their investigation. I was, that summer, the same age as my father when he was murdered. There was some resistance, some concern that my intentions were not personal but political; the police must be defensive about crimes they have never solved. A thin folder was recovered from the archives. The chief of detectives was surprised when he examined the file; he saw his name on a report and remembered that he was the first officer called to investigate the crime. He explained that he was a new police officer then and defended his trivial report. "We never spent much time on winos and derelicts in those days. . . . Who knows, one Indian vagrant kills another."

"Clement Vizenor is my father."

"Maybe your father was a wino then," he said, and looked at his watch. "Look kid, that was a long time ago. Take it on the chin, you know what I mean?"

I knew what he meant and closed the investigation on an unsolved homicide. The detective must have been the same person who told my mother to move out of town and forget what had happened. She tried to forget and left me with my grandmother in the tenement. Later, my mother placed me in several foster homes.

I hear my father in that photograph and imagine his touch, the turn of his hand on my shoulder, his warm breath on my cheek, his word trickeries, and my grandmother behind the camera. My earliest personal memories are associated with my grandmother and my bottle. She would hide my bottle to wean me in the trickster manner because, she said later, I carried that bottle around all day clenched between my front teeth. She reconsidered the trickster method, however, when I learned the same game and started to hide her bottles of whiskey. She might have forgotten where she placed the bottles, mine and hers, and then told stories, compassionate reunions of our past. I remember the moment, the bottles, and the stories, but not the camera. My father and that photograph hold me in a severed moment, hold me to a season, a tenement, more than we would remember over the dark river.

Alice Beaulieu continued her career downtown in a tenement, poor but never lonesome. She was in her sixties when she married a blind man in his forties. I was eighteen, home on leave from the military at the time, and proud to wear my new uniform to a reception. My grandmother was in the kitchen, in the arms of her new husband. "He's a lusty devil," she whispered to me, "and thinks I'm beautiful, so don't you dare tell him any different." She was a lover, favored in imagination, and she was plump and gorgeous that afternoon.

Alice and Earl Restdorf lived in a narrow dark apartment on LaSalle Avenue near Loring Park. Earl was pale, generous, and sudden with his humor. He repaired radios, a sacrament to sound, and collected radios that needed repair. Cabinets, chassis, tubes, and super-heterodynes were stacked at the end of the small dining room. My grandmother would sit on the side of a double bed, because she had never had a secured, private bedroom in the tenement, and chew snuff when she was older. Earl did not approve of her tobacco habits. Alice stashed soup cans in secret places to catch her brown spit; she pretended that her husband could not smell the snuff or hear the juice hit the bottom of the can. He smiled, folded in a chair near his radios.

My grandmother paid my son a dollar each time we visited to hold her pinches of snuff a secret. Robert was two and three years old when he learned the pleasures of secrets. She loved to tease and praise children, her grandchildren and great-grandchildren, and when she laughed on the side of the bed her cheeks bounced and her stomach leapt under the worn patch pockets on her plain print dresses. Alice Beaulieu was gorgeous. Robert has never told a soul about her juice cans at the side of the bed.

HAIKU IN THE ATTIC

Robert Vizenor was three months old when we moved into a narrow attic apartment in Prospect Park near the University of Minnesota. Judith Horns Vizenor had been an elementary school teacher and she would return to graduate school in education. Our apartment was a summer adventure; there was a kitchen area, but the sink was in the bathroom. We bathed and washed dishes in the bathtub. I copied hiragana and wrote haiku on the low slope of the ceiling. Fifty dollars a month included the back porch, a pleasant perch in the maple trees. Robert walked late that summer, in that apartment, for the first time.

I registered in summer school, four more courses to complete my degree, worked in the new anthropology library, and several hours a week attended animals in a special research program at the school of dentistry. More than a dozen dogs had their mandibles broken to observe the various methods of healing. I fed the dogs once a day, and assisted the doctor in surgery. One by one the dogs were sacrificed in the interests of science; my visits to the kennel became last rites on death row at the university.

Professor Edward Copeland opened his course on Japanese literature that summer with haiku in translation. The sense of impermanence, he said, is in the weather, the seasons, and in haiku; at the same time, we are aware of culture and tradition. The trees were in bloom near the windows. I was fortunate to have found a memorable course with an inspired teacher, and blest now to remember several distinguished teachers in four years at two universities.

Copeland nurtured literature, he turned poems over and over with a courteous hand. His voice was clear, the sound of mountain water, never strained; not a mere murmur at a blackboard. He would seldom complain, and never consumed literature. We met four times a week in the morning; the class was small, about fifteen students. He wore loafers and a sweater, the autumn colors rounded his thin shoulders, and he arrived one minute past the bell at the hour.

Copeland recited and translated one of the greatest haiku poems by Bashō: *furuike ya*, the ancient pond; *kawazu tobikomu*, frog leaps, or jumps; *mizu no oto*, sound of water, or splash. The poem shows the season, and suggests tradition and impermanence in the most subtle images and motions. Copeland paused, a natural silence, as a poem would score, and then he continued his introduction to the course.

Issa, we would understand, was near to nature, an elusive treasure in haiku imagination, and we wondered if our teacher had been the poet in one of his past lives. Copeland, Issa, and Takuboku seemed to be our teachers that summer. Literature, haiku, our seasons at the window were there in the imagination of our existence, and yet, and yet.

Japanese literature became the source of my second liberation; the first was in the military, and then in the summer of my senior year at the University of Minnesota. I studied culture, literature, art, and language with Edward Copeland.

We read introductions by Donald Keene, selections from diaries, and the *Manyoshu*, translations of haiku by R. H. Blyth, and Harold Henderson, and novels by Kawabata Yasunari, and Dazai Osamu. Someone mentioned Lafcadio Hearn.

Copeland was moved by the poems of Takuboku Ishikawa; a limited hand printed edition of *A Handful of Sand* was published, in translation, the year of my birth. Takuboku had traveled to Hokkaido. Later, his mother and wife suffered from tuberculosis; he wrote to a poet, "I have no money to take care of us and no courage to write. Really this has become a worthless world for me." He died at age twenty-seven. Copeland praised his poetry, the power of his dramatic images. I complained that the poet suffered so much to write, "and such a small book for so much hardship and death." My insecurities were on the rise. I worried that my life would be miserable, reduced to a thin volume of poems. My teacher paused, then he said, "Takuboku might have written nothing, how lucky we are that he left these poems." Then he read several poems from *A Handful of Sand*:

My father and mother are aged. . . .
O mosquitoes!
One and all,
Come and bite my skinny legs.

With the joy of meeting
A long lost friend,
I listen to the sound of water.

Coming home from my duties
Late at night,
I hold my child
Who has just died.

When I breathe,
There is a rolling sound in my chest,
A sound more desolate
Than that of a winter blast.

O, the sadness of lifeless sand!
Trickling,
It falls through my fingers
When I take it in my hands.

Copeland handed me a note at the end of the hour in the second week of class. The trees were rich and tender in their greens. The note, folded once with a deckle edge, was written in a gracious hand, "You have been looking out the window during my lectures. What do you see?" I waited, looked once more at the trees outside the window, and answered his note with this summer haiku:

In search of poems
How many trees have fallen?
Sound of the wind.

I read his note several more times and worried because two days had passed; he had not responded. I was vulnerable, my response was personal; would he think his lectures were the sound of wind? Copeland said nothing, and then on the third day he handed me a second note, folded once more on deckle paper; his response was a translation of a haiku by Buson:

Morning breeze
Fur
Seems to blow
Caterpillar!

I was warmed by his generous response with a poem, and heartened by his praise of imagination and literature. Copeland and Eda Lou Walton, my literature teacher at New York University, came together in my memories of the best teachers. His note and our poems started a friendship; several years later he contributed four of his translations of haiku by Bashō, Issa, and Buson, to introduce the seasons in my first important collection of original haiku, *Raising the Moon Vines.* I was a graduate student then, studying Japanese and Chinese history, art, and literature, and library science. *Two Wings the Butterfly*, a paperbound limited edition of my very first original haiku, with ink paintings by Judith Horns Vizenor, was printed in April 1962 by inmates at the Minnesota State Reformatory.

Did the old grey stump
Remember her strength today,
Raising the moon vines.

In the dark grass
Her gentle hands alight,
Two fireflies.

Peter Stitt published the first review of *Twio Wings the Butterfly* on October 15, 1962, in the *Ivory Tower*, a literary magazine at the University of Minnesota. He wrote, "Vizenor has an ability to capture the essence of a natural scene or object and concisely express it in some fine poems." Stitt was critical of the "anecdotes" and "lack of suggestiveness" in some poems. Roland Flint reviewed *Raising the Moon Vines*, and *Seventeen Chirps*, my third collection of haiku, for the *Minneapolis Tribune* on January 24, 1965: "The 'emptiness' in haiku is a positive, not a negative, characteristic; it is a succinctness, a deliberate restraint, an avoidance of clutter," wrote Flint. "It invites the reader to supply what is missing, and Vizenor is particularly good at its use. In one of his poems a child's angry grief is suggested but not quite spelled out:

Crack, crack
His hoe against the garden stones
Mother died.

I sold my meager properties, books, and car at the end of my second year at the University of Minnesota, and sailed on the *Nieuw Amsterdam* to Southampton, England. My closest companion on the ship was a bald retired iron worker. We had both sold most of what we owned to travel, but his idea was comic: he wanted to "cash out" on the road; he planned to travel to his death. Henry was certain that his life would run out sooner than his money. He tried to teach me how to drink aquavit with a flourish, but my breath was lost on the first sip. Henry won the popular vote in the tourist class hat contest, but he was disqualified in the end because of his gender. Women wore the hats in the contest; his was an apple and an arrow. I heard his raucous laughter several weeks later on a train in Switzerland. Henry tried once more to teach me how to down aquavit.

I was broke in five weeks and returned with stories, poems, and eight dollars. I was hired as an orderly at Homewood Hospital located at Penn and Plymouth avenues, a few blocks from my first rented room on Willow Street. The hospital admitted people with various mental problems and neurological disorders. There were wanderers in speech and hand, the wild, the touched, and the shocked, on the aisles, but the real lunatics were the orderlies and medical administrators. One man pretended to be a doctor: he wore a white coat, carried a stethoscope, and examined older women; he delighted in electroshock, and his comments were recorded with humor. One orderly was a certified kleptomaniac; theft was his best discourse. Roger would not feel good until he had stolen something, anything, from anyone. I pointed out, however, that he never stole flowers; he would steal whatever he could get his hands on at a flower shop, but never from nature. He stole from patients, friends, and the staff; the more he stole, the happier, but not with malice.

Roger had studied medicine; that is, he attended classes for more than a year before he was discovered and removed as an imposter. He took me on a wild medical tour of the University of Minnesota Hospital. We started in the locker room, white coats, hammers, but no names; he determined that no names indicated more significance. Roger demonstrated microtomy, and he moved a resident pathologist aside to show me a slice of tissue under a microscope. My tour ended in the operating room; we were dressed in greens and wore masks to observe an emergency appendectomy. The surgeon instructed an intern to make the first incision; there were at least a dozen interns and medical students crowded around the patient. I moved to the outside when the surgeon started to ask questions. Roger answered, he was the most impressive student there; he understood the manners of the game, but not the rules of the game.

Homewood Hospital was a circus; the nurses and orderlies were the trainers, the acrobats, and the patients were the animals, the sick animals. One of the nurses had an eye tic that stopped conversations; she would never answer a telephone because she saw fire shoot from the receiver. She took a patient home with her once, a former priest who was not able to leave a house on his feet because he saw fire on the threshold and believed that he would lose his soul if he crossed. We pretended that they were the perfect couple: he could answer the telephone, and she was secure that he would never leave the house. I delivered a parcel to their house once, and when he opened the door he moved back in fear. I was a demon in the fire.

I worked the late afternoon and evening shift. Most of the patients could not tell one orderly from another; we were the crazier ones in white coats, but some patients were sensitive, and more aware than others. Laura, for instance, was restrained, stranded in a mental hospital with advanced Parkinson's disease. She was strapped into a chair to hold her down in front of a television set with other patients. Laura twitched, and shuddered, her head was a wild pitch on the plastic chair, her neck strained, and clicked on the rebound. Laura moaned as best she could to warn me, and then pissed in the chair. She was humiliated once more as the warm urine ran on the floor. I took her to her room to change her gown. Her face was taut, and twisted, a Parkinson's mask, but her eyes pleaded with me to honor a simple moment of privacy. I was moved to tears. Laura held her beauty in her eyes; courteous turns and gestures, her warm touch, smiles, were lost in a nervous wilderness. We were both humiliated that she must wear a hospital gown, tied at the back. She had been deserted by her body and her family, but she held her freedom in her eyes. I left her alone behind a screen; later, she appeared in a lovely print dress with the buttons undone at the back; that moment of privacy, that small favor, brought her such joy in a cruel and inhuman mental hospital.

I worked there during the school year and into the summer. There were hours of great humor, compassion, and sadness, but most of the time the hospital administration was harsh, peevish, and tragic. The regular use of electroshock in the hospital troubled me; lonesome women lost their past, their best memories. The dubious causes of their depression were crossed with electric currents to the brain. Muscles leapt, and tightened, bodies pounded on the hard table; in the end these women, who could afford to be treated by men, learned to smile at the psychiatrist and were released to their husbands.

My reasons for leaving the hospital were connected to the use of electroshock and other medical abuses, but the actual decision was based on an unusual comic encounter one night with four male patients at the end of a hall.

Frank lived on the wake of a wild ritual, a circle of generous manners and then persecution and fecal decorations; the rituals were turned in about three weeks. He was on the rise, gracious, and concerned about others that night.

Robot Joe marched; rather, he did a hospital shuffle, from one end of the hall to the other. When he reached the end he moaned and marched in place until he was turned around. Robot Joe was a Thorazine man, an enormous beast; that night he was stopped, and marked time, behind a door at the end of the hall.

Super embodied the cruelest ironies; he had been the director of a mental hospital in North Dakota. He wore a tailored suit, vest, starched shirt, and conservative necktie; he was forever checking his pocket watch to be sure that his institution was run on time. He had fired me, and others, hundreds of times; every time we took his temperature, turned his pillow, or talked with him about the weather, we were fired for insubordination. Super fired me that night.

Heart Throb was a little man with nervous manners who simulated heart attacks three or four times a day. My first night as an orderly the nurses abandoned me in his room, with no information, when he had one of his many performance heart attacks. Heart Throb convinced me the first time. I climbed onto his bed, pressed, and pounded his heart. "Stay alive, you bastard, you're not dying on my first night," I shouted over his moist red chest. He was terrified and never again staged one of his heart attacks near me. He would rush out of his room nude, into the hall, and pretend short breath and chest pains.

Robot Joe was turned around and on his march back that night when Heart Throb opened his door, dropped nude to the cold floor, and moaned about chest pains. Robot Joe stopped at the door and moaned over Heart Throb. Frank heard the commotion and leaped out of his room to see what was the matter; his hairy ass stuck out of his hospital gown. He stood over Heart Throb and told Robot Joe how terrible it was that no one helped the patients in the hospital. Robot Joe seemed to moan his agreement, or at least Frank seemed to understand. I waited in the toilet at the end of the hall, watched myself in the mirror, and listened at a distance.

Super lived across from Heart Throb; he pushed his door open and investigated the cause of the disturbance in the hall. He was a born leader and took command of the situation. Frank asked him where he got the nice suit, and then agreed that hospital administrators should wear suits on duty. Heart Throb turned over, moaned louder, and held his chest; the more he was noticed the more he moaned. Super ordered Frank to read the pulse of the sick man on the floor, and he told Robot Joe to stand guard at the door. "You will be needed later," said Super. Robot Joe moaned and smiled; he seemed to understand.

"Show me, show me the pulse," said Frank.

"There, on his wrist," said Super. He wondered out loud about an orderly who could not read a pulse. Frank was nervous at first, not a good sign on his ritual circle, but when he heard that he was an orderly he proved that the times do make the man, even in mental hospitals.

"He's got a good one," said Frank.

"Damn nurses, you can't find one when you want one," said Super. He opened his gold pocket watch and read the time, "nine seventeen" one summer night in a mental hospital.

"What's the problem?"

"Who are you?" asked Super.

"I'm your nurse," I said and touched Heart Throb on the cold shoulder with the toe of my shoe. There was terror in eyes. No time to continue his heart attack when he saw me.

"You're fired," shouted Super.

"Who me?" I shrugged my shoulders and pretended to be concerned. Heart Throb was heartened by my dismissal and returned to his simulation on the cold hard terrazzo.

"Pick up your pay on the way out," said Super.

"Vacation time too?"

"You're fired," repeated Super.

"Wait a minute," said Frank. He was troubled, wild creases distorted his face and expressions. "You shouldn't fire us, we were just helping out." Frank pounded one bare foot on the floor, smack, smack, smack.

Heart Throb could not sustain his simulation under nurses who were to be fired by the director of the hospital, so he stood up and took part in the argument, still holding his damaged heart. "Frank's right," he announced. Later, he said Super was right, and Robot Joe was right, but he never included me in his tribute.

"I quit," I shouted.

"You can't quit," said Super.

"Why not?"

"Because you're fired," said Frank.

"No shit," I said.

"Yes, no shit," said Frank. He face loosened at the mere sound of the word. He delighted, at the bottom of his ritual circle, in the decoration of his room with shit; walls, windows, bed, chairs, and dishes, covered with his shit.

Super held his chin, raised his voice, and lectured us on the proper attitudes toward patients in his hospital. Frank agreed, but his mind was focused on shit, and he pranced in the circle; the urge was upon him to decorate his room that night. Robot Joe moaned; he even seemed amused for the first time. I closed the door but he would not move, he remained in the circle. Heart Throb said the director of the hospital was right, even "very right" that night. He described a heart attack and complained about the medical care in the hospital. They were right, very right, and it was time for me to leave before the charge nurse ordered me to clean more shit from the walls.

"The contemporary world makes schizophrenia possible, not because its events render it inhuman and abstract, but because our culture reads the world in such a way that man himself cannot recognize himself him in it," wrote Michel Foucault in *Mental Illness and Psychology*. "Only the real conflict of the conditions of existence may serve as a structural model for the paradoxes of the schizophrenic world."

I lived in Pioneer Hall my first quarter at the University of Minnesota. The next quarter I was hired as a residential counselor at the Ramsey County Home School for Boys, better known as Totem Town. Thomas Houle had been hired a few months earlier and we became close friends. There was as much humor as stress, as much pleasure as horror, and there was more than enough to loathe in an institution that promised to hold, nurture, educate, and reform boys who were wild and lost, even those who had committed the crimes of adults.

Stress is unforgiven, remembered on the run; the pleasures were common, generous emotions and honorable resolutions to troubles between some boys, their parents and teachers. The horrors haunt my memories. For instance, the boy who tortured and hanged domestic cats, chickens and then, years later, was convicted of the torture, mutilation, and murder of a woman. The easier memories and the best remembrance are the ironies, and the humor of human imperfections. One master social worker decided to manipulate an obvious condition of adolescence, masturbation.

Uncle, as he was known at Totem Town, organized small groups of boys, talked about sex, and sexual fantasies, and then he had a good group masturbation session. The older boys roasted the group masturbation and named them "Uncle Jacks," or the "Night Junkles," and the "Masterbeaters." Uncle was rather naive, to say the least; he was a lovable innocent, but the boys responded to peer pressure and were no longer interested in group beats. This was read as "maturation over masturbation."

Uncle was persuaded by the older boys, once they learned how to use his romantic notions, to hold an overnight camp in the woods behind Totem Town. The institution was located in rural Saint Paul. Uncle, in turn, persuaded the director to support the overnight. I opposed the inevitable with humor and my best wishes. The older boys insisted that some younger boys come along, a good plan. The campers cooked hot dogs over an open fire, and sang camp songs. Uncle waited until dark and then told stories to the younger boys around the fire; soon they were fast asleep. Meanwhile, the older boys had arranged for their friends to meet them at the nearest gravel road. More than a dozen boys roared around the cities that night with perfect alibis. They drank, fucked, stole cars, robbed stores, threatened people, and were back in their sleeping bags before dawn. Uncle counted his boys, and his blessings as a social worker; he was so pleased to report later that day to the county sheriff that his boys were fast asleep under his protection. Uncle was loose; he seldom brushed his teeth, and he had no shame to remember.

I lived in an industrial medical clinic during my third year at the university. I cleaned the clinic, stoked the coal furnace, shoveled snow in winter, and maintained the radiators for a monthly salary and an apartment in the basement of the converted mansion. The doctors were too serious to laugh; they examined and treated employees under contract with local business and corporations. However, there were rich ironies and humors in their practice. One doctor could not stand the sight of blood, and when there was an emergency he would call in the X ray technician, who was eager to play doctor. Once the doctor was alone and he called me to his office to assist him in treating a woman with a simple cut on her finger. The doctor invited her into his

office, declared a minor wound, and ordered me to treat it with prepared bandages; he claimed an emergency at the hospital and drove
away in his Mercedes-Benz convertible.

The medical clinic contracted to have the floor cleaned and polished
once a week by professionals. I met the cleaners once or twice on
weekends; the man who owned the company seemed familiar. We
shared the weather several times and then, at last, he asked me my
name. His mouth opened but he was silent for several minutes.

"Please, don't leave," he said. There were tears in his eyes, but he
assured me that everything was fine. He was very nervous and excited.
"Please, I'll be back in a minute."

He returned with his daughter, who was about my age. They both
touched me and then told me stories about my father Clement Vizenor.
They said we looked very much alike, and noted that my father was
about my age when he was murdered. This man was a painting
contractor twenty years earlier and he had hired my father and my
uncles as painters.

"I promised your father we would take care of you if anything ever
happened to him, and it did," he said. "But when he was murdered we
couldn't find you anywhere." They were burdened to remember the
death of my father, but that moment, a chance encounter at a medical
clinic, was a pleasant resolution to an old promise. They were strangers
to me; our memories were bound by the death of my father.

"You and my daughter should have grown up together," he said.

"Looks like we did all right anyway." We touched and promised to
plan a proper family visit. They never called me; I never called them.
We never got together as they had promised.

ENVOY TO HAIKU

The *Toya Maru* might have been the end of me.

The train ferry lost power and turned over in a typhoon between the islands of Honshu and Hokkaido. More than a thousand people died at sea that night. I was lucky. Our battalion had been ordered, at the last minute, to remain on the northern island and bivouac in the pristine Imperial National Forest.

"The vessel carried soldiers of the United States First Cavalry Division transferring from Hokkaido to new posts on Honshu," reported *The New York Times* on 27 September 1954. "The typhoon did widespread damage over the main islands of Japan."

The *Toya Maru* carried my typewriter and copies of my first stories to the bottom of Tsugaru Strait. I was wise to haiku that summer and would tote no more than a notebook. Naturally, that coincidence, and the loss of my typewriter, were trivial at the time.

I was a crossblood on the natural margins of a cultural contradance. My father was from the White Earth Reservation in Minnesota, a newcomer to the city, and my mother lived in Minneapolis. The chance union of my parents was a contradiction of suspensive racialism; neither war nor the ruins of representation in literature.

The woodland dream songs and trickster stories that would bear the humor and tragic wisdom of tribal experiences were superseded in the literature of dominance. Indians were invented to maintain the notions of savagism and civilization. The Anishinaabe, my ancestors of the woodland, were named the Chippewa. The oral stories and dream songs of the tribes were translated and compared as cultural evidence; scarcely with wisdom, humor or eminence. Biblical and classical references, the traces of dominance, encumbered the common pleasures of creation in literature.

"The sky loves to hear me sing" is a heartened invitation to the dream songs of the Anishinaabe. The dreamers listen to the natural turnout of the seasons, and the everlasting sky hears their voices on the wind. "With a large bird above me, I am walking in the sky" is a translation of an avian vision that was heard in woodland tribal communities. My interpretations of selected dream songs in translation were published in *Summer in the Spring: Anishinaabe Lyric Poems and Stories.*

Frances Densmore was one of the most honorable translators of tribal dream songs and ceremonies; these and other creations that she recorded at the turn of the last century would come to me later with a haiku nature.

as my eyes
look across the prairie
i feel the summer
in the spring

overhanging clouds
echoing my words
with a pleasing sound

across the earth
everywhere
making my voice heard

Chance and the contradictions of tribal and national identities would become my sources of incitation as a creative writer. I would have to leave the nation of my birth to understand the wisdom and survivance of tribal literature. How ironic that my service as a soldier would lead me to haiku, and haiku an overture to dream songs. Haiku would be my introduction to the pleasures of literature, a national literature that did not exclude the common reader by dominance, decadence, or intellectual elitism.

The Japanese would hear me in haiku, not at war; my first liberation in literature. Neither nation had me in mind at the end of the war or even later in narratives; nonetheless, the coincidence of suspensive maneuvers in the military and the assurance of haiku were assumed at Matsushima.

The United States Army trained me in combat simulations and guerrilla tactics, but the most elusive maneuvers of nations were overcome by chance, in the sensations of literature, not in the ruins of war.

The United States Steamship *Sturgis*, with more than three thousand soldiers on board, was bound for the port at Inchon, South Korea, an industrial center on the Yellow Sea. General Douglas MacArthur, commander of United Nations forces, had carried out an amphibious landing from the same port, behind the lines of the North Koreans.

Panmunjom, in the demilitarized zone between the nations, seemed so far removed from our troop ship, but we were certain at the time and that much out of fear, that our fate would be traded in measured words over a military blanket. Peace negotiations were down, checked over the absence and presence of names, and there were no indications that the war would end before we docked. Meanwhile, a hospital ship was delayed in the port at Inchon, so the *Sturgis* docked at Yokohama. Thereafter, several hundred soldiers were mustered each day from the top of the alphabet for military flights to the front lines in Korea.

That slow muster to combat was unbearable the closer my name came on the war list; then, by chance, near the end of the tees in the alphabet, there were no more musters. We waited at the end of the alphabet for a few days and then we boarded a train for Hokkaido, the northern island of Japan. Chitose was our destination, a small town cornered by two military bases near the city of Sapporo. The names at the lower end of the alphabet, about two hundred soldiers, were assigned to the Seventieth Tank Battalion, First Cavalry Division, a celebrated unit that had been decimated a few months earlier in Korea.

Three months later the war ended. An armistice was signed, after two years of negotiations, by officials of the United Nations and North Korea at Panmunjom on 27 July 1953.

The Japanese and their literature were my liberation. I was eighteen years old and saw haiku in calligraphy that summer for the first time, and read translations of poems by Kobayashi Issa and Matsuo Bashō. That presence of haiku, more than other literature, touched my imagination and brought me closer to a sense of tribal consciousness. I was liberated from the treacherous manners of missionaries, classical warrants, the themes of savagism and civilization, and the arrogance of academic discoveries. The impermanence of natural reason and tribal remembrance was close to the mood of impermanence in haiku and other literature. My poems and stories would arise as shadows, the evanescence of interior landscapes.

A haiku is "not explicit about what has been going on in the mind of the author," wrote Daisetz Suzuki in *Zen and Japanese Culture*. "He does not go any further than barely enumerating, as it were, the most conspicuous objects that have impressed or inspired him. As to the meaning of such objects . . . it is left to the reader to construct and interpret it according to his poetic experiences or his spiritual intuitions."

The haiku poem ascribes the seasons with shadow words, the sources of creation and visual memories, a moment of wonder in the natural world; the morning light that turns the leaves, the hands of children on the cold window, animals and birds in the first snow, the reach of waves at the end of an ocean storm. Shadow words and haiku thought are intuitive, a concise concentration of motion, memories, and the sensations of the seasons without closure or silence.

"In haiku, the two entirely different things that are joined in sameness are poetry and sensation, spirit and matter," wrote R. H. Blyth in *A History of Haiku*. "The coldness of a cold day, the heat of a hot day, the smoothness of a stone, the whiteness of a seagull, the distance of the far-off mountains, the smallness of a small flower, the dampness of the rainy season, the quivering of the hairs of a caterpillar in the breeze—these things, without any thought or emotion or beauty or desire are haiku."

These sensations are the tribal shadows of creation.

Donald Keene, in *Japanese Literature*, observed that a "really good poem, and this is especially true of haiku, must be completed by the reader. It is for this reason that many of their poems seem curiously passive to us, for the writer does not specify the truth taught him by an experience, nor even in what way it affected him. . . ." What haiku poems have sought, he pointed out, "is to create with a few words, usually with a few sharp images, the outline of a work whose details must be supplied by the reader, as in a Japanese painting a few strokes of the brush must suggest the world."

Earl Miner, and others, in *The Princeton Companion to Classical Japanese Literature*, defined the haibun as a prose composition, "usually with *haikai* stanzas . . . with an autobiographical" interest that "could treat many kinds of experiences. When it treats a journey, it becomes a species of kiko." Haikai is a form of linked poems, or "haikai no renga." The renga is linked poetry that "developed from a pastime in the twelfth century into serious art." The kiko is travel literature that expresses an "appreciation of famous places." Matsuo Bashō's *Oku no Hosomichi*, of *The Narrow Road to the Deep North*, in prose and haikai, "is no doubt the greatest." Haiku is an "abbreviation of haikai no ku, and a term seldom met in classical literature, although *hokku* were increasingly composed in ways highly similar."

Matsuo Bashō was born near Ueno in Iga Province. He wrote his first poems when he was eighteen years old, but his best haiku and haibun were composed during the last ten years of his life. He wrote about the common experiences of the world in a serious manner. Bashō created his haibun at the same time that my tribal ancestors encountered the colonists and their diseases.

Bashō visited Matsushima and wrote in his haibun diaries about the moon over the pine islands, the treasures of the nation. I was there three hundred years later, touched by the same moon and the master haiku poet. "Much praise has already been lavished upon the wonders of the islands of Matsushima," wrote Bashō in *The Narrow Road to the Deep North*, translated by Nobuyuki Yuasa. "Yet if further praise is possible, I would like to say that here is the most beautiful spot in the whole country of Japan. . . . The islands are situated in a bay about three miles wide in every direction and open to the sea through a narrow mouth on the southeast side. . . . Islands are piled above islands, and islands are joined to islands, so that they look exactly like parents caressing their children or walking with them arm in arm.

"The pines are of the freshest green, and their branches are curved in exquisite lines, bent by the wind constantly blowing through them. Indeed, the beauty of the entire scene can only be compared to the most divinely endowed of feminine countenances, for who else could have created such beauty but the great god of nature himself? My pen strove in vain to equal this superb creation of divine artifice."

Bashō died in October 1694 at the age of fifty. Four days before his death, one of his disciples wrote this about the master haiku poet: "Soon I heard the clatter of an ink bar rubbing against a slab. I wondered what manner of letter it was, but it turned out to be a poem." Bashō wrote this, his last poem:

> seized with a disease
> halfway on the road
> my dreams kept revolving
> round the withered moor

Matsushima is a natural remembrance, a dream of the moon over the pine islands in haiku. I considered his most frequently translated haiku, *an ancient pond, a frog jumps in, sound of water*, and wrote this original haiku in the autumn:

> calm in the storm
> master basho soaks his feet
> water striders

My haiku poems are read in the four seasons and there are three attributes of development. The haiku in my first three books, *Raising the Moon Vines, Seventeen Chirps*, and *Empty Swings*, were common comparative experiences in the past tense. Later, in *Matsushima*, my haiku were more metaphorical, concise and with a sense of presence.

> wooden bucket
> frozen under the rain spout
> springs a leak

> march moon
> shimmers down the sidewalk
> snail crossing

> hail stones
> sound once or twice a summer
> old school bell

> bold nasturtiums
> dress the barbed wire fences
> down to the wild sea

> acacia leaves
> rain on the construction site
> saved the bright trees

The third attribute in the development of my haiku widens the sentiment and attitude of the poem with an envoy, a prose concentration and discourse on the images and sensations. This practice combines my experience in haiku with natural reason in tribal literature, a new haiku hermeneutics. Tribal dream songs and haiku are concentrated in nature. For instance, the haiku poems that follow have an envoy, or a discourse on the reach of haiku sensations and tribal survivance. The envoy is interpretative; the three lines of the haiku are heard in shadow words and printed without punctuation. The envoy is in prose.

calm in the storm
master basho soaks his feet
water striders

The striders listen to the wind, the creation of sound that is heard and seen in the motion of water; the wind teases the tension and natural balance on the surface of the world. The same wind that moves the spiders teases the poets.

those stubborn flies
square dance across the grapefruit
honor your partner

Fat green flies dance on the back of spoons, turn twice, and reach for the grapefruit. The flies allemande left and right in a great breakfast dance, but the owners of the spoons in the restaurant would terminate the insects to save the grapefruit. We are the lonesome dancers over the remains of so many natural partners in the world.

redwing blackbirds
ride the reeds in a slough
curtain calls

The crack of bird songs and the flash of color on the wing is a comic romance in sloughs. We pose at lamp posts as the blackbirds might, cocked on the side of reeds with the wind close to our ears. Listen, audiences are better in the sloughs; the curtain calls never end.

cocksure squirrels
break the ice at the window
raid the bird feeder

My poems and stories about the squirrels were heard as a menace to neighbors, an invitation to honor mere rodents and tree rats. The squirrels must have heard the literature in their name that winter. Silence is not a natural world; the earth hears no balance in termination.

Haiku hermeneutics, that sense of haiku, is a natural habitude in tribal literature; the interpretations of the heard and written must consider the shadow words and sensations of haiku. The turn of the seasons, the course of spiders, the heat of stone, and the shadows of remembrance rush to the words laced in stories and poems. Stories must have their listeners and readers to overcome a natural imperma- nence. Oral stories must be heard to endure; haiku are shadow words and sensations of the heard. Words wait for no one on the page. The envoys to haiku are the silent interpretations of a "haiku spirit."

"The haiku never describes; its art is counter-descriptive, to the degree that each state of the thing is immediately, stubbornly, victo- riously converted into a fragile essence of appearances," wrote Roland Barthes in the *Empire of Signs*. "Hence the haiku reminds us of what has never happened to us; in it we recognize a repetition without origin, an event without cause, a memory without person, a language without moorings. . . . Here meaning is only a flash, a slash of light."

Bashō was a critical interpreter; he exercised, in a sense, the her- meneutics of haiku. He considered two attitudes of "poetic composi- tion," observed Makoto Ueda in *Matsuo Bashō*. "A good poet does not 'make' a poem; he keeps contemplating his subject until it 'becomes' a poem. A poem forms itself spontaneously. If the poet labors to com- pose a poem out of his own self, it will impair the 'soul' of his subject."

Uedo wrote that Bashō made use of the critical concept of "surplus meaning." The poem means more than the words; the meaning is "suggested" and "stated" at the same time. "According to Bashō's principle of 'lightness' then, a poem should present a picture of life objectively in familiar words, avoiding intensely emotional expression.A poet should not pour his passion into his work; he should rather detach himself from the passion and submerge it within an objective scene."

Bashō wrote that he "tried to give up poetry and remain silent, but every time I did so a poetic sentiment would solicit my heart and something would flicker in my mind. Such is the magic spell of poet- ry." Uedo noted that the haiku master "who considered poetry nothing more than a pastime in his youth, came to demand too much of it in his last years."

AVENGERS AT WOUNDED KNEE

Rodger Kemp was a dedicated teacher at the Pine Point School on the White Earth Reservation when the American Indian Movement was on the radical rise in the cities.

Kemp was summoned late one night by a local reservation radical who had been inspired by the media presentation of urban tribal militants. He pounded on the aluminum door of the house trailer and shouted, "Rog, open up, it's me."

"What's up?"

"I need a jump start," said the radical.

"Car's dead again?"

"Yeah, fuckin' white man's car."

"Come on in."

"Fuckin' battery's dead," he said.

"Sounds familiar, I better get dressed for this." Rodger had earned the reputation of being the most comfortable, reliable, and compassionate friend and teacher on the reservation. He listened, he taught children to imagine the world, he humored, he tutored, nurtured identities, coached, wrote proposals, loaned too much money, and jump started cars late at night with a wise sense of humor. I was there for the weekend, my house was under repair and renovation, and I listened to nurture my crossblood identities.

Rodger sat in the living room and laced his boots with deliberate care; the ersatz radical, a military veteran who could not find a good job on the reservation, paced back and forth near the door. He was high wired, and the aluminum trailer shuddered under his hard tread, tread, tread.

"Hurry up Rog."

"Right, one more boot."

"Someday I'm gonna drive to Park Rapids and shoot the fuckin' white bastards on the streets, and start the real revolution." The radical tried to provoke the calm teacher who laced his right boot. His mind was sudden, wild hits at violent scenes.

"Someday soon?"

"We're goin' in with rifles."

"By car?"

"Yeah, why?"

"Listen, could you do me a favor?"

"Sure Rog, what?"

"Could you get yourself a new battery before you start the revolution." Rodger smiled and waited at the door. The radical missed the humor, the trickster signature; he had assumed too much from the white teachers on the reservation.

Kemp connected his battery cables to the car and the radical roared down the reservation road in the dark with no praise; from a revolution in a trailer to racial insolence and loneliness on the road.

The American Indian Movement overturned the burdens of colonial education, and burned manners at the best institutions. Rather, the media-borne tribal simulations, and transvaluations, raised the romantic notions of a material and spiritual revolution in America. Media simulations and ersatz leaders have no real constituencies; the media men, and there were men under the media masks, had learned to rave in television scenes. Some of these men were paroled felons, seldom bound to praise and pleasure; some were wicked, and sold hallucinogens to tribal children. Some of these men were moved by personal power; literature and communal dreams were rare in their travels.

The media radicals encountered the material, not a liberation of the mind, or a revolution in literature. Most of the radicals were petulant about imagination and ideas, and were critical of tribal studies in colleges and universities. However, some of the radicals were eager to learn an older language of identities.

At that time most people understood the tribal name Chippewa, as in the Minnesota Chippewa Tribe, or in the assertion of an innocent child, "I'm very proud to be a Chippewa Indian." Chippewa was the colonial name imposed on a woodland tribal culture.

"The Anishinaabe are the people of the woodland in the language of those who have been known for more than a century in the dominant society as the Chippewa and Ojibway." My essay on the tribal name was published in the winter of 1971 in the *Indian Historian,* edited by Jeanette Henry. I proposed that we "relume the tribal identities of the woodland people by changing the tribal name back to the Anishinaabe." William Warren, the mixedblood historian, wrote in his *History of the Ojibway Nation* that the invented names of the tribe do "not date far back. As a race or distinct people they denominated themselves Anishinaabeg," the plural of Anishinaabe. Frances Densmore pointed out that the name "Chippewa is comparatively modern and is the only name under which the tribe has been designated by the government in treaties and other negotiations, but it has never been adopted by the older members of the tribe."

American Indian Movement leaders declared to the media that their members would return to the reservation to fight for treaty rights. They drove north from the cities by the hundreds armed with new pistols and rifles.

Russell Means, Dennis Banks, and thirteen other armed leaders filed into the tribal Headstart classroom on the Leech Lake Reservation and sat down on wee chairs. They sat in comic poses, their knees tucked under their chins, dressed in diverse combinations of cowboy clothes, simulated kitschymen, and traditional tribal vestments from the turn of the century. Dennis Banks, who was a charismatic wanderer then, wore his mountain man costume with a fur collar. Most of the leaders of the militant movement were from urban centers.

Simon Howard, then elected president of the Minnesota Chippewa Tribe, entered the classroom, eased down to a wee chair, and twirled his thumbs beneath his stout stomach. The leaders argued with each other about their places in the chain of command, who would sit beside whom at the scheduled television press conferences. Howard wore a thin nylon bowling jacket and a pork pie hat with a floral print in contrast to the media renascence of simulated vestments worn by the militants.

Howard was born on the reservation and his constituencies had been earned there. He was at the meeting as an elected tribal official to keep peace between white people and the militants. The militants were there for an armed confrontation with white people on the opening day of fishing. I was there as a press officer for the tribal government to modulate threats and rumors at scheduled press conferences. Walker was my home, and my work was understood on the Leech Lake Reservation. The militants were never at peace, the press conferences were mordant, and white people were terrified, but Howard managed with humor and astute observations to avoid a confrontation. Local units of the Minnesota National Guard had been placed on alert, and there were hundreds of state police and federal agents in motels around the reservation.

"All right boys, quiet down now and take your seats again," said Howard in the classroom. The tribal leader and the militants agreed to meet twice a day with each other and then with the press. "Now, I don't know everyone here, so let's go around the room and introduce ourselves." Howard looked around the room at the faces, but one by one the militants turned away. "Let's start with you over there. Stand right up, tell us who you are, and where you're from."

The man stood beside the wee chair; he dragged his feet forward and swung his rifle from side to side, a shy student with a weapon. "My name is Delano Western, and I'm from Kansas," he said. His voice trembled. Western leaned forward and looked down at the floor; he touched a spot on the carpet with the toe of his boot. He was dressed in a black hat with a wide brim and an imitation silver headband, dark green sunglasses with large round lenses, a sweatshirt with "Indian Power" printed on the front, two bandoliers of heavy ammunition, none of which matched the bore of his rifle, a black motorcycle jacket with military colonel wings on the epaulets. "Red Power" and "Custer Had It Coming" patches were on his jacket. A military bayonet was strapped to his body next to his revolver.

"We came here to die," said Western. He raised his voice and repeated his death wish once more. He and about six hundred militants had come to the town of Cass Lake on the Leech Lake Reservation to fight for tribal rights to hunt and fish on treaty land, rights that had already been argued by reservation lawyers in federal court and decided in favor of the tribe. How ironic that the militants were camped on treaty land given over to a church group by the federal government, land that should have been returned to the tribe.

The militants demanded money from public officials in Cass Lake; when the town refused to pay, the leaders held a press conference at a rifle range to scare the public. Means, the media man, smiled for television cameras, and fired his pistol or "white-people shooter" at cans. Banks, dressed in a black velvet shirt with ribbon appliqué, prepared for target practice; he stood in front of a collection of commodity food cans, or what he named "white fishermen," and attempted to fast draw his sawed-off shotgun. The peculiar weapon stuck on the rope holster attached to his belt. Banks stood up and tried again, but it still stuck. Frustrated, he untied the rope and walked away angry and embarrassed; he never carried his shotgun pistol again. Banks, a new shooter from the city, would never place in the fast-draw contests.

The church camp was used in the summer by urban families, but that spring the loudspeakers sounded from every cabin, on every tree: "We came here to die, to defend our red brothers and sisters from those white racist fishermen. Dinner will be served in one hour, and there will be a dance contest tonight. We need volunteers to help out in the kitchen, and some brothers and sisters who know how to hunt deer . . . make that just the brothers for now."

The media reported that deer were being slaughtered by militants on the reservation in violation of state laws. In fact, the brothers out hunting for two days missed every deer they shot at. One deer, the one pictured on television being dressed by militants at the church camp, had been killed in an accident with an automobile. The dead deer was delivered to the camp by the local game warden, who knew the militants needed food. While the militants were out "shining" deer one night, they fired seven rounds at the big round brown eyes of a cow. The militants missed and the owner of the cow fired back; the militant hunters scrambled a fast retreat to the church camp, declaring that they were under attack by white racist fishermen.

"We must go on living on this reservation after you leave," Howard told the militants at their last meeting. Kent Tupper, who represented the Leech Lake Reservation in federal court, told the militants several times during the week that the rights of tribal people must be won according to the law and not by violence.

I was convinced that the weather was the concord at the end of camp for the American Indian Movement on the Leech Lake Reservation. The cold rain distracted the urban militants who were armed for the first time with new weapons. Highway Patrolman Myles Olson said that "two days of rain was worth two slop buckets of Mace."

Dennis Banks was dressed in secular vestments two years later in federal court; he was on trial for alleged violations of laws in connection with the occupation of Wounded Knee on the Pine Ridge Reservation in South Dakota.

Banks told the federal jurors that he was called to a meeting on Monday, February 27, 1973, at Calico Hall on the Pine Ridge Reservation. "I attended this meeting, and the evidence will show that those who were in attendance at that meeting were Oglala Sioux chiefs, traditional headman, medicine man and councilman. . . . I heard an

Oglala Sioux woman, two women, address their chiefs and headmen in their own language. . . . The plea that they made to the American Indian Movement." Banks had not attended the meeting.

I was at that historic meeting at Calico Hall two days before the American Indian Movement occupied the village at Wounded Knee. The small cabin on the reservation was crowded with more than a hundred tribal people from several tribes, from cities and reservations. I was obsessed with a sense of spiritual warmth, and moved by the communal anticipation of the tribal people there; then, several drums sounded, slow beats, and then harder, spiritual harmonies, and we were transmuted by the power of the drums, the sound of the drums, the drums, the drums.

My heart responded to the drums, my chest became the drum, and my body was about to have me in that cabin on the reservation. I pressed to the outside, pressed shoulders, and thighs, closer and closer to chests, our breath the tribal drums, the drums, through the crowd to the door. Outside, the stars were silent, the air was clear, cold, and on the natural rise. I was liberated on the air, in the night sky, and said my name out loud, once, twice, and then the sound of the drums returned from a distance. My breath returned, and that time my body returned to me with a new awareness. I had been close to my own truth, the absolute truth of spiritual conversion that night; a few more minutes, hours, and my name might have been lost to the tribe behind a bunker at Wounded Knee. I might have raised my rifle to that airplane over the village in the morning; instead, my pen was raised to terminal creeds.

Then, ultimate realities, the scent of fried chicken that cold night. The only other journalist there, representing network television, had opened a box of fried chicken. He tried to hide in the back seat of his car, but in the end he shared conversation and one wing with me. I returned to the cabin with the night in me, and my mixedblood name. I listened to the voices, the racial politics, the ironies, and the lies, and tried to turn the sound of the drums in my heart into a dream song, into literature. I would not become a mixedblood true believer.

Dennis Banks was not seen at Calico Hall, where five traditional leaders gathered to consider a scheme to seize Wounded Knee. Banks was at Cherry Creek on the Cheyenne River Reservation with a television reporter; the media man was chauffeured to Wounded Knee by the reporter, but she departed when federal marshalls surrounded the area.

Russell Means was perched on a high platform behind a table at one end of Calico Hall. Lower, in front of him, the five traditional, or hereditary, leaders were seated in a row on benches. Means, who did not speak a tribal language then, spoke to the leaders through Leonard Crow Dog, a spiritual leader and translator. The traditional leaders listened to radical entreaties in translation and then retired to the basement to consider the plan to capture Wounded Knee. They conferred for two hours, and then postponed their decision until a second meeting could be held with elected reservation officials. Means was not pleased with their indecision, as he had expected the support of the hereditary leaders; he told them not to overlook his response to their needs on the reservation. We have been invited here, but remember, he admonished the leaders through the translator, we can leave to help people in other places.

March 1, 1973, Wounded Knee, South Dakota: "Members of the American Indian Movement held ten people hostage Wednesday at this Pine Ridge Reservation town where more than 200 Indians were massacred by Cavalry troops in 1890. The hostages were being held after a takeover Tuesday night by about 200 AIM supporters." That first paragraph to a story on the front page of the *Minneapolis Tribune*, under my name, was written by a reporter for United Press International. The rest of the story was mine, but the editors had decided to enliven the first paragraph with hostages.

My first paragraph indicated that there were no hostages; the owner of the store and the priest at Wounded Knee told me by telephone that there were no hostages. Leaders of the American Indian Movement were never charged with kidnapping or any other crime associated with the taking of hostages. I was close to the village, but the reporter for United Press International never moved from his motel room. He ordered a single-engine plane to circle Wounded Knee and filed his simulated story with an aerial photograph of the church, militants, and raised weapons. I was furious that sensational wire service lies had been attached to my news story. My vow never again to write for the newspaper lasted about two weeks. I was director of Indian Studies, an instructor at Bemidji State University, and a contributing editorial writer at that time.

"Killing Indians was once sanctioned by the military of this nation. Who can forget the slaughter of tribal people at Mystic River and Sand Creek and Wounded Knee in South Dakota," I wrote in a six part editorial series published in the *Minneapolis Tribune* in March 1973.

"We had sufficient light from the word of God for our proceedings," said John Underhill at Mystic River. "The only good Indians I ever saw were dead," said General Philip Sheridan at Fort Cob. "I have come to kill Indians, and believe it is right and honorable to use any means under God's heaven to kill Indians," said Colonel John Chivington at Sand Creek.

Killing Indians in South Dakota today is not sanctioned, but it is seldom viewed as murder. For example, Darld Schmitz admitted stabbing Wesley Bad Heart Bull in front of a cowboy bar at Buffalo Gap. Bad Heart Bull is dead. Schmitz is free.

The American Indian Movement could not survive as a revolutionary tribal caravan without the affinity of lawyers, and the press, and the sympathy of the church.

National television crews followed the revolutionary group to Custer, South Dakota, and were on hand to cover the burning of the county courthouse.

Thirty-eight people were arrested on charges of riot and arson. Ramon Roubideaux, a successful criminal attorney and member of the Rosebud Sioux Tribe, agreed to represent those arrested.

About a hundred young adventurers moved uninvited into a dormitory at the Mother Butler Center in Rapid City. The center is owned by the Catholic Church.

Without the press the death of Wesley Bad Heart Bull and the fires at Custer would have been less dramatic; without an attorney many people might still be in jail awaiting trial; and without the church there would be few places to stay. Most tribal people in Rapid City were not interested in taking a militant home for the night.

Many white residents of Rapid City responded to the presence of the young adventurers with a lump in the throat, a grimace on the face, and one hand on a gun. The city had not yet recovered from a terrible flood, and the arrival of the American Indian Movement was very bad timing.

But a few sensitive white people took the presence of young militants as a challenge to right a few wrongs. Most government officials were open for negotiations.

"I think you have a good message for this country," said Mayor Donald Barnett. The mayor seemed to be impressed by the intense dedication of the leaders of the American Indian Movement until he received the criminal files on the militants and discovered they were armed and staying in motels without paying the bills.

"Are these men serious civil rights workers, or are they a bunch of bandits?" Barnett asked during an interview. "People working for civil rights do not carry guns. I have seen the records on these men, and you can't sit and negotiate with a man who has a gun."

Comparing militant tribal leaders to the black civil rights movement, Barnett said: "Martin Luther King was a man of peace. He was never armed." Two dozen members of the American Indian Movement stayed in a downtown motel in Rapid City for two weeks. They were evicted by the police and left a bill of about $2,500 unpaid. No one was arrested, but police confiscated many weapons, including firearms.

"Now, I am no melodramatic martyr," the mayor said, "nor the great white hope, but I believe in communications and working things out through negotiations. . . . I could have done two things: violate their constitutional rights and jail every one of the militants, or try to negotiate."

And the mayor did his best to negotiate. He called and attended meeting after meeting. City officials were open and anxious to negotiate changes, but militant leaders changed the course of the arguments and demands from day to day in an effort to maintain a position of confrontation and confusion. The mayor and city council members moved to adopt a new ordinance establishing a racial conciliation board with investigative powers.

"We were making progress on the resolution," the mayor said, "when at a meeting of council members and militant leaders Vernon Bellecourt changed the demands and told white people to get out of Black Hills. . . . He was serious!

"Sure, I told him. . . . I looked at my watch. Let me see, I said, give me about two hours to pack some things up before I leave," the mayor recalled. "But they left, in anger. How can you talk to someone who responds like that? The war is over, and it happened everywhere in history. We won and you lost. There is no changing that and we are not leaving." But the symbolic war is real to the believers, and tribal people will not accept the loss.

There were many reports of shoplifting in supermarkets by young followers of the American Indian Movement. They were living at the Mother Butler Center with no money and no food. Rapid City merchants seemed to agree that it would cost less to put up with shoplifting than to make a legal complaint and suffer possible property damage.

Two weeks later the American Indian Movement moved to the Pine Ridge Reservation and then captured the village at Wounded Knee. At the same time the new racial conciliation board was negotiating in Rapid City, Dennis Banks was riding a horse, posing for photographers at Wounded Knee. Banks and Vernon Bellecourt are woodland tribal mixedbloods and members of reservations in Minnesota.

registered in the same motel as members of the American ...an Movement. I was awakened by the police the night the militants were evicted; my identification as a reporter saved me from the humiliation of being ousted, but at the same time it set me apart from tribal people in the motel. That was not a ripe moment for trickster signatures. The next morning several militant leaders complained that several lids of marijuana, and other hallucinogens, had been hidden and left behind in motel rooms when they were evicted.

The American Indian Movement put my name on their enemies list; four tribal goons, two of whom had once been friends of mine, were told to make life miserable for me at an education conference at the University of Minnesota at Duluth. The goons arrived at the back of the auditorium in the middle of my lecture and blocked the exits. I raised a radical pose and turned over the microphone to the goon who could not resist a chance to rave at an audience.

The confusion at the conference, my wild lunch invitation to the goons, and the unsolicited protection of the tribal students at the university, gave me time to leave down the back stairs and beat a retreat out of the city. When I got back home in Bemidji there were urgent telephone messages; my friends warned me that money had been paid by certain militant leaders to bash me around for the *Minneapolis Tribune* editorial series. The American Indian Movement leaders became the new tribal totalitarians and the least tolerant of dissidence.

Kent Tupper, the tribal attorney, advised me to seek a permit to bear a handgun. I resisted at first, but he persuaded me to at least have a gun in the house. I purchased a revolver and registered it with the county sheriff. Tupper pointed out that my resistance to a handgun was romantic, that my values were bound to an older ethic of street fights; the rules were better understood then, the weapons were fists and mouths, and there were negotiations and resolutions. "There is no reasoning with people who might be drug crazed," he said. A badly wired head is not a negotiable instrument, he pointed out. "You could be dead and right, and he'd be alive and wrong with a court appointed attorney, or you could be alive with a troubled conscience."

Clyde Bellecourt, one of the movers of the American Indian Movement in Minneapolis, appeared as a speaker two months later at Bemidji State University. I decided to be out of town when he was there. He was critical, as usual, of tribal studies programs, and he named me in particular. "Most Indian studies classes and courses throughout the United States are not controlled by the Indian students themselves," said Bellecourt. He was there for Indian Week, and his comments were reported in the local newspaper.

Bellecourt said that my views were not "the Indian view" and that my education was a cultural separation. "The way he writes I can sense he is not the man for the job here." He was disappointed that I was not present. "We didn't come here to condemn him, we came to bring unity."

Bellecourt asserted that some students told him that "they have no control or they are in an advisory capacity. When they do make a decision they usually don't get what they want anyway." He said: "Having rock and roll bands and baseball, that's not Indian to us. We feel that only through identity with our cultural background, that's the only thing we have to keep us, save us." Diane Brown, a student organizer of Indian Week, pointed out that Bellecourt had not been invited to the activities on campus.

FICTION

MIIGIS CROWNS

Stone Columbus brushed the blue meadow with the last tribal waves of summer birds. He heard the winter in the autumn, the rumors in the pine, the sorrow of birch, red wisps of sumac on the rise, and the eternal crows on the cold, cold roads; he heard the last touch of black flies in the trailer house and honored their slow burn to paradise.

The seasons leave their wild traces in memories at the headwaters; that winter the crows croaked and croaked in the birch. There were wicked stories to be told from the Old World.

Stone meditates on the precarious nature of the seasons to hold back the boreal demons. Tribal tricksters liberate the mind in winter stories, and the ice woman bares a seductive hand of summer at the same time; to be cold and lonesome is to be woundable.

The New World is heard, the tribal world is dreamed and imagined. The Old World is seen, names and stories are stolen, construed, and published. The trickster would be the seasons, neither mortal nor possessed in a cold sentence, neither delivered nor consumed, but heard and created in the crowns of miigis.

Stone hears the rush of buried rivers, the bounce of otter at the seams, and the primal silence of the ice woman, down to his avian bones. He listens to the wind in the cedar; and the seasons come closer and closer to be heard and remembered at the headwaters. The crows abide the demons and warn the heirs at a distance in the birch.

Miigis Flowers, the luminous child named for the sacred cowrie of creation, rescued the first snowflakes on the back of her black mittens. She leaned closer to hear them land on the wool, the creation of a season that would never be the same. She listened with the mongrels to the common touch of winter, and yet the blue snow shoulders on the meadow and the natural crowns near the headwaters became the incautious reach of the tricksters. She turned and rounded the meadow to the cedar; the new snow decorated the clowns she mocked and marched down to the great river.

Miigis was born in the autumn and remembers the seasons from her conception, and from her first winter at the headwaters; the crown that beaded the birch, the sunburst on the low window ice, and the mongrels bounded in the snow shrouds at dusk. She learned to meditate with her father under the cedar. Later that morning the snow crowns loosened on the embowed treès and bashed the tricksters, covered the animals and clowns, and traces of the ice woman.

Felipa was in town with her daughter to deliver wood to the elders and heirs, and to check the mail. She had received a letter from a collector of rare books in England. Miigis turned and brushed the return address, an embossed signature, *Treves Rare Books, Vindos de Portugal, London*, on a foxed envelope.

Pellegrine Treves, the antiquarian book collector, wrote that he had read "with keen interest and much admiration" about the Heirs of Columbus and the recent hearing in federal court. He enclosed a business card and a news article from the *Sunday Times* of London; the inside headline declared that "Red Indians Poach Columbus."

"Dear Madam Flowers," the letter began in a bold cursive hand. "The House of Life, as you most certainly know, is a metaphor that means a burial ground or cemetery in Hebrew. My relatives are buried in a House of Life here, in Spain, Portugal, Italy, Turkey, and in America.

"That you honor your dead with a metaphor from our language would be reason enough to reveal a ceremonial discretion, but the sacred burial site mentioned at the monumental Stone Tavern is the imperative that brings me to write, and to invite your attention to the remains of Pocahontas, otherwise remembered here as Lady Rebecca Rolfe."

Felipa read the letter a second time out loud as she closed the door of the trailer house. "I have acquired, due to unusual circumstances associated with an estate notice, the sealed, authentic remains of Pocahontas, who was thought to have been buried at Gravesend."

"Where is that?" asked Stone.

"Near London," said Felipa.

"Pocahontas at the House of Life," said Stone.

"I would be grateful, for reasons that cannot be wholly explained in this letter, if you would receive the remains of Pocahontas for proper burial by the Heirs of Columbus at the House of Life. Please indicate your interest by return post, and suggest a convenient time that we could arrange to meet soon in London."

"Not in the winter," said Stone.

"Signed, Pellegrine Treves," said Felipa.

"Not with me."

"Listen, he wrote to me," said Felipa

"Not with me," mocked Miigis.

"Pocahontas has been dead for more than three hundred years," said Stone. "Tell me, how does a book collector end up with her bones anyway?"

"Columbus has been dead . . ."

"What bothers me is that she was never buried in the church that celebrates her conversion and remains, or else this collector is playing a lost tribes number," said Stone.

"He asks for nothing," said Felipa.

"Collectors are never without a need for something," he said. Stone turned to the window in silence. The crows bounced on the highest branches of the birch. His was a spiritual burden, and he was suspicious of manners and intentions from the Old World. He wondered why the book collector would not travel to the headwaters with the remains of Pocahontas. "Why does he want you there?"

"Pocahontas is more important than his intentions," she said, and then read the letter a third time, searching for a word, a buried metaphor, that would reveal his avarice, romance, or racial conspiracies.

Felipa repeated the phrase "ceremonial discretion" several more times in various tones and dialects as she answered the invitation. She asked the book collector what he expected in return for the remains. She invited him to a ceremonial burial at the headwaters.

Pellegrine Treves responded that he, indeed, honored the dead and their names, but the "possession of human remains is a serious crime; hence, Lady Rebecca Rolfe is reposed but not abandoned in an uninviting parish. You may be assured that the vicar is unaware of these ironic circumstances. The remains, believed, by most accounts, to be buried in the chancel, are not there. However, she is stored there now by my attention in this instance.

"Your kind invitation would be all but impossible to accept, as much as I would be honored to attend her ceremonial burial at the House of Life." Treves concluded his letter, "Until we meet in London the manner of my acquisition of the remains of Pocahontas shall remain confidential."

Stone insisted that she court the wisest crows and tricksters and not leave the headwaters until the ice broke on the lakes in the spring. The winter was colder than usual, and the ice cracked and thundered late at night for more than two months. At last the river opened past the shallows; the otter pushed the hollow cones loose, and then two lines of geese secured the first shields of water on the lakes.

Miigis was four years old that spring and she could imitate crows, the various songs of more than seventeen birds, the sounds of mongrels, beaver, and the pout of weasels; once she was an otter, and then she turned to the sandhill crane as a vision. She told her mother, "Watch out for the jackdaws on the river, the jackdaws are demons." Miigis dreams the birds and their names in the places her mother travels, an avian vision of tribal landscapes. She was a crane, and jackdaws were a presentiment, not the birds of the headwaters.

Felipa Flowers arrived in London on the same day in March that Pocahontas, weakened with a fever, boarded the *George* anchored at Tower Steps on the River Thames. She stayed at the Belle Sauvage Inn on Ludgate Hill near Fleet Street. She had been in the city several times earlier as a fashion model, a presentation then of aesthetic features to the bourgeoisie, but now she was determined to rescue the remains of a young tribal woman who had died in service to the religious politics of the colonies; she had died in tribute to the noble fashions of the seventeenth century and would be buried at last in the tribal House of Life.

Pellegrine Treves had arranged to meet Felipa at the royal masque performance of *The Vision of Delight*, a spectacular dramatic and musical entertainment to honor the memory of Pocahontas. Treves had ordered a historical costume for her to wear, brocaded red velvet touched with gold and an elaborate white lace shoulder collar, based on an original engraving by Simon de Passe.

Felipa braided her hair with thin golden cords and, as usual, she wore a chocolate brown sweater, wool trousers, and blue moccasins. She would not pretend the time in brocade or red velvet, but she did borrow the splendid fan of three ostrich feathers that was part of the court costume.

Pocahontas was presented at a performance of *The Vision of Delight* and *Christmas, his Mask,* by Ben Jonson, on Twelfth Night at the end of the Christmas season in the Banqueting Hall of Whitehall Palace. King James and Queen Anne danced at the masque in honor of Rebecca Rolfe. Prince Charles, the new Earl of Buckingham, the Earl of Montgomery, Sir Dudley Carleton, ambassador to the Netherlands, John Chamberlain, and others in royal favor attended the masque. Chamberlain wrote to Carleton that "the Virginian woman Pocahontas, with her father's Counselor hath been with the King, and graciously used. And both she and her assistant well placed at the Masque."

Felipa was overawed by the costumes, the extravagant reproduction of scenes at the revised masque. She danced with kings, queens, pretenders to the crown, ambassadors, and clowns, and she was obliged to reveal the new tribal world. Pocahontas, she imagined, was a curiosity in the company of crown sycophants, bound in court costumes of the seventeenth century. The garments alone would have burdened the health of a tribal woman; the bad air and winter weather silenced a tender breath.

Philip Barbour wrote in *Pocahontas and Her World* that the spectacular presentations at the masque "would have been incomprehensible to almost anyone, the theatrical realism and pyrotechnics of such an extravaganza must have seemed the product of inconceivable sorcery. . . . But this was civilized England. The lords and ladies of the English court made up the audience." Pocahontas sat in rigid court dress, "attended by her unimpressionable Indian guard in 'exotic' Indian attire, His Majesty relaxed in gracious dignity, while Phantasy declaimed:

> Behold a King
> Whose presence maketh this perpetual *Spring,*
> The glories of which Spring grow in that Bower,
> And are the marks and beauties of his power."

Pellegrine Treves wore a blue mask and a crimson morning coat. He was stout above his waist with an enormous head and assiduous smile; his tongue teased the wide spaces between his short teeth, a wild creature in a sensuous cage. His cheeks were loose, his hands were warm and active, and the low tones of his voice were secure.

Felipa danced with the book collector twice before she heard his name, and then she remembered his hands and the assurance of his voice. "Names at first sight," he explained, "are the last remembered at a masque."

"Who are these people?" asked Felipa. More than a hundred men and women were dressed in lace and brocade to mock more than three centuries of court manners. The music and dancers were slow, the farthingales were authentic, the alcohol modern, and the humor was wild in costumes. Teams of men moved in comic combat, the complete cultural comedians who never touched each other.

"Once or twice a year the book dealers and collectors hold a masque, a spectacular celebration of the past in costumes," said Treves. "We honor you, in this instance, and the memories of Pocahontas."

"Not at first sight," mocked Felipa.

"Our ceremonial discretion," said Treves.

"Could we sit down?"

"Pocahontas was here nearly four centuries ago," he said as he moved through the dancers to a table at the side of the room. "Not at this exact place, of course, because Whitehall Palace was destroyed by fire in 1698." He moved his hands to sound each word, and his tongue pushed behind his teeth. "She boarded a ship on this very day, and tomorrow she would be dead at Gravesend."

Felipa heard that haunting sound of blue puppets. The chatter of their dance wavered over the laughter and music. The cornice and crowns over the entrance turned blue, and then she saw a woman enter with the puppets; she was a hand talker, the blue puppets were wild dancers, and the scarred tables were turned at the masque.

"Pocahontas was a hand talker," said Felipa.

"She was many things to many people, she saved the Virginia Colony from the Starving Time, and she was here to heal the royal wounds of the Old World," said Treves.

"The hand talkers are healers," she said. Felipa told him about the blue puppets and stories in the blood. Panthers purred on the blue tables; the mongrels wore masks, lace, and spiced powders, and danced the gavotte.

"The Old World celebrated death," said Treves.

"Where are the bones?"

"No one else must know," said Treves.

"Where are the bones?"

"Sealed in a church."

"You told me that much in your letter," she said. Felipa considered the advantages of rescuing the remains without the book collector, but the heirs had honored his compassion and romantic association with the House of Life.

"We can drive together," said Treves.

"To where?" asked Felipa.

"Gravesend on the River Thames," said Treves.

"How far from here?" asked Felipa.

"Less than an hour."

"I have a meeting in the morning and would rather travel by train," said Felipa. "Thank you for the offer, but name a time and place where we could meet at Gravesend."

"Tomorrow at the Three Daws on the corner of Crooked Lane and High Street," he said. "Near the Town Pier on the River Thames." Treves repeated the instructions and then asked her about the House of Life and the remains of Christopher Columbus. "Is it true that your people can hear the eternal human past in enclosures?"

Pellegrine Treves, a Sephardic Jew, is a descendant of renowned families who were merchants, traders, hand talkers, and rabbinical scholars in Spain, Portugal, and Turkey. He is related to Moses Mocatta, Abraham de Oliveira, and other seventeenth century founders of the first Sephardic Congregation in London.

Albert Hyamson wrote in *The Sephardim of England* that "the Jews, who left Spain in 1492 and Portugal five years later, settled for the most part in North Africa, Italy, and the Ottoman Empire." The marranos, or forced converts, "settled in increasing numbers in South and Central America and the West Indies where, although still under Spanish and Portuguese rule, they thought that the hand of the Inquisition and of its secular supporters would be lighter," and a number of these refugees escaped persecution in North America. Later, many families moved to New Mexico. Conversos and marranos such as these were the founders of the Sephardi community in England.

King Edward ruled on October 10, 1290, the "expulsion of the Jews from England. Practically every Jew left the country, and it was not until the middle of the seventeenth century that the lawyers gave the opinion that there was no bar to residence of Jews in England."

A few Jews, following the expulsion from Spain in 1492, settled in London. "The presence of this small group soon became known in Spain and protests against the harbouring of its members were made by his Most Catholic Majesty. The marriage of the Prince of Wales and Catherine of Aragon was then being negotiated, and as a part of the agreement Henry VII undertook to break up the small community. . . . In fact it was from the exiles from Portugal of 1496 more than from those from Spain four years earlier that the new Sephardi settlements in England and elsewhere were drawn." They had been prominent in international commerce. Francisco Mendes and his wife, Beatrice de Luna, for instance, were financiers in London and Europe. Christopher

Columbus was educated and influenced by marranos when he lived in Lisbon.

The Sephardi communities had endured religious and political persecution, avoidance and expulsion from nations in the Old World. Their heroic travail is shared in memories and literature with tribal cultures of the New World. Sephardi healers and tribal hand talkers bear their stories in the blood; the survivors are buried beside each other in the House of Life.

Samuel Pepys, the seventeenth century bigoted diarist, would have resisted the hand talkers and tribal ceremonies as much as he did a service in a synagogue on Creechurch Lane. He wrote on October 14, 1663, that "in the end they had a prayer for the King, which they pronounced his name in Portuguese; but the prayer; like the rest, in Hebrew. But, Lord! to see the disorder, laughing, sporting, and no attention, but confusion in all their service, more like brutes than people know the true God, would make a man forswear ever seeing them more; and indeed I never did see so much or could have imagined there had been any religion in the whole world so absurdly performed as this. . . ."

Pellegrine Treves, the first, moved to London in the early eighteenth century and married twice. Bathsheba, his second wife, was daughter of Moses de Paiba; their son Pellegrine rose to the rank of Postmaster General after forty years in the service of the East India Company.

The descendants of some of these families were settlers in the New World; some of the heirs might have been removed once more with tribal crossbloods in the harsh politics of race and wealth. Hyamson points out in *The Sephardim of England* that Sir Alexander Cumming, a Scottish lawyer who was "somewhat mentally unstable," moved to South Carolina in 1729; he was "inspired, so it was said, by a dream of his wife. He got himself appointed chief lawgiver of the Cherokee Nation of Indians and in the following year presented seven of the Cherokee chiefs whom he had taken to England to the King and also drew up a sort of British Government, further proposing a Jewish settlement on a large scale on their lands. His proposals included the settlement of three million Jewish families in the Cherokee mountains. . . .

"This project also proved abortive. Apart from Georgia it was not until 1750 that Jews began to settle in South Carolina, but there as independent not assisted immigrants." Lopez de Oliveira and other marranos, newcomers from Old World persecution, established a rabbinate and founded Charles Town. "Seven years later, in 1757, they acquired a cemetery," their first House of Life in the New World.

Pellegrine Treves folded his hands to listen at the masque; however, his hands could not bear the silence and moved into being as she told stories about her past career as a lawyer, her return to the reservation, and the trailer house at the headwaters with Miigis and Stone.

"Even here there is a shaman who knows you," said Treves. "He said you teased the bear in him and scared all the pets at Washington Square in New York."

"What are you saying?" asked Felipa.

"That's all he told me about you," said Treves.

"His name?" demanded Felipa.

"Transom," said Treves.

"Where is he now?" asked Felipa

"There, on the other side of the room near the door," he said. Treves pointed to a narrow man in a black leather cape; the man wore an enormous beaver felt hat, and his features were disguised by a mustache and thick beard.

"Does he know we are here?" asked Felipa.

"Yes, of course, he was kind enough to make available the news about the hearing, and he gave me your address at the headwaters," said Treves.

"Transom de Bear," she shouted twice from the table. He turned and moved toward her through the dancers. "He's a shaman who could vanish in his own clothes." She waved with excitement, but somehow, in the motion of dancers, and the shudder of the lights in the room, he vanished at the masque.

"He must be at the entrance," said Treves.

"Transom is no more," she said. Felipa would not reveal her worries, but she asked the book collector to escort her back to the Belle Sauvage Inn.

London was abandoned at that late hour; the lonesome horses, statues and stones carved in a lost summer, crewed at the circles under the waxen lights. Colors were hidden at the cold borders; here and there banners in blood and gold decorated a pallid facade to honor the glories of the crown.

Felipa telephoned the headwaters that night from under the covers of the narrow bed in her cold room. "Pellegrine Treves leans too much on manners, but he is an honest man," she told Stone.

"What does he say?" asked Stone.

"He wore a blue mask and talked with his hands," said Felipa.

"That's a start," said Stone.

"He listens," she said. "He even convinced me that Transom was at the party, dressed in a cape, and he said the shaman gave him our address."

"Who was he, then?"

"Transom could never grow a beard worth mentioning, he was too close to the bone, but the disguise worked on the book collector," said Felipa.

"The people in his books," said Stone.

"The imposter vanished when I called to him, and that worries me," said Felipa. "Transom was much too insecure to avoid me, he needed the attention of women and the acceptance of the tribe."

"So, what happens now?"

"Treves wants me to meet him late tomorrow at Gravesend," she said. "I'm sure there's more to the name than the place, but someone said it means the end of the grove."

"Better at first sight," said Stone.

"Where did you hear that?"

"Captain Treves Brink, who else?"

"Pellegrine Treves, names at first sight," said Felipa.

"So, where is Pocahontas?"

"Somewhere at Gravesend," she said, "but he won't tell me until we meet tomorrow at the Three Daws, and even then he might direct me to the church, or wherever, rather than handing over the bones himself, because he seems to be worried about criminal possession."

"Carry a sprig of white pine," said Stone.

"Naturally," she said. Felipa and the heirs carry a cut of white pine when they travel alone, as bald eagles have fresh sprigs in their nests. "If only white pine could heat this room."

"Where is Gravesend?" asked Stone.

"Near London on the River Thames," said Felipa.

"Call me the minute you hold her remains," said Stone.

"Listen to the mistle thrush," said Miigis.

"Did you see them?" asked Felipa.

"I dream you with mistle thrush last night," said Miigis.

"Miigis, count the crows in the morning until you see me in a few more days, and dream me with the birds and Admire," said Felipa.

The sun was smothered on the rise over London Bridge. The moist breeze carried the scent of sour limestone, carbon monoxide, pigeons, soiled cardboard, and burned plastics, down to the cold reach of the River Thames.

Felipa visited with a barrister at the Royal Courts of Justice to discuss the "pious intentions" decision over the ownership of the King of the Dancers statue, and then she ate lunch in a cafe at Neals Yard near Covent Gardens. That afternoon she inquired of Pellegrine Treves at an antiquarian bookstore on Cecil Street; she was reassured that he was the "most reputable and distinguished antiquarian book collector in the world."

Later she walked down Middle Temple Lane, around the gardens, east on Victoria Embankment to New Bridge Street near the Belle Sauvage Inn, and used the Underground between Blackfriars and Monument. She walked across London Bridge, over the River Thames, and on the north bank saw the haunting Tower of London; closer, she saluted the twin gothic bascules of Tower Bridge. The Tower of London, built in the eleventh century, was a royal residence when Pocahontas visited London. She boarded the *George* near the Tower of London that same day in 1617.

Felipa walked to London Bridge Station and boarded a British Rail train to Gravesend. The sun was low over the River Thames. She walked from the station to Stone Street, across King Street, and continued toward the Town Pier on Princes Street. She turned at St. George's Parish Church and admired in the garden the bronze statue of Princess Pocahontas, a replica of a statue in Jamestown, Virginia.

Gravesend was once the pilot port to London. The long ferry carried passengers between the two cities for more than four centuries. Black Elk, as others on ships from the New World, landed at Gravesend. Buffalo Bill Cody had hired more than a hundred tribal people for his Wild West Show, and chartered the steamer *State of Nebraska* for an exhibition in London.

Gravesend smelled of the sea, the pale mire on shore, and the scent of chalk and lime burners once located in Slave's Alley. The waterline was haunted by white chalkers, and river pilots, and the explorers who set sail for other worlds from the town piers. Sir Martin Frobisher attempted three times to discover the Northwest Passage. John Cabot also sailed from Gravesend; he discovered Cape Breton, which he thought was Asia, in 1497.

Richard Church wrote in *Kent* that "Gravesend is a maritime, one might say a saline, place. There is a robust, hornpipe character about its people. One expects to see a parrot in every front room, and a tattooist's shop round every corner." Pocahontas saw the last bright lights at Gravesend.

Pocahontas was born in 1595. Powhatan, the overlord of a tribal crescent on Chesapeake Bay, and his wife, Winganuske, named their daughter Matoaka, a tender metaphor. Pocahontas was a dubious colonial nickname that had sexual overtones, "a playful little girl." She married Kocoum in the tribal manner. Then, a short time later, she was betrothed to John Rolfe, a tobacco grower, and married on April 5, 1614, by Reverend Richard Buck. Grace Steele Woodward wrote in *Pocahontas* that the guests were "summoned to the ceremony by church bells, whose chimes echoed pleasantly on the Jamestown air."

The first converted tribal bride in the New World wore a "tunic of white Dacca muslin" and a "flowing veil and long robe of rich material. Her father sent her a chain of pearls and Sir Thomas Dale gave her an Italian ring," wrote Carolyn Thomas Foreman in *Indians Abroad*. The couple lived in a house on the shore of the James River near Bermuda Hundred. Rolfe was appointed Secretary of the Virginia Colony. Thomas Rolfe, their only child, was born a year later.

Some of these men of the Old World would have been dismissed, as their wives and children were tribal, but in the New World colonial survival condoned, in one instance, racial intermarriage. The Book of Ezra provides severe measures against mixed marriages. Ezra the priest said, "You have broken faith in marrying foreign women."

Alexander Whitaker, an educated and pious man, wrote to a minister of the Blackfriars in London: Pocahontas married "an honest and discreet English gentleman, Master Rolfe, and that after she openly renounced her country idolatry, confessed the faith of Jesus Christ, and was baptized; which thing Sir Thomas Dale had labored a long time to ground in her."

Pocahontas, John Rolfe, their son, and others sailed on the *Treasurer* and arrived at Plymouth on June 12, 1616. They stayed at the Belle Sauvage Inn on Ludgate Hill in London. She was praised by distinguished gentlemen, entertained, honored by royalty, and nine months later prepared to return to the civilization of the New World.

Pocahontas had been weakened by social observance and disease; she boarded the *George* with her husband and son. The ship sailed on the River Thames twenty five miles to Gravesend. There, "in painful simplicity," wrote Philip Barbour in *Pocahontas and Her World*, "as spring came to England, Princess Pocahontas begged to be taken ashore. She was deathly ill. . . . The *George* dropped anchor, and Pocahontas was carried onto the little wharf. A hundred yards or so away, the three-story inn rose massively before them. Pocahontas was hurried to a room, and a doctor was summoned—that much, at least, may be surmised, for there is no record.

"It was too late. Climate, that had killed many an Englishman in Virginia, took the life of Pocahontas in England. Climate, and a broken heart. There is no need to postulate some epidemic, some disease."

Charles Ap Thomas, in *Ye True Narrative of ye Princess Pocahontas*, wrote that she was buried "on the site, or in the close vicinity, of the then disused old parish church of Saint Marie's." Later her burial was ensured in the chancel of St. George's Parish Church; the register reveals that "Rebecca Wrothe wyff of Thomas Wroth gent a Virginia lady borne, here is buried in ye chanuncell." There has been no evidence to support the rumors that her remains were stolen by body snatchers in the seventeenth century and sold to collectors in London.

Miigis saw birds in the wild time of her dreams, and there in the garden near the church, a mistle thrush turned on the highest branch of a tree. The low sun brightened the brown thrush and the clock on the church tower. Felipa heard the thrush and watched her shadow lean with Pocahontas over the lush garden, broken on the iron gate; the sun wavered as the shadows reached out over the cold black road.

The mistle thrush is a storm cock, the watchers and dreamers say, as in the winter the songs, the sound of flute notes, are heard to warn of storms. The wind raised the mistle thrush on the branch, and the song wavered with the shadows. Then the shadows vanished in the garden.

Felipa walked down West Street past the New Falcon Inn to Crooked Lane; there, on the corner; across from the Pier Hotel, was the Three Daws on the River Thames.

Pellegrine Treves was seated at a small table near the window. "I just arrived myself," he said, and with chivalrous manners held her coat and directed her to a chair at the table. He ordered sherry, and she ordered a pint of bitter. In the distance, from the liquor bar at the entrance, she heard the matriclinous rancor and the haunting pities of Sinéad O'Connor.

"The weather has turned," said Treves.

"Yes, the mistle thrush sang down the sun," said Felipa.

"Are you a dedicated bird watcher?"

"My daughter dreams birds," said Felipa.

"The mistle cock, as you know, is our weather bird," said Treves.

"Yes, the storm cock," said Felipa.

"You were at the church then?"

"That statue laid a lonesome shadow," said Felipa.

"Lonesome, indeed," said Treves.

"The invention of a tourist civilization," said Felipa.

"Quite, not a pose in the proper sense, but a rather cruel and arrested romance, as if she might burst from the hollow bronze in full stride back to the New World," said Treves.

"She would be walking north," said Felipa.

"Indeed, and her remains are hidden at the church," said Treves.

"Hidden in the chancel after all?"

"No, her remains were first stolen from the rector's vault when a new chancel was built a century ago, and over the years, stolen once or twice again from the secret owners, but then, as others learned of my interests in rare books about American Indians, it was inevitable that the remains of Pocahontas would be offered to me," said Treves.

"But why hide her at the church?"

"Pocahontas touched me as a child, she was beautiful, courageous, so persecuted by manners, and she died so young, lonesome for her homeland," said Treves.

"The noble savage," she said in a cold and critical tone. Felipa resisted his romantic revisions of tribal cultures and women, but the tone of her mordant response was unclear: "Too much romance subdues our humor and miseries."

"I was in love at first sight of her in portraits, and then my adolescent love matured in the most unusual and personal way, as I learned that my relatives must have danced with her at the masque, she was touched by my family," he said, and pressed his hands on the table. "I was determined to prove that our families were related, that my relatives married hers in the New World, that we were of the same tribe, that we would be united in the House of Life."

"Who stole her bones?" asked Felipa.

"I considered the return of her remains to the church where she might have been buried, but then the matter was settled when I read about the headwaters and the Heirs of Columbus," said Treves.

"So, you could have delivered her remains to me at the masque or at the Belle Sauvage Inn," she said. "Instead, here we are near the inn of her death."

"Indeed, but the truth of the matter is my fear of death and human remains," he said, and moaned. Treves pressed his hands on the table each time he mentioned the remains of the woman he loved. "I could not bear to overturn my love of her with the reality of her remains under my arm." Treves cleared his throat. "You see, it was quite enough that she was locked in the boot of my car, but once at the church it took me hours and hours of consideration to overcome my fear and resistance to hide her remains in the church."

"Vindos de Portugal, what does that mean?" asked Felipa.

"The refugees, we were identified as marranos and refugees," he said. Treves was relieved that she had turned the conversation. "Now, of course, the adversities of the past are measures of honor and compassion."

"Marvelous, the turns of language," said Felipa.

"Indeed, however bold the revisions, there is much to admire in a civilization that turns the real world of rubbish tips into civic amenities, and other royal euphemisms for common trash."

"What books do you collect?" asked Felipa.

"I started my collection more than forty years ago with doublure and fore-edged painted books, but the obscure pastoral scenes did not hold my interest for long," said Treves.

"How is that done?" she asked. Felipa pretended that she had at least a basic knowledge of antiquarian books. "I mean, how many methods were there?"

"The edges of the pages are fanned and then painted, so that when the book is closed, unfanned as it were, the scenes on the edges are not seen," said Treves.

"But your interest turned to American Indians," said Felipa.

"Yes, but not straight away," he said. "I built a very good collection of first edition association copies, mostly in fiction, but with a few others in history and philosophy."

"Indian novels?"

"Yes, several first editions with signatures by James Welch, Louise Erdrich, Leslie Silko, and a special copy dedicated to me by the novelist and book collector Thomas King, but the most unusual association edition in my collection is *The Voice in the Margin*, by Arnold Krupat," said Treves.

"Krupat said he was an Indian?"

"No, not really, you see a first edition of his book was sold at public auction with marginal notes by N. Scott Momaday, winner of the Pulitzer prize, as you know," said Treves.

"He wrote *The House Made of Dawn*, *The Way to Rainy Mountain*, and, as you know, he won the first Native American Literature prize," said Felipa.

"Yes, I have signed copies of those and a first edition of his second novel the *Ancient Child*, as well as his autobiography, *The Names*, with notes he made for a public reading," said Treves.

"What does he say about Krupat?" asked Felipa.

"Well, as the marginal notes are attributed to Momaday, one would say he was not pleased with Krupat, rather captious, but ironies abound even in the staid relations of antiquarian book auctions," he said. "The marginal notes, you see, were by another distinguished novelist who pretended to be Momaday." Treves touched the pleasures of antiquarian tenure, the arcanum of association literature, the subdued glories of a book collector.

"What Momaday might have written?"

"Indeed, and the book was returned to auction," he said. "I acquired it at a real bargain and learned later that the marginal notes were by another notable novelist, so the copy has a double association, you might say."

"Who wrote the notes?" asked Felipa.

"That much is confidential," said Treves.

"The margins, then," said Felipa.

"Krupat wrote that Momaday offered an 'invariant poetic voice that everywhere commits itself to subsuming and translating all other voices,' and so on, to which the novelist made a marginal note, 'but not enough to subsume your arrogance and dialogic domination.'"

"Sounds like an esoteric word war to me, but at the same time the sense of oral stories in the printed word is mythic, the remembered poet over the noted critic," said Felipa.

"Indeed, but Krupat's discussion of 'racial memory' drew the sharpest marginal responses," said Treves. "The novelist noted, 'Krupat gives head to footnotes, how would he know about tribal memories?'"

"Krupat would be the trickster on the margins," said Felipa.

"The book is great, and the notes are cruel," said Treves.

"The politics of tribal creation stories never ends," said Felipa.

"Most of the editions in my collection are valued for their association rather than racial politics," he said. Treves checked his wrist watch several times. "Forgive me, but we must be at the church on the hour."

"Whatever you say," said Felipa.

"The church ladies open the door at seven o'clock for about fifteen minutes for the cleaners, otherwise the church is locked but for services," said Treves.

"So, tell me about your other books then." said Felipa.

"You're too kind," said Treves.

"No, really, the most interesting editions."

"I have acquired several novels and manuscripts by William Faulkner, first editions of *As I Lay Dying, Go Down, Moses*, and others, with perfect dust jackets, and a signed first edition of *Look Homeward, Angel*, by Thomas Wolfe," said Treves.

"How about Indian Bibles?" asked Felipa.

"John Eliot's famous *Upbiblum God* is in my collection," said Treves.

"How much is that worth?"

"You must mean at auction?"

"Yes," said Felipa.

"The 1663 Cambridge edition might bring more than thirty thousand dollars," said Treves. He smiled, folded his hands on the table, and checked the time. "We have forty minutes."

"Do you buy at auctions?" asked Felipa.

"Seldom, my collection is more selective and personal, for instance, several years ago I acquired from an antiquarian dealer the twenty volume set of *The North American Indian*, by Edward Curtis, with association signatures of the author and President Theodore Roosevelt," said Treves.

"Fascinating, but what's your most valuable edition?"

"The *Manabosho Bestiary Curiosa*, no doubt," said Treves.

"Stone told me about that book," said Felipa.

"A rare anonymous manuscript collection of wild erotic stories with original drawings in color of the vainglorious trickster posing with his enormous penis," he said. "The edition is cased and published at Madeline Island, Lake Superior, in 1653."

"Schoolcraft must be the author," said Felipa.

"No, he came later," said Treves.

"Could this be the work of a missionary?"

"Now there is a trickster story," said Treves.

"Stone would like a copy," said Felipa.

"Several publishers have invited me, over the years, to consider a special facsimile first edition of the manuscript, cased and stained," said Treves.

"How many manuscripts are there?" asked Felipa.

"One, no more," said Treves.

"Incredible, but how can it be that you own the only copy of a tribal manuscript that was written more than three centuries ago?" asked Felipa.

"An estate sale in London," said Treves.

"How does the only copy end up here?" asked Felipa.

"George Catlin may have obtained the manuscript from the Ojibway Indians who were brought to Paris by a Canadian, or at least that is one of the theories of how *Manabosho Bestiary Curiosa* landed in England, but even more complicated is the date of publication in 1653," said Treves.

"The trickster calendar," said Felipa.

"I have been told that the trickster bestiary was published as a tribal antidote to *Catechism in the Indian Language*, by John Eliot, the first book printed in an Indian language that same year," said Treves.

"Now that makes sense in trickster time," said Felipa.

"Prurient interests alone would seem insufficient motivation for a cleric or colonial factor to return with such an erotic manuscript on his own," said Treves.

"Black Elk might have brought the manuscript," said Felipa. "He was here with Buffalo Bill Cody in the Wild West Show and met Queen Victoria."

"I understand the Sioux and Ojibways were enemies," said Treves. "So why would he have possession of the bestiary, unless, of course, he intended to use the manuscript as a trickster coup count in the Old World?"

"Trickster stories and tribal enemies are not the same," said Felipa.

"Indeed, but someone would have remembered the manuscript," said Treves. He checked the time once more and paid the waiter for the beer and sherry.

"Have the ladies arrived?" asked Felipa.

"They should do in a few minutes," he said, and held her coat. Treves was a familiar face in the Three Daws. Once or twice a month he visits with rare book collectors, and a retired captain of a ship. Even as a child he was eager to hear stories about the sea, but he has never collected books about exploration or ships.

The River Thames soughed on the cold moist air, and the lights of the passenger ferry wavered in the distance. Treves turned and explained as they walked that the remains of Pocahontas were sealed in a narrow black metal case and hidden in a storage closet under the stairs at St. George's Parish Church.

"The closet is to the left as you enter the church," he said. "You enter through a small door near the toilets, so be careful not to hit your head."

"As *you* enter?"

"Yes, you must understand how much this has troubled me, and my only comfort now is that you will bury her in the House of Life," said Treves.

"Where will you be?" asked Felipa.

"Outside, in the garden by the statue," said Treves.

"You won't leave me alone?"

"Not until you have her remains in hand," said Treves.

"What about the ladies?" asked Felipa.

"The ladies will probably be in the small kitchen area to the left, if not, then appreciate the stained glass windows for a few minutes," said Treves.

Felipa listened at the black double doors; inside, the ladies raised their voices over a recent wedding. Treves waited near the statue in the garden. The trickster poacher pushed the door and entered the cold church. The ladies smiled on cue and directed the tourist to the stained glass at the sides of the chancel. Felipa studied the arched windows, but she was poised to rescue the remains of Pocahontas.

The two memorial windows were presented by the Colonial Dames of America in 1914. The Ruth window on the left shows Pocahontas in a rigid court costume, with a wide lace collar and an ostrich feather fan in her right hand; the stained glass image is similar to the seventeenth century engraved portrait by Simon de Passe, the only likeness made during her life, and the portrait of Lady Rebecca in the National Portrait Gallery. A facsimile of the engraving was published as the frontispiece to the *Generall Historie*, by John Smith, in London, 1624.

The Rebecca window on the right of the chancel shows Pocahontas in the lower right corner in baptismal attire, the representation of the first tribal convert married and buried as a curiosity in the traditions of the Old World.

Felipa heard the ladies in the kitchen area; she moved close to the wall and found the storage closet door open, and one of the ladies was inside. "The loo is over there, dear," she said, and pointed.

"Yes, thank you," she said, and smiled. Felipa waited in the toilet until she heard the storage door close; then she flushed the toilet and dashed to the area under the stairs. She found the black unmarked metal case behind a stack of portraits. The seams of the heavy case were sealed with wax, the only indication that it contained human remains.

Felipa walked out of the church unseen, closed the black door, and rushed to the statue of Pocahontas. "The ladies were too kind," she said out of breath as she rounded the statue, but no one was there. Pellegrine Treves had vanished in the night.

Felipa saw several people approaching the church on the garden path; she turned behind the statue and ran on the wet grass to the western gate at the back of the church. She had rescued a tribal woman from the cruelties of more than three centuries of civilization; she was at peace, unconcerned, and lonesome for the heirs at the headwaters. She closed the iron gate and walked back toward the train station on Princes Street.

She remembered the description of the port town, a saline place with a hornpipe character; she whistled a tune from the *New World Symphony*, by Antonín Dvořák, and tasted the saline air of Gravesend.

Felipa walked close to a row of abandoned buildings that fronted the narrow street. At Church Alley two men reached out, covered her head with a hood, and pulled her back into the darkness. She swung the metal case around and struck both men, one on the shoulder, a glancing blow, and the other man in the face; the metal cut his cheek to the bone. Felipa recovered hours later; she was tied to the pipes in a cold and dark room in a building near the church and the statue of Pocahontas.

Miigis dreamed an earlier season over the thin rose shadows at dawn; she counted the crows in the tender birch. She could hear them, but she could not reach the vast number that bounced and croaked near the trailer house; she could not reach the stories of the crows. Admire licked her hands and barked at the morning star, a blue radiance in the window.

Stone waited that morning for Felipa to telephone as she had promised before she left London. Later he called the Belle Sauvage Inn and learned from the desk clerk that "Madam Flowers has not yet returned to check out." The operator searched the directories, and at last he placed a call to the book collector Pellegrine Treves.

"Felipa has not returned to the hotel," shouted Stone.

"Who might this be?" asked Treves.

"Stone Columbus."

"Yes, forgive me, but we parted before dinner," said Treves.

"Where did she go from the Three Daws?" asked Stone.

"St. George's Parish."

"When did you see her last?"

"As she came out of the church," said Treves.

"Call me if you hear anything," he said, and slammed the receiver down. Stone stood at the window with Miigis and Admire. They could do nothing but wait for the telephone to ring.

Later in the morning a man telephoned and said in a disguised voice that "Felipa Flowers will be released unharmed when you trade the remains of Columbus for Pocahontas."

"Name the place," shouted Stone.

"Gatwick airport in London."

"I don't have a passport," said Stone.

"Boston International, then," said the man.

"When?" asked Stone.

"Tomorrow at midnight."

"Where is she now, put her on the phone," he shouted, but there was silence and then the connection was dead. Stone summoned the heirs to the stone tavern. Christopher Columbus was disinterred once more in the politics of racial terrorism and the shame of colonial fortunes.

Stone was instructed to place the silver casket in a duffel and wait near the curb in front of the departure terminal at Northwest Airlines. The heirs decided that he should travel with Miigis to Boston. He made reservations, packed the purple duffel, the one Felipa carried to New York, and drove to the airport in Minneapolis.

Miigis was awakened by jackdaws in a dream early the next morning, a presentiment. The jackdaws landed on a statue. An hour before their flight was scheduled to depart they learned that Felipa had been found dead in England.

Stone drove back to the headwaters in silence. Pellegrine Treves was the first to telephone with the morbid details of her death. Felipa, he said in a broken voice, was found in the morning at the base of the statue of Pocahontas at St. George's Parish Church in Gravesend.

"The cause of death has not been determined, but police have ruled the case a possible murder and have ordered an investigation," said Treves.

"Please, would you search at Gravesend?" asked Stone.

"I understand, say no more," he said, and drove to the church the next morning. He remembered their conversations, the moment she pushed the parish door open, and later, from a distance, her shadow near the statue.

Treves reported to Stone that Felipa was found with her back on the base of the statue, facing the river, her arms and legs were folded to the side, and her head was bent forward on her chest.

Felipa was found with no shoes; her blue moccasins and her leather purse were never located. The metal case had vanished, and was never mentioned to the police or the vicar of the parish. The ladies in the church remembered a late tourist, nothing more.

"I found faint marks in the grass and believe that she was dragged to the statue by two people from the street behind the church," said Treves. "She mentioned white pine that night at the masque, and there was such a cutting at the entrance to an abandoned building across from the church."

Scotland Yard homicide inspectors held the body for two weeks to schedule sophisticated forensic tests and studies to determine the cause of death; however, in the end the case was closed. There was no evidence of alcohol, barbiturates, alkaloids, or any other toxic chemi-

cals in her body fluids or tissue; there were minor bruises on her
shoulders, and more serious bruises and contusions on her wrists, but
no evidence of mortal wounds or asphyxiation. The cause of death was
ruled unintentional, and by natural but unresolved causes. The detective inspectors reported that the deceased, "Felipa Flowers, may have
died from exposure or loneliness at Gravesend."

VICTORIA PARK

Tianjin is partitioned in memories of lost relatives, colonial concessions, shadow capitalism, and painted faces from classical operas. Memories waver at night, never in the heart.

Griever considered the old street names on colonial maps. Marechal Foch, Saint Louis, Gaston Kahn, and then located the cathedral where the Lazarist Sisters of Saint Vincent de Paul had opened an orphanage.

John Hersey wrote that in their eagerness to win souls the sisters paid "a cash premium for each child brought in to them; and, what was worse, they were said to have paid to have sick and dying children carried to them, so they could baptize them *in articulo mortis*. In 1870, rumors were circulated that after conducting their mystic rites the nuns extracted the babies' eyes and hearts for purposes of witchery. Four men were arrested and beheaded. One man, under torture, confessed that he stole children and sold them to the verger of the cathedral."

"The city went wild," wrote Hersey, who was born in Tianjin, the child of missionaries. "The mob stripped the sisters naked, one by one, and in full sight of the surviving nuns ripped their bodies open, cut their breasts off, gouged their eyes out, and, finally, impaled them on long spears, hoisted them in the air, and threw them into the burning chapel of the orphanage."

Griever was astonished that the other missionaries survived that night; but he was even more surprised to find apple pie on the menu in the old colonial hotel restaurant. He folded the old map with care, pinched his ear, and ordered. The waitress returned with the last slice of pie. She stood at his side to practice her pronouns and verbs while he told stories from wild histories.

"Sian is beset with terra cotta warriors and inert tourists, cosmetic beasts in cold museums," the trickster muttered and searched for a wild hair on his temple, "but dreams never close down to serve the state."

"You eat pie."

"What kind of apples are these?"

"We eat pie."

"Not with chopsticks."

"You eat spoon."

"Confucius was a dream buried in wild histories," he said between enormous scoops of pie. "The old masters were buried with their eunuchs in fine fast dust. . . ."

"You like pie."

"Ceramic spears burst overhand."

"We like pie."

"Genealogies and reveries were cropped with each succession and revolution," he said and raised the spoon like a jade mace over the table.

"You mop up now."

"Where did you learn that?"

"You finish pie," she commanded. When she smiled, the mass of her cheeks rose close to her brows; she peered down at the white plate and tablecloth like an arctic hunter.

"Arenas, where millions of children are buried in unmarked graves, silent corners, streets and parks, have been renamed, but colonialism, that worm in the muscles of the heart, persists in more than memories and printed words," he said and then cleaned the plate with his thumb.

Griever is a tattler in restaurants; when he eats alone he lectures to waitresses. Communism, trickeries, and comedies are his public themes; at the guest house, he argues with the teachers over capitalism.

"Communist soldiers," he roared in the baronial restaurant, "burned the common markers between racial and cultural concessions, wrenched the opium dealers, craven cloud chewers, and dismembered them on the road.

"Place names were purged," he bellowed to the vacant tables, "but nine colonial nations succeeded in their vaults and domes, spires, groins, cusps and lobes on arches, and in their moats and stunted trees, sculpturesque gardens, monolithic markets, the same old pillars hauled back from the shadows."

Victoria Park is the atrium in colonial concessions, carved from class reveries. The Astor House Hotel loomed there on London Meadows and Victoria Road, one block from the Hai He. The river bears the same name, which means "ocean river," but the roads have been renamed the Jianguo and Chengdu.The Astor House is now the Tianjin Hotel and Victoria Park has become a number. The hedgerows and imperial gardens, once sculpted with the same dedication as a hand tied carpet, were razed during the revolution. Colonial names were removed from directories, and common street maps became state secrets.

Hua Lian is the secular verger of Victoria Park, as the tourists remember the green, and warden of the bicycle parking lot at the corner. This is a comfortable position for an old blind woman who paints her face red and white, and who has refused to alter her memories from the concessions to please the new masters and shadow capitalists. The numbered factories, hotels, technologies, and conversions were not visual; numbers, she told the cadres, are "blind, and repeated, not imagined."

Hua Lian, which means "picture" or "painted face," a traditional role for actors in classical operas, was born blind behind the park in a pleasant house where her mother was a servant to the president of the concession coal companies; her father served the green and the gardens and was a member of secret societies.

Zhou Enlai, Wu Chou, Hua Lian, and other celebrated actors attended the Nankai Middle School in Tianjin. The principal, Zhang Boling, encouraged men and women to be activists. Zhou Enlai became premier of the People's Republic of China; Wu Chou, the warrior clown who studied shamanism and dharma trickeries, is the overseer of the campus gate; and Hua Lian is the verger of concession memories, trees, and the elephant slide, but, she insists, not the public toilets at Victoria Park.

Zhou Enlai invited Hua Lian to march in student protests. She was known as Hua Ci then, a nickname which means "painted word," because she was favored with a sixth sense, an acoustic kinesthesia; she could remember total conversations and visual details from several perspectives. Now, at her booth in the park, she pictures the past and recounts conversations. Zhou Enlai is there, or Feifei, as he was known when he wrote editorials for the student newspaper. He was arrested when he crawled under a gate at the governor's offices to demand the release of other activists. He was in prison isolation for six months, she remembers, and wrote messages on toilet paper. "In the beginning everyone gathered for a lecture given by Zhou Enlai on Marxism and historical materialism," she remembered his words.

"Tianjin has never been the same when he moved," she said, "but he wrote to me from other places. He told me he talked with Ernest Hemingway, and I could see the two of them together in Shanghai. Zhou with his new Sam Browne belt, and Hemingway with his wide moustache, but in the end, you know," she whispered, "Hemingway was no more than a word shadow. He was nervous and weakened with words, and we were cautious with word capitalists who attended revolutions. Hemingway wrote that the Communists 'always try to give the impression that they are the only ones who really fight.' Some writers raise the dust and wash their hands at the same time."

Hua Lian endured the revolutions behind a painted face. Her father was murdered and her mother died from fear. For months Hua Ci lived in Victoria Park with other lost children and ate bark from the trees.

She has never dressed for the reformation of place names, nor has she pretended to be a second in the public duels between the pragmatists and ideologists in each generation of power; her denial of the new number place names was at once overlooked because her blindness was seen as an inner exile, an eternal prison in a new land.

The bright blooms in the atrium, the dark walnut beams in the old hotel, warm pear pie, the cries of children on the bund, the sounds of horses on the old roads that circled the park, and other tastes and fancies, she has stationed in her visual memories. These lucid interior visions were not altered in word shadows or the revolution. Time bends in her marrow, a natural arch; the radiant gestures she remembers from causeries cannot be measured in the politics of names or the philosophies of written grammars.

Griever could not remember where he parked his bicycle. The Flying Pigeon was the same color as dozens of others in the even rows; the locks were even similar, bolted to the rear frame. Several saddles were covered with bright cloth and there were red pennons tied to some, but he had neglected to mark his bicycle for easier identification in the public lots.

Griever approached the old woman in the narrow booth at the entrance to the park. He leaned over the high counter and asked the warden, who held her head down, if she understood his common problem. The booth was dark, humid, and smelled of cosmetic paint and Springtime Thunder, a popular fragrance. He asked a second time, but did not wait for an answer because he remembered a wide crease on the chain guard of his bicycle. He inspected each green Flying Pigeon from one end of the lot to the other and found seven with similar creases. When he leaned down for a closer examination, the verger appeared at his side. She wore black cloth shoes, faded blue trousers, and a canvas chimere. There was a hole at the end of her right shoe from an uneven bound toe. Griever raised his head and there was the woman with the picture face, the peculiar woman who waited at the bus stop with a horsehair duster.

Hua Lian paints her face in the tradition of the classical opera for her duties in the park. She wears a bright red and white cosmetic mask to forbear public pities. When she laughs two dark molluscoid sockets open on her round face. The missionaries awarded her dark glass eyes when she graduated from middle school, but her father buried them in the park during the revolution to avoid criticism. She weeds the garden in search of her cosmetic eyes.

She learned the moves and positions of traditional operas; she painted the blind sockets dark blue and touched the loose skin at the rims with gold and silver glitter. Now, when she smiles and moves, the hollows reveal a personal constellation.

"The numbered factories," she said.

"Creases?"

"Bruises, marred and broken parts, come out the same," she chanted," pragmatic designs from factory number two."

"Where did you learn that unusual accent," he queried and then examined the blue sockets and the rich red paint on her cheeks, chin, and thin neck. Her brows were luminous, like a light beneath the water, and she wore one braid down her narrow back.

"The owners of those with the red standards have not paid the fee, you see," she explained with her head turned to one side like a clown. When she spoke she picked at a black wart near her collarbone.

"Where did you learn to speak English?"

"Do you own a bicycle?"

"Yes, somewhere, but I never knew about a fee," he said and moved closer. He held his breath and looked deep into the dark blue hollows on her face.

"Ten fen, please," she said and held out her hand.

"For a bicycle, no less," he complained and searched his pockets. "Here," he said and watched her hand move toward him; her smooth brown fingers seemed to sense the space and distance to his hand, like an insect, and then with a sudden pinch she had the note.

"Would you be staring at me?"

"Nothing more than close regard," he parried.

"What is your *meng mingzi?*"

"Listen," he said to avoid the words and questions he did not understand, "the colors, the lines, how can you see to paint such perfect pictures on your face?"

"Look," she responded, an eschewal of his tributes, "was it your pleasure to taste the pear pie at the Astor House Hotel?"

"Not pear, the last slice of apple pie."

"Pear pie, to be sure."

"Do you ever answer questions?"

"Confucius was asked that question once."

"What was his answer?"

"Words are rituals, catechisms a slow dance."

"Shit, who are you?"

"The other ritual," she said and moved toward the booth at the end of the row. She pulled the door closed behind her and leaned over the high counter.

"Wait," he pleaded, "what other ritual?"

"Blind rituals," she said.

"Where is my bicycle?" he asked, but she had lowered her head in silence. "Listen, tribal tricksters gossip from the heart, give me that much," he appealed over the counter. The words bounced back from an invisible cultural seal.

Griever found his bicycle in the third row under a red plastic standard. He pedaled a few blocks back toward the guest house but he could not continue because the visage of the blind woman appeared on windows, on buses, and at corners he passed. He circled the Small White House District, once the concession of the United States, and returned to the park. He sat on a wooden bench with a view of the booth and waited for the woman to emerge.

Griever counted thirteen immature blossoms planted in the hard circle behind the bench. Two stems were broken and the petals brushed the dust like tired soldiers. The trees were painted with lime, white trunks poised like ceremonial dancers. Broad leaves shadowed the back of a ceramic elephant in the center of the park. Breaks in the shadows unraveled on children, sprouted in wild red and blue, pink and green, from a metal chute that curved down from the mouth of the elephant.

The trickster leaned back on the bench and watched the elephant, and then he traced the massive shadows, classic revival columns, from the old concession coal companies on the corner. The Communist Party has occupied the building since the liberation; soldiers in oversized uniforms protected the oak portals. The shadows danced between machines, over chalk line caricatures on the cracked concrete, over cold histories at the end of a worn tether.

Griever held his breath until the train lurched through the mountain tunnel in a dream. In the darkness the seats turned to cages and the soldiers to monkeys. He was alone, supine on the last hard bench at the end of the coach. The animals stared and pointed. He moved to avoid their attention; when he looked out the window to find his place in the middle world, his face was captured in a simian reflection on the uneven pane. He frowned, smiled, winked, and the animal cast back the same expressions in reverse order.

Griever cocked his thumb like a pistol and aimed; the train pitched to the side on a curve, his trigger finger shot between the bars, and an old monkey severed it at the second knuckle with her stained teeth. He pulled his hand back; the train leaned in the opposite direction, and the finger rolled back from the cage. He recovered the stub and pinched it back in place with his other hand.

The monkeys howled and bounded in circles when an anile figure with pictures on her face entered at the end of the car, three times the distance of a common coach. The animals were becalmed when the old woman walked near their cages. She raised her right hand to her ear, a salute, and the monkeys folded their hands in silence. She moved to the end of the coach with her head down.

Griever waited with his hands folded near the window, and then when he recognized the red and white lines and blue sockets, the wart on her neck, he leaped from the bench to the aisle. He reached to touch her hand and noticed that his trigger finger was upside down; the nail was turned down and brushed her wrist.

"What is your *meng mingzi?*" she asked and raised her head. There were small lanterns at the bottom of the blue sockets on her face. The light wavered when she moved her head.

"What does that mean?" he asked.

"Your name, dream name," she answered and turned back to the cages, "but it means more than that to the mind monkeys."

"More than what?" he asked and twisted his finger.

"What is your temper, show me your heart?"

"Listen," he responded, his standard salutation when he is troubled, "never mind my heart, my finger is on backward and nothing makes sense on this train."

Hua Lian touched the wart on her neck and the mind monkeys chattered while their cages turned back to seats. She moved down the aisle, stepped high over thresholds like an opera character, swished a horsehair duster in her hand, and when she passed their seats, the monkeys took the veil and became miniature nuns dressed in black habits and cowls with wide starched coifs shaped like speckled scallop shells.

"Jesus, Freud, Marx, and Mao," he said twice and counted the names with his fingers on the back of the seat, "this is a trick by the Gang of Four."

The train stopped at a crowded station. The nuns and other monkeys on the platform followed the old blind woman through the narrow streets of the town. Peasant women carried small lanterns and wailed behind the nuns. Children laughed at the monkeys under the veils.

Griever pushed through the crowd to be near the blind woman, but the closer he got the more animals he encountered. Then, when he reached to touch the braid with his turned finger, the nuns untied their cowls and stood naked; their bodies were covered with black hair.

"Yama, Yama, Yama, Yama," the monkeys chanted. Hundreds of them turned around him in a wide circle on the dirt road like a dark primal wheel.

Griever broke through the wheel and the dust shadows and ran to the end of the road. There, breathless in a small park, he clawed a panic hole between two fruit trees and screamed into the earth. The leaves shivered overhead. At the bottom of the hole he found one glass eye.

Hua Lian touched him on the shoulders, and then she moved back to watch him awaken. He stretched like an animal, rolled over on his back, handed her the glass eye, and cradled his head in his hands.

"Confucius screamed underwater," declared Hua Lian. She stood behind the bench near the panic hole and polished the dark eye. She wore a red silk coat with the faces of monkeys embroidered on the collar and the sleeves.

"Goldfish ponds?" he asked through his hands.

"Rain barrels," she answered.

"You answered a question," he said and then remembered the monkeys on the train. He watched her hands and recounted several fast scenes from his dream; he could not picture when he cut the panic hole in the hard earth behind the bench.

"Your finger has turned."

"The nail was down," he said and pinched his finger. He could not understand how she knew about the events in his dream. There were no marks on his finger.

"Broken thoughts?" she asked with a wide smile. "You must be the one who freed the pears at the street market."

"Chickens, not pears," he responded.

"Free the pears and cocks, free words, free the shadows," she said. Her teeth chattered like a small treed animal.

Wide shadows reached over the park and shrouded the booth and the elephant slide. The breeze that moved the broad leaves increased the acrid smell of urine from the open toilet at the corner.

"Must have pissed on the train," he whispered and pictured the steam down the hole and remembered how he tried to count the crossbeams that passed under the coach; more than a hundred ties before he closed and returned to his seat.

"Squeeze this under your nose," she said and handed him a small curved bundle of straw bound with a red ribbon.

"What is this?"

"*Da suan he ping*," she answered.

"What does that mean?"

"Garlic peace, for the toilet."

"No shit," he said and pinched the bundle. The scent raised his brows; his nostrils expanded with pleasure. He asked, but she would not reveal the herbal preparation.

Millions of fat flies swarmed over the dark mounds of human excrement in the toilet. The floor was wet with urine, several inches deep near the entrance. The servants who once cleaned the toilets are now the cadres; such menial duties were forbidden with liberation. The Gang of Four pressed doctors and teachers to serve socialism in public toilets, but since then the toilets have not been cleaned.

Griever held his breath and then pinched the garlic peace bundle under his nose to survive the stench; ammonia burned his eyes. He leaned back from the threshold and pissed hard and wide over the urine pond.

Hua Lian posed at the bus stop with a horsehair duster; exalted persons carried the duster, a token of refinement from the classical opera. She fingered the end and then swished the space around the double doors at the rear of each bus that stopped at the far corner of the park. Her manner was familiar to the regular passengers.

"Save this park," Griever said in a loud voice from behind. He pinched the garlic peace between sentences. "You said that last week when the bus stopped here, what did you mean?"

"Memories and trees."

"Why the trees?"

"Someone cuts parts from the trees at night."

"So, we can set a trap to catch the butchers," he suggested, "but why tell these strangers who pass on a bus?"

"Heart gossip," she said.

"Wait a minute," he insisted, "that's what I do, you got that line from me this afternoon."

"People will tell stories about that opera woman at the park and the person who cuts trees will hear and remember."

"Rather abstract conservation."

"Truth comes from peculiar places," she said as the next bus turned the corner near the park. "What I really do here is read faces on the bus."

"With one glass eye?"

"Watch me," she said and cut the space around his head with the horsehair duster, "like you watched those nuns on the train."

"Which reminds me," he said when he remembered a scene from the dark train, "in my dream this afternoon you had small blue lanterns in your eye sockets."

"Lantern is the word for eye in the cant of the old secret societies," she explained and then turned toward the street.

"Yama, what does the word mean?" he asked.

"Yama is the King of Darkness."

"Never mind," he said.

"The monkey nuns are on the bus," she said and cut small circles with the duster near the bus when it stopped.

"Where?"

"There, on the face of the driver."

"Never mind," he said.

"Who should we find on the next bus?"

"Confucius."

"The patient patriarch," she said and carved a figure from space with the horsehair duster, "the best voice for the rulers, the man of public altruism and filial pieties, the man who kissed stones but never broke them."

"Do you see him?"

"Wait, he is not yet on this bus," she said. The diesel bus shuddered to a stop at the corner but she turned from the street and aimed the duster back toward the park. She turned the duster in small circles and followed a stout man who carried a small leather suitcase. His feet never seemed to leave the concrete as he hurried to meet the bus. He paused at the double doors, tilted his head to the side, smiled, and then he entered. The doors snapped closed on his shadow.

"Confucius he is not," exclaimed Griever.

"Watch him move," she said. Her duster seemed to hold the bus at the corner while she construed his paternal moves. "Notice how he bends his head to women and children, how he kowtows to power, to those in uniforms."

"Kowtow indeed, how did you know that?"

"His heart gossip is bound in genealogies," she said and then lowered the duster. The engine started and the bus lurched from the curb. Hua Lian turned her head to the side and smiled; a child pressed her face to the window.

"Listen," he said, to avoid his insecurities, "let me see that duster, what's in that hair, some kind of radar?" She handed him the duster; he waved it around his head and pictured Hester Hua Dan.

"Buddhist on the next bus."

"Where?"

"The horsehair will find him," she said.

"What does a Buddhist look like?"

"Indifferent."

"Never mind," he muttered and waved the duster in circles around his head. Two soldiers watched from the opposite corner.

"Watch for the man who is detached," she said, "the one who has no interest in culture, women or children, the one who has a soul perched on his shoulder."

"How about those soldiers over there?"

"Communists are capitalists," she explained. "The soldiers serve the cadres, and the cadres down the line are the new shadow capitalists."

"Where are the Buddhists?"

"There," she said and pointed with her hand, "the man in the back with the uncombed hair and the basket of pears."

"Wait a minute," he moaned and lowered the duster, "that same man dropped his pears last week on the bus, and there are the old women who pushed me into a seat."

Griever moved closer but the double doors cracked closed; with the duster he conducted the bus as it pulled from the curb. The two old women remembered the trickster and covered their smiles. The woman with the puckered mouth was not wearing the black opal and blue stones.

SHADOWS

Bagese, as you must have heard by now, became a bear last year in the city. She is the same tribal woman who was haunted by stones and mirrors, and she warned me never to publish these stories or reveal the location of her apartment.

She was a wild bear who teased children and enchanted me with her trickster stories. She could be hesitant, the moves of an old woman, but her arms were thick, her hands were hard and wide, and she covered her mouth when she laughed because she was embarrassed that her teeth were gone.

Most of the time she celebrated her descent from the stones and the bears, wore a beaded necklace and blue moccasins that were puckered at the toes, but she would never be considered traditional, or even an urban pretender who treasured the romantic revisions of the tribal past. She was closer to stones, trickster stories, and tribal chance, than the tragedies of a vanishing race.

Bagese reeked of urine, and the marbled sweat on her stout neck had a wicked stench. She wore the same loose dress every time we met, and never washed her hair in more than a year. She was a strain on the nose, but even so she convinced me to believe in bears, and it seemed so natural at the time to hear her say that stones, animals, and birds were liberated at last in the city. She was a bear, and the bears were at war in her stories.

That bear woman warned me more than once, and with wicked

humor she hauled me close to her neck and pounded me on the head with her hard hands. I felt like a mongrel, and the smell of her body made me sick to my stomach. She was a bear and teased me in mirrors as she did the children, and at the same time she said that tribal stories must be told not recorded, told to listeners but not readers, and she insisted that stories be heard through the ear not the eye. She was very determined about the ear in spite of the obvious inconsistencies. The tribal world was remembered in the ear, but she never said anything about the nose.

I listened, held my breath, and promised not to publish what she told me. I was in her scent and could do nothing less, of course, and she told me stories about the liberation of animals, birds, and insects in the cities. She even encouraged me to tell my own stories, but my stories were lectures, or dead voices, so she told me to imagine in my own way the stories she had told me. I imitated her voice at first, practiced her hesitant manner, and repeated the sounds of her animal characters.

The secret, she told me, was not to pretend, but to see and hear the real stories behind the words, the voices of the animals in me, not the definitions of the words alone. I lectured on tribal philosophies at the university, and what she told me at first might have fallen on deaf ears in the classroom.

The best listeners were shadows, animals, birds, and humans, because their shadows once shared the same stories. She said there were tricksters in our voices and natural sounds, tricksters who remembered the scenes, the wild visions in the shadows of our words. She warned me that even the most honored lectures were dead voices, that shadows were dead in recitations. She said written words were the burial grounds of shadows. The tricksters in the word are seen in the ear not the eye.

She was such an incredible person, a natural contradiction in a cold and chemical civilization, and you will understand later why my promises were broken to remember her stories, the mirrors in her apartment, and the dead voices at the treeline. She became a bear and carved her image on a sacred copper dish the night before she vanished. She seemed to leave her mark, a signature, and that ended the game.

Bagese lived alone in a garden apartment on a busy street near Lake Merritt in Oakland, California. The front windows were below an untrimmed hedge and faced a bus stop. I visited her there many times over a period of two years. We first met on the street, and the other times were in her apartment. She wore the same clothes and never washed her hair or neck once in that time.

The city buses rattled the aluminum dishes in the sink, and overnight bits of paint and plaster were shaken loose from the ceiling and covered the table. The kitchen walls were touched with shadows of mold, the corners held their own natural traces. The ivy in a black plastic pot flourished at the windows, a lonesome brush with morning light, nothing more.

Bagese was born without a last name near a town on the crossroads at the border of the Leech Lake Reservation in Minnesota. She was born long before tribal bingo and remembered the rush of wild rice on the side of an aluminum canoe, the sound of the last cash crop in the autumn of her birth.

She learned as a child to hear the sounds of birds in their seasons. She pretended to be a bluebird, an oriole, and imitated a cardinal. Later, when she was thirteen, thin, silent, and alone, she told me she became a blue heron. She laughed when the herons mocked her moves in the cattails. She was too slow over the shiners in shallow water, and worried that she would never survive with the birds, because the birds were hunted and driven with the animals from the reservation. Their shadows were lost in lesson plans and irrefutable bird guides.

Bagese told me that she was born dead at the treeline, buried in tribal voices. I pretended to understand, but some of her stories were obscure and she never responded to my constant doubts. She was alone, silent most of the time, and never seemed to have any human friends, but she remembered too much of the natural world to ever live in isolation. At first that seemed to be a contradiction, the seclusion of her apartment and the separation of her stories about animals and birds driven to the city.

I was certain that she told no one else these stories, and that I was the only one who listened to her for more than a year. She should have been my discovery at the cages, but as you can see, she must have waited there to catch my ear. How else could she have finished her game?

Later, she convinced me that silence and isolation were learned with the eyes not the ears. She heard wild voices in the shadows, in the dance of leaves, in the pose of a cockroach on the bread board, and she remembered their stories with such pleasure, compassion, and imagination, that even a cockroach could be humbled with pride.

She remembered as a child how she turned to natural voices on the water, how she turned to nature when humans abused the silence, but more than once the loons and mallards mocked her in a canoe. She held an escape distance from the hunters and mechanical winters, practiced the manners of animals and the stories of birds. She learned to hear their shadows and survived on their stories.

I was never sure how to hear the stories she told me. I could see the scenes that she described, but meaning escaped me because the stories never ended. She just paused or stopped, and that was never certain either. She seemed to be more at ease with crows and bears than other birds and animals. There were real bears, remembered bears, bear voices, the bears in the mirrors, and the bears who returned to their shadows in the cities. She declared that the bears at last found a new wilderness in the city.

She told me the bears were tricksters in mirrors and stories in their own seasons, of course, but never more devious than humans. She was hunted with the bears by lonesome men that last autumn on the reservation. Their moves were sudden, mean, and measured in a cold and silent sight at the treeline.

Bagese remembered that one summer she was an otter on the great river, how she turned over and over in the bright water. She was an otter shadow in her stories and pretended that her coat would become a medicine bundle. She carried the sacred stones and the miigis of creation. She told me how inspired she was to give her body to the tribe, to hold that power in ceremonies, to shoot the spirit of the miigis shell that would heal the present. She said the past was stolen, the tribe was invented and recited in dead voices, and the present was hunted and driven with the animals and birds from the treelines. The animals and birds, and their shadows of creation, she insisted, had become outcasts and dreamers in the cities. She heard the dead voices, and became a bear in the mirror.

Bagese Bear assumed a surname when she moved from the treeline to Oakland, California. She said her uncle had been relocated there on a federal program. Sucker, a nickname that described his mouth and the way he inhaled his words, she said, learned how to weld at a government scrapyard on San Francisco Bay. A few years later he returned to the reservation and repaired automobiles with a blowtorch. She listened and remembered his trickster stories about freedom and demons in the city. His stories were shadows and sanctuaries in the winter, and the scenes he described were new tribal creations and relocations.

Bagese has lived in that same apartment at the bus stop for more than fifteen years because it was close to the caged birds at Lake Merritt. I first met her there, at an aviary near the lake. I heard her voice in the distance, a salutation early in the morning, and there she was at a cage with the crows. She held the attention of an elder crow in a real conversation. She even had a way with the wounded golden eagle in a round cage near the crows. I mean, she spoke in such a way that the eagle answered and bounced closer to the bars to hear her stories.

My grandmother carried on with lovebirds and caged canaries, but this was different. These were wild birds caged until their wounds healed, and they listened to her stories. I mean their shadows and her stories were in the same natural time. I thought she was a shaman, but in fact she had taken me into her stories and trickster game.

I followed her to a bench at the narrow end of the lake and asked her what she had told the crows and the golden eagle. She was slow to respond to me, as if the caged birds were a secret. I did not appreciate her natural hesitation at first, but later she told stories of the wanaki trickster game in the same slow, scrupulous manner, with pauses a mean listener would take advantage of at the verbs.

I knew she had me that morning because she hesitated, covered her mouth, and then turned to the side. She seemed to laugh, but the sound was no more than sudden breath.

The folds on her neck opened and closed when she turned to the side to avoid my doubts. She would have been more cordial, it was clear, if I had been a caged bird. I mentioned the cages, what a shame it was to cage wild birds, and she turned her head in the other direction. The hesitation was more than the season.

The magnolias spread their bright shadows overnight with petals behind the bench, and the bees rushed the tender wisteria blooms that embraced the arbor near the lake.

"No shame," she whispered.

"That crow heard you."

"So he did, and so did you," she said and turned toward me. She held her hands to her mouth and looked past me, to one side of my head, and then the other.

"Can you see me here?"

"Can you hear, are you a bear?" asked Bagese.

"Hardly, but please, don't let my human appearance hold back your imagination." I moved to catch her eyes, but there was no one there. I was certain that she had bad vision.

"Your animals are dead voices."

"No, not really, my cat complains every morning, but why would you ask me about my pets?" I was suspicious and leaned back on the bench to watch her hands. She laughed, and then she rushed me on the bench and pounded me on the head. Her mouth was uncovered, close to mine for the first time, and her wild tongue bounced from side to side on her gums.

"The animals in your stories," she shouted.

"What stories?"

"The stories you hear in the mirrors," she said and then gestured with her mouth toward the twisted wisteria bound to the arbor behind me. I turned to see the blossoms, and she was gone without a sound. I could not believe what had happened to me. I was the discoverer that morning and she turned me into a child on the bench. She tricked me and touched my sense of innocence.

Bagese has tried to lose me every time we got together, as she had done that first morning on the bench, but elusive or not, the more she hesitated and resisted my interest, the more winsome she became to me. No one ever carried on stories with caged birds the way she did, and no one could be so hard and soft at the same time, or so hesitant with such a wicked tongue. She was an old bear who teased insects with her body odor, and that was no mean distinction in the city.

I followed her that early morning to her apartment two blocks from the lake, but it was not as easy as it might sound. I never thought an old woman could trick me on the street, she could never walk that fast, but somehow she summoned two mongrels to rush me from behind, the perfect diversion. The mongrels barked, and when they retreated, she was gone.

I was certain she lived on the same block as the mongrels, and tried to imagine what she would have in the windows of her apartment. She was not behind the violets or animal figurines. I walked on both sides of the street, studied the buildings, even searched behind several homes, but there were no traces. She never told me her name.

I rested on a bench at a bus stop, and it was there, in a most unusual manner that I found her apartment. The city buses stopped at the corner, and when two students boarded they commented on the crazy bear behind the hedge. The bus roared from the curb, but there was only ivy in the window of the garden apartment. Closer, the interior came alive with mirrors, and a collection of stones, many stones, birds, leaves, flowers, insects, and other mysterious things spread out like a map on the floor. I learned later that she had laid out a wanaki game.

I crouched behind the hedge and waited at the window for a sign that she lived there. I was sure it was her apartment, but no one was there. The bright clouds of an ocean storm came ashore and rushed the eucalyptus trees. The rain came in bursts, cold and hard, and blurred the window.

Something moved in the mirrors, and the mirrors were everywhere, but the images were distant and obscure. The room was a dream scene, sensuous motions in the rain. The mirrors and stones seemed to be alive. I had no idea what the mirrors were reflecting because nothing seemed to be moving in the apartment. I would learn later, of course, that she was a bear in the mirrors, an image that escaped me for several months.

The buses roared, the windows rattled, the storm clouds passed, and at last she appeared in the mirrors. When she saw me at the window she covered her head with her hands and danced in the leaves and stones on the floor. I could not hear, but she must have laughed over my appearance at the window, a clever ruse. I was so determined to find this woman that nothing reminded me of my compulsive and stupid behavior at the time, crouched at her kitchen window like a peeper.

She might have struck me blind, but instead she taught me how to hear and see the animals in stories. Nothing comes around in chance when the best moments are lost to manners and the clock.

"Laundry," she said at the door, and that became my nickname. She laughed and pounded me on the head. "You smell like television soap, the sweet smell of laundry is a dead voice."

Bagese invited me in, of course, and over the threshold there was a transformation of voices in the apartment, nothing in my life has ever been the same since. She told me stories with wild voices that demanded my attention and imagination, stories she warned me to remember but never, never to publish. She cursed the dead voices of civilization, the word demons who hear no stories on the run. She praised chance and tricked the demons with dead pronouns.

The wanaki chance, for instance, was her game of natural meditation, the stories that liberated shadows and the mind. Chance is an invitation to animal voices in a tribal world, and the word "wanaki" means to live somewhere in peace, a chance at peace.

She turned seven cards in the game, one each for the bear, beaver, squirrel, crow, flea, praying mantis, and the last was the trickster figure, a wild card that transformed the player into an otter, a rabbit, a crane, a spider, or even a human. The animals, birds, and insects were pictured in unusual poses on the cards. The bear, for instance, was a flamenco dancer, the crow was a medical doctor, and the praying mantis was the president. The cards and creatures were stories, and she insisted that nothing was ever personal in a game of wanaki chance.

Bagese told me that the poses of the creatures were the common poses of civilization, the stories and shadows of the animals and birds in the mirrors. She compared the wanaki peace cards to tarot cards that depict the vices and virtues of human adventures, but tarot was in the eye and wanaki was in the ear. The fortunes were never the same as animal stories.

She has lived in a wanaki game since she moved to the city. Every morning she selects one of the seven cards and concentrates on the picture of the bird, animal, insect, or wild chance of the trickster. She explained that the players must use the plural pronoun *we* to share in the stories and become the creatures on the cards. That morning she had become the stories of the crow and gathered bits and pieces of nature, fallen leaves and feathers near the lake, and placed them in similar positions in her apartment, which was all part of the wanaki chance. The shape of the lake was obvious once she told me about the game. The objects were laid out as she had found them in the miniature shape of Lake Merritt.

The beaver and squirrel stones were placed in the north on the floor of her apartment, the bear in the east, the flea in the west, the crow and praying mantis in the south, and the last card was the trickster in the center of the wanaki game.

I was more than eager to remind her that the wanaki cards were an obvious contradiction to what she had told me. The pictures on the cards were the same as written words and could not be heard. I was certain she wanted me to ask obvious questions. "So, how can you hear stones and pictures?"

"The bear is painted not printed, and the praying mantis is seen as the president, this is a shadow, a chance not a word," she insisted.

"Written words are pictures."

"Printed books are the habits of dead voices," she said and turned a mirror in my direction to distract me. "The ear not the eyes sees the stories."

"And the eye hears the stories."

"The voices are dead."

"So, the wanaki pictures are dead."

"There are no others, these are my picture stories, no one sees them but hears my stories," she said and then drew one of the seven cards in the game. She held the picture to the mirror and the praying mantis became a bear.

The natural meditation scene was conspicuous, and the dead birds on the miniature bay were a bit much, but she enlivened my ambivalence with stories about a tribal woman who brought dead animals and birds back to life on the reservation.

"She must have been the resurrection shaman."

"You could say that," she responded.

"She could make a fortune at a chemical company."

"She already has on weekends," said Bagese.

"So, why are you playing miniature meditation with leaves and twigs in your apartment when you could bring back the dead and buy your own reservation?"

I never doubted that she had the power and the stories to bring back the dead, even dead voices at a great distance. The moment she appeared as a bear was more than enough power to transform the world, at least in my mind, but the mirrors that haunted her apartment were too much for me to understand.

The return of dead animals and birds was a story that made sense, but the mirrors that haunted her apartment were outside of my imagination and appreciation. These mirrors held images that were never in that room, and there were images that she could see, but not me. I avoided the mirrors for fear that my face would vanish, or that my image would tell me who the animals were in my past. My present memories and insecurities were more than enough for me to understand. The evolution of the animals in me, or as she said, the animal shadows that came to me as stories, would be too much to endure at rush hour, in line at the bank, or in a lecture at the university.

I was not surprised to learn that there seemed to be a hierarchy of mirrors in that apartment. There were round hand mirrors everywhere, beveled mirrors, suspended mirrors, table mirrors, tile mirrors, and framed mirrors covered the walls. She teased me to watch myself in the mirrors, the smaller mirrors. She even positioned a portable mirror to catch me when I sat at the kitchen table. When I refused to look into the mirrors she laughed and pounded me on the head.

I can never be sure, but there seemed to be something sexual about the mirrors in her apartment. There was never any doubt that her lust almost did me in when at last, after seven months of visits, she appeared to me as a bear in the tabernacle mirror. I will never forget that moment in her maw, and since then she has never pounded me on the head.

The Empire tabernacle mirror was mounted with distinction on a partition just inside the door to her apartment. As the door opened, there was the tabernacle. The distinctive decorated glass was the first mirror in her apartment. I have never seen anything like it, not to mention the haunting reflections of the other mirrors. The tabernacle frame was turned and painted black and gold with carved rosettes in the corner blocks. The upper part of the framed mirror was decorated with the creatures pictured on the wanaki cards. The face of the trickster, a bear in a human figure at the center of the scene, was a miniature metallic mirror. I saw her as a bear in that tabernacle mirror. The landscape was painted on the reverse side of the glass, and the main mirror was below the wanaki scene.

Bagese told me stories in the animal, bird, and insect voices of the wanaki game. She teased the trickster in the tabernacle, and pounded the mirrors that leaned too close to the dead voices. Two years later she was gone without a trace. The mirrors were down, the apartment was empty, but the ivy held to the window. I remember her stories as our stories now, and if she heard them told once more, even these published versions, she might return to pound me on the head as promised.

TERMINAL CREEDS AT ORION

Orion was framed in a great wall of red bricks. Behind the earthen wall the blades of seventeen windmills named for the states rattled like strident insects on the hot wind over the panhandle. The circus pilgrims gathered near the main gate in the long lean shadows of the wall to read the application and conditions for admission to the enclosed town.

"Let the bishop read the fine print."

"Getting out worries me," said Sun Bear Sun.

"Listen to this," said Double Saint, "visitors are welcome inside the Great Wall of Orion. Within the red walls live several families who were descendants of famous hunters and western bucking horse breeders. Like good horses, we are proud people who keep to ourselves and our own breed. We are amiable families within these walls and choose from time to time certain wanderers to share our food and conversation."

"Get this," said Bishop Parasimo, "it boasts that we should be prepared to eat eat eat and defend our ideas and views on the universe, narcissism is a form of isolation."

"Listen to this," said Belladonna. "Listen to this shit, terminal creeds are terminal diseases. The mind is the perfect hunter."

"Not a good place," warned Inawa Biwide.

"What does it say about getting in to eat something?" asked Double Saint. "How do we get through the gate?"

"This is Bishop Omax Parasimo," he called into the metal pipe extending through the red wall. He strained his voice. "Is there someone there there there? This is one of the circus pilgrim clowns, over."

"We should order what we want," Sun Bear Sun suggested. "This thing is like a restaurant. Tell them to hold the onions."

"Give me that damn thing," said Double Saint. "Behind the great red wall, this is Saint Saint Plumero with a hollow stomach and fantastic stories on the worlds outside these lonesome walls, over."

"Saint who?" a voice asked.

"Saint Saint Plumero!"

"How many are there out there?"

"Eight pilgrims, seven clown crows, two animals, one that glows, and various good spirits," said Double Saint into the pipe.

"Who are these pilgrims?"

"We are tribal mixedbloods with good stories and memories from thousands of good listeners," said Double Saint. "Open the gate and let us in before we knock the walls down, over."

"Let all the pilgrims speak for themselves."

"Me."

"Trickster and double saint."

"Parawoman."

"Keeper of the cedar fires."

"Mother of secrets and dreams."

"The great sun of sun bears."

"Conceived and born at Wounded Knee."

"The son of everlasting silence."

"Smile smile smile on strange faces."

"Most unusual, peculiar pilgrims," the voice in the pipe said. "Wait where you are and the guards will come to take you through the gate, we will find families where you can eat but you are too many to stay for the night."

In a few minutes the metal portcullis opened and several guards dressed in band uniforms escorted the pilgrims through the red wall. The dark tunnel inside the gate led to a large room with barred windows overlooking the center of the town. The pilgrims were examined. Information about places of birth, identities and families, education and experience, travels and diseases, attitudes on women and politics and ideologies and other descriptions were recorded.

The red door opened and several hunters and breeders stepped across the threshold with wide smiles and extended hands. The hunters and breeders looked forward to visitors to keep in touch with what was happening in the world outside the walls, but in the past few months killers and demons were lurking at the gates. To protect the families behind the Great Wall of Orion, the elder breeder explained, "we must ask questions about our visitors."

The pilgrims followed the hunters and breeders through the small neat town to one of the largest houses west of the bank and markets. Dozens of people were waiting on the front steps of the house. The pilgrims were introduced again and again and each time asked about their views on politics and news from the world outside the walls. The pilgrims were eager to please in return for the food but were troubled with the rapid questioning and disinterest in answers. Thousands of questions were asked before dinner was served in the church dining room. While the food was being served the hunters and breeders announced that one of the pilgrims would be obligated to speak after dinner. Belladonna agreed to talk about tribal values.

"Food at last," said Double Saint.

"My stomach forgot how to act in front of real food," said Sun Bear Sun as he stuffed several whole potatoes into his mouth with one hand. Onions, carrots, and thin slivers of pork he held in the other hand until his stomach took the potatoes.

The circus pilgrims sat in the church within the red earthen walls and ate and then ate more to avoid answering more questions. Bishop Parasimo was the first to shift the flow of conversation. He asked the hunters and breeders sitting at his table to discuss the meaning of the messages on the outside walls. "What does it mean mean mean narcissism is a form of isolation?"

"Why do you repeat certain words?"

"I am a tribal saint."

"I am a breeder."

"Narcissism . . ."

"Narcissism rules the possessor," said a breeder with a deep scar on the side of his forehead. "Narcissism is the fine art that turns the dreamer into paste and ashes."

"Could narcissism be survival?"

"Never, never!" explained a small boned hunter with thin lips. "Survival is not a possessive reflection. The turning under in the cold and snow, or the resignation to the forces of evil. Survival is a keen view, the vision of eagles, the forearm of a bear and the ritual of a spider building his web on the wind. That is survival!"

"Do the people here here here always ask so many questions?" asked the bishop. He had finished his meal and after wiping his hands and mouth he rested his hands on the table to share in the conversation.

"We cannot live without questions."

"We avoid terminal creeds with questions, there are no last words to this world," said the breeder with the scar.

"Questions and verbal doubts keep us from the voices of internal violence," said a woman breeder in a western shirt with pearl buttons.

"Internal violence?"

"The violence that comes from shaving conversations too close to agreements," she said with no facial expression. Her lips moved some, but the rest of her face, even her pearl colored eyes, could have been struck from cold stone. "Inside is no place to disagree with ideas. Inside is no place to be suspicious about the meaning of statements and actions."

"The church would never last last last in your hands," said the bishop. "What I mean is that it would never last through your questions."

"People are the living dead with the unquestioned church in them," the woman with the stone face said. "The church kills people inside with terminal creeds, terminal creeds, disliving lightning in the antelope hills."

"Which reminds me," said the bishop, "what does it mean mean mean that the mind is the perfect hunter?" His hands followed and marked a question on the table.

"Your hands are interesting," said a breeder with thin blond hair and a sharp nose bone. "Do your hands ever disagree with what you are saying?"

"With themselves perhaps."

"Then your hands must suffer the terminal disease of terminal creeds. What use are your hands if they never question your view on the sides and shapes of time and experience?"

"I need someone to agree with me me me," said Bishop Parasimo. His humor was tense. "What would the celebrants think if the bishop blessed them and drew the sign of the cross with quarreling hands?"

"They should be quarreling if they bless terminal creeds," said the woman with the stone face. "Did you say the celebrants?"

"Yes, the celebrants."

"Celebrants, diseases of sheared sheep."

"But sheep have no evil."

"Evil is not a disease, evil is a state of being," said the woman. "Sheep are terminal followers with or without evil doing."

"Your brand of survival is making it on hard words behind this red wall. Your wall is more terminal than the church," said the bishop in his best liturgical voice. To please the listeners he turned his hand gestures in disagreement with his words. "Now how about the perfect hunter, what is your answer to that terminal phrase?"

"The perfect hunter leaves himself and becomes the animal or bird he is hunting," said a hunter on the other side of the table. He touched his ear with his curled trigger finger. "The perfect hunter turns on himself. He lives on the edge of his own meaning and humor. The humor is in the contradictions of the hunter being close and distant at the same time, being the hunter and hunted at the same time, being the questioner and the questioned and the answer. The believer and the disbeliever at the same moment of mental awareness."

"Mea culpa culpa culpa," chanted the bishop but his hands did not follow his words. His hands shunned the hunters and breeders. "Spare me the rest of the universe in your contradictions. May the terminal believers of this good earth spare your voices hiding behind these walls."

"The wall saves us from terminal creeds."

"What you need are terminal fools."

"Pitter patter."

The breeders and hunters at the table smiled and nodded and then turned toward the head table where the bald banker breeder was tapping his waterglass. Ting ting ting ding ding dong. Belladonna was sitting next to the banker. She was nervous and touched the two beaded necklaces around her neck. Resting his hand on her right shoulder, the banker breeder introduced Belladonna as the speaker and then reviewed the practice of the hunters and breeders challenging the ideas from visitors outside the walls. The families applauded when the banker spoke of their mission against terminal creeds. "Depersonalize the word in the world of terminal believers and we can all share the good side of humor in our own places. Terminal believers must be changed or driven from our dreams. Until then we will continue our mission against terminal creeds wherever and whenever we find them." Belladonna could feel the moisture from his hand resting on her shoulder. Then he referred to her as the good spirited speaker who has traveled through the world of savage lust on the interstates, "this serious tribal woman, our speaker, who once carried with her a tame white bird." He released her shoulder when he said her name. Belladonna Darwin-Winter Catcher.

Belladonna leaned back in her chair. The muscles on her chest and thighs twitched from his words about the tame white bird. The banker did not explain how he knew that she once traveled with a tame dove until the medicine man told her it was an evil omen to be seen with a white bird. She turned the dove loose in the woods but the bird was tame and returned to her shoulder. She cursed the bird and locked it out of her house, but the white dove soared in crude circles and hit the windows. The dove would not leave. One night, when she was alone, she squeezed the bird in both hands. The white dove took the pressure for affection and wriggled with contentment in her hands. She shook the dove. Behind the house, against a red pine tree, she severed the head of the white dove with an axe. Blood spurted in her face. The blood-stained headless dove flapped alone through the last white world into the dark woods.

"We are waiting," said the banker.

Belladonna was still shivering when she stood at the table next to the banker breeder. She fumbled with her beads. "Tribal values and dreams is what I will talk about," she said in a gentle voice.

"Speak up, speak up!"

"Tribal values is the subject of my talk!" she said in a loud voice. She dropped her hands from her beads. "We are raised with values that shape our world in a different light. We are tribal and that means that we are children of dreams and visions. Our bodies are connected to mother earth and our minds are part of the clouds. . . . Our voices are the living breath of the wilderness."

"My father and grandfathers three generations back were hunters," said the hunter with the trigger finger at his ear. "They said the same things about the hunt that you said is tribal. Are you telling me that what you are saying is exclusive to your mixedblood race?"

"Yes!" snapped Belladonna. "I am different than a whiteman because of my values and my blood is different. I would not be white."

"Do tell me," said an old woman breeder in the back of the room. "We can see you are different from a man, but tell us how you are so different from whitepeople."

"We are different because we are raised with different values," Belladonna explained. "Our parents treat us different as children. We are not punished because our parents give us the chance to experience limits. We are never yelled at as children, our parents use their eyes to tell us what we have done wrong. We live in larger families and never send our old people to homes to be alone. These are some things that make us different."

"What else is so different?"

"Tribal people seldom touch each other," said Belladonna folding her arms over her breasts. "We do not invade the personal bodies of others and we do not stare at people when we are talking. Indians have more magic in their lives than whitepeople."

"Wait a minute, hold on there," said a hunter with an orange beard. "Let me find something out here before you make me so different from the rest of the world. Tell me about this Indian word you use, tell me which Indians are you talking about, or are you talking for all Indians. And if you are speaking for all Indians then how can there be truth in what you say?"

"Indians have their religion in common."

"What does Indian mean?"

"Are you so hostile that you cannot figure out what and who Indians are? An Indian is a member of a recognized tribe and a person who has Indian blood."

"But what is Indian blood?"

"Indian blood is not white blood."

"Indians are an invention," said the hunter with the beard. "You tell me that the invention is different than the rest of the world when it was the rest of the world that invented the Indian. An Indian is an Indian because he speaks and thinks and believes he is an Indian, but an Indian is nothing more than an invention. Are you speaking as an invention?"

"Mister, does it make much difference what the word Indian means when I tell you that I have always been proud that I am an Indian," said Belladonna "proud, proud to speak the voice of mother earth and the sacred past of the tribes."

"Please continue."

"Well, as I was explaining, tribal people are closer to the earth, the meaning and energies of the woodlands and mountains and plains. We are not a competitive people like the whites who competed this nation into corruption and failure. We are not competitive because we share our lives and dreams and use little from the earth."

"When you use the collective pronoun," asked a woman hunter with short silver hair, "does that mean that you are talking for all tribal people?"

"Most of them."

"How about the western fishing tribes on the ocean, the old tribes, how about including them in your collective generalizations. Those tribes burned down their own houses in potlatch competition."

"The exceptions are not the rule."

"But the rule has too many exceptions," said the woman with silver hair. "You speak from terminal creeds. Not a person of real experience and critical substance."

"Thank you for the meal," said Belladonna. She smirked and turned in disgust from the hunters and breeders. The banker placed his moist hand on her shoulder again. "She will speak in good faith," said the banker, "if you will listen with less critical ears. She does not want her beliefs questioned. Give her another good hand." The hunters and breeders applauded her until she stood again to speak. She smiled, accepted apologies for hard questions and started again.

"The tribal past, our religion and dreams and the concept of mother earth, is precious to me. Living is not good for me if a shaman does not sing for shadows in my dreams. Living is not important if it is turned into competition and material gain. Living is hearing the wind and speaking the languages of animals and soaring with eagles in magical flight. When I speak about these experiences it makes me feel powerful, the power of tribal religion and spiritual beliefs gives me protection. My tribal blood is like your great red walls. My blood moves in the circles of mother earth and through dreams without time. My tribal blood is timeless and it gives me strength to live and deal with evil."

"Right on sister, right on," said the hunter with the trigger finger on his ear. He leaped to his feet and cheered for her views.

"Hallelujah!" shouted another hunter.

"This is a bad place," whispered Inawa Biwide.

"Powerful speech," said a breeder.

"Truth in beautiful words," said a hunter.

"She deserves her favorite dessert," said a hunter in a deep voice. The hunters and breeders did not trust those narcissistic persons who accepted personal praise.

"Shall we offer our special dessert to this innocent child?" asked the breeder banker of the hunters and breeders gathered in the dining room. "Let me hear it now, those who think she deserves her dessert, and those who think she does not deserve dessert for her excellent speech. Let me see a show of hands for those opposed. Three opposed. Well, she wins her favorite dessert."

"No dessert please," said Belladonna.

"Now, now, how could you turn down the enthusiasm of the hunters and breeders who listened to your thoughts here. How could you turn down their vote for your dessert. What is the dessert tonight?"

"Sugar cookies."

"Bring the cookies for the speaker of dreams," said the banker breeder. "She will lead us all in our just desserts." The banker breeder put his hot hand on her shoulder again.

The hunters and breeders cheered and whistled when the cookies were served. The circus pilgrims were not comfortable with the shift in moods and excessive praise.

"The energies here here here are strange," said Bishop Parasimo. The hunter with the scar frowned. "What is the meaning of their sudden shift in temperature, what does all this cheering mean?"

"Quite simple, mister bishop," said the breeder with the scar. "You see, when questions are unanswered and there is no humor the messages become terminal creeds, and the good hunters and breeders here seek nothing that is terminal. So the questioners become celebrants when there is nothing more to learn. Terminal creeds are terminal diseases and when death is inevitable celebration is the best expression."

"Here come the sugar cookies."

"Speakers first."

"Here, here, for our mixedblood from the plains, this is a sugar cookie toast to our speaker, a forever toast to her precious tribal past and to the freedom into the present," said the banker breeder. The hunters and breeders cheered her when she nibbled her cookie.

The families smiled when she stood to tell them how much she loved them. "In your smiling faces I can see myself. This is a good place to live and I admire your courage and your care for the living. Thank you for this special moment on our journeys." The hunters and breeders cheered her again.

"But you applaud her narcissism," said the bishop to the breeder with the scar.

"She has demanded that we see her narcissism," said the breeder. "You heard her tell us how she saw in our faces her own. Your mixedblood friend is a terminal believer and a victim of her own narcissism."

"But we are all all all victims."

"The histories of tribal culture have been terminal creeds and narcissistic revisionism. If the tribes had more humor and less false pride then the families would not have collapsed under so little pressure from the whiteman. Show me a solid culture that disintegrates under the plow and the saw?"

"Your views are terminal."

"Who is serious about the perfections of the past? Who gathers around them the frail hopes and febrile dreams and tarnished mother earth words?" asked the hunter with the scar. "Surviving in the present means giving up on the burdens of the past and the cultures of tribal narcissism. No other culture has based social and political consciousness on terminal creeds. Survival is not narcissism."

"You must be burning at the stake."

"All terminal creeds fail. Economics has taken over the values of the church. If the church could not survive the dollar then tell me how can a tribal culture survive when it sounds like the past took place in the nave of a church?"

"Tell me, where do the terminal believers gather with their tolerance for the views of others? Your speaker cannot give up her frail bromides without facing the fear of collapsing inward," said the breeder. His voice was harsh. He touched the scar on his forehead. "You see, mister bishop, when we challenge terminal creeds here behind the protection of our great wall, we collapse outward, not inward. Outward because we never internalize the blame for ideas that did not work in the real world whenever the world was real. We are not tribal victims seeking those who will punish us for what we believe so that we can be sure we are good believers."

"Tell me, mister bishop, will you collapse inward, or will you collapse outward? Will you choose the questions and hard words of your collapse, or will the precious words choose you from the burdens of the revised past?"

"Dominus vobiscum."

"Inward collapses at lightning hills."

"Lightning hills?"

Belladonna nibbled at her sugar cookie like a proud rodent. Her cheeks were filled and flushed. Her tongue tingled from the tartness of the cookie. In the kitchen the cooks had covered her cookie with a granulated time release alkaloid poison that would dissolve in minutes. The poison cookie was the special dessert for narcissists and believers in terminal creeds. She was her own victim. The hunters and breeders have poisoned dozens of terminal believers in the past few months. Belladonna nibbled at the last crumbs, in her effort to be polite, unaware that she would be dead before morning. She smiled and nodded her appreciation to the hunters and breeders.

"But before you and this fine circus resume your pilgrimage," said the banker breeder, "please, as our special dessert speaker, you must sign your name and write a one line thought in our book for us to remember this moment together."

The banker breeder handed her a large leather bound book with a red ribbon. The banker opened the book to the ribbon marker. Belladonna paused to think out her precious line. The circus pilgrims and hunters and breeders waited in silence. Then she took the thick pen and wrote her message. The banker read her message to the hunters and breeders.

"Our hearts soar with the eagles of our people," he said and then closed the book on the ribbon marker. The audience cheered her once more. She blew them kisses and then removed one of her beaded necklaces. She slipped it over the stout bald head of the banker. He raised his voice over the cheering and said that the best times were still to come.

The circus pilgrims expressed their appreciation and were escorted out of town under the state windmills and through the portcullis. The sun had dropped beneath the great earthen wall. The pilgrims walked around the shadows. There were no clouds on the horizon. The seven clown crows hopped and flew and hopped and flew near the pilgrims until it was dark.

"The orange sun still bounces behind my eyes like a bunch of circus balloons," said Belladonna. "The starts are never bright enough to burn through our vision like the sun, hopping down a road with orange balloons, and just when I focus on them they float upward, and the more I try to catch them in focus the quicker they disappear."

"We should have started walking at night when we were on the interstate," said Bishop Parasimo. "It feels good to be alone in the cool darkness without facing the sad faces of all those wanderers."

"Feels like an adventure," said Double Saint.

"My father took me into the sacred hills," chanted Belladonna. "We started when the sun was setting, because Old Winter Catcher had to know what the setting sun looked like before he climbed into the hills for the night. The sun was beautiful, it spread great beams of orange and rose across the heavens. He said it was a good sunset. No haze to hide the stars. He said it was good and we climbed into the hills. I feel like that now. I feel like we are climbing into the hills for the visions of the morning. The morning when the first and last colors of the heavens are turned around."

"So talkative in the dark," said Double Saint.

"Bigfoot, tell me one thing?" Belladonna asked turning and walking backwards. "Have you ever walked up a hill backwards? Have you ever lifted your feet with visions in the back of your head?"

"Never . . . but in dreams. You see, with the size of my feet, nothing abnormal you understand, but with the length and breadth of these beautiful feet," he said looking down at his huge feet thumping on the cool black asphalt. "It is a must to take the world straight out, not to mention hills, in the forward position. Have you ever seen a bird walking backwards?"

Belladonna leaped and turned before she landed. She whistled at the stars and the darkness between them while she walked with her head pitched backwards. The crows rode on her shoulders and hopped beside the pilgrims on the road. Perfect Crow hopped and flapped in four or five spurts ahead and then waited for the pilgrims. The crows never hopped backwards.

"Backward flight?"

"We walked up part of the hill backwards," Belladonna said with her head turned backwards. "Then he told me that the world is not as it appears to be frontwards. To leave the world and see the power of the spirit on the hills we had to walk out of the known world backwards. We had to walk backwards so nothing would follow us up the hill. Things that follow are things that demand attention. Do you think we are being followed now?

"When I do this we are walking into the morning with Old Winter Catcher," she said walking backwards down the road. "The first to come into morning with no demands on our attention."

"Another nice thing about walking backwards," said Double Saint while he smacked his hands on his leather covered thighs, "is that when you fall you fall on your ass and not on your face. Ass falling is a lot less embarrassing."

"There go the balloons again," she said turning around. "When will the balloons leave me behind?" She waved her arms in the motion of flight ahead of the pilgrims. She hopped and flapped like the crows and then, with a high pitched moan, she started running. She disappeared into the darkness. The sound of her feet and breath came back to the pilgrims. Then there was silence. The pilgrims walked for several hours without seeing or hearing her. Their fear increased when they heard her gentle laughter but could not find her. Proude called out to her but she did not answer. When she laughed again her voice seemed miles ahead of them.

Pure Gumption, with Private Jones following at her side, trotted in giant circles through the fields and trees. Her golden aura was visible from a great distance, like a swarm of fireflies appearing and disappearing in the deep dark grass. Pure Gumption stopped and began to howl. When the pilgrims ran toward her glow they found Belladonna on her stomach with her face buried in the grass. Her hands were over her ears. She was trembling in fear.

"We are here," said Proude, putting his hands on her shoulders. Her fear and tension seemed to leave her muscles when he spoke. When she rolled over her once smooth and sensitive face had turned to pale wrinkles and deep lines. Her dark eyes seemed to be pulling inward into darkness, avoiding sight and light.

"The demons were here, the demons were in the grass all around me," she repeated several times. The pilgrims carried her from the grass back to the road.

"Back to the good road again," she sighed as her feet touched the rough asphalt. Her muscles were more relaxed. She seemed to slide as she laughed harder and harder until the pale wrinkles on her face turned deep red. The pilgrims were silent watching her face change.

"Back to the roads again," she chanted. "Roads are good black lines into the future, but are there no red lines to follow somewhere? What use are we without colored roads into the unknown?" She spoke in short sentences while she walked in short uneven spurts. Her manner and expressions were strange even to the pilgrims.

Belladonna was falling inward from the circles of creation. She was passing through time again over the rim of humor. The pilgrims did not fear her interior journeys, but they feared the demons who were waiting for her to fall on the road. She could no longer walk with ease.

"We have come . . . to this little night nation . . . in short little steps," Belladonna chanted as she laughed between phrases and dragged her feet on the asphalt. "Short steps . . . short steps . . . dragging our little short steps." Breathless she turned and stumbled backwards down the road.

While the pilgrims carried her to the grass at the side of the road she whispered and laughed between disconnected phrases. "Damn the whitefeet in tribal governments, curses on blonds who travel with the tribes, curse the curses, moan home when the wars are done . . . moan home . . . moan home . . . our fathers love our bodies . . . magic medicine on our bodies . . . medicine in our blood and the trees . . . mind trees and mind leaves changing colors with our time."

The pilgrims comforted her in the grass while she continued talking in short phrases. Proude started a fire to hold back the moisture rising from the earth. Belladonna crawled so close to the flames that she singed her hair. When she was pulled from the fire she laughed and chanted the words, "father father fire fire perfect father perfect father fire," over and over again.

Proude heated water and made herbal tea. Belladonna chanted and then laughed. Double Saint said she made "no sense and not listening to meaning made sense." The herbal tea put the pilgrims to sleep before the bishop had finished his lecture on listening. "Sometimes we listen to ourselves so well well well that we have no need for others to listen. She is speaking and listening at the same time."

Proude and Inawa Biwide rested beside Belladonna near the fire. She moaned in her half sleep and mumbled unrelated words without moving her lips. The words seemed to speak through her from some unknown power. The night passed in word dreams.

STORIES

ALMOST BROWNE

Almost Browne was born on the White Earth Indian Reservation in Minnesota. Well, he was *almost* born there; that much is the absolute truth about his birth. Almost, you see, is a crossblood and he was born on the road; his father is tribal and his mother is blonde.

Marthie Jean Peterson and Hare Browne met on the dock at Sugar Bush Lake. He worked for the conservation department on the reservation, and she was there on vacation with her parents. Marthie Jean trusted her heart and proposed in the back of an aluminum boat. Hare was silent, but they were married that year at the end of the wild rice season.

Hare and Marthie had been in the cities over the weekend with her relatives. The men told stories about fish farms, construction, the weather, and automobiles, and the women prepared five meals that were eaten in front of the television set in the amusement room.

Marthie loved fish sticks and baloney, but most of all she loved to eat orange Jell-O with mayonnaise. She had just finished a second bowl when she felt the first birth pain.

"Hare, your son is almost here," she whispered in his ear. Marthie did not want her parents to know about the pain; naturally, they never would have allowed her to return to the reservation in labor.

Marthie never forgot anything; even as a child she could recite the state capitals. She remembered birthdates and presidents, but that afternoon she packed two baloney sandwiches and forgot her purse. She was on the road in labor with no checkbook, no money, no proof of identity. She was in love and trusted her heart.

The leaves had turned earlier than usual that autumn, and the silent crows bounced on the cold black road a few miles this side of the reservation border. Ahead, the red sumac burned on the curve.

Hare was worried that the crows would not move in time, so he slowed down and honked the horn. The crows circled a dead squirrel. He honked again, but the crows were too wise to be threatened. The engine wheezed, lurched three times, and then died on the curve in the light of the sumac.

Almost earned his nickname in the back seat of that seventeen-year-old hatchback; he was born on the road, almost on the reservation. His father pushed the car around the curve, past the crows and red sumac, about a half a mile to a small town. There, closer to the reservation border, he borrowed two gallons of gas from the station manager and hurried to the hospital on the White Earth Reservation.

The hatchback thundered over the unpaved government road; a wild bloom of brown dust covered the birch on the shoulders. The dust shrouded the red arrow to the resort at Sugar Bush Lake. The hospital was located at the end of the road near the federal water tower.

Wolfie Wight, the reservation medical doctor, opened the hatchback and reached into the dust. Her enormous head, wide grin, and hard pink hands frightened the crossblood infant in the back seat.

Almost was covered with dust, darker at birth than he has ever been since then. Wolfie laughed when the child turned white in his first bath. He was weighed and measured, and a tribal nurse listened to his heartbeat. Later, the doctor raised her enormous black fountain pen over the birth certificate and asked the parents, "Where was your child born?"

"White Earth," shouted the father.

"Hatchback?" The doctor smiled.

"White Earth," he answered, uncertain of his rights.

"Hatchback near the reservation?"

"White Earth," said the father a third time.

"Almost White Earth," said the doctor.

"White Earth," he repeated, determined that the birth of his son would be recorded on the reservation. He was born so close to the border, and he never touched the earth outside the reservation.

"Indeed, Almost Browne," said the doctor, and printed that name on the birth certificate. Wolfie recorded the place of birth as "Hatchback at White Earth" and signed the certificate with a flourish. "One more trail born halfbreed with a new name," she told the nurse. The nurse was silent; she resisted medical humor about tribal people.

Almost was born to be a tribal trickster. He learned to walk and talk in the wild brush; he listened to birds, water, lightning, the crack of thunder and ice, the turn of seasons; and he moved with animals in dreams. But he was more at home on cracked polyvinyl chloride in the back seats of cars, a natural outcome of his birth in a used hatchback.

Almost told a blonde anthropologist one summer that he was born in the bottom of a boat and learned how to read in limousines; she was amused and recorded his stories in narrow blue notebooks. They sat in the back seat of an abandoned car.

"I grew up with mongrels," he told the anthropologist. "We lived in seven cars, dead ones, behind the house. One car, the brown one, that was my observatory. That's where I made the summer star charts."

"Indian constellations?" asked the anthropologist.

"Yes, the stars that moved in the sunroof," he explained. "I marked the stars on cards, the bright ones that came into the sunroof got names."

"What were their names?" asked the anthropologist.

"The sunroof stars."

"The names of the constellations?"

"We had nicknames," he answered.

"What were the names?"

"The sunroof charts were like cartoon pictures."

"What names?"

"Moths are on one chart."

"What are the other names?"

"Mosquitoes, white lies, pure gumption, private jones."

"Those are constellations?"

"The sunroof charts are named after my dogs," he said and called the mongrels into the back seat. White Lies licked the blond hair on the arms of the anthropologist.

Almost learned how to read from books that had been burned in a fire at the reservation library. The books were burned on the sides. He read the centers of the pages and imagined the stories from the words that were burned.

Almost had one close friend; his nickname was Drain. They were so close that some people thought they must be brothers. The two were born on the same day near the same town on the reservation border. Drain lived on a farm, the fifth son of white immigrants.

Drain was a reservation consumer, because he believed the stories he heard about the tribe. He became what he heard, and when the old men told him to shout, he shouted; he learned to shout at shadows and thunderstorms.

Almost told stories that made the tribe seem more real; he imagined a trickster world of chance and transformation. Drain listened and consumed the adventures. The two were inseparable; one the cross-blood trickster, the other a white consumer. Together, the reservation became their paradise in stories.

Almost never attended school; well, he almost never attended. He lived on the border between two school districts, one white and the other tribal. When he wanted to use the machines in school, the microscopes, lathes, and laboratories, he would attend classes, but not more than two or three times a month. Each school thought he attended the other, and besides, no one cared that much where he lived or what he learned.

Almost learned four natural deals about life from his grandmother; he learned to see the wild world as deals between memories and tribal stories. The first deal, she told him, was chance, where things just happen and that becomes the deal with animals and their languages; words were pictures in the second natural deal; the third deal, she said, was to eat from the real world, not from the pictures on menus; and the last deal, she told him, was to liberate his mind with trickster stories.

"In natural deals," he explained to his best friend, "we act, bargain, agree, deliver, and remember that birds never eat monarchs in our stories."

"What monarchs?" asked Drain.

"The milkweed butterflies."

"So, what's the deal?"

"We're the deal in our stories."

"Some deal," moaned Drain.

"The deal is that whites are fleas and the tribes are the best dealers," said Almost. "Indians are the tricksters, we are the rabbits, and when we get excited, our ears heat up and the white fleas breed."

Almost converted a reservation station wagon into a bookmobile; he sold books from a rack that unfolded out of the back. The books, however, were not what most people expected, not even in trickster stories, and he needed a loan to expand his business.

"We're almost a bookstore," said Almost.

"Blank books?" shouted Wolfie. "You can't sell books on a reservation, people don't read here, not even blank ones."

"Some of them are burned," said Almost.

"You're crazy, blank and burned books," said the doctor, "but you do have gumption, that much is worth a loan." She polished her black pen on the sleeve of her white coat and signed a check to the crossblood.

Almost the whole truth:

Almost is my name, my real name, believe that or not, because my father ran out of money and then out of gas on the way back. I was born in the back seat of a beatup reservation car, almost white, almost on the reservation, and almost a real person.

White Jaws, the government doctor who got her cold hands on my birth certificate, gave me my name. Imagine, if we had run out of gas ten miles earlier, near a white hospital, my name might be Robert, or how about Truman? Instead, White Jaws made me Almost.

Listen, there must be something to learn in public schools, but not by me. My imagination stopped at the double doors; being inside a school was like a drain on my brain. So, my chance to learn came in bad nature and white books. Not picture nature in a dozen bird names, but road kills, white pine in eagle nests, fleas in rabbit ears, the last green flies in late autumn, and moths that whisper, whisper at the mirror. Nature voices, crows in the poplars, not plastic bird mobiles over a baby crib. So, nature was my big book, imagination was my teacher.

Classrooms were nothing more than parking lots to me, places to park a mind rather than drive a mind wild in the glorious woods, through the dangerous present in the winter when the whole real world struggles to survive. For me, double doors and desks are the end of imagination, the end of animals, the end of nature, and the end of the tribes. I might never have entered the book business if I had been forced to attend a white school.

The truth is, I almost got into the book business before my time. A blonde anthropology student started a library on the reservation and she put me in charge of finding and sorting books. I found hundreds of books that summer, what a great time, books were like chance meetings, but the whole thing burned down before I learned how to read. The anthropologist told me not to use my finger on the page but we never practiced in any real books. She talked and talked and then when the building burned down she drove back home to the city. People always come here with some other place in mind.

Drain, he's my best friend, said it was a good thing the library burned because most of the stuff in there was worthless digest books that nobody wanted to read in the first place. Drain is a white farm kid who lives on the other side of the road, on the white side of the road, outside the reservation. He learned how to read in another language before he went to school.

I actually taught myself how to read with almost whole books, and that's the truth. I'd read with my finger first, word for word out loud right down to the burned parts and then I'd picture the rest, or imagine the rest of the words on the page. The words became more real in my imagination. From the words in pictures I turned back to the words on the center of the page. Finally, I could imagine the words and read the whole page, printed or burned.

Listen, there are words almost everywhere. I realized that in a chance moment. Words are in the air, in our blood, words were always there, way before my burned book collection in the back seat of a car. Words are in snow, trees, leaves, wind, birds, beaver, the sound of ice cracking; words are in fish and mongrels, where they've been since we came to this place with the animals. My winter breath is a word, we are words, real words, and the mongrels are their own words. Words are crossbloods too, almost whole right down to the cold printed page burned on the sides.

Drain never thought about real words because he found them in books, nowhere else. He taught me how to read better, and I showed him how to see real words where we lived, and the words that were burned on the pages of my books. Words burned but never dead. It was my idea to open a bookstore with blank books, a mobile bookstore.

Doctor Wolfie gave us a loan, so we packed up and drove to the city, where we started our blank book business near the university. Drain somehow knew the city like the back of his hand. I told him that was the same as finding words in animals. Everything was almost perfect; we were making good money on the street and going to parties with college students, but then the university police arrested us for false advertising, fraud, and trading on the campus without a permit. The car wasn't registered, and we didn't have a license. I think that was the real problem.

Drain played Indian because the judge said he would drop the charges if we went straight back to the reservation where we belonged and learned a useful trade.

"Almost Browne, that's my real name," I told the judge. "I was almost born in the city." The judge never even smiled. These men who rule words from behind double doors and polished benches miss the best words in the language, they miss the real words. They never hear the real words in court, not even the burned words. No one would ever bring real words to court.

Drain was bold and determined in the city. He drove right onto campus, opened the back of the station wagon, unfolded our book rack, and we were in business. That's how it happened, but the judge was not even listening. Wait, we played a shaman drum tape on a small recorder perched on the top of the car. The tape was old; the sound crackled like a pine fire, we told the judge.

Professor Monte Franzgomery was always there, every day. He would dance a little to the music, and he helped us sell blank books to college students. "Listen to that music," he shouted at the students. "That's real music, ethnic authenticity at the very threshold of civilization." That old professor shouted that we were real too, but we were never sure about him because he talked too much. We knew we were on the threshold of something big when we sold out our whole stock in a week, more than a hundred blank books in a week.

Monte said our blank books made more sense to him than anything he had ever read. This guy was really cracked. Our books were blank except on one page there was an original tribal pictomyth painted by me in green ink, a different pictomyth on a different page in every blank book. Yes, pictomyths, stories that are imagined about a picture, about memories. So, even our blank books had a story. I think those college students were tired of books filled with words behind double doors that never pictured anything. Our blank books said everything, whatever you could imagine in a picture. One pictomyth was almost worth a good story in those days.

Well, we were almost on our way to a fortune at the university when the police burned our blank books. Not really, but a ban on the sale of blank books is almost as bad as burning a book with print.

So, now we're back on the reservation in the mail-order business, a sovereign tribal blank book business in an abandoned car. Our business has been brisk, almost as good as it was at the university; better yet, there's no overhead in the back seat of a station wagon on the reservation. Listen, last week the best edition of our blank books was adopted in a cinema class at the University of California in Santa Cruz. Blank books are real popular on the coast.

Monte promised that he would use our blank books in his seminar on romantic literature. He told a newspaper reporter, when we were arrested, that the pictomyths were a "spontaneous overflow of power-ful feelings."

Drain said we should autograph our blank books, a different signa-ture on each book. I told him the pictomyths were enough. No, he said, the consumer wants something new, something different from time to time. The stories in the pictomyths are what's new, I told him. He was right, and we agreed. I made pictures and he signed the books. He even signed the names of tribal leaders, presidents, and famous au-thors.

Later, we published oversized blank books, and a miniature edition of blank books. Drain bought a new car, we did almost everything with blank books. We even started a blank book library on the reservation, but that's another story for another time.

ICE TRICKSTERS

Uncle Clement told me last night that he knows *almost* everything. Almost, that's his nickname and favorite word in stories, lives with me and my mother in a narrow house on the Leech Lake Chippewa Indian Reservation in northern Minnesota.

Last night, just before dark, we drove into town to meet my cousin at the bus depot and to buy rainbow ice cream in thick brown cones. Almost sat in the back seat of our old car and started his stories the minute we were on the dirt road around the north side of the lake on our way to town. The wheels bounced and raised thick clouds of dust and the car doors shuddered. He told me about the time he almost started an ice cream store when he came back from the army. My mother laughed and turned to the side. The car rattled on the washboard road. She shouted, "I heard that one before!"

"Almost!" he shouted back.

"What almost happened?" I asked. My voice bounced with the car.

"Well, it was winter then," he said. Fine brown dust settled on his head and the shoulders of his overcoat. "Too cold for ice cream in the woods, but the idea came to mind in the summer, almost."

"Almost, you know almost everything about nothing," my mother shouted and then laughed, "or almost nothing about almost everything."

"Pincher, we're almost to the ice cream," he said and brushed me on the head with his right hand. He did that to ignore what my mother said about what he knows. Clouds of dust covered the trees behind us on both sides of the road.

Almost is my great-uncle, and he decides on our nicknames, even the nicknames for my cousins who live in the cities and visit the reservation in the summer. Pincher, the name he gave me, was natural because I pinched my way through childhood. I learned about the world between two fingers. I pinched everything, or *almost* everything, as my uncle would say. I pinched animals, insects, leaves, water, fish, ice cream, the moist air, winter breath, snow, and even words, the words I could see or almost see. I pinched the words and learned how to speak sooner than my cousins. Pinched words are easier to remember. Some words, like government and grammar, are unnatural, never seen and never pinched. Who could pinch a word like grammar?

Almost named me last winter when my grandmother was sick with pneumonia and died on the way to the public health hospital. She had no teeth and covered her mouth when she smiled, almost a child. I sat in the back seat of the car and held her thin brown hand. Even her veins were hidden, it was so cold that night. On the road we pinched summer words over the hard snow and ice. She smiled and said, *papakine, papakine,* over and over. That means cricket or grasshopper in our tribal language and we pinched that word together. We pinched *papakine* in the back seat of our cold car on the way to the hospital. Later she whispered *bisanagami sibi,* the river is still, and then she died. My mother straightened her fingers, but later, at the wake in our house, my grandmother pinched a summer word and we could see that. She was buried in the cold earth with a warm word between her fingers. That's when my uncle gave me my nickname.

Almost never told lies, but he used the word almost to stretch the truth like a tribal trickster, my mother told me. The trickster is a character in stories, an animal, or person, even a tree at times, who pretends the world can be stopped with words, and he frees the world in stories. Almost said the trickster is almost a man and almost a woman, and almost a child, a clown who laughs and plays games with words in stories. The trickster is almost a free spirit. Almost told me about the trickster many times, and I think I almost understand his stories. He brushed my head with his hand and said, "The almost world is a better world, a sweeter dream than the world we are taught to understand in school."

"I understand, almost," I told my uncle.

"People are almost stories, and stories tell almost the whole truth," Almost told me last winter when he gave me my nickname. "Pincher is your nickname and names are stories too, *gega.*" The word *gega* means *almost* in the Anishinaabe or Chippewa language.

"Pincher *gega,*" I said and then tried to pinch a tribal word I could not yet see clear enough to hold between my fingers. I could almost see *gega*.

Almost, no matter the season, wore a long overcoat. He bounced when he walked, and the thick bottom of the overcoat hit the ground. The sleeves were too short but he never minded that because he could eat and deal cards with no problems. So there he was in line for a rainbow ice cream cone, dressed for winter, or almost winter he would say. My mother wonders if he wears that overcoat for the attention.

"*Gega, gega,*" an old woman called from the end of the line. "You spending some claims money on ice cream or a new coat?" No one ignored his overcoat.

"What's that?" answered Almost. He cupped his ear to listen because he knew the old woman wanted to move closer, ahead in the line. The claims money she mentioned is a measure of everything on the reservation. The federal government promised to settle a treaty over land with tribal people. Almost and thousands of others have been waiting for more than a century to be paid for land that was taken from them. There were rumors at least once a week that federal checks were in the mail, final payment for the broken treaties. When white people talk about a rain dance, tribal people remember the claims dancers who promised a federal check in every mailbox.

"Claims money," she whispered in the front of the line.

"Almost got a check this week," Almost said and smiled.

"Almost is as good as nothing," she said back.

"Pincher gets a bicycle when the claims money comes."

"My husband died waiting for the claims settlement," my mother said. She looked at me and then turned toward the ice cream counter to order. I held back my excitement about a new bicycle because the claims money might never come; no one was ever sure. Almost believed in rumors, and he waited one morning for a check to appear in his mailbox on the reservation. Finally, my mother scolded him for wasting his time on promises made by the government. "You grow old too fast on government promises," she said. "Anyway, the government has nothing to do with bicycles." He smiled at me and we ate our rainbow ice cream cones at the bus depot. That was a joke because the depot is nothing more than a park bench in front of a restaurant. On the back of the bench was a sign that announced an ice sculpture contest to be held in the town park on July Fourth.

"Ice cube sculpture?" asked my mother.

"No blocks big enough around here in summer," I said, thinking about the ice sold to tourists, cubes and small blocks for camp coolers.

"Pig Foot, he cuts ice from the lake in winter and stores it in a cave, buried in straw," my uncle whispered. He looked around, concerned that someone might hear about the ice cave. "Secret *mikwam*, huge blocks, enough for a great sculpture." The word *mikwam* means ice.

"Never mind," my mother said as she licked the ice cream on her fingers. The rainbow turned pink when it melted. The pink ran over her hand and under her rings.

Black Ice was late, but that never bothered her because she liked to ride in the back of buses at night. She sat in the dark and pretended that she could see the people who lived under the distant lights. She lived in a dark apartment building in Saint Paul with her mother and older brother and made the world come alive with light more than with sound or taste. She was on the reservation for more than a month last summer, and we thought her nickname would be Light or Candle or something like that, even though she wore black clothes. Not so. Almost avoided one obvious name and chose another when she attended our grandmother's funeral. Black Ice had never been on the reservation in winter. She slipped and fell seven times on black ice near the church and so she got that as a nickname.

Black Ice was the last person to leave the bus. She held back behind the darkened windows as long as she could. Yes, she was shy, worried about being embarrassed in public. I might be that way too, if we lived in an apartment in the cities, but the only public on the reservation are the summer tourists. She was happier when we bought her a rainbow ice cream cone. She was dressed in black, black everything, even black canvas shoes, no, almost black. The latest television style in the cities. Little did my uncle know that her reservation nickname would describe a modern style of clothes. We sat in the back seat on the way back to our house. We could smell the dust in the dark, in the tunnel of light through the trees. The moon was new that night.

"Almost said he would buy me my first bicycle when he gets his claims money," I told Black Ice. She brushed her clothes; there was too much dust.

"I should've brought my new mountain bike," she said. "I don't use it much though. Too much traffic and you have to worry about it being stolen."

"Should we go canoeing? We have a canoe."

"Did you get a television yet?" asked Black Ice.

"Yes," I boasted, "my mother won a big screen with a dish and everything at a bingo game on the reservation." We never watched much television though.

"Really?"

"Yes, we can get more than a hundred channels."

"On the reservation?"

"Yes, and bingo too."

"Well, here we are, paradise at the end of a dust cloud," my mother announced as she turned down the trail to our house on the lake. The headlights held the eyes of a raccoon, and we could smell a skunk in the distance. Low branches brushed the side of the car; we were home. We sat in the car for a few minutes and listened to the night. The dogs were panting. Mosquitoes, so big we called them the state bird, landed on our arms, bare knuckles, and warm shoulder blades. The water was calm and seemed to hold back a secret dark blue light from the bottom of the lake. One loon called and another answered. One thin wave rippled over the stones on the shore. We ducked mosquitoes and went into the house. We were tired, and too tired in the morning to appreciate the plan to carve a trickster from a block of ice.

Pig Foot lived alone on an island. He came down to the wooden dock to meet us in the morning. We were out on the lake before dawn, my uncle at the back of the canoe in his overcoat. We paddled and he steered us around the point of the island where bald eagles nested.

"Pig Foot?" questioned Black Ice.

"Almost gave him that nickname," I whispered to my cousin as we came closer to the dock. "Watch his little feet; he prances like a pig when he talks. The people in town swear his feet are hard and cloven."

"Are they?"

"No," I whispered as the canoe touched the dock.

"Almost," shouted Pig Foot.

"Almost," said Almost. "Pincher, you know him from the funeral, and this lady is from the city. We named her Black Ice."

"*Makate Mikwam*," said Pig Foot. "Black ice comes with the white man and roads. No black ice on this island." He tied the canoe to the dock and patted his thighs with his open hands. The words *makate mikwam* mean black ice.

Black Ice looked down at Pig Foot's feet when she stepped out of the canoe. He wore black overshoes, the toes were turned out. She watched him prance on the rough wooden dock when he talked about the weather and mosquitoes. The black flies and mosquitoes on the island, special breeds, were more vicious than anywhere else on the reservation. Pig Foot was pleased that no one camped on the island because of the black flies. Some people accused him of raising mean flies to keep the tourists away. "Not a bad idea, now that I think about it," said Pig Foot. He had a small bunch of black hair on his chin. He pulled the hair when he was nervous and revealed a row of short stained teeth. Black Ice turned toward the sunrise and held her laughter.

"We come to see the ice cave," said Almost. "We need a large block to win the ice sculpture contest in four days."

"What ice cave is that?" asked Pig Foot.

"The almost secret one!" shouted Almost.

"That one, sure enough," said Pig Foot. He mocked my uncle and touched the lapel of his overcoat. "I was wondering about that contest. What does ice have to do with July Fourth?" He walked ahead as he talked, and then every eight steps he would stop and turn to wait for us. But if you were too close you would bump into him when he stopped. Black Ice counted his steps, and when we were near the entrance to the ice cave she imitated his prance, toes turned outward. She pranced seven steps and then waited for him to turn on the eighth.

Pig Foot stopped in silence on the shore where the bank was higher and where several trees leaned over the water. There, in the vines and boulders, we could feel the cool air. A cool breath on the shore.

Pig Foot told us we could never reveal the location of the ice cave, but he said we could tell stories about ice and the great spirit of winter in summer. He said this because most tribal stories should be told in winter, not in summer when evil spirits could be about to listen and do harm to words and names. We agreed to the conditions and followed him over the boulders into the wide cold cave. We could hear our breath, even a heartbeat. Whispers were too loud in the cave.

"Almost the scent of winter on July Fourth," whispered Almost. "In winter we overturn the ice in shallow creeks to smell the rich blue earth, and then in summer we taste the winter in this ice cave, almost."

"Almost, you're a poet, sure enough, but that's straw, not the smell of winter," said Pig Foot. He was hunched over where the cave narrowed at the back. Beneath the mounds of straw were huge blocks of ice, lake ice, blue and silent in the cave. Was that thunder, or the crack of winter ice on the lake? "Just me, dropped a block over the side." In winter he sawed blocks of ice in the bay where it was the thickest and towed the blocks into the cave on an aluminum slide. Pig Foot used the ice to cool his cabin in summer, but Almost warned us that there were other reasons. Pig Foot believes that the world is becoming colder and colder, the ice thicker and thicker. Too much summer in the blood would weaken him, so he rests on a block of ice in the cave several hours a week to stay in condition for the coming of the ice age on the reservation.

"Black Ice, come over here," said Almost. "Stretch out on this block." My cousin brushed the straw from the ice and leaned back on the block. "Almost, almost, now try this one, no this one, almost."

"Almost what?" asked Black Ice.

"Almost a whole trickster," whispered Almost. Then he told us what he had in mind. A trickster, he wanted us to carve a tribal trickster to enter in the ice sculpture contest.

"What does a trickster look like?" I asked. Trickster was a word I could not see, there was nothing to pinch. How could I know a trickster between my fingers?

"Almost like a person," he said and brushed the straw from a block as large as me." Almost in there, we have three days to find the trickster in the ice."

Early the next morning we paddled across the lake to the ice cave to begin our work on the ice trickster. We were dressed for winter. I don't think my mother believed us when we told her about the ice cave. "Almost," she said with a smile, "finally found the right place to wear his overcoat in the summer."

Pig Foot was perched on a block of ice when we arrived. We slid the block that held the trickster to the center of the cave and set to work with an ax and chisels. We rounded out a huge head, moved down the shoulders, and on the second day we freed the nose, ears, and hands of the trickster. I could see him in the dark blue ice; the trickster was almost free. I could almost pinch the word trickster.

Almost directed as we carved the ice on the first and second days, but on the third and final day he surprised us. We were in the cave dressed in winter coats and hats, ready to work, when he told us to make the final touches on our own, to liberate the face of the trickster. Almost and Pig Foot leaned back on a block of ice; we were in charge of who the trickster would become in ice.

Black Ice wanted the trickster to look like a woman. I wanted the ice sculpture to look like a man. The trickster, we decided, would be both, one side a man and the other side a woman. The true trickster, almost a man and almost a woman. In the end the ice trickster had features that looked like our uncle, our grandmother, and other members of our families. The trickster had small feet turned outward, he wore an overcoat, and she pinched her fingers on one hand. He was ready for the contest, she was the ice trickster on July Fourth.

That night we tied sheets around the ice trickster and towed her behind the canoe to the park on the other side of the lake. The ice floated and the trickster melted slower in the water. We rounded the south end of the island and headed to the park near the town, slow and measured like traders on a distant sea. The park lights reflected on the calm water. We tied the ice trickster to the end of the town dock and beached our canoe. We were very excited, but soon we were tired and slept on the grass in the park near the dock. The trickster was a liberator; she would win on Independence Day. Almost, anyway.

"The trickster melted," shouted Almost. He stood on the end of the dock, a sad uncle in his overcoat, holding the rope and empty sheets. At first we thought he had tricked us, we thought the whole thing was a joke, so we laughed. We rolled around on the grass and laughed. Almost was not amused at first. He turned toward the lake to hide his face, but then he broke into wild laughter. He laughed so hard he almost lost his balance in that heavy overcoat. He almost fell into the lake.

"The ice trickster won at last," said Black Ice.

"No, wait, she almost won. No ice trickster would melt that fast in the lake," he said and ordered us to launch the canoe for a search. Overnight the trickster had slipped from the sheets and floated free from the dock, somewhere out in the lake. The ice trickster was free on July Fourth.

We paddled the canoe in circles and searched for hours and hours but we could not find the ice trickster. Later, my mother rented a motorboat and we searched in two circles.

Almost was worried that the registration would close, so he abandoned the search and appealed to the people who organized the ice sculpture competition. They agreed to extend the time, and they even invited other contestants to search for the ice trickster. The lake was crowded with motorboats.

"There she floats," a woman shouted from a fishing boat. We paddled out and towed the trickster back to the dock. Then we hauled her up the bank to the park and a pedestal. We circled the pedestal and admired the ice trickster.

"Almost a trickster," said Almost. We looked over the other entries. There were more birds than animals, more heads than hips or hands, and the other ice sculptures were much smaller. Dwarfs next to the ice trickster. She had melted some overnight in the lake, but he was still head and shoulders above the other entries. The competition was about to close when we learned that there was a height restriction. Almost never read the rules. No entries over three feet and six inches in any direction. The other entries were much smaller. No one found large blocks of ice in town, so they were all within the restrictions. Our trickster was four feet tall, or at least she was that tall when we started out in the ice cave.

"No trickster that started out almost he or she can be too much of either," said Almost. We nodded in agreement, but we were not certain what he meant.

"What now?" asked Black Ice.

"Get a saw," my mother ordered. "We can cut the trickster down a notch or two on the bottom." She held her hand about four inches from the base to see what a shorter trickster would look like.

"Almost short enough," said Almost. "He melted some, she needs to lose four more inches by my calculations. We should have left her in the lake for another hour."

Pig Foot turned the trickster on his side, but when we measured four inches from the bottom he protested. "Not the feet, not my feet, those are my feet on the trickster."

"Not my ear either."

"Not the hands," I pleaded.

"The shins," shouted Black Ice. No one had claimed the shins on the ice trickster, so we measured and sawed four inches from his shins and then carved the knees to fit the little pig feet.

"Almost whole," announced Almost.

"What's a trickster?" asked the three judges who hurried down the line of pedestals before the ice sculptures melted beyond recognition.

"Almost a person," said Black Ice.

"What person?"

"My grandmother," I told the judges. "See how she pinched her fingers. She was a trickster; she pinched a cricket there." Pig Foot was nervous; he pranced around the pedestal.

The judges prowled back and forth, whispered here and there between two pedestals, and then they decided that there would be two winners because they could not decide on one. "The winners are the Boy and His Dog, and that ice trickster, Almost a Person," the judges announced.

The ice trickster won a bicycle, a large camp cooler, a dictionary, and twelve double rainbow cones. The other ice cave sculptors gave me the bicycle because I had never owned one before, and because the claims payment might be a bad promise. We divided the cones as best we could between five people, Almost, Pig Foot, Black Ice, me, and my mother.

Later, we packed what remained of the ice trickster, including the shin part, and took him back to the ice cave, where she lasted for more than a year. She stood in the back of the cave without straw and melted down to the last drop of a trickster. She was almost a whole trickster, almost.

TULIP BROWNE

Windmills and Crazy Papers

Tulip Browne is obsessed with wind and natural power; she builds miniature windmills in her new condominium in the hills. She throws open the windows and listens to the ocean wind over the copper blades of seventeen windmills; at dawn she attends a palace of whirs and secret twitters.

Once a week she wanders on the lower streets to encounter poor and destitute people; to brush with contention and common pleasures. The rude misconnections, wild separations, and blame shouted on the streets remind her of natural power and her untamed relatives in woodland reservation dreams. "Those down and out people," she told her mother, "are overlooked thunder storms in the cities, and we need their storms and stories to remember we are alive."

Tulip reveals no secrets and she bears no confessions from the reservation baronage or her mixedblood identities; her sensitive moves are secluded, but she haunts memories with her personal power. She invites people to dinner at the best restaurants and challenges them to a "persona grata rencounter."

"Do you know what that means?"

"Listen," he sighed behind his shopping cart.

"What is your name?"

"No," he shouted and waved his arms. His wild voice aroused two white cats in a cardboard box lashed to the top of his cart.

"No what?"

"No I don't know what you mean," he said.

"How about dinner?"

"When?"

"Down the block at the Krakow on the Vistula."

"You name it, you got it, you pay it," he said and pushed his cart down the sidewalk at her side. He parked under a bright red canopy at the entrance to the restaurant and covered the white cats with a broken parasol. "This place never leaves any garbage out, did you know that?"

"Have you ever eaten here?"

"Persona grata, what does that mean?" he asked and folded a thick slice of black bread over three butter cones. He lowered his head and leaned closer to the table, an animal over bread and butter.

"Persona grata means one is acceptable and welcome," she said, "and rencounter means to meet, an unplanned meeting, that's what I'm doing with you."

"Chance, you mean?"

"Yes, you could put it that way."

"Ronin Bloom," he mumbled over his bread.

"What?"

"Ronin Bloom," he shouted, "that's my name, not my real name, but my name, persona nongrata in the uppity hills where you come from sister." He finished the sentence and the black bread at the same time.

"Sir, could you leave your rope outside," said the black waiter. His forehead wrinkled when he spoke; he pinched his nose. "The rope, man, the rope, out, out, now."

Ronin wore a blue leather necktie, a paisley shirt, an oversized matted wool coat, threadbare, wide-ribbed corduroy trousers, black boots with no heels, and thick canvas knee pads. He had not violated the liberal dress code in the restaurant, but the rope and his pungent odor would have been enough to remove him with reasonable cause.

"The rope, man, now."

"My cart's on the end of this," he said with the rope in his hands. One end of the thin orange tether was tied to two shopping carts parked under the canopy, and the other end encircled his waist in the belt loops.

"Could he bring his carts inside?" asked Tulip. She cocked her head and folded her hands on the rim of the table.

"I'm afraid not."

"Give me one good reason."

"Well, the stench is enough," said the waiter, his hand over his nose. He moved back from the table and summoned the owner of the restaurant.

"The shopping carts block the entrance, which in case of fire is very dangerous, but that's not the real problem," said the stout owner in rapid speech. "The cats are in violation of the city health code."

Ronin pushed his chair back in preparation to defend the honor of his two shorthairs, but the chair was on rollers and the gesture was lost in a collision with another table. "Man," he said to the owner, "I'm a streetwiser and nobody talks about my family like that, but nobody. Whistle and Black Duck were born on my carts."

"Perish the thought," the owner smirked.

"The carts are their home and my place too, our place, the carts are a sovereign place, we got everything we need on eight wheels," he shouted at the owner.

Ronin moved around the restaurant, from table to table, and repeated his stories about his sovereign carts. The customers were overwhelmed and covered their noses with monogrammed napkins when he landed too close to their tables. One woman covered her head and whimpered. "Sure, you can sit there with your keys to a house in the hills. Well, this rope is my key, man," he said to the shrouded woman. "So, who's crazy around here, me and my rope or you under that dumb napkin?"

"Please, sir," said the owner.

"Ronin is my name."

"Mister Ronin, sir, would you please step outside with us now?" The owner and three waiters surrounded the streetwiser, pushed him down into a chair, and rolled him out of the restaurant. The owner tripped on the orange rope and cursed street people; he hated the destitute and even denied them garbage from the restaurant.

Tulip paid for the two meals; the owner delivered the food outside in decorative cartons embossed with an imperial seal and Krakow on the Vistula. The cartons were tied with cotton braids. She cocked her head and assured the owner that she would return soon, but her gestures were lost in the confusion. The owner and three waiters rushed to the back of the restaurant to block the streetwiser and his carts.

Ronin Bloom had pushed his tandem shopping carts through the restaurant and parked between two tables at the rear. There he presented his collection of lost shoes and told stories about Black Duck and Whistle to seven customers. The waiters rushed the streetwiser and pushed his carts out the back door onto the trash landing.

"Whistle does but Black Duck is white . . . listen, I've got my crazy papers, you can't treat me this way," were his last words when the owner cursed him once more and slammed the steel door closed.

Ronin and Tulip pushed the carts down the main street to a park bench between a hotel and a bank. He ate with his fingers from the embossed carton and repeated his best lost shoe stories. Tulip listened and fed the cats on a thick golden napkin.

"My uncle has a shoe collection," she said.

"So, what's his name?" he asked and wiped his mouth on his matted sleeve. He wiped his hands on the shorthairs.

"Mouse Proof Martin."

"Never heard of him," he mumbled.

"No one has a better lost shoe collection," she boasted. "He even travels around and shows his shoes at colleges and museums."

"Maybe so," he shouted over the roar of a diesel bus, "but no one has a better lost shoe collection in a shopping cart, you can count on that."

"What got you started?"

"Sylvan Goldman."

"Relative?"

"Better than that, he was a grocer," he sighed and teased the short-hairs on their tethers. "Goldman's invention changed the world."

"Plastic clothes?" she teased in response.

"Shit no, he invented the shopping cart, the nesting cart, my tandem wheels, my mobile home where the urban buffalo roam," he chanted and waved his hands.

"Nice tune. Still hungry?"

"No, that crack on the river place was too much," he said and then turned his hands over and over on his knees. "Street people eat faster than the uppity hill people, you know."

"Why do you wear knee pads?"

"Balance," he shouted.

"You mean weights?" she said and ducked his breath.

"No, no, you know," he hesitated, "like two gloves, same shoes, balance like that, balance on the run, because I only have to wear one."

"Tell me, which one?"

"Look at this knee," he said and raised his right trouser leg. He wore no socks and his ankles were marbled black. "See, the patella is gone, broken and removed. The doc said wear a pad or lose my leg, so, two pads for me, balance."

"Ronin, you have nice legs."

"No woman ever said that to me before," he mumbled and covered his knee. "You got nice legs too. Do you live in the hills or something?"

"Yes, with a mongrel."

"What's his name?"

"White Lies."

"Shit, is that a real name?"

"Reservation name."

"You heard about crazy papers?"

"No, but you said something about that back at the Krakow on the Vistula," she said. "Should I have crazy papers?"

"Definitely. With a dog named White Lies, you definitely need your own crazy papers," he said and laughed. His teeth were stained and marked with caries. "Did you ever take your hound to a black hangout and call his name?"

"Never."

"Then you need crazy papers," he said and stretched his hands. Ronin opened a blue folder and removed an official certificate. He touched a pencil stub to his tongue and asked, "So, what's your real name?"

"Tulip Browne."

"Twolips and White Lies," he repeated and printed it on the document. "Now, with this, you can hangdog the street, wander into restaurants and search for food, and stay out of jail because the cops will know you're a wacko lodge member and not a case from club mental."

"Do I get a cart with crazy papers?"

"You ever heard about Terry Wilson?" he asked and propped his boots on the back of the carts. Black Duck pawed the holes in his soles.

"Does he have crazy papers?"

"He wrote *The Cart That Changed the World: The Career of Sylvan Goldman,* and that book and the cart changed my world," he said. "Goldman invented the nest cart, and I declared the tandem cart a sovereign state on low wheels.

"Sylvan made a seven-minute movie about how to use his invention because men would not be seen behind a cart. Well," he said and scratched his ear, "my mother saw that movie when I was born and it changed our lives, she decided that the cart was a perfect baby nest. She was the first person to buy her own cart to keep me in. So here I am, over twice as many wheels now."

Ronin unloaded a down sleeping bag, pushed several bundles of soiled clothes aside, and revealed his library and personal files wrapped in black plastic at the bottom of one cart.

"Here's my mother with me and our first nest cart," he said and selected several other photographs from a cigar box. "This one was my first elevator ride in my cart, the sides were decorated with crepe paper."

"Wait a minute."

"What?"

"Who's that with the beaded belt buckle?" she asked. Tulip pointed to an enormous stomach at the side of the photograph.

"Rainbow, that's my uncle, he lived with us for a time," he said and turned the photograph to read the inscription on the back. "Mogul's Department Store, October 23, 1939, with Rainbow, the day he said we're going to Oklahoma."

"You traveled in your cart," she mocked.

"Right, on the train," he said and passed her several photographs of his mother and various new carts painted in bright colors. "Rainbow got a job at the Folding Carrier Corporation in Oklahoma City because Sylvan Goldman owned the company and he liked to hire Indians way back then."

"Where is his face?"

"Who?"

"Rainbow, nothing but his stomach here."

"Well, somehow, he never got his face into a picture," he said and sorted through a stack of irregular shaped photographs, "nothing but his gut, you're right, and that beaded belt, except this one where you can see his boots and the brim of his cowboy hat. He always wore that hat, even to bed."

"Rainbow with no head."

"Listen," he said as he closed the cigar box, "you're a really nice person, you can borrow my cart book to change your world too." The book was covered with plastic, an unmarked treasure. "This is the only book that really counts, the only one I ever read cover to cover."

"Ronin, do you like windmills?"

"You got a windmill book that changed your world?"

"I build miniature windmills."

"No shit, where?"

"Meet me here on this bench in one week," she said. Tulip leaned forward and buttoned her coat. "I'll return your book then and give you one of my windmills. You can mount it on the front of your cart."

"Whistle loves the wind."

"Next week, then?"

"Tulip, what a name for a streetwiser, and she even makes little windmills," he shouted as she crossed the street.

"Who cares? I got my crazy papers right here," she shouted back and then disappeared behind a bus at the intersection.

Terrocious and the Dead Head

Tulip Browne opened the windows and listened to the ocean wind turn the blades on her windmills. She remembered a humid night on the blue meadow when she heard voices but no one was there.

White Lies raised his head and moaned when the telephone chimed over her memories. Tulip has two numbers, one personal, and the other as a private investigator; the business line has a recorded message. She touched the copper blades as she passed and answered the personal chime.

"The windmills whir down to the bone this morning," she said, certain that no one but relatives and close friends would call on her unlisted number.

"Sounds wild to me," said a male voice.

"Who is this?" she demanded.

"Terret Pan Anna, listen . . ."

"How did you get this number?" she asked and then pressed a button to record the conversation. "Who are you, why are you calling me at home?"

"Tulip, is this Tulip Browne?"

"Answer me," she insisted.

"Tune, your brother, he gave it to me," he said with less humor. "He gave me your number, he said it was a secret and told me to eat the number. Anyway, when do you answer your machine?"

"Who are you?"

"Professor Pan Anna," he announced, "chairman of the Native American Indian Mixedblood Studies Department at the University of California, but you can call me Terrocious."

"Terrocious?"

"Listen, we need your help to investigate a serious problem of witchcraft and a stolen computer here," he pleaded. "We can talk about the details later."

"Witchcraft?"

"Owl heads, dead heads, rattles, whistles, and crackpot shamans," he chanted, "have the faculty and students on the edge of their seats. Will you meet me for lunch to at least talk about our problem?"

"Where?"

"You name it this time," he said with confidence.

"Krakow on the Vistula."

"Fantastic, tomorrow at noon then," he said. Later he called her business number, listened to her recorded voice several times, and then he dictated, "I promise to eat your personal number when we meet if you promise to answer my calls and tell me more about the windmills close to the bone."

"How much?" she asked and considered the menu.

"Lunch is on me," he said and smiled.

"No, not the lunch," she said and closed the menu. "I mean how much money do you have set aside to pay me as a private investigator?"

Pan Anna explained that Professor Marbell Shiverman, the author of *Native Americana Feminine Folklorica* and other studies of shamanic stories, had received in the mail a dead owl head, but the university police were reluctant to investigate tribal religious practices as criminal activities. He construed that urban shamans had became more material than spiritual and their stories more humorous. "But then," he whispered, and leaned closer to the private investigator, "we lost a new computer and other equipment." Terrocious touched her arm and watched the goose pimples rise; but he did not understand, the papillae response was an aversion not an adduction.

"Why are you telling me this?"

"Simple," he sighed, "would you investigate?"

"Have you notified the police?"

"No, no," he said and then leaned closer to whisper. "That's part of the problem, you see, we would like some solid evidence to take care of this ourselves. We're a new department and what we don't need now is bad publicity about our faculty to feed the racists."

"Two thousand dollars, minimum," she announced.

"What?" he shouted.

"My fee to investigate," she said and repeated the amount, "in consideration of what you have told me so far. You can be sure that not one dollar of that amount is based on idealism, racialism, or revisionism."

"You're right about that," he said and wiped his mouth. He pushed the plate of sour sausages aside and spread his fingers down on the table, a sign that he had reached the bottom line in the conversation. "We have only a thousand, but how do we know you'll provide the information we need to solve this problem?"

"Why did you call on me then?"

"You're right again," he mumbled and closed his hands. The little finger on his right hand was doglegged from a childhood injury.

"One thousand cash or your personal check in advance," she said and then mocked his hand movements. She spread her small hands down on the table.

"Tune never told me his sister was such a hard driver," he said and turned from side to side in the swivel chair. "His humor has been a real treasure on the campus, especially at our last graduation when he came down on the anthropologists."

"Tune spends too much time under his hat to suit me," she said and smiled, "but he's a real trickster. Listen now, here are my conditions."

"Surprise me."

"First, my report will be in the oral tradition and told to you, no one else, in less than a week," she emphasized. "I will describe several scenes and imagined events as stories, but the interpretation and resolution of the information will be yours, not mine. There will be no written report unless the same information is given to the police at the same time. You must agree to these conditions."

"Why do I feel like I've just bought a special stretch of blue sky over a swamp," he said. Terrocious stared at her and then he laughed, but he was nervous and uncertain.

"Because you have, but the stretch is a baronage."

"Could we get personal for a minute?" he asked and turned in his chair. "Tell me about your windmills, what whirs close to the bone?"

"I build windmills," she said and sliced a meatball on her plate. "Miniature windmills to catch the wind, natural power."

"Catch me," he pleaded and spread his hands.

"Too much wind," she said and laughed.

"How did you become a private investigator? You must be the only mixedblood in the business, and from a reservation no less."

"Eat my personal number."

"That was a joke," he said and raised his doglegged finger.

"Not to me."

"I don't have the number with me."

"Here, eat my business card then; your promise is recorded," she said. Tulip wrote her personal number on the back of an embossed card.

Pan Anna examined the folded card, then he cut out the number, soaked it in sour sauce, and ate it with a morsel of sausage. "You're a hard woman," he said and swallowed. He might have pouted as a child, an expression that was marked on his forehead. He craved the attention of women.

"Now, tell me about your names," she said with her elbows on the table. When the black waiter cleared the dishes, he recognized her and wrinkled his brow. "Tell me, is your nickname an adjective like ferocious?"

"Terrocious was a short sentence in public school," he said, pleased to tell stories about himself. "When I was in high school the principal was so angry with me once that he combined the words terrible and atrocious when he cussed me out. Well, I made the mistake of telling that story at a faculty party and the name stuck, as you might have imagined."

"How about Pan Anna?"

"Now that is an interesting story," he said and expanded his chest. He had gained some weight over his academic worries and the winter; his shirt buttons were strained. "But tell me about your name first."

"No, not now."

"Pan Anna goes back a long way, back to the Pan-American Exposition of 1901 in Buffalo, New York," he said and touched her bare arm and then her shoulder.

Tulip shivered and rubbed her arm. She is fascinated with natural power, wind and water, but she hates most tribal men, even mixed-bloods when they assume a racial connection, an unnatural privilege based on pigmentation and tribal cultures. Blond women, she has observed, have become the new material possession and are treated better than tribal women. When she resists a tribal man, her features become haunted, an animal at the treeline. Tulip moved back from the table when his wild breath touched her hair.

"Better that my grandfather was inspired with the birth of Pan Anna than the death of William McKinley at the Pan-American Exposition," he said and moved closer. "Can you imagine my name being Terrocious McKinley?

"My grandfather was part of the Indian Congress at the exposition, one of the human types in an ethnological village, but he never seemed to mind," he said and cleared his throat several times. "He loved it, he told us stories about walking around the Evolution of Man exhibit with Geronimo, and the time he met William Jennings Bryan, the lawyer and politician, that gentleman chimpanzee Essau, and my grandfather was there at the Temple of Music when President McKinley was shot by the anarchist Leon Czolgosz.

"But what impressed him the most at the exposition was when Vice

President Theodore Roosevelt named a tribal child, the first born at the concession," he said and raised his hands to enhance the suspense. "Roosevelt named that baby Pan Anna, and my grandfather was so impressed with that exposition name that he adopted it as our surname."

"Did he consider Czolgosz?"

"No, not even the vice president, but my grandfather was touched in a most unusual way, a religious experience of sorts, with the birth of that child at the exposition," he said in a solemn tone. "That child was the beginning of something new for him, a new tribal time, a new culture, and a new name."

"Luster Browne, my grandfather, was a tribal baron," she said and moved closer to the table. Tulip opened one of her business cards and drew on the back a map of the White Earth Reservation. "Patronia, the name of his federal allotment, is right here, not far from the source of the great Mississippi River."

"Fantastic," he said and touched her shoulder.

"Shadow Box, my sweet father, gave us all nicknames, such as Tune, China, Ginseng, Slyboots, Mime, and Garlic, and mine was Tulipwood, because my skin was the color of tulip wood at birth," she said and looked around the restaurant. The owner and one black waiter watched her from a distance. "We are all wild heirs to that reservation baronage."

"Fantastic," he swooned.

"Mime was silent, the most beautiful person in our family," she whispered and folded her arms. "I love her more than anyone. We were twins, and she was born with no palate, no voice, no spoken words. Mime learned the most honest gestures in language, and she brought us closer together with her silent play and imitations. She mocked me, but she knew our mother better than anyone, she moved her hands and winked just like our mother. Her face was radiant with humor, her eyes were a dance, she had no fear, she was at peace with the world, and it was her pure love and trust, her innocence and silence that brought her to a violent death."

Tulip leaned forward in silence. Her breath was short and sudden; she turned her head to one side. She folded her hands. The overhead fan churned the thick air in the restaurant. "Garlic was killed by lightning on the meadow and the next night my beautiful sister Mime was raped and murdered behind the old mission house."

"Tulip, no more now."

"Well, listen, that's how I became a private investigator," she said and shivered. "I was nineteen then, home from college for the summer, and it took me more than a year of investigation to convict three white men and one mixedblood of rape and murder, four drunken bastards on a hunting trip, looking for a savage, but they hated what they found because she was pure, a silent voice that reminded them of their own savagism."

"Please, no more now," he pleaded and then covered her hands with his; he was gentle and warm. "This is when a trickster would resolve the moment with tribal stories, a wild turn in a cruel world."

Tulip waited for his personal check to clear before she started her investigation. She called each faculty member in the department and asked them about dead owls, shamanism, and the stolen computer; she recorded each conversation and studied the voice patterns on oscillographs.

Professor Marbell Shiverman was the last person she called late that afternoon. Tulip asked her about owls and other dead heads; she was eager to discuss evil possession and moved the conversation with her own rhetorical questions.

"How many heads have you received?"

"One, an owl head, dead."

"Naturally."

"Cruel and unusual," said Shiverman.

"Do you have pets?"

"Moan."

"Moan?"

"Our black cat."

"Of course."

"Siamese mixedblood."

"Where did you receive the dead head?"

"Where?"

"I mean, at home?"

"No, the office," said Shiverman.

"Who delivered the owl head?"

"The postman."

"Was the package postmarked?"

"Well, the owl head was in my box when I arrived at the university that morning," she said in a monotone, "but we never thought to keep the postmark."

"There was someone else there?"

"The secretaries."

"Did you keep the dead head as evidence?"

"We put it in the freezer."

"Who would send you an owl head?"

"Tulip, what a beautiful name, listen, let me put it this way," she said and then inhaled through her nose, a low whistle, "I am a gay feminist, need I say more?"

"Feminists mailed you a dead head?"

"Men, men, that's who," said Marbell Silverman.

"Why would a man send you a dead head?" she asked in a firm tone of voice. Tulip turned more pleasure on the wind, the wind over copper blades on her miniature windmills, than she ever did in bed with men; but even so, she would never crib her own real experiences with crude ideologies based on gender.

"Listen, the men in the department hate me, they have tried, believe me, to get rid of me because they refuse to accept gays or feminists," she said. The words were aggressive signifiers, but her voice was monotone, a cold heart on the oscillograph.

"Professor Pan Anna has hired me to investigate the origin of the owl head and the loss of the computer," she said. "Do you know anything about what happened to the computer?"

"Nothing, why do you ask?" Her voice wavered and rose three tones on an octave. "Pan Anna loaned the computer to a male friend of his, and now he's trying to blame me for it, but we know what he's up to this time, we know about his sexism."

"He told me he would rather have the computer returned, with no blame," she said with precision. "Pan Anna told me he would rather avoid the university police and a stolen property report."

"That man is a liar, you can take my word for it," she said with a whistle and then paused. "Listen, once a week we have a tribal healing ceremony for women here at our home, why don't you come over and relieve your burdens?"

"Perhaps, next week then?"

"Pan Anna is an evil man, and if you don't believe me then come over and you can hear for yourself what the women in the department have to say about him."

"No man is a saint, but evil is a cruel measure of human experience," she said and stopped the conversation. The voice patterns were smooth over the dead head conversation but peaked when the stolen computer was mentioned.

Tulip visited the department the next morning; she obtained an accurate description of the stolen computer, the weight and measurements of the carton, and estimated the distance from various offices to the loading dock behind the building. She examined scratch marks on the polished tile floor where the carton had been dragged in the main office. The marks ended at the door.

"Has the hallway been polished since the computer was stolen?" she asked. Tulip pointed at the marks and held her distance from the chairman.

"No, once a year in summer," he answered. "First it was my secretary and now you both seem obsessed with the marks on the floor. So what do the scratches tell you?"

"Nothing."

"Terrific, what else is new?"

"Marbell Shiverman said you were a sexist."

"Of course."

"That's what I said too."

"Wait a minute, whose side are you on?"

"Mine."

"I like a woman on her own side."

"Of course," said Tulip.

"Never mind the rest," he moaned.

"She said you and the other men in the department were trying to force her out because she is gay," she said. Tulip browsed in his office, examined his library and tribal artifacts. She read the introduction to a book on the woodland trickster.

"What did you tell her?"

"The truth," she said with a smile.

"But the truth is the problem."

"My intent is to tell her the truth, enough to make her nervous if she is guilty, and if she is nervous enough she might make a mistake and return the computer."

"Of course," said Terrocious.

"Now, where were you on the night of the crime?" she asked and turned from the bookcase. Tulip sat down at the side of his desk and crossed her legs. She wore a loose cotton blouse with wide sleeves.

"In bed with a blonde," he boasted. Terrocious leaned back in his swivel chair and watched the dark space between her legs, under her short skirt.

"What kind of car does she drive?"

"The blonde?"

"No, Shiverman."

"Something small and foreign," he mumbled with marginal interest.

"I can picture her corpulent arm pressed against the side window, and, come to think of it, she drives an old pink pickup too."

"Does she have a reserved parking place behind this building?" she asked. Tulip uncrossed her legs and turned in the chair.

"Yes," he sighed.

"Fantastic," she mocked and departed.

"Wait a minute," he shouted and followed her down the hall to the stairs. He watched her narrow thighs reel down the steps to the rear entrance of the building.

Terrocious told her there, on the loading dock, that a few days after the computer was stolen, "Shiverman reported to the police that her office, less than a hundred paces from this very spot, had been burgled. Her long list of stolen things was unbelievable, the owl head was first, followed by a cat litter box, an ash tray, and last but not least, an expensive electric typewriter that belonged to the department."

"She reported the owl head?"

"Not only that," he said with mock excitement, "but she reported that the official file on the investigation of the owl head was stolen."

"Too obvious."

"That's what the university police thought, accustomed as they are to peculiar professors," he said and moved closer. He brushed her right thigh. "Shiverman, however, was a real test of their imagination."

Tulip was admired as an honest private investigator; in eight years she had established confidential contacts in police agencies and most public services institutions. She obtained university police records that reported a pickup parked behind the building the morning after the computer was stolen; the report was a routine investigation because several pickups had been stolen that month. She obtained copies of service bills from Pacific Gas and Electric and reports on Marbell Shiverman's telephone charges in the past three months; she also located a computer store where supplies had been purchased for the same computer model that was stolen.

Terrocious hemmed and hawed on the telephone; he called several times to remind her that she had promised an oral report in less than a week. Tulip increased the volume of his recorded message and then opened the windows to listen. "Remember, never mind, but listen, would you like to get together, well, when your report is prepared in the oral tradition, or sooner, anytime, how about tonight? How about dinner?" he droned. He used most of the time on her recorder that week.

White Lies barked at his recorded voice.

Tulip agreed to meet him for lunch on the patio at the faculty club; there, on the campus, she would present her oral report over a tuna salad sandwich. She spread horseradish on the dark bread and told her stories about the owl head and the computer.

"Once upon a time there was a professor who could never remember the postmark on a package that contained an owl head, even though she said it was delivered to her mail box at the university," explained the trickster detective. "This is hard to believe because the professor considers it to be so serious, and because she had invited secretaries and students down to her office to witness that dead heads had been delivered. The secretaries confirmed that she opened her mail, letters, and packages before she left the main departmental office."

"So, what does that mean?"

"She delivered her own owl head," she said and nibbled at her sandwich. "This professor is not an imaginative person, that much can be determined from her publications."

"The gay victim with a dead head," he mumbled and sliced a melon. "And men wear the black hats and owl masks in these wicked stories."

"She was so hated, one faculty member told me, that an owl head would never be enough, maybe a horse head or a barrel of pig umbles," said Tulip. "But what are umbles?"

"Umbles, animal guts, like eating humble pie."

"That's what he meant?"

"What else?" said Terrocious.

"Her voice oscillograph crested on computers."

"You analyzed her voice?"

"The whole faculty."

"And me, describe my oscillograph then."

"The phallic mountains," said Tulip.

"Of course, what else can be raised by words?"

"She is more concerned about computers than owl heads, men, or even sexism, and that surprised me when she cursed men as evil," she said and turned toward the sun. "The professor has a monotone voice, expressionless at times, but she seems to attract extremes to break her own madness."

"Well, tell me then, how did she get the computer out of our offices and then out of the building without being seen by somebody that night?"

"She ordered a master key when she served on the building security committee," she explained. "The police have a record of that, and she used that key to enter the main office to steal the computer. Someone dragged the carton across the floor while she held the door, then the two of them carried the carton down to her office where it remained that night. The university police identified her pickup by chance in the parking lot behind the building the next morning, but she did not have classes that day and the secretaries said she did not come in for her mail. That morning she pulled up to the dock and loaded the computer into the pink pickup."

"More, more, this is circumstantial evidence."

"Correct, but the units of electric power she used at her home have increased since the computer was stolen, more than twelve kilowatt hours a month, which is what a new color tube would use, but she does not own a new set and the increase is closer to a computer than anything else," she explained. Tulip ordered coffee and then continued her oral stories. "Her telephone records show an increase in long distance calls, which could be associated with the use of a computer modem, and she purchased computer supplies for the same model of computer that was stolen, and she made her first charges at that store on the day after the computer was stolen."

"How on earth did you find that out?"

"The oral tradition," she mocked.

"Now what?" asked Terrocious.

"Tell her what you have learned, and promise her that no one will know if she returns the computer she borrowed, but remember, she does not seem eager to hear male voices."

"Borrowed is the functional word here," he said, "and if she refuses, then we have no choice but to turn over the information to the university police. What do you think she will do?"

"You're a sexist, of course," she mocked, "and she's gay, and a victim who harvests owl heads, which means she will never appreciate your politics on this one."

"We could borrow back the computer," he said and moved down in the chair. Terrocious shaded his eyes with his hands and watched the muscles on her neck and cheeks move when she sipped her coffee. "That's what we can do, borrow it back one night, that would take care of the problem, no report to the police, no criminal investigation to embarrass the department, and no more problem."

"Would she sue?"

"Embellish the dead head stories and she might."

"Do you like windmills?" asked Tulip.

TRICKSTER PHOTOGRAPHY

Tune Browne is that crossblood trickster who boards with mongrels and claims to hold pure reason on a lunge line. You remember, the tribal photographer who pictured stoical whites and focused on their noses, necks, ears as a journalist?

Since then his photographic studies of pain, silence, and pretension, have won national attention, grants, and prizes. The trickster photographer became known as the Edward Curtis of the white pretenders. Even so, his most recent collection of photographs was removed from the "Ethnographic Present Photographers" exhibition at the P. W. Wonder Museum of the Family in Saint Paul, Minnesota.

Browne had loaned nineteen portraits, or stoical simulations, to the Wonder Museum. The photographs focused on white people who pretended to be tribal in the Boy Scouts of America, Indian Guides, the Pure White Hopi Snake Dance, and other social organizations.

Petrel Gray, the curator of photographs at the Wonder, told reporters that the special ethnographic exhibition was "reorganized with cultural references, not with malice or bias, and we are dedicated to the images of minorities, but we have never supported postmodern tribal satire, and we are certain about a sense of ethnographic presence."

"Break that down to the ethnographic here and now," said a newspaper reporter.

"The Browne photographs were neither ethnographic nor present, in the sense of our exhibition, and we received complaints from our patrons that the photographs were racist simulations."

"Was that a joke?" asked a reporter.

"Wonder directors never joke about public responses and our responsibilities to photography," said Gray.

"Wonder, then, has no simulations?"

"Yes, that would be our position, no racial simulations," said Gray. "To be sure, the subject of his photographs is the issue here, not the race of the photographer."

Tune Browne laughed with the mongrels in the darkroom. He enlarged a portrait of his grandmother dressed in a Boy Scout uniform and mailed it to Petrel Gray.

"The subject is the object in my portraits, as white people pretend to be tribal," said Browne. "The pretenders and mock dancers have become their own racial enemies, but then the subjects and objects have always been white, pure white simulations, and soon they will want their own federal trust reservations."

Tune Browne was born at the White Earth Reservation in Minnesota. He graduated in business from a community college and then turned to photography when he worked as a security guard at the Cadillac Bingo Casino in Park Rapids.

Browne wears white shirts with photographs printed over the pockets and on the sleeves; his favorite is a snapshot of himself at four hours old in a cradleboard.

The Cadillac Casino sponsored the first show of his photographs, more than a hundred portraits of white senior citizens concentrating on various tribal games of chance; the losers were the winners.

Browne, one reviewer commented, "has become the Indian Edward Curtis, believe it or not, because he has captured the vanishing white man at his own game." His prints were soon sold in private galleries; the public shows of his "pure white pretenders" drew thousands of tribal people to museums.

The trickster photographer, much to his surprise, had impressed his peers and the academic nihilists at the same time; one show became another and he earned the first doctorate in tribal simulations, an advanced degree with no referent, in the History of Consciousness from the University of California, Santa Cruz. His dissertation, "The Pure White Hopi Snake Dance and the Order of the Arrow: Comparative Photographic Studies of Cultural Simulations and Racial Pretenders," was rejected by several university publishers.

The Associated Press reported that the white snake dancers "claim they are trying to preserve dying traditions." Naturally, the Boy Scouts praised the Order of the Arrow, a simulation that honored white boys who pretended to be tribal; a simulation with no real reference and better than the remains of the real.

"Traditions never die, they only change," said the trickster. "Death comes to the subjects not the objects, because my photographs capture the white dancers as pretenders, pure simulations."

Tune Browne the trickster photographer is the onlie begetter of the last pure white pretenders of tribal traditions; his pictures are an invitation to simulations. The satires and cultural ironies are in the observer; the emulsion has no predicate, no racial real, no ethnographic presence.

SEPARATISTS BEHIND THE BLINDS

The Bureau of Indian Affairs has been wished dead more times than evil, but colonial evil is better outwitted than dead because someone would be sure to create a more depraved form of tribal control.

One of the oldest colonial bureaus in the federal government, planned first under the War Department and later transferred to the division of Land Management in the Department of the Interior, revealing federal ambivalence toward tribal people, has survived all death wishes like pale cockroaches from the old cities.

The Bureau of Indian Affairs continues to feed on linear words from field reports, swelling on white paper, indifferent research, while children hunger down five generations of tribal memories.

No one is alive now who remembers from personal experience the vernal morning when the cedar still stood and the rivers were wild and clean; the good time before the federal government created tribal exclaves through treaties and appointed tactical separatists, colonial administrators, to exploit native people and their resources. What the federal government has done to native tribes with humorless trickeries and faithless promises should never be forgotten.

Thousands of tribal people moved from reservations to urban centers, meaning to leave behind evil, their hunger and grim memories, but the federal colonialists were waiting like the cockroaches to define tribal places in the cities. The sons and daughters of those who had first settled on urban reservations demanded programs and services to change the limits of their lives.

The time was spring in the middle sixties. The place, in the morning,

was the Edward Waite Neighborhood House on Park Avenue in Minneapolis, and in the afternoon, the Minneapolis Area Office of the
Bureau of Indian Affairs located on Lake Street. The event was the first
organized protest against the federal colonialists. The participants
were tribal children, the unemployed, several high school dropouts,
old tribal people with walking sticks, college students, drinkers and
wanderers from the streets, and one white lawyer, who marched in the
picket line in his suit and conservative tie.

"When we hit the lines leave these plain brown sacks of cockroaches
in the federal buildings. We will be moving in a few minutes," said
Clement Beaulieu to the tribal people waiting in the garage behind the
Neighborhood House.

Clement Beaulieu was a tribal advocate on the urban reservation.
He organized, with the assistance of George Mitchell, Mary Thunder,
and several others, the Urban American Indian Protest Committee and
the first national protest, demanding that the Bureau of Indian Affairs
offer services to tribal people in the cities. "The urban reservation is the
largest in the state," said the advocate, "and tribal people should be
served wherever they live."

Protests and picket lines were new experiences on the urban reservation, and some were opposed to demonstrations. Dennis Banks, for
one, before his radical transformation as one of the political and spiritual leaders of the American Indian Movement, when his hair was cut
short, martial short, and he wore summer suits with white shirts and
ties, said that "demonstrations are not the Indian way."

Banks was right, but not for the right reasons. Holding a sign
bearing protest bromides was not a traditional tribal experience for
either clowns or warriors, but because it was immature, simple-
minded, and embarrassing to proud people, white urbanites understood the messages and supported the event. Picketing was not tribal,
but it was the language of white natives stuck on television in the
suburbs. Banks, who in the middle sixties avoided demonstrations and
protest rhetoric, later learned the power of televised bromides. Conservative as he seemed then, his views were shared by most tribal people,
which made the organization of a demonstration a serious challenge.

Beaulieu, determined to state the troubles of urban tribal people
through demonstrations and other means, called upon his friends and
relatives for assistance. Some served as drivers to transport tribal
people to and from the demonstration site at the area office, and others
printed bromides and messages and fixed them to sticks. It was a good
time, people were not without fear, but the memories have lasted and
those who were there live with a certain historical praise.

Beaulieu asked Mary Thunder to find as many tribal children as she could lead on the picket line. She walked into several elementary school classrooms, interrupted the teachers, and left with all the tribal children. She was also responsible for encouraging other tribal mothers to participate, which was important then because the slogan for the demonstration was "AIM AGAINST BIAS," "American Indian mothers against the Bureau of Indian Affairs' stupidity."

Late in the morning there were nineteen tribal people, most of them children, waiting in the garage behind the Neighborhood House. The people played pool and ate rolls while they waited for the first protest to begin. Dozens of tribal people who promised to be at the protest did not appear or call in their regrets. At the last minute, before the protest began, Beaulieu drove through the urban reservation looking for tribal people on the streets. When he found an individual, or a couple, he promised free dinners and a place in tribal histories for demonstrating their feelings against colonialism and federal separatists. Thirteen strangers picked up on the streets participated in the protest.

When the drivers lined up their cars waiting to transport the tribal protesters to the area office, the receptionist at the Neighborhood House told Beaulieu that a man named Gus Hall was waiting outside for permission to join the demonstration. Gus Hall was the general secretary of the Communist Party in America.

"Gus Hall, are you certain he said his name was Gus Hall?" Beaulieu asked the receptionist. She said she was certain that was his name.

"Gus Hall is a Communist," said Beaulieu.

"Who cares?" said the receptionist.

"Senator Humphrey, and television and the newspapers will too, . . . not to mention the rednecks and racists on the prairie," said Beaulieu. "Tell him to wait, tell him to wait a few minutes for me."

Beaulieu closed his office door and looked out the window while he considered the consequences of permitting the general secretary of the Communist Party in America to participate in the first demonstration against the Bureau of Indian Affairs. The movement would be associated with communism and unpatriotism. Gus Hall was free from federal restrictions and had mellowed with time, but politicians and old union members would not forget his brash management of the Young Communist League in Minnesota and his condemnation of capitalism when he was arrested during the Minneapolis Teamsters strike. The nation would side with the federal government and not with tribal people if a communist leader were seen at the demonstration. But would television and newspapers report the protest? A communist on the line would make it news, national and international news. Gus Hall in a new war dance. Gus Hall adds the tomahawk to the hammer and sickle. Gus Hall would make the protest news and then, once the issues were in the news, the protest committee could exclude and dispossess communism.

"Mister Hall," said Beaulieu, introducing himself. "This is a pleasure. . . . We will be leaving for the area office in a few minutes and we would be pleased to have you march with us this afternoon."

Hall smoked a pipe and was dressed in a tweed suit coat. He wore plastic-framed spectacles. He looked down when he spoke and when he listened, showing his bald head, and glanced up when he paused between sentences. He was slow to answer questions, gesturing with gentle hand movements.

Beaulieu pinched his nose and smiled over the smell of imported pipe tobacco.

"Douglas Hall, there, it is you," exclaimed Archie Goldman, executive director of the Waite Neighborhood House, as he came around the corner of the building. Douglas Hall is a lawyer who has been active in labor organizations—too active for some conservative managers—and human rights movements, and persuasive in liberal politics. "Douglas, you *are* looking good, trim there at the waist, and how is your wife? Listen, are you here for the beginning of this incredible revolution?"

"Yes, as one of the demonstrators," said Hall.

"Goldman told me you were Gus Hall," said Beaulieu.

"Never, forked tongue talk," said Goldman.

"Goldman speaks with ease now," said Beaulieu, "but wait until tomorrow when his board learns that the revolution was started in the garage."

"Listen, this is a good thing," said Goldman, huffing and puffing too hard on his pipe. He was enveloped in his own smoke.

"So much for communism," said Beaulieu.

Beaulieu did not issue the protest signs until the tribal people were at the area office. The children were eager to hold signs and march in front of the government windows, but the older tribal people, those on walking sticks, the elders with grim memories from the federal boarding schools, were hesitant and embarrassed to be seen in a protest demonstration. The elders had not forgotten the power of the colonial separatists. Most of the demonstrators were uncomfortable until three white men in a red car passed the picketers several times, shouting "go back to the reservation . . . dirt and savages never work . . . get your asses off welfare . . . savages suck . . . you got enough hands out now."

The tribal children stuck out their tongues and waved their signs like crosses at the passing white men. The signs had several misspelled words. One misspelled word, proglem for problem, was given meaning in print. The definition of a proglem (combining the meaning of problem and program) is that which is rendered from federal programs designed to solve people problems from a distance. The signs were printed in black and brown and red ink: No More Apologies . . . Negotiate Don't Dictate . . . We Don't Want to Return to Reservations . . . Stop Studying the Indian Problem—The Bureau of Indian Affairs Is Not under the War Department Anymore . . . Serve Indians Not Lands . . . Give Us Jobs and Training Not Commodities . . . The Bureau of Indian Affairs Can't Get Along without Us Now.

The demonstrators were given facts about the Bureau of Indian Affairs and instructed how to respond to questions about the purposes of the demonstration. The tribal protesters were told to express their emotions first and then the critical facts. White federal officials had no position from which to debate emotional statements.

George Mitchell and Mary Thunder prepared a two-page statement which was distributed during the demonstration. The statement listed the annual budget and the total number of employees in the Bureau of Indian Affairs. Other information was critical of federal services.

"One-third of the total Indian population in Minnesota lives in urban centers. Therefore, the Urban American Indians demand that the Bureau of Indian Affairs direct one-third of its programs to the Urban Center Indians in this area.

"We do not want to live in the depressed reservation areas. We want to live and work in normal American urban communities, but the Bureau of Indian Affairs will not serve the needs of the Indian unless he is somehow identified with reservation Indian trust lands, living in rural poverty.

"We want to be served like humans and not like quantities of land. We are Indians, that should be enough to be served by the Bureau of Indian Affairs.

"We wonder what the Irish, the Swedes, or the American Negro would have to say about a Bureau of Irish Affairs, a Bureau of Swedish Affairs, or a Bureau of Negro Affairs, which did not serve the needs of urban citizens.

"The Bureau of Indian Affairs does more for land, roads, and trees, than it does for Indian people. We demand that the Bureau of Indian Affairs negotiate not dictate.

"These are the things we demand:

"Assistance in orientation to city life . . .

"Assistance in finding housing . . .

"Assistance in using legal and medical facilities . . .

"Assistance in forming and developing effective Indian community organizations representing urban Indian interests and needs.

"Job training and education in *this* area, not in another part of the country. We don't want to be relocated. We like it here and we would like to be trained, live, and work in this area.

"Assistance in finding and adjusting to employment . . .

"The Bureau of Indian Affairs should send their employees into the community where the Indians live, to understand the urban Indian needs. There have been enough studies and statistics about the Indian. We are tired of being talked about, it's time for the Bureau of Indian Affairs to get to work."

The demands were not unusual, the need for services to urban tribal people had been established in simple emotions at the demonstration, but demanding that a portion of federal funds allocated to the tribes be redirected to urban centers was not a popular view on reservations. Elected tribal leaders had their own problems on the reservations and could not support urban diversions. Tribal politicians were in tacit agreement with the Bureau of Indian Affairs.

Clement Beaulieu wrote to Robert Bennett, then Commissioner of Indian Affairs, about the problems of tribal people being denied services in urban centers.

"I have your letter," Bennett responded in a letter, "relating to the picketing of the Area Office of the Bureau of Indian Affairs in Minneapolis as a protest of the discontent by Indian people with the Bureau's inability to work on urban Indian problems.

"I am sure that you and many other Indian people feel that you should not be dependent upon the Bureau of Indian Affairs for services, particularly when you have established residence in cities throughout the country. I know that you would not want the Bureau of Indian Affairs to follow Indian people wherever they may go in this country but that you would rather share in the community life wherever you establish your home.

"The ability of the Bureau of Indian Affairs to provide services to Indians who have established residence away from the reservation is a matter of law as well as policy in that funds appropriated by Congress are for particular services, primarily for those on or near Indian reservations. It would seem to me that Indian people who are residents and citizens of communities and States throughout the country who have need for services should apply to the same agencies that provide services to other citizens of the community. They are certainly entitled to these services."

Glen Landbloom, then area director of the Bureau of Indian Affairs office in Minneapolis, summoned his best and smoothest tongue to invite the protest organizers into his office for a talk. "My door is always open," he said, but no one accepted his offer. "We came here to change policies not to cultivate conversations," responded Beaulieu.

Landbloom issued an order that the blinds be drawn during the picketing of the building. Notwithstanding the order, some tribal employees, like prisoners behind horizontal bars, separated the metal blinds and smiled at the demonstrators. Visiting hours had ended.

"Those bastards sit at their desks while our children are starving," said George Mitchell to Sam Newlund, staff writer for the *Minneapolis Tribune*. "Outside on the street the arrowstocracy is on the move and inside they hang around the office. . . . They're dumb on one end and numb on the other."

Robert Treuer, former labor organizer and Bureau of Indian Affairs official at the office in Bemidji, Minnesota, wrote to Beaulieu following the demonstration, that "one of these days we'll have to get together and I'll give you a cram course on social protest, direct action techniques, with particular emphasis on picketing. I'm not enamoured of the picketing stunt—it just gave the Bureau of Indian Affairs hierarchy a chance to look good with their superiors in Washington."

The demonstration was reported in newspapers and on radio and television. Liberal politicians supported the general demands of the protesters and white people rallied behind the tribal underdogs who seemed to be fighting a heroic battle against the evil federal colonialists. The demonstration was the first passionate tribal drama that served to focus some attention, however limited, on the adverse living situations of tribal people in urban centers of the dominant culture.

Several months later the Bureau of Indian Affairs announced that it would provide funding for an urban employment and social services center in Minneapolis. When the demonstration ended, people and programs changed.

Glen Landbloom was transferred from the area office to a reservation post. Mary Thunder continued working in a good humor with tribal children and writing an urban reservation newsletter. George Mitchell organized an urban tribal teen center and expressed more interest in local politics. Douglas Hall, who was first introduced to tribal people on the picket lines, became active in tribal organizations as a result of the demonstration. Sam Newlund turned his attention to tribal people. His writing was balanced and accurate. Joe Rigert, then an editorial writer for the *Minneapolis Tribune*, followed news stories with sensitive editorials supporting a new tribal consciousness.

Gus Hall, or Arvo Kusta Halberg as he was named at birth by his Finnish immigrant father when the family lived near Virginia, Minnesota, never made the demonstration at the area office of the Bureau of Indian Affairs. But several months later, following the first convention of the Communist Party in America in seven years, where Hall was elected general secretary by acclamation, he asked tribal people to write about their experiences with federal colonialism for communist newspapers.

Tribal people have a passionate attachment to their land and an unusual sense of patriotism for the nation, which bounds between love and hate, but is not without good humor. The tribal protest committee refused to write for the communists because—in addition to political reasons—there was too little humor in communist speech, making it impossible to know the hearts of the speakers.

ESSAYS

DOUBLE OTHERS

Native American Indian medical doctors are scarce, and for that reason they were once the measure of assimilation and invitational civilization. Tribal healers and shamans were counted as the representations of both demonic and noble savagism; these men and women were studied and romanced as evidence of the other, or the exotic double other, in an "authentic" culture.

These considerations and the transvaluations of cultural values are the means that belie the histories of tribal names and simulations of identities in the literature of dominance.

The postindian shaman is an ecstatic healer in literature and culture, the shadow of tragic wisdom outside the humdrum of time and manners. The shamans bear precarious visions and hear curious stories that are both separations and ministrations to common tribal communities; however, a mere ecstatic vision is not an endorsement because shamans must heal, and the performance of healers must be sanctioned by those who trusted the performance and were healed. Otherwise, the rush to natural reason in the cities could become an avaricious simulation! The double others are the discoveries of the ecstatic separations of one other from the simulations of the other in the representations of an "authentic" tribal culture. Truly, the shamanic double others are the ironic absence of romantic antiselves.

The medical doctor, on the other hand, is a certified simulation bound to time and institutions with traces of tribal culture and dominance; the manifest manners of performance are honored more than ecstatic visions as a healer. The decadence of healers has caused a revolution in the state of simulations; tribal identities have been misconstrued as salvation and other countersanctions.

Robert Bellah argues in *The Broken Covenant* that the romantic "trans-valuation of roles that turns the despised and oppressed into symbols of salvation and rebirth is nothing new in the history of human culture, but when it occurs, it is an indication of new cultural directions, perhaps of a deep cultural revolution."

There are more specious shamans and tribal healers in urban areas than on reservations. In the cities natural reason has been superseded by contrived performances, the simulations that have no shadows of survivance. Medical doctors, the obverse of shamans, the double others in the cities, are weakened as healers in certain tribal communities because they have no stories.

"Caring and curing go hand in hand," wrote Michael Harner in *The Ways of the Shaman*. "Through his heroic journey and efforts, the shaman helps his patients transcend their normal, ordinary definition of reality, including the definition of themselves as ill. The shaman shows his patients that they are not emotionally and spiritually alone in their struggles against illness and death."

Santiago, a tribal leader at the Santo Domingo Pueblo, asked Carl Hammerschlag, the medical doctor in the Indian Health Services, "Do you know how to *dance*?" Hammerschlag humored the patient, "And will you teach me your steps?" Santiago danced at the side of his hospital bed and said, "You must be able to dance if you are to heal people."

Hammerschlag learned to hear stories with natural reason in the course of his practice. "Indian traditions have a strong belief in spirits and the healing presence of sacramental objects," he wrote in *The Dancing Healers*. "Witchcraft is just the opposite side of that view; it explains the concepts of evil. A concept of evil is necessary to give us a sense of right and wrong, a way of knowing how to treat others. . . . When you believe in witchcraft you also believe that you can get rid of the evil spirit. The task is to find a power greater than that of the witch; it may be a totemic animal, a psychic, a medicine man, a ceremony, surgery, or the confessional."

Charles Alexander Eastman, Ohiyesa, was raised by his paternal grandmother with a tribal name in the traditions of the Santee Sioux. He graduated with distinction from Dartmouth College and the Boston University School of Medicine.

Eastman was one of the first tribal medical doctors determined to serve reservation communities; he became the physician at the Pine Ridge Reservation. A few months later, on December 29, 1890, he treated the few tribal survivors of the Wounded Knee Massacre. The

Seventh Cavalry murdered hundreds of ghost dancers and their families at the encampment of Big Foot. Two weeks earlier the tribes mourned the death of Sitting Bull.

Eastman was raised to be a traditional tribal leader, but that natural course would not be honored. His father, Many Lightnings, was imprisoned for three years in connection with the violent conflict of settlers and the Minnesota Sioux in 1862. He would have been hanged but the death sentence was commuted by President Abraham Lincoln. Christianity touched his tribal soul and he chose the name Jacob Eastman.

Charles was about twelve years old when he and his relatives escaped to avoid possible retributions by the military. His sense of a traditional tribal world was never the same after his father was sentenced. His new name, education, and marriage were revolutions in his time; moreover, he was burdened with the remembrance of violence, the separation and conversion of his father, and the horror of the massacre at Wounded Knee.

Eastman and others of his generation, the first to be educated at federal boarding schools, must have been haunted and mortified by the atrocities of the cavalry soldiers. Wounded Knee caused even more posttraumatic burdens than other horrors of war because the stories of the survivors were seldom honored.

The Vietnam Veterans Memorial honors the names of those who lost their lives in the war; their names are shadows in the stone. The names are the remembrance of stories, and the shadows of the names wait to be touched. A Wounded Knee Memorial would honor the names of those who were murdered by the soldiers; the shadows of the ancestors could come to their names in the stone to hear the stories of survivance.

"He arrived one cold and windy day," as the medical doctor at Pine Ridge, South Dakota, wrote H. David Brumble III in *American Indian Autobiography*. "Just one month later he was binding wounds and counting frozen corpses at Wounded Knee."

Eastman reported later that the survivors "objected very strenuously to being treated by army surgeons, alleging as a reason that it was soldiers that had been the cause of their wounds, and they therefore never wanted to see a uniform again."

Brumble rushed to representations in his interpretations; he tied nine lines from *Indian Boyhood* by Eastman into the manifest manners of the vanishing tribal pose. The lines he construed as dismissive of the tribal simulation contain these past-tense phrases: the "Indian was the highest type of pagan and uncivilized man" who possessed a "remarkable mind," but "no longer exists as a natural and free man," and the remnants on the reservations are "a fictional copy of the past."

Brumble strained over these lines; he seemed to be insensitive to the burdens of the manifest manners of discoveries, the presence of antiselves, and the duplicities of assimilation policies, tribal ironies, and countersimulations. He asserted that "*Indian Boyhood* reflects evolutionist ideas," and the autobiography assumes that "the races may be ordered, that some are higher, some lower." Eastman "believed that differing races have different instincts," and "saw himself as an embodiment of Social Darwinist notions about the evolution of the races."

Brumble overstated the assumed influences of evolutionism at the time; his interpretations arise from the distance of literature and are imposed as representations of the intentions of a tribal medical doctor. Brumble traced Eastman with the most controversial notions of evolutionism and determinism. Clearly, the harsh debates over the monogenetic or polygenetic creation and evolution of humans have landed in the interpretation of tribal autobiographies.

"By the end of the first two decades of the nineteenth century, when philanthropy and the churches could show few positive results from their efforts to lift the Indians, doubts were raised about whether they could really be civilized," wrote Robert Bieder in *Science Encounters the Indian*. "Many such critics began to question the monogenetic assumptions, set forth in the Bible, that all mankind shared the same origin. Increasingly they began to explain Indians' recalcitrant nature in terms of polygenism. To polygenists Indians were separately created and were an inferior species of man."

Eastman wrote, "I have never lost my sense of right and justice." He endured the horror of a massacre, the melancholy of racialism, and resisted federal policies on reservations and in government schools. His resistance to manifest manners and dominance was honorable, and more assured than to tease once more the antiselves of evolutionism.

Frederick Hoxie, director of the D'Arcy McNickle Center for the History of the American Indian, pointed out that Eastman carried out his objective of a "universal quality" and "personal appeal" in *The Soul of the Indian*. "Significantly, his writing avoided identification with a particular tribal tradition, emphasizing instead a generalized and idyllic past." Eastman was an author of the soul, not a servant of the science of racialism at the time; he would counter antiselves and the simulations of savagism.

"Those soldiers had been sent to protect these men, women, and children who had not joined the ghost dancers, but they had shot them down without even a chance to defend themselves," wrote Luther Standing Bear in *My People the Sioux*. "The very people I was following—and getting my people to follow—had no respect for motherhood, old age, or babyhood. Where was all their civilized training?"

Historical mention of that massacre more than a century ago remains scarce. The *American Heritage Dictionary* notes in the geographic entries that Wounded Knee was the "site of the last major battle of the Indian Wars." That a massacre of tribal women and children would become the "last major battle of the Indian Wars" is an instance of manifest manners and the literature of dominance. Elaine Goodale, a poet and teacher from Massachusetts, became the dedicated supervisor of Indian education in the Dakotas. She met the young doctor at Pine Ridge. They were married later that year in New York City. Eastman was troubled by federal authorities and policies on reservations; he tried a private medical practice for a time, and then, after several other positions in federal service, he turned to writing. Later, Charles and Elaine purchased a summer camp in New Hampshire.

"The Indian no more worshipped the Sun than the Christian adores the Cross," he wrote in *The Soul of the Indian*. "The Sun and the Earth, by an obvious parable, holding scarcely more of poetic metaphor than of scientific truth, were in his view the parents of all organic life. From the Sun, as the universal father, proceeds the quickening principle in nature, and in the patient and fruitful womb of our mother, the Earth, are hidden embryos of plants and men."

Eastman endured the treacherous turns and transvaluations of tribal identities, the simulations of ferocious warrior cultures, the myths of savagism and civilization, federal duplicities, assimilation policies, the rise of manifest manners, and the hardhearted literature of dominance. He wrote to teach his readers that the tribes were noble; however, he would be reproached as romantic and censured as an assimilationist. Others honored his simulations of survivance.

"Eastman spent the balance of his long life making his way along the narrow path that bridged his two cultures," wrote Sam Gill in *Mother Earth*. "He was extremely influential and became a major model for the way of resolving the tensions that existed between cultures. . . . He attempted through government service, through lecturing and writing, through participation—often in founding and formative roles—in many organizations such as the YMCA and the Boy Scouts of America, to build bridges of understanding between cultures."

Eastman embraced metaphors over truistic translations to describe tribal religions; he was romantic, but he would disabuse those who pronounce that tribal cultures created the notion of the sun and mother earth as deities. Gill pointed out that his "statement is motivated by the need to counter this view, which he sees is as misplaced as declaring that Christians worship the cross."

Eastman was an outstanding student, and he learned to use metaphors as the simulations of survivance. He celebrated peace and the romance of tribal stories to overcome the morose remembrance of the Wounded Knee Massacre. Could there have been a wiser resistance literature or simulation of survivance at the time? What did it mean to be the first generation to hear the stories of the past, bear the horrors of the moment, and write to the future? What were tribal identities at the turn of the last century?

"I made a promise to my grandfather never to lose touch with his Coast Salish traditions, never to abandon our cedar roots, never to forget any creature that shares this world, and never to allow or participate in a rape of the earth or the sea," wrote Duane Niatum in *I Tell You Now: Autobiographical Essays by Native American Writers.* Niatum, a poet and teacher, mentions that his surname was given to him by his great-aunt and recorded in court documents. "Because I feel this is a sacred trust, I have reason to suspect that if I live long enough, this name will turn out to be what ultimately changed my character and life."

Mary TallMountain, Koyukon Athabascan, the author of poems and stories who lives in San Francisco, wrote in the same collection of autobiographical essays, that "Alaska is my talisman, my strength, my spirit's home. Despite loss and dissolution, I count myself rich, fertile, and magical. I tell you now. You *can* go home again."

Native American Indian identities bear the tribal memories and solace of heard stories. Postindian identities are inscrutable recreations, the innermost brush with natural reason, and, at the same time, unbounded narcissism and a rush of new simulations of survivance.

The sources of tribal remembrance, tragic wisdom, creation, personal visions, and the communal nature of the heard are precarious, but the nuances of posted names are burdened more with colonial discoveries, duplicities, and simulations in the literature of dominance than with the menace of silence, the inaccuracies of memories and histories, or the uncertainties of stories out of season.

The distinctive salutations of a personal tribal nature, however, are more than the mere translations and possessions of memories and names. Consider the untold influences and choices of names and metaphors of remembrance in specific cultural experiences, and the various sources of identities in public, private, intimate, and sacred circumstances; the choices become even more enigmatic with the vagaries, pleasures, and treasons of cultural contact, and the transvaluations of such wicked notions as savagism and civilization in the course of manifest manners and histories.

The literature of dominance, narratives of discoveries, translations, cultural studies, and prescribed names of time, place, and person are treacherous conditions in any discourse on tribal consciousness. Nature has no silence. The poses of silence are never natural, and other extremes, such as cultural revisionism, the ironic eminence of sacred consumer names, and assumed tribal nicknames, are dubious sources of consciousness; these distinctions, imitations, and other maneuvers are unsure stories heard over and over in common conversations.

The postindian warriors of simulations are not the insinuations of either humanism or "radical empiricism." Postindian simulations are the absence not the presence of the real, and neither simulations of survivance nor dominance resemble the pleasurable vagueness of consciousness.

William James wrote in *The Meaning of Truth* that one of the "main points of humanism" is that an "experience, perceptual or conceptual, must conform to reality in order to be true." Realities are preserved as the possible, but this world would not embrace simulations because the real in humanism is not a contradiction of other realities.

"My present field of consciousness is a centre surrounded by a fringe that shades insensibly into a subconscious more," asserted James in *A Pluralistic Universe*. "I use three separate terms here to describe this fact; but I might as well use three hundred, for the fact is all shades and no boundaries."

Postindian simulations are the absence of shades, shadows, and consciousness; simulations are mere traces of common metaphors in the stories of survivance and the manners of domination.

Luther Standing Bear was one of the first tribal students at the new government school at Carlisle, Pennsylvania. "One day when we came to school there was a lot of writing on one of the blackboards," he wrote in *My People the Sioux*. "We did not know what it meant, but our interpreter came into the room and said, 'Do you see all these marks on the blackboard? Well, each word is a white man. They are going to give each one of you one of these names by which you will hereafter be known.' None of the names were read or explained to us, so of course we did not know the sound or meaning of any of them. . . . I was one of the 'bright fellows' to learn my name quickly. How proud I was to answer when the teacher called the roll! I would put my blanket down and half raise myself in my seat, all ready to answer to my new name. I had selected the name 'Luther'—not 'Lutheran' as many people called me."

Captain Richard Pratt, who experimented with the education of tribal political prisoners at Fort Marion, Florida, became the first superintendent of the industrial school at Carlisle. He told the eleventh annual meeting of the Lake Mohonk Conference, three years after the massacre at Wounded Knee, that "the Indian has learned by long experience to believe somewhat that the only good white man is a dead white man, and he is just as right about it as any of us are in thinking the same of the Indian. It is only the Indian in them that ought to be killed; and it is the bad influences of the bad white man that ought to be killed too. How are these hindering, hurtful sentiments and conditions of both sides to be ended? Certainly, never by continuing the segregating policy, which gives the Indian no chance to see, know, and participate in our affairs and industries, and thus prove to himself and us that he has better stuff in him, and which prevents his learning how wrong is his conception of the truly civilized white man."

Luther and his generation were the last to hear the oral stories of their tribal families before the stories were translated, and they were the first to learn how to write about their remembrance and experiences.

The Indian became the other of manifest manners, the absence of the real tribes, the inventions in the literature of dominance. The postindian simulations of survivance, on the other hand, arose with a resistance literature. However, there are serious and notable distinctions in the comparison of tribal identities in the past century. Those tribal men and women who heard oral stories and then wrote their stories would not bear the same sources of consciousness as postindian warriors of simulations who are heard and written about by others.

Personal names and tribal nicknames are stories. "The idea that personal names might comprise a literary genre in some cultural contexts does not seem immediately obvious," wrote Peter Whiteley in his essay "Hopitutungwni: 'Hopi Names' as Literature." He points out that some Hopi names are "tiny imagist poems." The translation of nicknames would not reveal the obvious in tribal communities, the context and figuration of names in heard stories.

Luther Standing Bear, for instance, chose his names, and the stories of the bear are heard even in the translations of his surname. He wrote in *My Indian Boyhood* that "the Indian very seldom bothers a bear and the bear, being a very self-respecting and peaceful animal, seldom bothers a human being." The bear is the shadow in the memories and the trace in his names. The bear is "so much like a human that he is interesting to watch." The bear is "wise and clever and he probably knows it."

Not only is the bear "a powerful animal in body, but powerful in will also." The bear "will not run, but will die fighting. Because my father shared this spirit with the bear, he earned his name," wrote Standing Bear. "While in battle he was badly wounded, yet with blood streaming from his body, he did not give up and for this bravery earned a name of which he was ever after proud."

Standing Bear mentioned the caution of hunters because of the "bear dreamers" of the tribe. "They are the medicine men who, during their fast, have had a vision in which the bear had come to them and revealed a useful herb or article with which to cure the sick."

The postindian first person pronoun is a salutation to at least nine simulations of tribal identities in the literature of dominance. The simulations are the practices, conditions, characteristics, and the manifold nature of tribal experiences. The simulations would include tribal documentation, peer recognition, sacred names and nicknames, cultural anxieties, crossblood assurance, nationalism, pan-tribalism, new tribalism, and reservation residence.

- The inheritance of tribal traits and the traditional use of an oral tribal language, recognition of peers, and documents of family connections to a reservation or tribal community are simulations of identities.
- Tribal nicknames are heard in oral stories; the names are given by others and are associated with communities, not the separate and autistic induction of the individual. The translation of nicknames as surnames is the closure of tribal stories and the remembrance of communities in the association of names and pronouns; translated names are misconstrued identities in the literature of dominance.
- The historicism of tribal cultures and the indispensable linear representations of time, place, and person, in the absence of the real are simulations of manifest manners.
- The manifold anxieties and desires that arise from the tension announced in the binary of savagism and civilization are other simulations in the literature of dominance.

- The notions of crossbloodism, determinism, and racialism, maintain the sentiments of weakness, that crossbloods are a descent from pure racial simulations.
- The manifest manners of nationalism as sources of tribal identities are both means of association and resistance; some tribes are simulated as national cultural emblems, and certain individuals are honored by the nation and the tribes as *real* representations.
- Pantribalism, an institutional and personal simulation, presents a source of identities for tribal governments and professionals, such as tribal teachers and medical doctors, and a common source of individual recognition and association for those who have no other sources of tribal identities; pantribal associations are common at universities and tribal community centers in cities.
- Tribalism is an essential source of identities; the notion that tribal identities are inherited as a universal connection in the blood determines political and cultural unities in the literature of dominance.
- The reservation simulations are the notion that reservation experiences determine obvious tribal identities. Thousands of tribal people have moved from reservations to cities in the past century to avoid poverty, sexual abuse, and the absence of services, education, and employment.

Nationalism is the most monotonous simulation of dominance in first person pronouns of tribal consciousness. The stories of tribal names chase new metaphors as the simulations of survivance. Homi Bhabha argued in "DissemiNation: time, narrative, and the margins of the modern nation," an essay on the "strategies of cultural identification" in *Narration and Nation,* that the "nation fills the void left in the uprooting of communities and kin, and turns that loss into the language of metaphor."

The concerted creations of tribal cultures are in continuous translations as stories, and the situation of hermeneutics remains the same in simulations; the silence of heard stories in translations, and the absence of the heard, antecedes a presence in the shadows of names. Has the absence of the heard in tribal stories turned to the literatures of dominance? What are the real names, nouns, and pronouns heard in the fields of tribal consciousness? How can a pronoun be a source of tribal identities in translation? How can a pronoun be essential, an inscription of absence that represents the presence of sound and a person in translation?

Paula Gunn Allen, the most honored postindian warrior of simulations in literature, pronounced in *The Sacred Hoop* that "the major difference between most activist movements and tribal societies is that for millennia American Indians have based their social systems, however diverse, on ritual, spirit-centered, woman-focused worldviews." Moreover, she wrote, "American Indian thought is essentially mystical and psychic in nature."

Allen conceived the word "cosmogyny" in *Grandmothers of the Light: A Medicine Woman's Sourcebook.* Cosmogynies are simulations that uncover "a spiritual system that is arranged in harmony with gynocratic values." The stories in this sourcebook "connect us to the universe of medicine," she announced in the preface. "Gynocentric communities tend to value peace, tolerance, sharing, relationship, balance, harmony, and just distribution of goods."

The crystal skull, a spectacular carving of a head in a clear rock crystal is the source of incredible postindian medicine stories. Allen avowed that she "channeled information" from the "immortal" remains of the skull, a "being" with a "powerful and beautiful presence." She named the carved rock head Crystal Woman.

The spiritual simulations in crystal were the cause of creation and medicine stories. Allen "channeled" to understand that Crystal Woman was a "priestess, a shaman, a medicine woman." She came before "the human beings, before the five-fingered beings."

Allen revealed that two men found the skull in Belize. "In the fullness of time, they found the place where the skull had come to light, and after a time they discovered its present home. they made their way far to the north, to the crisp, suburban home of Sun Woman, Daughter of Light. . . . It is said that the Mother of All and Everything, the Grandmother of the Sun and the Dawn, will return to her children and with her will come harmony, peace, and the healing of the world." Everything must be more obscure on the channel, the encounter with an absence, otherwise these names would lose their postindian significance.

The crystal skull was purchased from "Tiffany of New York in the late 1890s" and may have "originally been brought from Mexico by a Spanish officer," wrote Mark Jones, the editor of *Fake? The Art of Deception.* "Past speculation has suggested that the skull is in fact of Far Eastern origin, but at the time of its entry into the collections of the British Museum it had generally come to be accepted as being from pre-Hispanic Mexico." The skull appears to be Aztec. When it was last examined, however, "the conclusion was that some of the incised lines forming the teeth seemed more likely to have been cut with a jeweler's wheel than to have been produced by the techniques available to Aztec lapidaries." The skull could have been created by a tribal artist for a church or cathedral. "Other speculations as to the origins and possible use of the crystal skull are legion. The question remains open."

Crystal Woman and the crystal skull have more than one simulation in common with the medicine woman, Agnes Whistling Elk, created by Lynn Andrews. The authors, their simulations, crystal manners, and arcane stories arouse millions of readers, most of them women who are reassured once more that literature is "authentic," the real, a source of presence, "gynocratic" medicine, and simulations of utopian peace.

"When I first met Agnes, I asked her if she thought it was strange for someone from Beverly Hills to be sitting in her quiet cabin in Manitoba asking for help," wrote Lynn Andrews in *Flight of the Seventh Moon.* She describes how "Agnes initiated me into my womanliness and self-hood" with visions and ceremonies.

"No, it is not surprising that you are here. Many omens have spoken of your coming, and I would be surprised if it were any other way. You know that enlightenment is arrived at in a different way for a woman than for a man," reported Andrews.

"I asked Agnes if she taught men the same as woman. She laughed and said I should discover that answer for myself. 'Teach the next ten men you meet how to have a baby.'"

Agnes "said that it had been told to her in a prophecy that I was to become a warrioress of the rainbow of black, white, red, and yellow peoples, and that one day I would become a bridge between the two distinct worlds of the primal mind and the white consciousness," Andrews wrote in *Jaguar Woman.*

Andrews pursues racialism and rainbows, to be sure, but she has never been a warrior of postindian survivance; she is the absence of a warrior, the headmost simulator of manifest manners and ersatz spiritualism in the literature of dominance.

The postindian warriors and posers are not the new shaman healers of the unreal. Simulations and the absence of the real are curative by chance; likewise, to hover over the traces of the presence in literature is not an ecstatic vision. The turns of postindian remembrance are a rush on natural reason. Some simulations are survivance, but postindian warriors are wounded by the real. The warriors of simulations are worried more by the real than other enemies of reference. Simulations are the substitutes of the real, and those who pose with the absence of the real must fear the rush of the real in their stories.

The missionaries of manifest manners have flourished for centuries with such ease in politics, education, communications, and literature. The simulated realities of tribal cultures, the most unsure representations, have informed presidents, journalists, college teachers, and publishers for several centuries.

Charles A. Lindbergh, the aviator and adventurer, wrote in his lucid *Autobiography of Values* that his grandfather, who had emigrated from Sweden and settled in Minnesota, "started the community's first school in his farm granary." The school, of course, is an admirable remembrance, but the land, the stolen land and removal of tribal families to reservations, was a mere mention in the literature of dominance. "Children of those days lived in constant fear of Indians, though the Chippewa were friendly and even if, as grownups told them quite truthfully, there was no longer any danger from the Sioux. Now and then, when parents were out of hearing, boys would hide in bushes and whoop like savages to frighten sisters and their friends." The manifest manners were the tired simulations of savagism, at least, that his parents would not hear but in the pleasure of his memories.

"When the real is no longer what it used to be, nostalgia assumes its full meaning," wrote Baudrillard in *Simulacra and Simulations*. "There is a proliferation of myths of origin and signs of reality; of second-hand truth, objectivity and authenticity." Nostalgia, and the melancholia of dominance, are common sources of simulations in manifest manners; mother earth and the shamans of the other are summoned to surrender their peace and harmonies in spiritual movements.

Ed McGaa, the postindian warrior of simulations and sun dance ceremonies, nominated a new rainbow tribe to counter savagism and manifest manners. "The red people had no need to consider migration from their nature-based system," he wrote in *Rainbow Tribe*. "Their land was kept pure and clean. It was still very productive and was not overpopulated." He claims that such "treasures" as "harmonious sociology, unselfish leadership, warm family kinship, and honest justice" proliferated in traditional tribal cultures. The simulations of his rainbow tribe are treacherous, in one sense, because nostalgia is the absence of the real, not the presence of imagination and the wild seasons of peace. The rainbow tribe is a diversion, it would seem, a simulation marooned in the romance of the noble savage and the unattainable salvation of absolute boredom and melancholy.

"We invent the real in the hope of seeing it unfold as a great ruse," wrote Baudrillard in *Fatal Strategies*. People "seek a fatal diversion." No "matter how boring, the important thing is to increase boredom; such an increase is salvation, it is ecstasy."

McGaa, however, had not invented the salvation of the rainbow tribe when he was a law student at the University of South Dakota. Then he lectured in public schools and on reservations about his missions as a combat fighter pilot in Vietnam.

"I remember a touching scene when I was in law school and flying helicopters" for the Marine Corps Reserves. "We circled to land and were met formally by a marching contingent of Sioux warriors" on the Standing Rock Reservation. "We were told to march at the head of the contingent" into the packed gymnasium. "I told the excited crowd that it was an honor to return to a land of tribal people who appreciated the sacrifice of their warriors. I told them how they had salved my spirit with their honoring medicine and how this medicine was deeply appreciated by all the living who returned" from Vietnam.

"Many Sioux warriors from this Hunkpapa and Minnecoujou Sioux reservation had been killed," continued McGaa. "A flag for each departed warrior was raised on its own sapling staff, and the Sioux anthem and our national anthem were played. . . . In the background, draped from two taller poles, the American flag and a tribal flag waved. It was an extremely moving scene cast upon the computer of life."

McGaa, at that time, was the secret witness for the prosecution in a commutation hearing on a capital punishment case before the South Dakota Board of Pardons and Paroles. Thomas White Hawk had been sentenced to death for a brutal murder, and the defense counsel had enlisted more than a hundred tribal witnesses to testify against capital punishment. The combat aviator testified that he was a second-year law student and "half Indian."

"Have you formed an opinion as to the commutation of White Hawk's sentence?" asked the prosecutor, Charles Wolsky.

"Yes, I have formed an opinion," he testified at the commutation hearing. "Well, the old-time Indian had three main methods of punishment. We had outright capital punishment. We had banishment or we had forgiveness. . . . banishment was usually when you did something to your people. They would banish you from the tribe," he explained, and compared banishment to capital punishment. "The outright death penalty was when the tribe would kill you for a real grave serious crime where you brought tremendous disgrace and despair upon your people."

McGaa, on a mission of manifest manners, was the sole witness for the prosecution. Later, outside the hearing room, he was nervous and troubled. He looked back and asked, "Who was that old man in there?" Charles White Hawk, uncle of the condemned murderer, attended the hearing; he sat with his arms folded over his chest and stared at the witness when he testified.

"White Hawk, White Hawk," shouted McGaa, "that old man is a medicine man and he was doing his power on me in there." Indeed, the tribal medicine of survivance, and the man who would simulate a rainbow tribe had lost the seasons.

Governor Frank Farrar announced that he had reviewed the case of Thomas White Hawk and, on 24 October 1969, "commuted his sentence of death in the electric chair to a sentence of life imprisonment for as long as he shall live with the personal request to future Boards of Pardons and Paroles that all petitions for further commutation of the sentence" be denied.

"The Indian is a true child of the forest and the desert," wrote Francis Parkman in *The Conspiracy of Pontiac.* "His haughty mind is imbued with the spirit of the wilderness, and the light of civilization falls on him with a blighting power."

Parkman, one of the masters of manifest manners and the simulations of savagism, considered civilization a blight to the other; such adversities as alcohol, uncouth missionaries, wicked debaucheries, avarice, fraud, corruption, violence, and colonial melancholy, in the occupation of the new nation, were the overload, not the light of civilization. The tribes must have perceived the heart of darkness, not the light of blight, in manifest manners and the cruelties of civilization.

"The shadows of his wilderness home, and the darker mantle of his own inscrutable reserve, have made the Indian warrior a wonder and mystery," continued Parkman. His romantic and sinister simulations that the "generous traits are overcast" by "sleepless distrust" and suspicions of "treachery in others," are the histories and literature of dominance.

"Ambition, revenge, envy, jealousy, are his ruling passions; and his cold temperament is little exposed to those effeminate vices which are the bane of milder races. With him revenge is an overpowering instinct; nay, more, it is a point of honor and a duty."

Parkman mentions the unscrupulous trade in diluted and poisonous alcoholic beverages in *The Old Régime in Canada.* "The drunken Indian with weapons within reach, was very dangerous, and all prudent persons kept out of his way. This greatly pleased him; for, seeing everybody run before him, he fancied himself a great chief, and howled and swung his tomahawk with redoubled fury. If, as often happened, he maimed or murdered some wretch not nimble enough to escape, his countrymen absolved him from all guilt, and blamed only the brandy. . . . In the eyes of the missionaries, brandy was a fiend with all crimes and miseries in his train; and, in fact, nothing earthly could better deserve the epithet infernal than an Indian town in the height of a drunken debauch."

Evelyn Waugh observed the tribes with an obverse curse of racialism and manifest manners, but with an ironic touch, that the tribes were similar, in certain respects, to the English. "The Indians, I learned later, are a solitary people and it takes many hours' heavy drinking to arouse any social interests in them," he wrote in *Ninety-two Days: The Account of a Tropical Journey Through British Guiana and Part of Brazil.* "In fact the more I saw of Indians the greater I was struck by their similarity to the English. They like living with their own families at great distances from their neighbours; they regard strangers with suspicion and despair; they are improgressive and unambitious, fond of pets, hunting and fishing; they are undemonstrative in love, unwarlike, morbidly modest; their chief aim seems to be on all occasions to render themselves inconspicuous; in all points, except their love of strong drink and perhaps their improvidence, the direct opposite of the negro."

Native American Indians bear the burdens of a nation cursed with the manifest manners of alcoholism. Once thought to be nutritious, alcohol has been the earnest measure of temperance, and the source of enormous excise revenues from the sale of beverage alcohol.

Alcohol has "crossed regional, sexual, racial, and class lines," asserted William Rorabaugh in *The Alcoholic Republic.* Manifest manners, however, have never understated the racialism of alcohol, or the savage simulations that the tribal other had the real burden, a genetic weakness to alcohol and civilization. Indians are the wild alcoholics in the literature of dominance.

"Americans drank at home and abroad, alone and together, at work and at play, in fun and in earnest," wrote Rorabaugh. The early nineteenth century was a "great alcoholic binge." Americans drank over time, fashion, and their economic miseries, and the tribes became the simulated measure of the national curse of alcoholism; the public has been hesitant to discern the real cost of alcoholism, and reluctant to abandon the stereotype of the drunken savage.

"The colonial view of Indian drinking, that red men could not hold their liquor, was in fact the beginning of a long-standing stereotype of the impact of alcohol on the tribes," wrote Mark Lender and James Martin in *Drinking in America.* The colonial settlers simulated the tribes as savages, and "any sign of intemperate behavior served to confirm that image. Some modern anthropologists have termed the so-called Indian drinking problem the 'firewater myth.'" The authors explain that "some tribes learned to drink from the wrong whites: fur traders, explorers, or fishing crews, all of whom drank hard and, frequently, in a fashion not condoned" by missionaries and other colonists.

"Perhaps no stereotype has been so long-lasting and so thoroughly ensconced in our social fabric as that of the 'drunken Indian.' Our federal government gave it official recognition by prohibiting the sale of beverage alcohol to Indian people for over a century," wrote Joseph Westermeyer in "'The Drunken Indian': Myths and Realities" in the *Psychiatric Annals*.

The premise that prohibition can subdue alcoholism on reservations has never been renounced. Russell Means, for instance, once declared as a candidate for the presidency of the Oglala Sioux Tribal Council that he would establish "customs checkpoints" around the entire reservation, prohibiting the transportation and sale of beverage alcohol in tribal communities. The advocates of prohibition seem to have increased with the incredible rise of tribal casinos, and even more because some casinos have opened liquor bars on the reservation.

Prohibition is neither a cure nor a resolution of the "firewater myth" in the literature of dominance; however, prohibition espoused by postindian warriors is a simulation of survivance. Means would abolish the institution and manifest manners rather than punish the victims of beverage alcohol.

Louise Erdrich, the poet and novelist, has pronounced one of the most extreme prohibitions as a resolution to the menace of alcohol in the lives of women and children. Fetal Alcohol Syndrome, the situation of acute alcohol poisoning on some reservations, "has grown so desperate that a jail internment during pregnancy has been the only answer possible in some cases," she wrote in the foreword to *The Broken Cord* by Michael Dorris. The use of the word "internment" is a curious euphemism for incarceration, and without the patent due process of law in a constitutional democracy.

"If a woman is pregnant and if she is going to drink alcohol, then, in simple language, she should be jailed," asserted Jeaneen Grey Eagle. Dorris interviewed her on the Pine Ridge Reservation. She was then the director of Project Recovery. He wrote that "her words were shocking, antithetical to every self-evident liberal belief I cherished, yet through my automatic silent denial I felt some current of unexpected assent," and then he asked, "What civil liberty overrode the torment of a child?"

Indeed, alcohol is poison, but must tribal women bear once more the moral burdens of manifest manners? Must tribal women bear the burdens of the distribution of beverage alcohol and the excise revenues on the sale of alcohol? The "internment" of poor tribal women would be an autocratic salvation for the moral crimes of a nation.

Native American Indians have endured the envies of the missionaries of manifest manners for five centuries. The Boy Scouts of America, the wild simulations of tribal misnomers used for football teams, automobiles, and other products, Western movies, and the heroic adventures in novels by James Fenimore Cooper, Frederick Manfred, Karl May, and others are but a few examples of the manifold envies that have become manifest manners in the literature of dominance. The shamans of the tribes have been envied by urban spiritualists, military men have envied the courage of the tribes, and now, on some reservations, the outrageous riches from casino operations are envied by untold posers in organized crime and politics.

UNNAMEABLE POSTINDIANS

Native American Indian identities bear the memories and solace of heard stories; the cultures of tribal identities are elusive and inscrutable creations, an innermost brush with natural reason; at the same time, tribal identities are unbounded narcissism and the tease of user simulations.

William Least Heat-Moon, for instance, the celebrated author of *Blue Highways*, assumed an uncommon surname and then embraced pronouns that would undermine his own postindian identities.

Heat-Moon, in the foreword to the new edition of *Old Indian Trails* by Walter McClintock, simulated the presence of the tribal other with a rhetorical wish to "live as the Indians did before the Europeans descended here. Perhaps even better, to join a tribe with old ways and discover whether life with people only slightly beyond a stone-age culture is sweeter than ours, to learn whether tribal Americans truly built their lives around a harmony and balance between humankind and the rest of nature." The romance of nature and the other is a mode of dominance in literature.

The sources of some postindian identities have become texts, the unheard consumer renaissance of scriptural practices. Kenneth Lincoln, and others, have celebrated uncommon, but nonetheless modernist, communal adoptions of postindian identities. Hertha Wong, on the other hand, in the introduction to her book on tribal narratives, seemed to search for a discoverable and essential tribal connection. Jamake Highwater, the most tiresome postindian poser, simulated his tribal descent in the promotion of his publications.

Native American Indian traditional names are heard in visions and conceived in performances: Sacred names are the assurance of identities, and most nicknames are based on performances and communal experiences. Traditional nicknames, however, are seldom autoinscriptions; most descriptive nicknames are given by peers, not publishers.

The autoinscriptions of postindian nicknames are tracts, commercial instruments that endorse the simulations of identities in the absence of the heard, and the absence of performance, shadows and memories of the tribal real. The observance of heard stories once situated tribal names and remembrance. Now, as identities become textual commodities, certain authors inscribe their own descriptive names and then, as a postindian reversal of a traditional encore, enact the text or autoinscription as a simulation of identities. Doubtless some "traditions" are invented as evidence to support the texts of postindian identities. Traditions and names, in this sense, serve the literature of dominance, not the remembrance of tribal survivance.

Autoinscriptions are language, to be sure, but not stories; nicknames are the presence of the heard, the shadows of natural reason and trickster shimmers in stories. Names hold no breath but shadows and memories; languages bear human solace and consume the scriptural at the same time. Tribal nicknames are stories, not definitions; autoinscriptions are the poses not survivance. We are the stories, not the adoption of scriptures; we are the shadows in our names.

Postindian autoinscriptions are hoarse similes, and tragic, in the sense of ruinous scriptures, because there are no tragedies outside of literature; the pose of silence is a tragic name. The nature of tragedy "cannot be determined without reference to tragic works of literature—there is no *tragedy* without them," wrote Suzanne Gearhart in *The Interrupted Dialectic*. The similes of autoinscription have no tragic source of reason but in the transitive structures of literature that become the notions of culture. Postindian autoinscriptions are escape distances, and even the distances are poses.

The sources of tribal remembrance, creation, personal visions, tragic wisdom, and the communal nature of the heard are precarious, but the capacities and nuances of posted names are burdened more with colonial discoveries, the duplicities of dominance, and pretentious simulations, than with the menace of silence, the inaccuracies of memories, or the uncertainties of stories heard out of season.

The distinctive salutations of a personal tribal nature, however, are more than the mere translation and possession of memories and names. Consider tribal chance, the untold influences and choices of cultural experiences, and the various sources of unnameable identities in public, private, intimate, and sacred circumstances; the choices become even more enigmatic with the vagaries, pleasures, and treasons of cultural contact, and the transvaluations of such wicked notions as savagism and civilization in the course of colonial histories.

The literature of dominance, the histories, narratives of discoveries, translations, cultural studies, and prescribed names of time, place, and person, are treacherous conditions in any discourse on tribal consciousness. The poses of silence are not natural, and other extremes, such as cultural revisionism, the ironic eminence of sacred consumer names, and assumed tribal nicknames, are sources of identities besides the obvious associations; these distinctions, poses, adoptions, imitations, and other maneuvers are unsure scriptural stories told over and over in common conversations of dominance.

Natural reason, tragic wisdom, and survivance are active represen tations of the rights of consciousness; the romantic adoption of tribal names and identities is passive and serves the causes of dominance. Postindian simulations must be seen as ironic overtures; otherwise the reason praises dominance.

Sacred names, those secure ceremonial names, were scarcely heard by missionaries or government agents and seldom translated as surnames; nicknames were assured in tribal stories, but the stories were lost in translation as surnames. Later, most surnames were chosen and dictated at federal and mission schools. Some tribal names endure in stories, and nicknames are identities learned and ascertained in the performance of stories; moreover, descriptive names seem to be more esteemed in translation, and certain choices of names are mere simulations with no active memories or stories.

Snowarrow is but one recent name that has been chosen by a teacher to augment his postindian identities. Youngblood is another; some nicknames are ostentatious, and others are read with no ascriptions. Some names are eschewed and renounced for countless reasons. Thomas Edward Kill, for instance, petitioned a court for legal permission to change his surname because he hoped to become a medical doctor and he did not think his tribal name in translation would inspire confidence.

Kenneth Lincoln avows adoption as a source of significance as a scholar. He noted in *Indi'n Humor* that "he was adopted into the Oglala Sioux." The sapient humor of adoption is elusive, a passive simulation, and a dubious endorsement of authenticity.

Some names and associations are chance, to be sure, an ironic observance, or the break even consciousness of apostates; for all that, tribal stories and natural reason are unanimous, memorable even in translation, and descriptive names are so celebrated in this generation that thousands of "wannabee" romantics pursue an obscure tribal connection, an adoption, a passive wisp of ancestral descent in a document or name. Others bear consumer simulations and pretensions as personal identities, for various reasons, and pretend to be tribal in the name, blood, and remembrance of those who have endured racialism and the literatures of dominance.

Native American Indian identities are created in stories, and names are essential to a distinctive personal nature, but memories, visions, and the shadows of heard stories are the paramount verities of a tribal presence. The shadows of names are active and intransitive, the visual memories that are heard as tribal stories; these memories are trusted to sacred names and tribal nicknames.

Tribal identities would have no existence without active choices, the choices that are heard in stories and mediated in names; otherwise, tribal identities might be read as mere scriptural simulations of remembrance. The literatures of dominance are dubious entitlements to the names in other cultures, simulations that antecede the shadows of the real and then unteach the mediations of tribal names and stories.

Luther Standing Bear chose his names, and the stories of the bear are heard in the translation of his surname. Not only is the bear "a powerful animal in body, but powerful in will also." The bear "will stand and fight to the last. Though wounded, he will not run, but will die fighting. Because my father shared this spirit with the bear, he earned his name."

N. Scott Momaday, the novelist, wrote in *The Way to Rainy Mountain* that his tribal grandmother "lived out her long life in the shadow of Rainy Mountain, the immense landscape of the continental interior lay like memory in her blood. She could tell of the Crows, whom she had never seen, and of the Black Hills, where she had never been. I wanted to see in reality what she had seen more perfectly in the mind's eye, and traveled fifteen hundred miles to begin my pilgrimage." Aho, his grandmother, heard stories of a migration that lasted five centuries; the stories she heard became the shadow distance of tribal imagination and remembrance.

Momaday honored the memories of his grandmother and touched the shadows of his own imagination; shadows that traced his identities and tribal stories in three scriptural themes in *The Way to Rainy Mountain.*

Tribal nicknames are the shadows heard in stories; the pleasures of nicknames, even in translation, are an unmistakable celebration of personal identities. Nicknames are personal stories that would, to be sure, trace the individual to tribal communities rather than cause separations by pronouns of singular recognition.

Brian Swann and Arnold Krupat, the editors of *I Tell You Now: Autobiographical Essays by Native American Writers*, pointed out that the "notion of telling the whole of any one individual's life or taking merely personal experience as of particular significance was, in the most literal way, foreign to them, if not also repugnant." Nothing, however, is foreign or repugnant in personal names and the stories of nicknames. The risks, natural reasons, and praise of visions are sources of personal power in tribal consciousness; personal stories are coherent and name individual identities within communities, and are not an obvious contradiction to communal values.

The shadows of personal visions, for instance, were heard and seen alone, but not in cultural isolation or separation from tribal communities. Those who chose to hear visions, an extreme mediation, were aware that their creative encounters with nature were precarious and would be sanctioned by the tribe; personal visions could be of service to tribal families. Some personal visions and stories earn the power to heal, to liberate the spirit, and there are similar encounters with tribal shadows in the stories written by contemporary Native American Indian authors.

Nicknames, shadows, and shamanic visions, are tribal stories that are heard and remembered as survivance. These personal identities and stories are not the same as those translated in the literatures of dominance.

"My spirit was quiet there," Momaday wrote in *The Names*, a meticulous memoir of his childhood at Jemez, New Mexico. "The silence was old, immediate, and pervasive, and there was great good in it. The wind of the canyons drew it out; the voices of the village carried and were lost in it. Much was made of the silence; much of the summer and winter was made of it."

"I tell parts of my stories here because I have often searched out other lives similar to my own," wrote Linda Hogan in *I Tell You Now*. "Telling our lives is important, for those who come after us, for those who will see our experience as part of their own historical struggle."

"I was raised by an English-German mother. My father, one-quarter Cherokee, was there also, but it was my mother who presented her white part of my heritage as whole," wrote Diane Glancy in *I Tell You Now*. "I knew I was different, then as much as now. But I didn't know until later that it was because I am part heir to the Indian culture, and even that small part has leavened the whole lump."

"Facts: May 7, 1948. Oakland. Catholic Hospital. Midwife nun, no doctor. Citation won the Kentucky Derby. Israel was born. The United Nations met for the first time," wrote Wendy Rose in *I Tell You Now*. "I have heard Indians joke about those who act as if they had no relatives. I wince, because I have no relatives. They live, but they threw me away. . . . I am without relations. I have always swung back and forth between alienation and relatedness."

"So I was born in Southern California but I don't remember it. At least not consciously. My mother used to tell me how the roar of the ocean disturbed her at night when we lived in Oceanside, made her feel uneasy somehow. But I have always loved the sound of the ocean," wrote Janet Campbell Hale in *Bloodlines: Odyssey of Native Daughter*. "In June, when I was six months old, when northern Idaho's harsh winter had ended, my family packed up the car again and left sunny Southern California and went home to where their hearts were.

"I first saw the light of day in California, but the first place I remember is our home in Idaho. There is no place on earth more beautiful than Coeur d'Alene county."

"George Raft was an inspiration to my mother and, in a sense, he was responsible for my conception," I wrote in *Interior Landscapes: Autobiographical Myths and Metaphors*. "She saw the thirties screen star, a dark social hero with moral courage, in the spirited manner of my father, a newcomer from the White Earth Reservation. . . . I was conceived on a cold night in a kerosene heated tenement near downtown Minneapolis. President Franklin Delano Roosevelt had been inaugurated the year before, at the depth of the Great Depression. He told the nation, 'The only thing we have to fear is fear itself.' My mother, and millions of other women stranded in cold rooms, heard the new president, listened to their new men, and were roused to remember the movies; elected politicians turned economies, but the bright lights in the depression came from the romantic and glamorous screen stars."

Native American Indian creation stories are in continuous translations, interpretations, and representations; at the same time, postindian simulations and pretensions are abetted as lateral sources of identities. The absence of the heard in translation antecedes a presence in the shadows and hermeneutics of tribal names and stories.

Has the absence of the heard in tribal stories come to be the literatures of dominance? What are the *real* stories, the *real* names, nouns, and pronouns, heard in the *unnameable* cultures of tribal consciousness? How can a pronoun be a source of tribal identities in translation? How can a pronoun be essential, the inscription of an absence that represents the presence of sound and the other in translation?

Postindian simulations of dominance are silence, the absence of shadows and tragic wisdom; autoinscriptions, the pretensions of traditions, and political adoptions are passive postscripts without tragic wisdom or the common rights of consciousness.

Kenneth Lincoln mentions his adoption on the cover of *Indi'n Humor.* The allusion to a tribal presence suggests that the interpretations of the author are more authentic. Why else would a university professor pose as the other by adoption?

The insinuation of authenticity by adoption is obscure, passive, and indecorous; the pose is a renaissance language game. The mere written words, of course, are postindian simulations not tribal representations. The diverse and unnameable cultures of tribal identities are not heard as the passive pretensions of adoption.

Brian Stock pointed out in *Listening for the Text* that in the occidental world, as "the written word came to play a more important role in law, administration, and commerce, existing oral traditions either declined or adapted to a new environment." In the tribal world, however, the burdens of colonialism, translation, and racialism denied the natural reason of shared values in the new environment of scriptural dominance.

Luther Standing Bear enacted survivance over dominance at the turn of the last century; he and many other tribal people performed with distinction at federal schools and enacted written words to bear the shadows of their own traditional heard stories.

"Performative acts in language remained verbal, and individualistic, as they had always been," argued Stock. "But they were increasingly contextualized by writing in a manner that implied shared values, assumptions, and modes of explanation." Later, these natural connections between literature and society were weakened by structuralism and other theories. "The leading proponents seemed to say: if social relationships cannot be revealed through texts, then we will study the properties of texts for their own sake and pretend that we are studying society." The context of this observation, and the denial of tribal imagination, would embolden textual simulations, the pretensions of adoption, and the autoinscriptions of tribal names in the absence of heard stories.

Indi'n Humor: Bicultural Play in Native America is a contradiction in humor: The poses and intimations of the adoptee become the very ironies of trickster literature. The author is his own reduction, an unwitting reversal of the aesthetic trickster. The simulations of the adoptee are both the subject and the object of his own interpretations; the poses of a schlemiehl or trickster sycophant of the modern canon. The author could have been more self-reflexive of his adoption and the distinctions of communal humor, and he could have been more aware of postcolonial tragic wisdom. "My own argument for tribal comic wisdom takes heart from the heyoka, or sacred clown, vision on the western high plains, among the Lakota where I grew up in Nebraska," wrote Lincoln. "*Indi'n Humor* takes its cues from literary craftspeople. It is less about criticism than culture, more in search of imaginative spark than speculative certainty." Lincoln and other postindian adoptees and posers are shied by the unnameable and the uncertainties of simulations.

George Steiner observed in the introduction to a recent edition of *The Trial* by Franz Kafka that "nearly all mature aesthetic form" is self-reflexive. Kafka, in this sense, has more in common with the imagination of Native American Indian authors than the intimations and interpretations of Kenneth Lincoln. "There is a sense in which works of the imagination of sufficient seriousness and density always enact a reflection on themselves," wrote Steiner. "Almost always, the major text or work of art or musical composition tells critically of its own genesis." The imagination of trickster stories enacts a similar reflection and awareness of creation.

Franz Kafka was heir to an "unending analysis," noted Steiner. "The techniques of teasing out the abyss, of circling the unnameable, of weaving meaning on meaning, of labouring to make language wholly transparent to a light which consumes that through which it passes, having their antecedent and validation in the twice-millennary debates of Judaism with itself." Native American Indian literature teases the same imagination of the unnameable, and the light passes through translation, interpretation, reductions, and the insinuations of authenticity.

"Schlemiehls are fools who believe themselves to be in control of their fictive world but are shown to the reader or audience to be in control of nothing, not even themselves," wrote Sander Gilman in *Inscribing the Other.* "Schlemiehls are fools who are branded with the external sign of a deranged language, a language that entraps them." The avowal of adoption brands the author with simulations, the "external signs" of his own interpretations. The trickster created the schlemiehl and the practice of political adoptions to distract those who lack the imagination and tragic wisdom of their own culture of identities.

Hertha Dawn Wong declared an obscure connection to tribal identities in the preface to *Sending My Heart Back Across the Years,* a study of "nonwritten forms of personal narratives." She wrote that "according to the Oklahoma Historical Society, my great-grandfather may have been Creek or Chickasaw or Choctaw or perhaps Cherokee." That whimsical sense of chance, "may have been" one of four or more distinct tribes, is not an answerable choice or active source of credible identities. "I had little idea," she observed, when she began writing her book, "that I was part Native American, one of the unidentified mixed-bloods whose forebears wandered away from their fractured communities, leaving little cultural trace in their adopted world." The racialism of these romantic notions is the simulation of dominance.

Elizabeth Cook-Lynn, editor of *Wicazo Sa Review,* argued that the "wannabee sentiment" that clutters *Sending My Heart Back Across the Years* "is a reflection of a growing phenomenon" at universities in "the name of Native American Studies." The "unnecessary claim of this scholar to be 'part Native American' is so absurd as to cast ridicule on the work itself." She pointed out that curriculum development at universities "has been reduced to offerings which might be called 'What If I'm a Little Bit Indian?'" The pretensions of some scholars, however, are not even a little bit Indian.

Jack Anderson, in a column released by the Universal Press Syndicate in 1984, reported that Jamake Highwater, "one of the country's most celebrated Indians has fabricated much of the background that made him famous." Highwater, the columnist revealed, "lied about many details of his life. Asked why someone of such genuine and extraordinary talent felt he had to concoct a spurious background, Highwater said he felt that doors would not have opened for him if he had relied on his talent alone." Anderson pointed out that "Vine Deloria Jr. and Hank Adams say flatly that Highwater is not an Indian."

Highwater, author of *The Primal Mind* and other books about tribal cultures, may have opened doors with his spurious identities, but he also stole public attention, and his bent for recognition may have closed some doors on honest tribal people who have the moral courage to raise doubts about the unnameable cultures and simulations of their own identities. "The greatest mystery of my life is my own identity," Highwater wrote in *Shadow Show: An Autobiographical Insinuation,* published two years after the column by Jack Anderson. "To escape things that are painful we must reinvent ourselves. Either we reinvent ourselves or we choose not to be anyone at all. We must not feel guilty if we are among those who have managed to survive."

Highwater was very active in his tribal simulations, but the poses were in the cause of dominance. Imagination and active reflection would be honorable considerations if the author had not been deceptive about his past. Alas, he could write about the myth of the other, and the ease of his lonesome poses in the theater of dominance.

"I was *hot* for crime," wrote Jean Genet in *The Thief's Journal*. He would not create the silence of autoinscriptions; he was a *hot* shadow, an erotic shimmer in trickster stories. "Erotic play discloses a nameless world which is revealed by the nocturnal language of lovers. Such language is not written down. It is whispered into the ear at night in a hoarse voice. At dawn it is forgotten."

Genet would not create a work of art, "an object detached from an author and from the world, pursuing in the sky its lonely flight. I could have told of my past life in another tone, in other words. I have made it sound heroic because I have within me what is needed to do so, lyricism."

Jean-Paul Sartre noted that *The Thief's Journal* assumed the "most *natural* form" of the "myth of the double," but the portrait is not familiar. "But Genet is never familiar, even with himself. He does, to be sure, tell us everything. . . . His autobiography is *not* an autobiography; it merely seems like one; it is a sacred cosmogony. His stories *are not* stories. They excite you and fascinate you; you think he is relating *facts* and suddenly you realize he is describing rites."

Genet was *hot* for survivance not dominance. "Genet is the Poet, Sartre the Philosopher, a distinction Genet insisted on," wrote Edmund White in *Genet*. "As Sartre remembered, 'He considered himself to be a poet. *The* poet, in fact as I was *the* philosopher. . . .' Genet is the peasant, Sartre the bourgeois. Genet espouses the peasant's simple-minded theological morality, whereas Sartre invents a new atheistic morality."

Anthony Kerby argued in *Narrative and the Self* that the loss of the "ability to narrate one's past is tantamount to a form of amnesia, with a resultant diminishing of one's sense of self. Why should this be so? The answer, broadly stated, is that our history constitutes a drama in which we are a leading character, and the meaning of this role is to be found only through the recollective and imaginative configuring of that history in autobiographical acts. In other words, in narrating the past we understand ourselves to be the implied subject generated by the narrative."

In other words, the cultures of tribal identities are heard in names and stories; otherwise the simulations that antecede tribal stories and tragic wisdom would be tantamount to the amnesia of discoveries in the literatures of dominance.

ISHI OBSCURA

Ishi was never his real name.

Ishi is a simulation, the absence of his tribal names. He posed at the borders of the camera, the circles of photographers and spectators, in the best backlighted pictures of the time.

Ishi was never his real name, and he is not the photographs of that tribal man captured three generations ago in a slaughterhouse in northern California. He was thin and wore a canvas shirt then, a man of natural reason, a lonesome hunter, but never the stout pretense of a wild man lost and found in a museum. Two tribal men were captured, two pronouns in a museum, one obscure and the other endured in silence. Ishi the obscura is discovered with a bare chest in photographs; the tribal man named in that simulation stared over the camera, into the distance.

Ishi is not the last man of stone. He is not the obscure other, the mortal silence of savagism and the vanishing race. The other pronoun is not the last crude measure of uncivilization; the silence of that tribal man is not the dead voice of racial photographs and the vanishing pose. He came out of the mountains in an undershirt; later, he was redressed in Western clothes in the museum, and then he was told to bare his chest for the curious writers and photographers.

Ishi told stories to be heard, not recorded and written; he told stories to be heard as the sounds of remembrance, and with a sense of time that would never be released in the mannered silence of a museum. Overnight he became the last of the stone, the everlasting unknown, the man who would never vanish in the cruel ironies of civilization.

Ishi was given a watch "which he wore and kept wound but not set," wrote Theodora Kroeber in *Ishi in Two Worlds*. He understood time by the sun and other means, but his "watch was an article of pride and beauty to be worn with chain and pendant, not a thing of utility."

This tribal survivor evaded the barbarians in the mountains, the summer tourists, and the unnatural miners in search of precious minerals; now, as a captured portrait, he endures the remembrance of their romantic heirs. The gaze of those behind the camera haunts the unseen margins of time and scene in the photograph; the obscure presence of witnesses at the simulation of savagism could become the last epiphanies of a chemical civilization.

He was invited to return to the mountains and asked by his admirers to start a fire in the natural way; he was reluctant at first, but then he showed his reentry students, an anthropologist and a distinguished medical doctor, how to hunt with various bows and arrows. He heard the rush of mountain water, the wind over stone, and he told stories the bears were sure to hear, but he could have told his students even more about the violence of civilization. The miners were the real savages; they had no written language, no books, no manners of providence, no sense of humor, no natural touch, no museums, no stories in the blood, and their harsh breath, even at a great distance, poisoned the seasons. They were the agents of civilization.

Ishi came out of the mountains and was invited to a cultural striptease at the centerfold of manifest manners and the histories of dominance; he crossed the scratch line of savagism and civilization with one name, and outlived the photographers. His survivance, that sense of mediation in tribal stories, is heard in a word that means "one of the people," and that word became his name. So much the better, and he never told the anthropologists, reporters, and curious practitioners his sacred tribal name, not even his nicknames. The other tribal pronoun endured in silence. He might have said, "The ghosts were generous in the silence of the museum, and now these men pretend to know me in their name." Trickster hermeneutics is the silence of his nicknames.

"Ishi is the absence," he might have said.

"He was the last of his tribe," wrote Mary Ashe Miller in the *San Francisco Call*, September 6, 1911. He "feared people" and "wandered, alone, like a hunted animal. . . . The man is as aboriginal in his mode of life as though he inhabited the heart of an African jungle, all of his methods are those of primitive peoples."

Ishi became the absence of his stories of survivance, the wild other to those he trusted in silence. There were other names in the mountains. The motion of the aboriginal and the primitive combined both racialism and postmodern speciesism, a linear consideration that was based on the absence of monotheism, material evidence of civilization, institutional violence, and written words more than on the presence of imagination, oral stories, the humor in trickster stories, and the observation of actual behavior and experience.

Miller wrote that hunting "has been his only means of living and that has been done with bow and arrow of his own manufacture, and with snares. Probably no more interesting individual could be found today than this nameless Indian." Indeed, the simulation and pronoun of absence in the stories of survivance.

Ishi smiled, shrugged his shoulders, and looked past the camera, over the borders of covetous civilization, into the distance. The witnesses and nervous photographers, he might have wondered, were lost and lonesome in their own technical activities. Whatever they valued in the creation of the other they had lost in the causal narratives of their own lives.

Susan Sontag wrote in *On Photography* that photographs are "experience captured, and the camera is the ideal arm of consciousness in its acquisitive mood." The camera captures others, not the experiences of the photographer; the presence of the other is discovered in a single shot, the material reduction of a pose, the vanishing pose, and then invented once more in a collection of pictures. The simulation of a tribe in photographs.

The tribes have become the better others, to be sure, and the closer the captured experiences are to the last wild instances in the world, the more valuable are the photographs. Nothing, of course, was ever last that can be seen in a picture. Nothing is last that are stories of remembrance; nothing is last because the last is the absence of stories.

The camera creates an instance that never existed in tribal stories; the last and lost was not in tribal poses but in the remembrance of the witnesses who died at the borders of their possessions behind the camera. To be heard was once a course of survivance in tribal imagination; now, however, the tribes must prove with photographs the right to be seen and heard as the other. Mere presence is never the last word at the borders and margins of civilization; the sounds of stories, the human touch of humor and silence, and visions must be documented with photographs. Simulations are the outset and bear our tribal presence at the borders.

Sontag argues that "there is something predatory in the act of taking a picture. To photograph people is to violate them, by seeing them as they never see themselves, by having knowledge of them they can never have; it turns people into objects that can be symbolically possessed."

The absence of the tribes is sealed, not real, in a photograph; the absence is a simulation, the causal narratives of museum consciousness, and the remorse of civilization. Photographs are the discoveries of the absence of the tribes. Tribal stories, on the other hand, are mediations, and more is heard, seen, and remembered in oral stories than in a thousand pictures.

"The primitive notion of the efficacy of images presumes that images possess the qualities of real things," wrote Sontag, "but our inclination is to attribute to real things the qualities of an image." The simulation supersedes the real and remembrance.

Ishi told an interpreter, "I will live like the white people from now on." The Bureau of Indian Affairs had promised him protection, but he would remain with his friends in the museum. The ironies of "protection" have weakened the language of government. Ishi would not hear the promise of the miner, but he had no reason at the time to be suspicious of an agency created to represent his interests. "I want to stay where I am, I will grow old here, and die in this house." Tuberculosis ended his life five years later.

Alfred Kroeber, the anthropologist who cared for Ishi, wrote that "he never swerved from his first declaration." He lived and worked in the museum. "His one great dread, which he overcame but slowly, was of crowds." Ishi said, "hansi saltu," when he saw the ocean and the crowded beach for the first time. The words were translated as "many white people."

Kroeber, an eminent academic humanist, is seldom remembered for his nicknames. Ishi, on the other hand, remembered the anthropologist as his "big chiep," which was his common pronunciation of the word "chief." Ishi used the tribal word "saltu," or "white man," a word that could be used as a nominal nickname commensurate with his own— Big Chiep Kroeber, the anthropologist, and Ishi, the mountain man who told survivance stories.

Ishi was captured and possessed forever by the camera, not the agencies of a wild government. The sheriff secured "a pathetic figure crouched upon the floor," the *Oroville Register* reported on August 29, 1911. "The canvas from which his outer shirt was made had been roughly sewed together. His undershirt had evidently been stolen in a raid upon some cabin. His feet were almost as wide as they were long, showing plainly that he had never worn either moccasins or shoes. In his ears were rings made of buckskin thongs."

Sheriff Webber "removed the cartridges from his revolver" and "gave the weapon to the Indian. The aborigine showed no evidence that he knew anything regarding its use. A cigarette was offered to him, and while it was very evident that he knew what tobacco was, he had never smoked it in that form, and had to be taught the art."

Alfred Kroeber confirmed the newspaper report and contacted the sheriff who "had put the Indian in jail not knowing what else to do with him since no one around town could understand his speech or he theirs," wrote Theodora Kroeber in *Alfred Kroeber: A Personal Configuration*. "Within a few days the Department of Indian Affairs authorized the sheriff to release the wild man to the custody of Kroeber and the museum staff. . . ." Ishi was housed in rooms furnished by Phoebe Apperson Hearst. She had created the Department and Museum of Anthropology at the University of California.

Alfred Kroeber wrote in *The Worlds' Work* that at "Eleven o'clock in the evening on Labor Day, 1911, there stepped off the ferry boat into the glare of electric lights, into the shouting of hotel runners, and the clanging of trolley cars on Market Street, San Francisco, Ishi, the last wild Indian in the United States."

Kroeber named the lonesome hunter and natural philosopher who had survived the barbarian miners in the mountains. Ishi is a modern nickname, not a sacred name. "Ishi belongs to the lost Southern Yana tribe that formerly lived in Tehama County, in northern California. This tribe, after years of guerilla warfare, was practically exterminated by the whites by massacre. . . ."

He wrote in the *San Francisco Call*, December 17, 1911, that when "Ishi, the last 'uncontaminated' aboriginal American Indian in the United States, left the Oroville jail, which had been the first home civilization was able to offer him, for his new abiding place at the University of California Museum of Anthropology at the Affiliated Colleges in San Francisco he brought with him much primeval and tribal lore of the most ancient of arts which will prove as romantic to the student of the future as it is fascinating to the twentieth-century American of today."

Kroeber pointed out that "he has perceptive powers far keener than those of highly educated white men. He reasons well, grasps an idea quickly, has a keen sense of humor, is gentle, thoughtful, and courteous and has a higher type of mentality than most Indians."

Thomas Waterman, the linguist at the museum, administered various psychological tests at the time and concluded in a newspaper interview that "this wild man has a better head on him than a good many college men."

These college men, however, were the same men who discovered and then invented an outsider, the last of his tribe, with their considerable influence and power of communication. They were not insensitive, to be sure, but their studies and museums would contribute to the simulations of savagism. At the same time, some of these educated men were liberal nihilists, and their academic strategies dispraised civilization. These men who represented civilization would find in the other what they had not been able to find in themselves or their institutions; the simulations of the other became the antiselves of their melancholy.

"The bourgeois literary scholar who strikes a pose and stigmatizes boredom as a cross the aristocracy has to bear forgets that it was boredom that engendered literature," wrote Wolf Lepenies in *Melancholy and Society*. "Bourgeois melancholy signifies a form of loss of world which is considerably different from that entailed in aristocratic melancholy. The latter resulted from a loss of world, the former from having relinquished a world that had never been possessed."

Ishi trusted his new world, and those who honored him were bettered in their careers. He had been liberated from violence and starvation in the mountains; a wild transformation from the silhouette of the hunted to the heuristic pleasure of a museum.

Kroeber wrote that he "put on weight rapidly after coming within reach of the fleshpots of civilization and their three times a day recurrence. In a couple of months he had gained between forty and fifty pounds."

At the University of California a week later, "the unknown refused to obey orders" for the first time. "He was to be photographed in a garment of skins, and when the dressing for the aboriginal part began he refused to remove his overalls," reported Mary Ashe Miller in the *San Francisco Call*. "He say he not see any other people go without them," said the tribal translator Sam Batwi, "and he say he never take them off no more."

Miller wrote that the "battery of half a dozen cameras focused upon him was a new experience and evidently a somewhat terrifying one. He stood with his head back and a half smile on his face, but his compressed lips and dilated nostrils showed that he was far from happy. . . . His name, if he knows it, he keeps to himself. It is considered bad form among aboriginal tribes, I am told, to ask any one's name, and it is seldom divulged until a firm basis of friendship is established."

Theodora Kroeber wrote that "Ishi was photographed so frequently and so variously that he became expert on matters of lighting, posing, and exposure. . . . Photographs of him were bought or made to be treasured as mementos along with family pictures and camera records of a holiday or an excursion."

You hear his name now in the isolation of his photographs. You must imagine the lonesome humor in the poses that pleased the curators in the natural light near the museum at the University of California. Their dead voices haunt the margins of our photographs. You were not the last to dream in his stories. You were not the last memories of the tribes, but you were the last to land in a museum as the simulations of a vanishing pose in photographs.

Ishi may have undressed above the waist to pose for the photograph supervised by Joseph Kossuth Dixon, or one of his assistants, in connection with an incredible enterprise to capture the last images of a vanishing race: the Rodman Wanamaker Expedition of Citizenship to the North American Indian in 1913.

Dixon outfitted a private railroad car and traveled to many tribal communities and museums around the country. Later that year he published a portrait of Ishi and more than a hundred other photographs from his collection in *The Vanishing Race*.

"The Wanamaker expeditions took place at a time when the sense of national guilt about what had been done to the Indians was rising," wrote Charles Reynolds, Jr. in *American Indian Portraits from the Wanamaker Expedition of 1913*. "The Indians were seen as noble savages whom the white man had turned into a vanishing race." Ishi and Bluff Creek Tom are the only two "noble savages" who are not dressed to the neck in the collection of photographs.

Ishi posed for this "given" photograph, one of the few with his chest bared. The apparent tattoo on his chest does not appear in any other photographs of him published in *Ishi in Two Worlds* by Theodora Kroeber. The tattoo, an intentional retouch or accidental stain on the negative, has never been explained. The simulated tattoo, or negative stain, enhances the image of a naked savage.

Saxton Pope, the surgeon at the medical school near the museum, was a student of tribal archery and other tribal activities. He took Ishi to Buffalo Bill's Wild West Show when it was in the city. "He always enjoyed the circus, horseback feats, clowns, and similar performances," he wrote in "The Medical History of Ishi." Later, a "warrior bedecked in all his paint and feathers, approached us. The two Indians looked at each other in absolute silence for several minutes. The Sioux then spoke in perfect English, saying: "What tribe of Indian is this?" I answered, 'Yana, from Northern California.'

"The Sioux then gently picked up a bit of Ishi's hair, rolled it between his fingers, looked critically into his face, and said, 'He is a very high grade of Indian.' As we left, I asked Ishi what he thought of the Sioux. Ishi said, 'Him's big chiep. . . .'"

Ishi was a winsome warrior of survivance, not a religious leader or a warrior chief on the road to complement the tragic simulations and representations of tribal cultures. His personal power was more elusive than the political poses of a tribal leader. He was never obligated to speak as a leader or the last hunter of his tribe; otherwise, his stories might not have been heard, not even in the museum. His stories were his survivance, and not an obligation to be a tribal leader. He had a natural smile, but he never learned how to shake hands.

Pierre Clastres wrote in *Society Against the State* that a tribal chief must "prove his command over words. Speech is an imperative obligation for the chief." The leader "must submit to the obligation to speak, the people he addresses, on the other hand, are obligated only to appear not to hear him."

Some tribal leaders were captured as proud warriors in photographs; they were heard, overhead as simulations too much, and translated without reason, and out of season; their stories were lost to manifest manners, and lost at inaugurations and postmodern performances in wild west shows. The simulated leaders lost their eminence in the discourse of tribal power, "because the society itself, and not the chief, is the real locus of power."

Clastres overturns the rustic notions of tribal leaders with a new sense of political responsibilities in communities. "The chief's obligation to speak, that steady flow of empty speech that he *owes* the tribe, is his infinite debt, the guarantee that prevents the man of speech from becoming a man of power."

Ishi was never heard as a tribal leader. He bared his chest and posed for photographs, but he was never decorated as a warrior. His portrait was published with a collection of other simulated tribal people. He posed for friends and photographers, but he was never invited to bare his chest at a wild west show.

"En route to the inauguration of President Wilson in 1913, thirty-two chiefs stopped in Philadelphia for the day to be entertained at the Wanamaker Store," wrote John Wanamaker in *American Indian Por-*

traits. The special luncheon of warriors was followed by a "war dance" in a private corporate office.

Ishi lived and worked in a museum. He never wore leather clothes or feathers, and he was not invited to pose at the presidential inauguration. He was not a chief, but as a tribal survivor he could have been seen and heard as a leader. In a sense, he had more power than those who were invited to the inauguration as decorated warriors. Tribal power is more communal than personal, and the power of the spoken word goes with the stories of the survivors, and becomes the literature of survivance.

Ishi was at "ease with his friends," wrote Theodora Kroeber. He "loved to joke, to be teased amiably, and to tease in return. And he loved to talk. In telling a story, if it were long or involved or of considerable affect, he would perspire with the effort, his voice rising toward a falsetto of excitement." His stories must have come from visual memories, and he should be honored for more than his stories, his humor, and survivance: he should be honored because he never learned how to slow his stories down to be written and recorded.

"The Rodman Wanamaker Expedition of Citizenship to the North American Indian concluded in December 1913 with a ceremony on the Staten Island site where ground had been broken for the Indian memorial ten months earlier," wrote Charles Fergus in *Shadow Catcher*, a novel based on the unusual photographic expedition.

"At the Panama-Pacific Exposition of 1915, in San Francisco, former president Theodore Roosevelt opened the exhibit of expeditionary photographs, and Joseph Dixon lectured three times a day for five months to more than a million citizens. Prints were sold from the three Wanamaker expeditions, perhaps the first photographic print sales on record," wrote Fergus in the epilogue. "Dixon's illustrated book, *The Vanishing Race*, was also selling briskly; it has been reprinted several times over the years, with critics favorably comparing his photographs to the famous Indian portraits of Edward S. Curtis."

The Wanamaker photographs were forgotten in a few years' time; the collection landed in an attic and later in museums and archives. Those behind the cameras have vanished, but the last wild man and other tribal people captured in photographs have been resurrected in a nation eager to create a tragic history of the past.

The Indian agent James McLaughlin, wrote Fergus, "was instrumental in persuading Franklin Lane, Secretary of the Interior under President Wilson, to speed the granting of citizenship to qualified Indians." The tribes were discovered, captured, removed to reservations, and photographed as outsiders in their own land. Ishi died eight years before he might have become a citizen of the mountains he remembered and told in many, many stories. "McLaughlin designed tokens of citizenship that were presented in 1916 and 1917. These consisted of a purse . . . a leather bag, a button."

Ishi and then his photograph ended in a museum. The photographers were lost on the margins; those who gazed at his bare chest and waited to shake his hand would vanish three generations later in a lonesome and melancholy civilization.

Ishi has become one of the most discoverable tribal names in the world; even so, he has seldom been heard as a real person. Ishi "looked upon us as sophisticated children," wrote Saxton Pope. "We knew many things, and much that is false. He knew nature, which is always true," and his "soul was that of a child, his mind that of a philosopher."

Theodora Kroeber wrote that "Ishi was living for the summer with the Waterman family where Edward Sapir, the linguist, would be coming in a few weeks to work with him, recording Ishi's Yahi dialect of the Yana language. . . . They noticed that he was eating very little and appeared listless and tired. Interrupting the work with Sapir, they brought Ishi to the hospital where Pope found what he and Kroeber had most dreaded, a rampant tuberculosis."

Ishi died at noon on March 25, 1916. Kroeber was in New York at the time and wrote in a letter, "As to disposal of the body, I must ask you as my personal representative to yield nothing at all under any circumstances. If there is any talk about the interests of science, say for me that science can go to hell. We propose to stand by our friends. . . . We have hundreds of Indian skeletons that nobody every comes near to study. The prime interest in this case would be of a morbid romantic nature."

Four days later the *San Mateo Labor Index* reported that "the body of Ishi, last of the Yana tribe of Indians, was cremated Monday at Mount Olivet cemetery. It was according to the custom of his tribe and there was no ceremony." Saxton Pope created a death mask, "a very beautiful one." The pottery jar that held the ashes of Ishi was placed in a rock cairn.

THE TRAGIC WISDOM OF
SALAMANDERS

Mother, mother earth, the names honored as tribal visions, could become our nonce words near the sour end of a chemical civilization. That naive and sentimental nickname, a salutation to a common creation of nature, is the mere mother of manifest manners and tractable consumerism.

The names that mediate natural actions could unbosom the earth from the notions of maternal nonce words. The salamander and the natural mediation of amphibians, for instance, could be an unpretentious signature of the earth, the trace between land, water, and our stories. Consider the stories and memories of salamanders as the natural traces of survivance.

The salamander earth is a wiser name than obtuse tribute to an abused mother. The earth sustains the nonsense romance of the commons and the curses of science, and the earth must crave new narratives to heal the mortal wounds of objectivism and the incoherence of nuclear dominance.

"Scientific knowledge has lost its objective privilege and its epistemology has collapsed into incoherence, and yet our social theorists continue to grant it analytic privilege," wrote Will Wright in *Wild Knowledge*. "I am arguing that the scientific ideas of knowledge and nature are incoherent." Moreover, "nature must be understood reflexively, through a reference to language, not objectively," and "rationality must be criticized in the name of reflexive nature, not accepted in the name of objective nature."

The best tribal stories were never rushed to their extinction in nature or reason. The wise hunters honored the salamanders and endured the winter in the sure memories of their natural survivance. Not even the wicked shamans or predacious hunters in the fur trade could chase the breath of nature out of their own stories. Starvation, disease, and soul death were worries of the heart, but honorable hunters were liberated in the shadows of their natural mediations, memories, visions, and stories. The radioactive ruins and chemical wastes of our time are new worries and without the narratives of regeneration. The winter memories of survivance are denied in the ruins of a chemical civilization.

The earth must bear, as no mother would, the abuses, banes, and miseries of manifest manners. To name the wounded earth our mother, the insinuation of a wanton nurturance, is the avoidance of our own burdens in a nuclear nation.

Mother earth, the earth as our abused mother, is a misogynous metaphor; once more, the narratives of our parents have been abandoned in the ruins of sentimental representations. We are the heirs, to be sure; at the same time we are the orphans of our own dead tropes and narratives. We are the earth mutants, the lonesome survivors, who convene at night on the borders of tribal memories, creation, and treacherous observance.

"It is an indisputable fact that the concept of the earth goddess has grown strongest among the cultivating peoples," wrote Åke Hultkrantz in *The Religions of the American Indians*. "Many hunting tribes in North America manifest the same primitive belief in 'our mother,' 'mother earth.' The more recent peyote religion has accommodated Mother Earth to some extent under the influence of the Catholic cult of the Virgin Mary." The manifest notion of "primitive belief" is due no doubt to his patent on objective nature.

"Mother Earth will retaliate, the whole environment will retaliate, and the abusers will be eliminated," Russell Means maintained in *Mother Jones*. "Things will come full circle, back to where they started." He announced that "it is the role of American Indian peoples, the role of all natural beings, to survive."

Åke Hultkrantz and Russell Means seem to accede to the tribal creation notions of mother earth. Means avouches a natural order in the language of functional religion and resistance. Hultkrantz inscribes the notion of mother earth as a universal representation of tribal favors and succors. He wrote in *Belief and Worship in Native North America* that "Mother Earth is a common idea among Indians over large parts of North America."

Sam Gill, however, wrote in *Mother Earth* that the "origins of Mother Earth as a Native American goddess were in some measure encouraged by the exigencies of the emergence of an 'Indian' identity that has complemented and often supplanted tribal identities." He pointed out that until "after the middle of this century, there is scant evidence that any Native American spoke of the earth as mother in any manner that could be understood as attesting to a major figure or a great goddess."

The earth as our mother would never endure the nuclear silence of the seasons in our stories, or the death count of natural reason in the common abuses of the earth in our name. We must be remembered as the earth with names that mediate natural actions, and new creations must be heard in our narratives.

Laban Roborant, the salamander man, and other characters in these stories are the tribal tricksters of the mundane, the traces of the marvelous, and the solace of an escape distance. These trickster stories are aired to creation, natural reason, human unities, and the earth in the wild literature of survivance.

Roborant was born in the lonesome winter on a woodland reservation; he studied philosophies, established his own school of amphibian meditation, and ruled a boat dock at the tribal marina.

The salamander is a man of natural reason, and he holds attributive names and culture at an escape distance. The stories heard in his nickname are the trickster shadows of creation, the stories of mythic creatures. He would misuse the obvious over and over to hear common ecstasies in winter stories at the treelines.

Roborant is a trickster healer who would overturn the sentiments of mother earth to embrace the traces of the moist snails on cold concrete. Early every morning he copies the snail trails at the marina and traces them on fish location maps for the tourists.

"We cast our hearts to the cold water, and the snails smear the same stories on the concrete overnight," he said on the boat dock. "Here we are at the end of the dock, domestic animals who prey to be lonesome humans so we can name the earth our culture, and then we poison our natural relatives, poison the memories of our own creation in the literature of dominance, and that literature is no more original than the traces of snails."

"The traces of silence?"

"Survivance meditation," he whispered on the cold wind.

"Sounds like a lonesome literary theory."

"Meditation is not theoretical," said the salamander.

"Snails were never my signature."

"Their traces end in our memories," said the salamander. He watched my hands and mocked my signature moves. Then he laughed and the wind carried the sound of his amphibian stories back over the water.

I was touched by this man with the amphibian nickname, this salamander of the tribal marina. He told elusive trickster stories, traced the terrestrial snails, and menaced the black flies on the dock. No one has ever demanded more of my emotions and reason at the same time than this salamander. No wild children, no sure advocates of the heart, no wicked shamans have reached into the silence of my memories, shadows, and creation with such worrisome stories as the salamander man. I learned in time that he was more treacherous than nature, more elusive than winter bears, more obscure than spiders at the seams of civilization, more audacious than crows in the birch, and more memorable than the salamanders in his meditation. He was the natural reason and ironies of the earth in his own stories.

Mother earth is the nickname of a tribal man who once lived in a paradise of black flies on a woodland reservation. The lake near his cabin was decorated with rich ribbons of natural light that summer. The rush of dawn touched the stones on the natural shore at the tribal marina and landed later in weakened shadows behind the medicine poles. Hundreds of black flies waited on the boat dock for the first glance of the sunrise, the sudden beams that would warm their wings into graceless flight.

"Black flies remember our creation," said the mother earth man.

"Not on this dock," said the salamander of the marina. He beat the sun to bash the black flies on the rails of the wooden dock, and then he brushed their remains into the water. The bodies of the flies floated near shore without honor, even the fish seemed to wait for the wings to move as a lure. The sun bounced on the water and roused the bodies of the wounded flies; their wings buzzed and turned in wild circles.

"There, listen to the flies, the signatures of creation even at their death," said the mother earth man. He leaned over the water and handed the cold bodies to the warm stones. The flies buzzed in the sun on the stones.

"Flies are bait, not stories," said the salamander.

"Black flies are the earth mothers," said the mother earth man.

"No mothers here," said the salamander.

"Black flies are my relatives," said the mother earth man.

"Must be your cousins," said the salamander of the marina. He crushed more flies on the dock with his wide hand. "There, more relatives to mourn over on the stones." He raised three flies to the sun and then pulled out their wings.

"Black flies are my stories," said the mother earth man.

"Now you tell me," said the salamander.

"Thousands of black flies live on my name."

"You must mean live on your body," said the salamander. He covered his nose with his hands to notice the stench of the mother earth man. Mother earth man never washed and he wore the same stained shirt for more than a year. The fetor of the mother earth man raised hundreds of generations of grateful black flies. When he moved into the light the flies circled his head and crotch in great black orbits.

"They land on my middle name."

"Do the flies have nicknames?"

"More than one," said the mother earth man.

"Then you are the man of this house of mother flies?"

"You boast, but the earth hears the flies."

"Mother, my stories are about salamanders."

"Black flies are the same."

"Wash your body once and your relatives are gone."

"Once, many years ago, there were four flies caught in a bottle right on my desk," said the mother earth man. "We heard them buzz and watched them weaken day after day, and near the end, one after the other, they marched in circles close to the rim and then died upside down."

"Mother, are you ready to fly?"

"Almost every morning, summer and winter, for months and months after their death, the wings of the flies would buzz when the first blaze of sunlight bounced in the bottle," said the mother earth man.

"Weird suckers," said the salamander.

"Those black flies were the sound of creation."

"What kind of bottle was it?"

"Something in clear glass," said the mother earth man.

"Black flies sound much better in aluminum."

"To the ordinary person, the body of humanity seems vast," wrote

Brian Walker in *Hua Hu Ching*, the teachings of Lao Tzu. "In truth, it is neither bigger nor smaller than anything else. To the ordinary person, there are others whose awareness needs raising. In truth, there is no self, and no other. To the ordinary person, the temple is sacred and the field is not. This, too, is a dualism which runs counter to the truth."

The salamander and the mother earth man were never the other in their stories of black flies, snails, ants, and crows; never the outsiders on the uncommon fields of tribal consciousness. The mother earth man returned to the reservation in silence; no one heard his stories but the black flies and the salamander; no one else could chase him out of his human silence. The mother earth man teased the salamander that there is no reason for silence in nature.

The stories of the salamander were worrisome to be sure, but he countered the names of dominance over natural reason, and he teased the mother earth man right back that the earth could become an absolute human silence, a nuclear silence.

The salamander boat man was the crossblood mandarin of the tribal marina. The solace of his natural memories was burdened with the remains of the causal philosophies that he had studied at more than seven universities; lonesome, and morose, he dreamed his creation out of the ocean, founded the new school of amphibian meditation, and returned to the reservation. He envisioned natural reason over tribal silence and he worried that the stories of amphibian creation had landed in mean translations. He teased the mother earth man that "some of our best stories died over and over again in romantic confessions to blond anthropologists."

"The earth mothers," he announced on his return to the reservation, "were much too intricate and bewildered to hear their own creation and regeneration as salamanders." So, he became the tribal master of amphibian meditation moves. The salamander lived alone in the boat house over the water at the marina; he ate alone once a day, either baked walleye or venison stew with boiled potatoes. His thick white hair bounced with each move as he roamed the shores with the seasons, and the reservation mongrels were close at hand.

The salamander creates and remembers descriptive names, nothing more since the time he flushed out philosophies and the cruelties of the mind at the universities. No one ever heard his sacred name, and he never responded to his birth name since he returned to the reservation as the salamander.

He is awakened by the natural rise of water and tours the dock at dawn. He hears the motion of the waves, that certain amphibian rush with the sunrise, and senses the natural hour even over wind and storms. That salamander bashes flies to feed his favorite fish near the dock. Later in the morning he rents boats and motors to the tourists.

"You must be the boat man," said the number woman.

"I am the salamander," declared the boat man.

"Greek surname, to be sure," said the number woman. Even on vacation she wore a badge that indicated she was a corporate real estate sales executive. Numbers became her nickname that second season at the marina because she would announce the time on clocks, dates, numbers on menus, road signs, and every number she noticed in the world. She mounted an electronic muskie sounder on the rented tribal boat and then read the numbers out. She turned the codes and sounded the numbers.

The salamander provided her with a snail map of the best fishing sites, one of the original snail trails he had traced earlier. He insisted that the snails knew more than machines, and the traces of snails as the best locations to catch muskies had at least the same chance as the usual fish stories. So, he told the mother earth man, "what does it matter that the snails are my original source of the best locations?"

"Then the snails deserve the credit," said mother earth man.

"The trace is not the catch," said the salamander.

"But the catch is in the name," said the mother earth man.

"Salamander the Greek Indian, seven meters, now that's an unusual combination, there's a writer who makes such a claim, nine, thirteen, now what was his real name?"

"Thomas King," said the salamander.

"Right, he wrote *Medicine Creek*," said the numbers.

"No, *Medicine River* is the name of his novel."

"Right, damn good stories about softball."

"No, basketball," said the salamander.

"Right, natural players," said the numbers.

"Salamander is not a surname."

"First name, seventeen?"

"No, salamander is a meditation move."

"Right, what's the word on the catch?" asked the numbers.

"Try your sounder," said the salamander.

"Right, this mother sounder can locate a minnow in a rain storm," said the numbers. She turned toward the marina and waved to the mother earth man who paused between two medicine poles. Two wide belts of black flies shrouded the blue poles "Now that is a strange man, so many flies follow him around he must be the best shit trick of the season."

"Black flies are his relatives," said the salamander.

"Right, think of all those mouths to feed," said the numbers.

"He does, and they eat together."

"Spare the flies and spoil the meal," said the numbers.

"The marina restaurant refused to let him through the door at first, because his families were sure to follow," said the salamander. "The tourists were sick when he was in the restaurant, but the owners soon changed the rule and turned him into the best fly catcher on the reservation."

"Right, he ate his relatives."

"No, mother earth was rushed through the back door without his relatives, and then when the inside flies circled the table in his honor he wiped his mouth with his hand and marched them right out the front of the restaurant," said the salamander. "He led those flies away without poisons, swatters, or tanglefoot paper."

"Give me some numbers," said the numbers.

"Ten thousand black flies waited outside the restaurant, and a hundred or so were at the tables inside," said the salamander. "Mother earth is related to every black fly on the reservation, so the ones in the restaurant were distant cousins and ever so pleased to be back in the circle of his stench."

"Mother earth could make a fortune on fleas, ants, and crows, not to mention rats and cockroaches," said the numbers. "The ants would march by the thousands to his odor, and the crows would circle mother earth right out of the corn fields."

I fired at those crows over and over on the wing, and nothing died but natural reason and the stories of the earth in me. The crows were the enemies of the farmers not the corn, but the crows outwitted me that autumn and became my enemies. I was slow to learn that we heard the same seasons and survivance on the earth. My shotgun was cold, the crows were wiser, and that was a truer measure of the incoherence in the causal rush to science.

The corn honored the crows in some stories. The corn cursed the farmers and shouted to be liberated from science and human machines. The corn teased the crows to be taken into their wise paradise. Otherwise, the corn would be dried and stored for the pigs to eat.

I tried to shoot those crows to save the corn, to land my honor as a hunter, and the corn tried to save the crows. The farmers hated the crows, poisoned the corn, and braced the hunters to terminate his enemies. The earth was poisoned, songbirds died in silence, and investors dickered over the corn futures; the futures that no other creatures could endure.

I shot at those crows over and over on the wing. I roamed the corn fields and cursed the wind that carried the crows out of my range of fire. The crows outwitted me with such ease, and tormented the farmers. The crows were in my sights, but the crows could see me much better and turned on the wind, a natural survivance, when the shots exploded.

The corn teased the crows to the bitter end of that season in my memories. The crows raided the machines over winter, the farmer lost his land to the bankers, not the crows, and the crows in me were wise not to aim and shoot at the real enemies of this salamander earth.

"Children stationed in the fields or on the platforms of watch houses among the corn rows drove away blackbirds, crows, and chipmunks from the seed and young plants," wrote Carolyn Merchant in *Ecological Revolutions*. "Seed soaked previously in hellebore caused drunkenness in the marauding birds."

"Indian poke harrowed the settlers," said the salamander.

"That mother earth man would be a natural monarch of the cockroaches and the crows," said the numbers. "Can you imagine, the tribal marina and the dock secured by thousands of wise crows?"

"They talk too much," said the salamander.

"Imagine hordes of cockroaches marching out of their seams in the concrete, out of their cracks in bathrooms, out of ceilings, out of the woodwork everywhere to be in the wicked scent of this strange man," said the numbers.

"Indian poke enticed the anthropologists," said the salamander.

"Right, we could borrow his clothes and do the same."

"Some tourists were out here drinking one night and they stole his shirt because they could not understand why any woman, much less an attractive blonde, would touch the mother earth man," said the salamander.

"Right, clothes are not the man," said the numbers.

"Anyway, mother earth was under the dock with a woman and the tourists stole his shirt," said the salamander. "The shirt was not his power, but it did have the wicked stench of power, and in the morning his abandoned shirt was covered with brown ants, millions of ants marched to touch his shirt and then return to the earth."

I came back from a visit with relatives on the reservation and was horrified to discover that two armies of brown ants had invaded my house. The armies marched in two columns, one marched through the house to the pantry, and the second column turned around and marched out under the front door.

I crushed the armies under my shoes. I walked on the ants in both directions of their march, but there were millions of ants in two wide brown columns. My house was occupied by two cruel armies of brown ants. I worried that the ants would cover my shoes and climb up my legs. I needed a new weapon to kill the ants.

The armies were no match for a straw boom. I beat the ants with the side of the broom and then swept their crushed bodies into brown piles on the dinning room floor. I was a warrior and beat the armies from one end of the house to the other. These ants would claim no rations in my pantry.

I had wounded hundreds of brown ants and hundreds more were dead on the hardwood floors. Brown bodies blocked the columns that moved near the baseboards to the pantry. I was furious that my house had been invaded, and tormented, at first, by the comeback of the ants. Their certain moves were not separation or panic in the face of the enemy; rather, the ants carried their dead and wounded from the battlefield. The enemy had attached their columns with superior weapons and the ants carried their dead away. This was a body count, not a coup de main with the earth.

I moved closer to the armies and watched the soldiers honor their dead in battle. Their disaster was mine. I became the lonesome witness in the literature of solace and domination. The distance of my violence haunted the earth in my memories. I cried over the miseries my violence had caused in the lines of the ants. They might have carried me away if the earth had been turned in other stories.

The ants were in search of nothing more than a meal that summer. I discovered at last the most obvious conditions of their invasion. My superior weapons held the line between humans and the ants, otherwise the ants might have driven me out of my own house. At the turnaround in the pantry the armies were nourished by the remains of cola in several overturned bottles. These ants wanted nothing more from me than a taste of cola that summer and they landed in these stories.

I had terminated hundreds of ants, and then, struck by the obvious, moved the cola bottles outside near the front door. The ants were spared the dangerous march through the house of their enemies.

Later that summer, I convinced a friend, who was about to spray ant killer on the kitchen counter, to give me two days to solve the problem without poison. Not only the ants, but humans would be poisoned with the spray. I placed a bottle cap filled with strawberry jam near the crack in the brick wall over the counter where the ants had entered. The next morning we discovered that the ants had gathered around the jelly and not the crumbs on the counter.

That night, over dinner, my friends told the story about my war and peace with the ants. Later we poured a few drops of liqueur into the bottle cap with the preserve. The next morning the ants were gone. Not one could be found in the kitchen. My friends reasoned that several scouts came home drunk and the ant families decided it was time to leave that decadent house forever. There was much laughter over my stories.

"Mother earth man's shirt in a bottle cap," said the numbers.

"New meaning to ants in one's pants," said salamander.

"Mother earth man is my happy camper," said the numbers.

"Why do you say that?" asked the salamander.

"Well, because the earth loves him without a bath."

"This earth is a wounded man," said the salamander. "He is the mother cant of misused memories, the unwashed mother of trickster humor and romantic abusement, the wise hunter of liberation stories."

"Right, mother earth the transvestite," said the numbers.

"Never, mother earth is a holosexual trickster."

"Right, mother earth with the lonesome nickname."

"The earth has no name or reason," said the salamander.

"Whatever, but mother earth is my man."

"You and that horde of relatives."

"Never mind, the black flies are unmanned at night."

"Remember to hold your breath over his shirt," said the salamander as he traced an original snail trail on a new fish locator map. The map was plastic covered and embossed with a corporate real estate seal. "Not even the reservation mongrels can stand to be near his clothes for more than a few minutes at a time, so when do you plan to leave?"

"Does mother earth like to fish?"

"He would rather fly than catch a fish," said the salamander.

"Right, fly is his number," said the numbers.

"Mother earth landed once in Santa Cruz, California."

"Were the flies there?"

"No, he was at the university."

"The paradise of acute humdrum," said the numbers.

"That's where he earned his clever nickname," said the salamander. He turned and watched the mother earth man rush through the backdoor of the marina restaurant. "Who would believe that he was once a professor of literature and provost of a college at the university there?"

"Fantastic, the provost mother earth," said the numbers.

"Mother earth owned a townhouse in a faculty community on university land, and that is the reason he is here with the flies," said the salamander. "He lost his humor and returned to the reservation in silence when his learned colleagues and neighbors voted to use toxic chemicals on the common areas."

The earth as our mother has been wounded, and the rivers, birds, animals, and insects have been poisoned near the universities. We are the salamander earth, and no other names mean as much as the mediation of our names in stories. We bear the wounds of the earth, and that must be an obscure suicide. We are the mutants of a chemical civilization.

I lived in a new faculty housing area on the campus and discovered on a casual evening walk that the university had been dumping toxic chemicals from the science laboratories within several hundred feet of family residences.

I called the campus fire department and was told that no one there knew anything about a toxic dump or how dangerous a mixture of the chemicals might be in a fire or earthquake. No one knew what had been dumped there, and no one seemed worried about the families who lived nearby. The faculty homeowners would not support a demand to remove the toxic dump from a housing area. These were the same faculty members who would subscribe to various ideologies and manifest manners, but they would not act in their ultimate identities as the earth. They were orphans who had lost their stories of survivance.

Ordinary citizens were able to understand the risks and use their common sense and communal interests to correct hazardous conditions, but the most learned faculty homeowners would not confront the university administration over the toxic dump, not even in the interests of their own families.

Clearly, in this instance and many others that year in the glorious redwoods of the University of California, Santa Cruz, a higher education was not in the best interests of families or the earth. The faculty was burdened with careerism, the humdrum of elitism, and an unwise contract with objectivism. The earth cries to be heard and the faculty critiques radical environmentalism. Not even the radical feminists, who ruled a separatist house on campus close to the toxic dump, would support the petition to remove the chemicals from a residential area. Other recourse identities, such as race, class, and gender, were much more significant in their series of considerations.

Several months later the earth around the trees in the faculty housing area was removed by the landscape company, and then the holes were filled a few weeks later with a special chemical mixture of earth. So special, and so toxic, that when rain flooded the circles around the trees the chemical mixture killed the grass. The lawn was marked with dead trails of grass from the trees to the drains.

Animals, birds, cultured pets, and children were drawn to the fresh earth around the trees. How would the children and other creatures know that the earth of our creation had become an attractive nuisance at a university?

Dare we breathe?

Dare we eat?

Dare we drink the water?

Dare we touch the poisoned earth?

Dare we touch ourselves?

Dare we listen to the sycophants of science?

I was closer to silence when the faculty homeowners once more voted down my proposal not to use toxic chemicals to maintain the common areas. The faculty seemed to have no other sources of wisdom than the minimal realities of objectivism. The president of the homeowners association, an anthropologist and former marine, told me that lawn chemicals are not dangerous in the least. "Listen up," he shouted, "water is a chemical, do you want us to stop drinking water?"

"Indian poke is the best medicine for anthropologists."

"As a formal structure, language mediates between actions and the world, between social life and natural processes, and if this structure is to sustain its own possibility, then it must generate and legitimate actions that will successfully sustain this mediation," wrote Will Wright in *Wild Knowledge*. "In order to sustain itself, language must generate practices that are ecologically coherent, which means that if knowledge is referred to language then the formal criteria for knowledge must include a reference to ecological coherence, to sustainability."

The University of California has established environmental policies that provide for "applicable health and safety standards." The regulations assure that "continuous attention shall be paid to the identification, monitoring, and control of potentially harmful substances and physical agents in the campus environment. The scope of this program shall include but not be limited to toxic materials, air quality in controlled environments, and elements of physical exposure such as lighting, noise, and temperature."

The Santa Cruz campus is a scene of entranced duplicities over the environment. The university administration there has failed in certain considerations to "maintain a reasonably safe environment for its students, academic appointees, staff, and visitors." The recourse of environmentalism on this campus is unusual because of the delusions and, at the same time, there are chastened sermons on separatism; a withered inheritance of the last hurrah of elitism in the redwoods.

Michael Tanner, the academic vice chancellor, told me not to be concerned about the hazardous electrical transformers located on the campus. Hundreds of students could be exposed to polychlorinated biphenyls and many other toxic compounds from an electrical equipment fire. The provosts of the eight colleges on the campus reported to the academic vice chancellor, and we reported that the recent earthquake in the area was a reminder that the risks of chemical and electrical fires could never be underestimated.

"Professor Vizenor," announced the vice chancellor in a tense and avuncular tone of voice. "May I ask, are you a man who is afraid of snakes?" He leaned back from the conference table, pleased with the interrogative and the advantage he assumed as a senior administrator.

"No, not really, why would you ask me that?"

"Well, let me put it this way," he continued with no obvious sense of the ironic turn of his representation. "If you were afraid of snakes, surely you would not want us to kill all the snakes on the campus because of your fear, would you?" At last his provincial arrogance overcame his obtuse and unreasonable consideration of the issue.

"Would you be serious?"

"We cannot act on your fear of snakes," he assured me.

"These are electrical transformers, not snakes, and they use toxic compounds that may be carcinogenic if burned, and many industrial accidents have documented that polychlorinated biphenyls are dangerous and can cause birth defects in humans."

Michael Tanner listened but he would not respond to my formal recommendation to remove the transformers that used polychlorinated biphenyls. He must have reasoned that his snake ruse would resolve my concern as a provost to "maintain a reasonably safe environment" for students on the campus.

Two years later, and much to my surprise, the *San Francisco Chronicle* reported that the United States Environmental Protection Agency reached an agreement with the University of California that resolved "violations of federal regulations that govern the proper management of polychlorinated biphenyls" and the "university agreed to pay a civil penalty of $150,000." Moreover, the university agreed to remove the hazardous electrical transformers from several campus, including Santa Cruz.

The federal regulators, to be sure, would not have been touched by the simulated snake stories that slithered in the office of the academic vice chancellor. Michael Tanner misused and abused natural reason as a method of institutional management; he might have used the weather as an execration of environmental issues. There are, of course, many dubious stories about the mutations of other creatures in academic administration.

"We have changed the atmosphere, and thus we are changing the weather," wrote Bill McKibben in *The End of Nature*. "By changing the weather, we make every spot on earth man-made and artificial. We deprive nature of its independence, and that is fatal to its meaning. Nature's independence *is* its meaning; without it there is nothing but us."

We have misused the narratives of natural reason as we have the environment; we have abused the names of the seasons, the weather, salamanders, bears, crows, and ants in our creation stories, and that has weakened our survivance. The earth is burdened with our memories. We are the anomalous orphans who would ruin the narratives of natural reason and our own survivance.

The salamander is the new signature of the earth because we must learn to hear once more the tragic wisdom of natural reason and survivance. That humans turn to silence does not menace the earth, but the silence of the salamander could be the end of our nature and evolution.

Over and over "scientists say amphibians represent the global equivalent of the proverbial canary in the coal mine," wrote Emily Yoffe in "Silence of the Frogs," an article in *The New York Times Magazine*. The reasons for the silence of the salamander and the sudden decline of frogs are not understood by scientists.

Yoffe pointed out that herpetologists, those who study reptiles and amphibians, or frogs, toads, and salamanders, "with perhaps not the greatest objectivity, say frogs are the ideal creature to reflect the health of the environment. In their view, frogs are living environmental assayers, moving over their life cycles from water to land, from plant-eater to insect-eater, covered only by a permeable skin that offers little shield from the outside world."

The outside world has misused natural habitats and the narratives of amphibian survivance. We are the heinous other in the outside world of the salamander, the other in habitat destruction, the other in the ruins of our own stories about the atmosphere, the weather, the oceans, and our stories have turned to ultraviolet burns, pesticides, acid rain, sour snow, deforestation, soil erosion, radioactive waste, the dubious management of the environment, and the introduction of nonnative species of fish into rivers and pristine mountain lakes. "No pristine place can protect a species," wrote Yoffe. "At the top of the list is an increase in ultraviolet radiation. Among the hardest-hit amphibians are those that live at high altitudes." Many highland species of frogs "lay black eggs and have a black peritoneum and, in the male, black testes," a survival strategy "to protect themselves from harmful radiation."

The salamander earth must hear many great stories to regenerate our survivance in a chemical civilization. The silence of our nature is heeded with the salamanders. The lost creatures and mutations are phantom memories that may be too much even for the giants of amphibian meditation to endure.

The salamander hears the water rise to the sun over the tribal marina. He crushes the slow black flies, but never to extinction, and teases the mother earth man who liberates the same number of flies from the restaurant every morning. We do this over and over again because the stories hold us to natural reason and our mortality. The salamander earth is a story of liberation.

"For unless you own the whale, you are but a provincial and sentimentalist in Truth," wrote Herman Melville in *Moby Dick*. "But clear Truth is a thing for salamander giants only to encounter; how small the chances for the provincial then?"

CASINO COUPS

Luther Standing Bear must have wondered about a civilization that would count coup with coins. He seemed to envision, on his way to a government school with other children, the contradictions that would ensue in the creation of casinos, and the contention over tribal sovereignty on reservations.

The Lakota activist and author was raised a century ago to be a hunter and warrior, but the federal government had terminated the buffalo and then removed tribal families to reservations. He was one of the first children to be educated at the government school in Carlisle, Pennsylvania.

"I was thinking of my father," he wrote in *My People the Sioux*, "and how he had many times said to me, 'Son, be brave! Die on the battlefield if necessary away from home. It is better to die young than to get old and sick and then die.' When I thought of my father, and how he had smoked the pipe of peace, and was not fighting any more, it occurred to me that this chance to go East would prove that I was brave if I were to accept it."

Standing Bear wrote that when "the train stopped" in Sioux City "we raised the windows to look out." The "white people were yelling at us and making a great noise," and they "started to throw money at us. We little fellows began to gather up the money, but the larger boys told us not to take it, but to throw it back at them. They told us if we took the money the white people would put our names in a big book. We did not have sense enough then to understand that those white people had no way of discovering what our names were. However, we threw the money all back at them. At this, the white people laughed and threw more money at us."

Five generations later many of the tribes that endured colonial cruelties, the miseries of hunger, disease, coercive assimilation, and manifest manners are now moneyed casino patrons and impresarios on reservations.

The white people are throwing money at the tribes once more, but not to tribal children at train stations; millions of dollars are lost each month at bingo, blackjack, electronic slot machines, and other mundane games of chance at casinos located on reservation land. The riches, for some, are the new wampum, or the curious coup count of lost coins. The weird contradiction is that the enemies of tribalism have now become the sources of conditional salvation; this could be the converse of an eternal tribal millennial movement that was last heard in the Ghost Dance.

This preposterous carnival of coup coins has transformed tribal communities. The reservation governments throw nothing back to the states in fees or taxation, and that is one of the serious concerns of tribal sovereignty.

More than a hundred tribes are reported to have casinos or gaming facilities on and near reservations in the nation; the losses by the patrons at these operations, estimated to be several billion dollars a year, have become the extreme sources of tribal revenue. The ironies of panindian casino reparations could become the wages of sovereignty.

The Indian Gaming Regulatory Act, passed in 1988, recognized that the tribes have the "exclusive right to regulate gaming" if the activity is not prohibited by federal or state laws. The new gaming regulations established a National Indian Gaming Commission to meet congressional concerns and to "protect such gaming as a means of generating tribal revenue."

The new law established three classes of gaming: the first, traditional tribal games; the second, games such as bingo, lotto, and pulltabs; the third, and the most controversial of the classes, includes lotteries, slot machines, blackjack, pari-mutuel betting, and other casino type games. The tribes with the third class of casino games are required to negotiate with the state to enter into a "compact governing the conduct of gaming activities."

In the past few years there have been more news stories about tribal casinos than any other tribal activities. *The New York Times* has published numerous reports on the enormous Foxwoods Casino, owned and operated by the Mashantucket Pequot Indians. Governor Lowell Weicker of Connecticut reached an agreement with the new casino to permit slot machines, required, in part, by the new federal gaming laws. The envies are unnatural when a tribal casino has the riches to negotiate with the governor; this agreement weakens possible legislation that would allow other casinos to operate as a source of much needed revenue in the state. The Pequot Indians agreed to contribute at least a million dollars a year "in gambling profits to a fund to aid troubled cities and towns."

The governor has resisted casinos in the state, including those located on reservations, "on moral and economic grounds," reported *The New York Times*. His agreement with the tribe was a concession that resisted an "even greater evil; the building of casinos throughout the state." The Mirage Resorts of Las Vegas had "offered to build a casino in Hartford or Bridgeport."

Minnesota has negotiated agreements with thirteen casinos on eleven reservations in the state. The *Minneapolis Star Tribune* reported that tribal gaming employed more people in the state than United Parcel Service or Burlington Northern Railroad. "Lump the six casinos together, and they are the 20th largest employer in Minnesota," with about five thousand employees." The Mystic Lake Casino, owned by the Shakopee Mdewakanton Sioux, seats more than a thousand people at bingo and operates at least as many slot machines. The Shooting Star Casino on the White Earth Reservation cost more than sixteen million dollars to build, and the tribe has plans to build an addition that would double the size of the casino.

Many tribes "contracted with private gambling firms to set up and manage their gaming operations," reported Iri Carter for The Center for Urban and Regional Affairs at the University of Minnesota. "Several of these firms took the lion's share of the profits and left outstanding debts. Tribes had no choice but to ask for federal assistance."

The National Indian Gaming Commission was established to review contracts and to protect "gaming as a means of generating tribal revenue." The Inspector General for the Department of the Interior reported last year that management companies and some contractors had diverted millions of dollars from tribal casinos. "There may be some ticking time bombs" out there, said the inspector, James Richards.

Chris Ison reported in the *Minneapolis Star Tribune* that "the manager at Fortune Bay Casino" in northern Minnesota was replaced "after some tribal members alleged a conflict of interest. The manager, Cyril Kauchick, and an attorney for the casino, Kent Tupper, held an interest in the company that leased slot machines to the casino." Later, casino representatives said that "the federal report criticizing Indian gambling operations was 'political sabotage' intended to feed public mistrust of the industry." The Minnesota Indian Gaming Association "called the report inaccurate, paternalistic and part of a broad campaign by Las Vegas interests and others to 'weaken tribal gaming and undermine the sovereignty of tribal governments.'" Those named in the report denied that their interests and profits were improper. Tupper said he "had disclosed his ownership interests in Creative Games and stepped down as tribal attorney at the end of 1991."

The Bureau of Indian Affairs reported in *Indian News* that last year twenty tribes in two states, Michigan and Minnesota, provided close to eight thousand jobs with an annual payroll of more than ninety million dollars. The report indicated that the casinos generate more than eleven million dollars in annual social security and medicare tax revenue, more than two million dollars in state and federal unemployment compensation, and the casinos have reduced the cost of welfare in the two states. The new riches of the tribes translate as political power, and that in a slow and envious economy.

The number of casinos and employees grows by the month, and the estimated several billion dollars in the losses of patrons has increased at a rate that could save several state budgets from ruin.

Anishinaabe singers are the heirs of a rich tradition of chance and games, the moccasin games. Four objects are covered with two pairs of moccasins; one object is marked and becomes the chance of the game. None of this is done without music and the beat of a drum. The songs have no words; some of the best music of the tribe was inspired by the chance of the moccasin games. The best moccasin game songs were heard in dreams and visions, and the song, with the beat of the drum, accented beats and then hesitation, enchanced the game, and teases the players to choose the moccasins that covered the unmarked object.

There are no traditional songs to tease the electronic machines; the coins are the sounds of technology, the possession of time and place without music. The tease of chance is in the casino stories not the songs. The chance has no association of communities, no dreams of the hidden objects, and the winners lose their stories at the tribal casinos.

Standing Bear was naive on that train to a government school, but later he wrote several books and weathered the contradictions of his time. His name was entered in the "big book" for other reasons, but he, and other tribal leaders, might have warned the impresarios of the tribes that the riches of casinos entice the envies of others and could be the ruin of tribal sovereignty.

The casinos have raised new contradictions, the bereavement of traditional tribal values, and the envies of outsiders. The more money that is lost at casino games, the greater the revenues, and because of the riches, the elections of tribal leaders become more extreme on reservations.

The Mohawks at Akwesasne, for instance, came to violence over the casinos located on their reserve. One side fought for casinos and sovereignty, and the other side, the elected tribal leaders, opposed gambling operations in their communities. Two tribal people were killed and a casino was damaged before the onslaught ended several years ago.

"The allure of fast tax-free money inflamed and emboldened the Mohawks who entered the gambling business, even as it weakened those holding on to the old ways," wrote Rick Hornung in *One Nation Under the Gun: Inside the Mohawk Civil War*, "A new class of bingo chiefs were beating the odds, dealing with the white economy on favorable terms. The traditionalists counterattacked, claiming that Mohawk life was being corrupted by men who profit from games of chance rather than work. White bureaucrats and politicians, police and prosecutors initially saw this dispute as a brawl over gambling." The Mohawks, however, saw this as a threat to their traditional way of life.

The Red Lake Band of Chippewa Indians in Minnesota and the Mescalero Apache Tribe of New Mexico have sued agencies of the federal government to declare the new gaming laws unconstitutional and to prohibit the appointment of the National Indian Gaming Commission. The essential issue is tribal sovereignty.

The claim of the tribes is that the Indian Gaming Regulatory Act "violates their sovereign prerogatives to conduct affairs on their lands as permitted by treaties and the Indian Self Determination Act," wrote William Thompson in *Indian Gaming and the Law*. "They especially object to the fact that the Act determined the legality of their gaming enterprise on the basis of state law." To conduct casino games, the third class of gaming, the tribes must "make agreements with state governments. Their claim is that their standing is a matter of federal and not state law, and that any matters governing their commercial activities must be established through federal, not state law."

Most tribes have either avoided or disputed the regulation that the third class of games, those that have raised the most revenue at casinos, must be negotiated with state governments. Tribal leaders maintain that casinos are located on sovereign tribal land, outside of state jurisdiction. Nonetheless, federal agents raided casinos and seized machines to enforce the gaming laws on five reservations in Arizona. The seizure was blocked by angry tribal people on one reservation until the government agreed to negotiate the issue.

At the "Fort McDowell Yavapai Reservation, outside nearby Scottsdale," reported *The New York Times*, "a group of about 100 Indians used three dozen or so pickups, big earth-movers and other vehicles to surround eight trucks that were preparing to carry game machines away from the parking lot of the casino there.

"The blockade by the Indians, none of whom appeared to be carrying weapons, trapped not only the trucks but also dozens of F.B.I. agents. The ensuing standoff lasted five hours and was not broken until" the governor agreed to negotiate.

Tim Giago, editor of *Indian Country Today*, said, "There is a lot of anger in Indian country over this. The Indian nations are sick and tired of being treated like children. These are sovereign lands. Why in hell should these lands need the state's permission?"

Governor Fife Symington was concerned about violence over casinos on tribal land. "We could be headed for a real crisis and showdown," he told a reporter for *The New York Times*. "This is just the fuse that leads to a larger keg of dynamite. Let's face facts: What we're dealing with here is the terribly emotional issue of sovereignty on these lands." The governor negotiated a seven-year compact with the tribe and the video poker machines were returned to the casino.

Governor Symington, however, signed a new statute several months later that prohibits casino gambling within the borders of Arizona. "The measure, which outlaws even casino nights sponsored by churches and small charities to raise money," reported *The New York Times*, "is the latest example of a backlash in a number of states against" the third class of casino games on reservations. Some tribal leaders indicated that "they would begin a petition drive seeking a referendum to have the measure overturned." The new law has brought some churches and casino reservations together in a common cause. "John Lewis, head of the Arizona Intertribal Council, said the petition drive would be backed by a 'broad coalition' of Indians and charitable organizations."

Nelson Rose, a law professor, wrote in *Indian Gaming and the Law* that one part of the new criminal statutes "revolutionizes Indian and criminal law by making it a federal crime to violate any state law involving gambling on Indian land." He concludes, however, that "the reality will probably be no enforcement at all, since even the federal government has limited resources and gambling crimes are the lowest priority offenses."

William Thompson argued that the essential "control over Indian gaming should be national." The issues of tribal sovereignty "are difficult and they are clearly controversial. What is clear, though, is that the vast majority of tribes do not want any state regulation whatsoever. They should not be required to come under state regulations."

Tribal sovereignty is inherent, an essential right that has been *limited* but not *given* by the government. Congress, however, negotiated the original treaties with the tribes and has the absolute power to terminate reservations. That tension, between the idea of limited sovereignty and assimilation, could be resolved in federal courts or by congressional resolutions in favor of state governments. Casinos could be the last representation of tribal sovereignty. The winners hear the envies and could become the losers.

Tribal sovereignty is inherent, and that sense of independence and territorial power has been the defense of sovereignty on tribal land and reservations. Federal courts and congressional legislation have limited the absolute practices of sovereignty, such as certain criminal and civil responsibilities on reservations, but that sense of inherent sovereignty prevails in the many interpretations of the treaties with the federal government. The Indian Gaming Regulatory Act has placed tribal sovereignty in competition with the sovereignty of the states. Sovereignty is not, however, a limited issue or idea in the histories of other states and nations.

"The concept of sovereignty originated in the closer association of the developing state and the developing community which became inevitable when it was discovered that power had to be shared between them," wrote F. H. Hinsley in *Sovereignty.* "The function of the concept was to provide the only formula which could ensure the effective exercise of power once this division of power or collaboration of forces had become inescapable."

The Coalition to Protect Community and States' Rights has been active in the defense of state sovereignty. The stated mission of the Coalition is to "seek clarification of the federal Indian gaming law so as to restore a level playing field between Indian gambling and other forms of legalized gambling, and to protect communities and states which oppose it from having unwanted and untaxed gambling thrust upon them." There is nothing in their stated mission, objectives, or proposed action that mentions treaties or the inherent sovereignty of the tribes.

The envies of casino riches incite the enemies of the tribes and those who oppose the sovereignty honored for more than a century in treaties with the federal government. The envies, of course, are the manifest manners of domination, the oppression, and the miseries of racialism. Tribal sovereignty, in this sense, could be weakened only if the casino tribes were enervated by their own new wealth, and were seen as being powerless.

"Only wealth without power or aloofness without policy are felt to be parasitical, useless, revolting, because such conditions cut" the associations of people, argued Hannah Arendt in *Antisemitism*. The envies of others, those who would hate the tribes for their wealth without power, are terrible burdens of tribal sovereignty.

Standing Bear heard the last of the Ghost Dance, worked at the famous Wanamaker department store in Philadelphia, toured with Buffalo Bill's Wild West show in Europe, and acted in Western movies; these, and other adventures, endowed him with a wider vision of the world. He, and tribal leaders who matured in the last century with a sense of tragic wisdom, might have warned the tribes to throw some of their casino millions to others as an association of power, and as an honorable mandate of sovereignty.

To endure the adversities of political lobbies the tribes must do more for others in the world than the government has done for them in the past. The rich casino tribes must demonstrate the power of their sovereignty to the world. Otherwise, the unresolved issues of state taxation, the enforcement of criminal statutes on reservations, and the resistance to casinos on reservation land could cause more contention among the tribes, communities near casinos, and state governments.

The Italian word casino means either "country house" or "gaming house," and "pleasure establishment." The definitions have varied over the years, but the sense of taboos over the pleasures of casinos has endured. Gambling is human, an ancient practice, and the outcome of the passion of chance could be determined in tribal casinos. Sovereignty has been won and lost, to be sure, over cards and other games of chance, but casinos have never been represented as the measure of tribal sovereignty. The future generations of the tribe may wonder what became of the billions and billions of dollars that were lost, and lost, and lost at the postindian pancasinos on reservations.

The tribes could name ambassadors to various nations and establish an international presence as a sovereign government; the creation of embassies would be a wiser test of sovereignty than casino riches with no honorable power. Then the tribal embassies could negotiate with casino monies the liberation of hundreds of stateless families in the world.

The liberation of Kurdish, Tibetan, Haitian, and other families, for instance, would sustain the moral traditions of tribal cultures. The relocation of these families to reservation communities would situate an undeniable tribal sovereignty and earn the international eminence of a government.

Casinos are the wages of wealth, morality, and sovereignty, but tribal courage and an international presence could secure more than the envies of casino riches and the limited sovereignty determined by federal courts and the government. Casino avarice with no moral traditions is a mean measure of tribal wisdom.

five centuries later in postindian resistance histories and trickster stories. Denied the fortunes of his tragic adventures, he became a marvelous reversal of his own discoveries.

Stephen Greenblatt argued in *Marvelous Possessions* that Columbus had read books by Sir John Mandeville and Marco Polo. Mandeville was a marvelous liar and a fantastic anatomist; he mentioned the "Indians whose testicles hang down to the ground," and other textual envies. Greenblatt observed that "these marvels served as one of the principal signs of otherness and hence functioned not only as a source of fascination but of authentication." Columbus and tribal tricksters were interested in the marvelous stories of testicles.

"Why did Columbus, who was carrying a passport and royal letters, think to take possession of anything, if he actually believed that he had reached the outlying regions of the Indies? It did not, after all, occur to Marco Polo in the late thirteenth century to claim for the Venetians any territorial rights in the East or to rename any of the countries; nor in the fourteenth century did Sir John Mandeville unfurl a banner on behalf of a European monarch," wrote Greenblatt. "The difference may be traced of course to the fact that, unlike Marco Polo or Mandeville, Columbus was neither a merchant nor a pilgrim: he was on a state-sponsored mission from a nation caught up in the enterprise of the *Reconquista*. But the object of this mission has been notoriously difficult to determine." Tribal cultures could not dispute colonial claims because they were "not in the same universe of discourse."

The reversal of that discourse was heard in trickster stories and seen in the wild nature of countercultures. The fortunes and manifest manners of dominance were overturned in the postindian literature of survivance. The nation could no longer sustain the racial simulations of a universal discourse. The government had become a serious language crime that weakened humor and natural reason. The cultural detractions, political corruption, and violence turned the nation tribal, a reversal of fortunes.

Robert Bellah pointed out in *The Broken Covenant* that the "transvaluation of roles that turns the despised and oppressed into symbols of salvation and rebirth is nothing new in the history of human culture, but when it occurs, it is an indication of new cultural directions, perhaps a deep cultural revolution."

The tribes were *heard* at last, five centuries after colonial *discoveries*, and the tragic wisdom of the tribes became the sources of salvation in the ruins of constitutional representations of democracy. When the humor of the nation died with fear the voters turned to the tribes for

REVERSAL OF FORTUNES

Aristotle, in that tribal connection of fate and a theatrical "reversal of fortune," wrote in *Poetics* that a "discovery is, as the very word implies, a change from ignorance to knowledge, and thus to either love or hate, in the personages marked for good or evil fortune. The finest form of discovery is one attended by reversal, like that which goes with the discovery in *Oedipus*."

The Oedipus who was abandoned at birth in tribal stories. The same trickster who killed his father, unaware of who his parents were at the time, and then married his mother. She committed suicide when she learned that her second husband was her own trickster son, a tragic reversal of tribal reason and discovery in the classical ruins of representation. Oedipus blinded himself with the discovery.

Christopher Columbus was no Oedipus, but in a tribal sense of mythic fate he was blinded by his own tragic discoveries, and his fortunes have become an ironic reversal. The Curia impeached his character, to be sure, but his actions were *discoveries* in a constitutional democracy several centuries later and commemorated as cultural entitlements in an intractable reversal of fortunes.

Aristotle wrote that "tragedy is essentially an imitation not of persons but of actions and life." The action, or the plot, "is the end and purpose of the tragedy; and the end is everywhere the chief thing. Besides this, a tragedy is impossible without action, but there might be one without Character."

Columbus, son of a wool weaver, a restive and adventurous character, would become the governor of the tragic imitations of his own discoveries. He weighed anchor with a royal commission and landed their natural reason, tragic wisdom, and trickster discourse. The once despised became the new survivance leaders, the reversal discoveries of a postindian tribal nation. Such transvaluations were postindian reversals of fortune in the nick of time.

My stories were the shimmer of trickster reason and language games for more than a generation, and at best the nicknames bounced once or twice on the rim of revolution. Overnight the trickster discourse of my fiction and critical essays became the discourse of the new government. Suddenly, the turns of my fiction became the trickster discourse of my service to the new government.

There never was much of a distance between the heard and the seen in the natural world of the trickster and the tragic wisdom of the real; tribal dreams were the same as the seasons in my tribal stories. Trickster stories were the heard memories and loose seams that historical time would accuse in the representations of dominance. My postindian stories of survivance and casino coups became the trickster discourse and liberation policies of a new tribal administration. Trickster stories were the brush of a new government in a marvelous reversal of fortunes.

The President of the United States named me the first crossblood Secretary of State. Literature and trickster discourse became the metacenter of the revolution of state policies in the world. The nation was named a tribal state and we conducted our business in the humor of trickster discourse. Never mind the narrow and contested election that year, because the humor of contradictions must be closer to the cure than surveillance and the political strategies of terminal believers. The stories of our time matter the most in contradictions, transformations, and the liberation of imagination; not the lies and poses of gender dominance, but the humor of trickster discourse.

Creations and nations are stories, and we created a new tribal state in stories, a third gender nation, a state of humor that would heal those who had been abused in constitutional language crimes and stranded in a lonesome civilization without a vision or a nickname.

"Secretary of State Goes Domestic," was the newspaper headline about my policies and first decisions at the summit on tribal sovereignty and commonwealth reservations held in Georgetown, Guyana.

My press releases were elusive stories, and the reporters were forever curious about the meaning of tribal scenes and common metaphors. Trickster discourse was a test of their imagination, but some writers were never able to understand that fact and fiction arise in the same action of language.

When a reporter asked, "Mister Secretary, you said that tribal sovereignty was a commonwealth, a republic, a tribal state, not a colonial exclave, was that fact or fiction?" The sound of stories is my witness, I responded. "So, what does that mean?" That you heard me, facts are political, and fiction is a better story. Resurrection would be my confirmation that the truth of language is in the reversal of fortunes.

Ludwig Wittgenstein was mentioned more than once in my responses at press conferences, in the sense that if one knew the answer to the question that was asked, the question would not be asked in the same way, or there are no answers to any questions. The reporters were bored to hear me say that language is an art not a science, and that my responses were no more evasive than their questions. Evasion, of course, became the verbal mole in their critical revisions of trickster discourse. I pointed out that nothing was more evasive than a question, not even silence, because the worldview of mere questions was proto-human fascism. The reporter wrote, "The Secretary of State, a former journalist, accuses reporters who question as protofascist, in his best 'trickster humor,' of course."

"The Secretary of State ruled in the first month of his administration that Indian reservations were no longer reservations but commonwealth states," reported the *Native American Press*. "So, what does that do for our roads, schools, and reservation casinos, and our precious cues of sovereignty?"

My policies on sovereignty were liberation stories that overturned colonial exclaves and dominance with the humor and pleasures of a tribal commonwealth, and these stories were heard everywhere in the world. Those reservations and tribal communities that were established by treaties with various colonial governments would become commonwealth states until such time that these states held elections to determine their future as nations.

The representatives of tribal commonwealth states established diplomatic missions with other governments and terminated the dominance of colonial *interior* policies. The tribes negotiated as nations, not federal dependent reservations. The termination of the Bureau of Indian Affairs was much easier once the commonwealth states were established and recognized by the Department of State. Moreover, we were pleased to create a new national holiday, the Colonial Termination Day.

In time the tribal children of the commonwealth nations created new stories about the airplanes that released thousands of dollar bills over their remote communities. The airborne cash was a symbolic reference, a reversal of fortunes, to the centuries of racial dominance and wasted money on the administration of reservations and colonial exclaves. The holiday became known as Postindian Liberation Day, the more popular name in the Americas. Millions of tribal families sailed money folded into airplanes at their children and celebrated the end of the colonial invention of the *indian* by Christopher Columbus.

The Ishi Center for the Study of Tribal Survivance was established, funded, and in operation by the end of my first year in office as the Secretary of State. This institution supported the creation of imaginative literature on the natural reason and tragic wisdom of tribal communities, in other words the imagination of survivance over dominance. A natural antidote to the thousands of social science studies of tribal cultures published by the Bureau of American Ethnology. At the same time human remains held by state and federal institutions were returned to tribal communities; and if the remains could not be identified at hearings in bone court, burial ceremonies were held in the new national cemetery dedicated to the memories of tribal survivance.

Ishi is the nickname of a tribal man who was captured three generations ago in northern California. He lived and worked in an anthropology museum at the University of California. He had evaded the barbarians in the mountains, the unnatural miners in search of precious minerals; these miners had no natural reason, no stories that would sustain the visions of communities. The miners and those who based their wealth on stolen tribal land were the savages, the men and women of national violence and language crimes. The crimes continued in the causal notions of the social sciences.

The painters, dancers, poets, musicians, and other artists were commissioned to imagine the tribes and overturn the dominance of social science research and publications sponsored for more than a century by universities and the Bureau of American Ethnology.

Professors Kimberly Blaeser and Louis Owens were the first two tribal scholars and creative writers to be sponsored by the national Ishi Center for the Study of Tribal Survivance. They had both published critical interpretations of my literature, and for that reason they were invited by a magazine to write about me and my views on tribal survivance.

"Why do you continue to use the word 'tribal' when people around the world are resisting the suggestion of primitivism?" asked Blaeser. She had written earlier about this question of usage and the manners of the word.

"There is no better word to get past the colonial invention of the *indian,* and besides it makes more sense to use words in contradiction than in association with dominance."

"What do you mean by tribe?"

"Tribal survivance, the conditions and worldviews of families that have endured in the face of dominance and language crimes of colonialism, nationalism, and the policies based on the causal reason of the social sciences."

"Why do you bother to fault the social sciences with such rancor when you have written that there is no real distinction between fact and fiction?" asked Blaeser.

"But there is a distinction between imagination and methodology."

"Of course, but you must explain," said Blaeser.

"Imagination is tribal survivance, the methodologies of the social sciences have served dominance and the academic tropes to power in institutions."

"You often use the expression 'natural reason,'" added Blaeser.

"Imagination is natural reason and tribal survivance, and tragic wisdom is the experience of survivance over dominance, but the social sciences have served dominance and denied the wisdom of tribal survivance."

"Naturally, we are pleased that you have created this national institution in support of imagination, but what would prevent the federal government, or even the new tribal commonwealths, from using imaginative literature in the same way that it used social science deductions?"

"Causal methodologies are the language crimes."

"That's a causal response," said Blaeser.

"Myths are the action, metaphors are tribal survivance."

"More than a decade ago you wrote in an essay that the tribes with casinos would suffer from the envies of their wealth, and you warned that sovereignty was threatened by the very success of casinos as a test of their tribal sovereignty, so how would you write about sovereignty now?" asked Blaeser.

"As you know, various states competed with casinos on reservations then, and several states sued the tribes to determine the constitutional meaning of state and tribal sovereignty, all of which was the result of those who were envious of tribal wealth."

"What happened?"

"Well, with the creation of commonwealths and the end of colonial reservations and exclaves, the tribes hold the same reason of sovereignty as the states, and neither state nor tribal commonwealth is within the same treaty boundaries."

"How can a resolution to these problems seem so easy, when the tribes have died over sovereignty and casinos?" asked Blaeser.

"Imagination, and sometimes the shadow of a single word can be the creation, and in this case the word was 'commonwealth,' an international idea that invited the most imaginative responses from public officials who were exhausted by the rhetoric of victimization and the legacy of manifest manners."

"The Bureau of Indian Affairs was terminated within a year, and the word 'terminated' is an ironic signification in this sense," said Louis Owens.

"No, they were done in a few weeks, because once the metaphor of commonwealth was heard with such enthusiasm, no one could bear to listen to colonial revisions."

"Why did you hold the first tribal summit in Guyana?"

"Guyana is a crossblood nation, a rich and diverse culture of contradictions, and the tribes are burdened with a colonial document that does not honor their imagination, tragic wisdom, or determination."

"And you announced the creation of tribal commonwealths there, in a nation that has not yet honored the tribes as nations," said Owens.

"Survivance was the mission, and we were certain that the presence in the country of so many tribal leaders from other nations would be an inspiration to demand the negotiation of treaties and some measure of commonwealth status."

"You never seem to be bothered that fact and fiction come out the same in your stories, but now that you are the first crossblood Secretary of State, an esteemed position that must be more powerful than fiction, have you changed your views about fact and fiction?" asked Owens.

"I am even more inspired that stories, that brush of imagination, are the truth in every human situation, and the rest is either bad television or the facts that pose as the tropes to power and dominance."

"Can you say that in some other way?" asked Blaeser.

"Trickster discourse is the source of tragic wisdom."

"Why is that?"

"Stories are the truth, facts are the vacuous end."

"And there are no ends in tribal stories," said Blaeser.

"There are no ends but this one."

"You once said that even the classical authors are marginal because they are borrowed for introductions in the same way that tribes have been borrowed as cultural evidence by the social sciences," said Owens.

"Yes, and this must be a reversal of fortunes?"

"Aristotle, but why the introduction to classical tragedy?"

"Owens, you discovered the reversal of fortune and now we are in the same trickster discourse of our own commonwealth creation."

"Aristotle is a crossblood, right?" said Blaeser.

"Yes, and he had enormous testicles."

"Trickster envies are the troubled waters of tragic wisdom," said Owens. "All the rest, you wrote, was bad television."

"You could say that, but not on television."

CROSSBLOODS

The main interest in life and work is to become someone else that you were not in the beginning. If you knew when you began a book what you would say at the end, do you think that you would have the courage to write it? What is true for writing and for a love relationship is true also for life. The game is worthwhile insofar as we don't know what will be the end.

Michel Foucault *Technologies of the Self*

The new woodland tribes bear their agonistic totems from that wild premier union with the fur trade and written languages, and earlier, a brush with lethal pathogens; that first touch, the deceptions of missionaries, the phraseologies of treaties, and the levies of a dominant consumer culture induced postmodern emblems and discourse.

The agonistic survivors are crossbloods; their stories and totems are indwelt, a new survivance that enlivens an interior landscape. Crossbloods hear the bears that roam in trickster stories, and the cranes that trim the seasons close to the ear. Crossbloods are a postmodern tribal bloodline, an encounter with racialism, colonial duplicities, sentimental monogenism, and generic cultures. The encounters are comic and communal, rather than tragic and sacrificial; comedies and trickster signatures are liberations; tragedies are simulations, an invented cultural isolation. Crossbloods are communal, and their stories are splendid considerations of survivance.

The reports and essays in this collection were first published in newspapers, magazines, and journals. The earliest reports arise from my experience as an advocate in tribal communities, urban and reservation, and as an editorial writer for the *Minneapolis Tribune;* later, from my encounters as director of Indian Studies at Bemidji State University, and as a professor at the University of Minnesota and the University of California at Berkeley.

More than a century ago my crossblood relatives published the first newspaper on the White Earth Reservation; my reports in this collection and my remembrance of that time are a continuation of an agonistic tradition of crossblood journalism.

The first issue of *The Progress,* edited by Theodore Hudon Beaulieu and published on March 25, 1886, was critical of land allotment legislation and the Bureau of Indian Affairs. Federal agents confiscated the newspaper and ordered that the crossblood editor and publisher be removed from the reservation. Several months later, following a trial in federal district court, the second issue of the newspaper was published.

The United States Indian Agent at White Earth saw the newspaper as a threat to his fascist control of activities on the reservation. He wrote to the publisher that the newspaper was circulated "without first obtaining authority or license so to do from the honorable Secretary of the Interior, honorable Commissioner of Indian Affairs, or myself as United States Indian Agent."

The editor wrote, "We began setting the type for the first number of *The Progress* and were almost ready to go to press, when our sanctum was invaded by T. J. Sheehan, the United States Indian Agent, accompanied by a posse of the Indian police. The composing stick was removed from our hands, our property seized, and ourselves forbidden to proceed with the publication of the journal. . . . We did not believe that any earthly power had the right to interfere with us as members of the Chippewa tribe, and at the White Earth Reservation, while peacefully pursuing the occupation we had chosen."

At the turn of the last century metropolitan newspapers advanced the racist notions of savagism and civilization at the same time that the editor of *The Progress* opposed the Dawes Severalty Act, or General Allotment Act, the federal legislation that allotted communal tribal land to individuals and opened the White Earth Reservation, and other tribal communities, to timber companies. The editor wrote, "We shall aim to advocate constantly and without reserve, what in our view, and in the view of the leading minds upon this reservation, is the best for the interests of its residents."

The *Minneapolis Journal,* on the other hand, reported on July 16, 1906, that "with the minds of the White Earth Indians muddled by liquor, and their eyes dazzled by money, of which they know little . . . the White Earth Indian Reservation will soon be a thing of the past." The Dawes Severalty Act, not beverage alcohol, was the problem; in any case, the reservation is not a "thing of the past." Such racialism has turned to liberal fascism in the present; however, in recent newspaper and television stories, the romantic simulations of tribal people have been overturned by more critical attention to economic development and the politics of reservation governments.

Some of my reports center on paraeconomic survivance in the past two decades, from tribal entrepreneurs, and reservation services, to the political management of tribal enterprises; for instance, the rise of bingo games as a new cash crop. High-stakes bingo operations on reservations, and tribal rights to hunt and fish within the boundaries of original treaties, have been reported in newspapers and magazines more than other issues in the past few years.

Bingo casinos have blazoned reservation communities in more than a dozen states for the past decade; the high-stakes game has tested tribal sovereignties, state jurisdictions, and traditional tribal world-views; the returns, incredible cash crops, have changed the way some people think about Native American Indians.

The five letters of bingo have been teased in church basements for several decades, the new monotheism, and even children learn to play the game in public schools; however, tribal bingo is a high-stakes game that takes millions of dollars from compulsive gamblers, and the cash debases some tribal communities.

The Lucky Knight casino, for example, was burned in August 1989 by tribal members who opposed gambling at the St. Regis Mohawk Reservation on the Canadian border in northern New York. Victory Adams, the owner of the casino, said the mob tried to burn other casinos on the reservation. The Associated Press reported that the "Mohawks contend they are not bound by state or federal gambling laws since they consider their reservation a sovereign nation."

Jake Swamp, a member of the traditional council, told *The New York Times* that the Mohawk Great Law of Peace "says you always must look seven generations into the future. . . . That's the only way we've been able to survive this far. But we're having a really hard time keeping our traditions intact." Casino gambling has divided the reservation between those who favor economic development, and those who fear the corruption of tribal cultures.

President Reagan signed legislation in October 1988 that established a commission to regulate gambling on reservations or federal trust land. The National Indian Gaming Commission monitors bingo and other games of chance in tribal casinos. Roger Jourdain, the trenchant chairman of the Red Lake tribal council in Minnesota, opposed the new legislation. "We are not going to stand by and let the federal government assume unauthorized and unconstitutional jurisdiction over our reservation," Jourdain told the *Minneapolis Star and Tribune*. "Tribes have the inherent right to govern themselves in all local matters, including the very important area of gambling."

The Fond du Lac Reservation, on the other hand, has turned the smoke and mirrors of state dominions, treaties, and tribal sovereignties into a festive gaming casino in downtown Duluth, Minnesota. The Fond du Luth Gaming Casino is a preposterous postmodern reservation; the fabrication of this gaming reservation insinuates the signature of a tribal trickster.

The tribal council at the Fond du Lac Reservation, and the mayor of the city of Duluth, proposed a venture casino as a source of revenue for economic development. The enticements were not racial, colonial, cultural, or savagism over civilization in a theater of inversions. Bingo was not a mismeasure of worldviews, or economic trust; wild cash was the lure, and two governments dared to propose the creation of a brand new reservation, a place to gamble downtown on trust land. This reservation was based on bad habits, even postmodern casino vengeance, an unusual measure of tribal paraeconomic survivance. "Gambling Abuse and Addiction Treatment" is a new subject heading in the local telephone directory, and there is a new listing for professional services located a few blocks from the casino.

The Sears building was purchased and converted to a casino that seats more than twelve hundred gamblers downtown under thousands of beveled mirrors. The new commission regulations limit the games to pull tabs, video poker and fruit machines, keno, lotto variations, and other games based on bingo, such as bingolette and bingo jack.

Telly Savalas, the television actor, and other entertainers were hired to celebrate the opening of the three million dollar urban reservation casino in September 1986. The Fond du Luth Gaming Commission reported that "never before in history had off-reservation land been taken into trust as Indian land for the purpose of gaming."

William Houle, the elected chairman of the tribal council at the Fond du Lac Reservation, pointed out that the creation of the casino had the support of state and federal politicians, James Watt, then secretary of the Department of the Interior, and the Bureau of Indian Affairs. "I don't believe there will ever be a project as unique as this one. You're never going to be able to find a relationship between a tribe and a city to rival the one we have here," said Houle, "Gaming has always been part of our culture, and now it is an integral part of our economy as well."

Indeed, but bingo as the new cash crop is based on losers, compulsive behavior, and most of the downtown gamblers are white; bingo and pull tabs are not moccasin games, and bingo is far from a traditional tribal giveaway to counter materialism. Moreover, the fabricated reservation could break the tribal bank. The tribal council borrowed more than three million dollars to renovate the building, and the city issued bonds to build a parking ramp next to the casino. The *Minneapolis Star and Tribune* reported that the tribal council, or band, stands to lose their investment if the "venture flops. In that case, the city could gain control of the building for its own use and take possession of the band's assets." In the first year of operation the casino had fallen short of expected revenues and was behind in loan payments.

Norman Crooks, former chairman of the Shakopee Mdewakanton Sioux Reservation in Prior Lake, near Minneapolis, established the Little 6 Bingo Palace in 1982, the first high-stakes bingo operation on tribal land in the state and one of the first in the nation. In the first few years the reservation was transformed by new community investments and payments to individuals. Eighteen years later each tribal member might have been paid a total of more than a hundred thousand dollars. The worldviews of tribal children must be altered by so much cash from games; unemployment and poverty turned to wealth and leisure in a decade.

Little 6 Bingo Palace is now the Mystic Lake Casino. The name appears on a huge outdoor sign at the entrance to a suburban shopping center; bus loads of white people arrive each night from various parts of the city to play bingo and other games on the reservation. Sweet Shawnee, one of the new video fruit machines, stands in the wide, air conditioned and carpeted trailer, waiting to be played. The simulated tribal woman pictured on the machine is dressed in a bikini and mounted bareback on a pinto; she wears a feathered headdress. Several other tribal casinos have the same machine. Such racial and cultural detractions might have been challenged in a white-owned establishment, but certain issues seem to lose their importance when the games turn a higher profit on reservations.

The American Indian Movement held the most headlines on tribal issues in the late sixties and seventies, a romantic inversion of racialism, and praise for generic cultures. These urban radicals were tribal simulations with dubious constituencies, and their stoical poses, tragic and lonesome, were closer to photographic and video images familiar to a consumer culture; these ersatz warriors were much closer to the invented tragedies of a vanishing race than were the crossbloods who endured the real politics and weather on reservations. My editorial series in the *Minneapolis Tribune* was the only critical report on the racial duplicities of the leaders of the American Indian Movement.

Donald Barnett, mayor of Rapid City, South Dakota, responded with concern to the radical leaders, but then he read their criminal records and changed his mind. "Are these men serious civil rights workers or are they a bunch of bandits?" the mayor asked in an interview. "People working for civil rights do not carry guns. I have seen the records on these men, and you can't sit and negotiate with a man who has a gun." A few days later the American Indian Movement occupied Wounded Knee, South Dakota.

United Press International reported on March 1, 1973, that "members of the American Indian Movement held ten people hostage . . . at this Pine Ridge Reservation town where more than 200 Indians were massacred by Cavalry troops in 1890." There were never hostages, and leaders of the American Indian Movement were never charged with kidnaping or any other crime associated with the taking of hostages. I was close to the village that day, but the reporter for United Press International never moved from his motel room. He ordered a single-engine plane to circle Wounded Knee and filed his simulated romantic story with an aerial photograph of the church, militants, and raised weapons.

The American Indian Movement is more simulation than dread in the eighties, and the crossblood leaders are as close to retirement as those who financed their movement and adventures. The church and state contribute to other causes now, and the media cover bingo, education, reburial, the legal interpretations of treaties, and other tribal issues, with more enthusiasm than the peevish revisions of urban revolutionaries.

Russell Means, however, reappeared in a recent national report on corruption and fraud in tribal programs. "Within the past two years, I have personally attempted to assist seven Indian reservations . . . with economic development," Means told an investigative committee of the Senate Select Committee on Indian Affairs. "I know that the tribal governments do not want economic development unless graft is a major ingredient." Means was hyperbolic, as usual, and did not name the seven reservations.

Dennis Banks, the venerable leader of the American Indian Movement, has returned to the business world and corporate investments in tribal communities. Twenty years ago, before his transformation as a political activist, he wore a necktie and was a recruiter for Honeywell. Banks was a fugitive in California for nine years; he returned to serve a three-year prison sentence in South Dakota. He moved to the Pine Ridge Reservation.

The *St. Paul Pioneer Press Dispatch* reported on January 4, 1987, that Banks borrowed money from the tribal council on Pine Ridge to establish his company, Loneman Industries. "Banks spends many of his days working the phone in his cluttered office, an abandoned portable classroom. . . . He's got meetings scheduled with IBM and an appointment with Nissan executives in Japan.."

"I should have been a capitalist years ago," he told James McGregor, a reporter for the *St. Paul Pioneer Press Dispatch*. Banks said, "I just click with ideas. There's an excitement to it. I like that excitement." In the past, he needed more stimulation than the mere click of economic ideas; once he posed as a traditional woodland warrior and, with hundreds of other urban militants, armed with new weapons, threatened to attack white fishermen on the opening day of the season and clouded a court decision in favor of the Leech Lake Reservation.

Federal Judge Edward Devitt ruled in January 1972 that the Leech Lake Reservation of the Minnesota Chippewa Tribe had the right to hunt, fish, and gather wild rice on the reservation without restriction from the state of Minnesota. The governor, elected tribal officials, and the state legislature reached an agreement that has become a model of good sense, a wise measure of treaties, and the best management of natural resources. Leech Lake tribal members relinquished the right to commercial fishing, and the agreement established a special licensing system; the proceeds from license fees, in the millions, have been turned over to the tribal government.

The American Indian Movement, and Vernon Bellecourt in particular, has opposed most agreements with state and federal governments and cash settlements for land and resources; some tribal radicals, supported by romantic liberals and anarchists, would oppose any government and hold to an absolute return of tribal land.

Bellecourt told a congressional committee that he was a "member of the White Earth Anishinaabe nation and the Anishinaabe Akeeng, which means 'the people's land.' We are a coalition of allottees and heirs to the White Earth Anishinaabe nation organized to stop the further taking our treaty-guaranteed lands and to recover what has been illegally taken from us." White Earth is a reservation, not a separatist nation, and most tribal people are proud to defend constitutional democracies. Once more, tribal radicals have dubious tribal constituencies.

Darrell Wadena supported the White Earth Land Settlement Act in 1986, which would reimburse tribal members whose allotments were lost to state tax forfeitures and illegal land transactions at the turn of the century. More than ten million dollars was awarded to the heirs who lost tribal land in various swindles; moreover, the settlement would provide six million dollars in economic assistance to the reservation, and ten thousand acres of land would be returned to White Earth.

Bellecourt is a leader of Anishinaabe Akeeng. He was once an elected member of the tribal government, but lost the election for tribal chairman to Darrell Wadena. Bellecourt told the *Minneapolis Star and Tribune* that the settlement was "the most terrible injustice." Wadena indicated that Anishinaabe Akeeng was urban, not reservation, born; he pointed out that Bellecourt has traveled to Nicaragua and Libya, and "people don't believe that his association with Gadhafi has any real importance here."

Panama has been added to the nations that Vernon Bellecourt has visited, according to a newspaper published at the Minneapolis American Indian Center. *The Circle* reported in September 1989 that Bellecourt sued the Federal Bureau of Investigation for "illegally obtaining copies of pictures he took" at a Congress of Indians Conference in Panama City. "The day after Bellecourt returned to the Twin Cities he took two rolls of film that he shot while in Panama to the F-Stop One Hour Photo Store . . . in Minneapolis on March 22, 1989. When Belle—court returned for his photos, the store manager informed him" an agent had demanded that an employee "give him copies of Bellecourt's pictures." A federal judge ruled in favor of the government; his decision was based, in part, on the type of machine that allows the public to view the process of printing the photographs. Bellecourt said, "If we allow the judge's order to stand, it'll be a threat to the basic, fundamental constitutional rights of all Americans."

Bellecourt has accused tribal leaders of "selling treaty rights." Three reservations, Bois Forte, Fond du Lac; and Grand Portage, agreed to an annual cash settlement of five million dollars to limit hunting and fishing rights on original treaty land in the Arrowhead region of Minnesota. The reservations agreed to restrict commercial fishing and to abstain from spear fishing. The agreement between the three reservations and the Minnesota Department of Natural Resources was approved by a federal judge in June 1988. The agreement was negotiated, not forced; reservations were permitted to withdraw with proper notice to exercise rights to hunt and fish in the original treaty area outside the reservations. One year later, in June 1989, Fond du Lac voted to withdraw from the agreement with the state and the other two reservations.

Robert Peacock, tribal leader at Fond du Lac, told the *Minneapolis Star and Tribune*, "If one has agreed not to do something, in essence you've put a price on doing it. Once you've put a price on it, it implies it's for sale." He said land was a "gift from the creator. . . . You can't measure love in dollars. You can't measure religion in dollars." The Fond du Lac Reservation would have been paid almost two million dollars annually to abstain from commercial fishing and not to spear fish, which has caused so much racial rancor on lakes in northern Wisconsin.

"The Dairy State has turned sour about fishing," wrote Ron Schara in the *Minneapolis Star and Tribune*. "Specifically, spear fishing in the name of Chippewa treaty rights. . . . Retaining treaty rights that destroy sport fishing and threaten a tourism economy is a hollow victory for Indian leaders. And they ought to know that."

Schara is a popular sports columnist, but his condescension and racialism is misdirected and malicious, a reversion to earlier colonial reports on tribal cultures. Schara has the right to publish racial notions, the tribe has a right circumscribed in treaties; he reports the rancor, the tribe exercises an aboriginal right.

"The story of Native American claims to aboriginal land within what is now the United States is not a story of broken treaties, amended statutes, or breach of the sacred duty of guardianship. Rather, it is the story of the unbridled, unabashed, and undisguised power of the conqueror over the conquered," Michael Kaplan wrote in *Irredeemable America*.

The Chippewa in Wisconsin spear muskies and walleye pike when the ice breaks on the northern lakes in the spring. The tribe has done this for centuries. The rights to hunt and fish are natural tribal practices, neither conferred nor alienated, in the tribal sense, by state or political dominions; however, the tribal rights to hunt and fish and gather wild rice have been contained by treaties with the government of the United States. In recent court decisions these tribal rights have been sustained.

The problems over land use started with conquest, political abuses, and racism, not with the aboriginal rights of tribal cultures; the dominant poses are economic, a manifest protectionism, macho tourism, and the patriarchal possession of natural resources. The tribal practices are natural rights that arise from aboriginal worldviews; the domination and possession of the earth is a Western custom that is not the same as the natural tribal right to use the land.

"Aboriginal title is a political issue, for the most part, not a legal one," wrote Michael Kaplan. "The United States government continued to extend sovereignty over tribal lands but sustained Indian rights to use and occupancy. Such use and occupancy has normally been based on exclusive possession antecedent to conquest or negotiated acquisition of title, as by treaty, and it is not a property right protected under the Fifth Amendment."

National sovereignties begin with tribal cultures; the modern sense of tribal sovereignties has been determined by treaties, state and federal statutes, court decisions, and other implications, such as land use agreements. Charles Wilkinson points out in *American Indians, Time, and the Law* that the existence of a tribe is maintained independent of "any federal action." Tribalism is aboriginal, not a federal source, "but it has become entwined with the federal government. . . . Congress established a comprehensive matrix of laws regulating Indian affairs and effectively limiting the scope of tribal sovereignty. . . . The power exists to enact everything from the debilitating allotment and termination programs to the beneficent child welfare and tax status laws that offer so much promise to Indian people."

The Chippewa are a tribal culture, and their aboriginal rights to hunt and fish on original treaty land in northern Wisconsin were settled in the United States Court of Appeals in 1983. The court recognized the rights mentioned in several treaties more than a century ago when vast territories were ceded to the government and reservations were established. Chippewa rights to hunt, fish, and gather wild rice on lakes, rivers, and lands in the ceded territories of the treaties were restored by the court. Nancy Lurie in the epilogue to *Irredeemable America* points out that at the time of the treaties the tribe "had long engaged in commercial fishing as well as hunting for the fur trade, so commercial activities were covered as a customary right in the treaties. The decision evoked bitter denunciations from white sportsmen's groups supported by generally anti-Indian whites claiming the Indians would wantonly wipe out all the fish and game."

Treaties determined the relations between the tribes and the federal government for several generations. Then, in 1871, Congress declared that the previous treaties would be honored, but in the future the tribes would form agreements with the federal government; legislation, not treaties, would arise from proposals and agreements to manage reservations and the tribes. The cessation of treaties was the end of tribal independence and the sense of national sovereignty. The General Allotment Act of 1887, for instance, provided individual land allotments; the tribes lost a hundred million acres of communal land on reservations. Moreover, Public Law 280 extended state, civil, and criminal jurisdiction on reservations.

The University of Minnesota sponsored the first conference on Indian Tribes and Treaties in 1955. Public officials, anthropologists, lawyers, and tribal representatives from various reservations attended the conference. John Killen, then a member of the *Minnesota Law Review*, reviewed several treaties and the legal issues that arose with state jurisdiction on tribal land.

Joe Vizenor, who was then an elected representative of the Minnesota Chippewa Tribe, argued that when Public Law 280 was presented to the tribe, "we went on record approving it with the provisions whereby we reserved our rights to fish, hunt, trap, and rice on our reservations. That was written in that law, and it seems to me that should clarify it." Vizenor continued, "Well, we have game wardens up there who are pinching Indians right and left for setting nets. We went to our Indian Office and we contacted the United States Attorney and we haven't a decision yet. We should like to know where we're standing, as quick as we can find out." The tribal right to hunt, fish, and gather wild rice was decided in federal court a generation later; the state did not have jurisdiction to enforce state game and fish laws on treaty land.

"To prove a point," Schara wrote in the *Minneapolis Star and Tribune*, "Wisconsin tribal leaders are giving their people old traditions instead of future hope. This isn't 1854. The way of their forefathers was not headlamps and electric trolling motors. . . . Or to put it another way: Does anybody really believe that what the American Indian people need today is all the fish they can spear?" Schara proved a racist point, but he should have asked about the ways of his own forefathers.

Dean Crist is president of Stop Treaty Abuse and the inventor of

Treaty Beer, the "true brew of the working man." His partisan beer, and the organization, represent the formal opposition to tribal rights on treaty land. Stop Treaty Abuse, a non sequitur, and other protest associations seem to assume that federal courts created tribal rights to torment white people who fish and hunt for wild game. Rather, federal courts based their decisions on the treaties, an interpretation of aboriginal rights and territorial enclosures that had been abused by state governments for more than a century. Tribal rights were restored, not created, by recent court decisions. Some protesters argue that treaties should be rescinded; in that case, the ceded territories would be restored to the tribes, and white settlers could become criminal trespassers.

"Our argument is not with the Chippewa Indians," Larry Grescher told Kurt Chandler of the *Minneapolis Star and Tribune*. Grescher was executive director of Protect American Rights and Resources; his dubious disclaimer would not ease the racial duplicities of his organization. "We recognize that the Chippewa Indians are doing only what the law allows them to do. We are attempting to put pressure on federal legislators to take a look at . . . rescinding treaties."

An "Annual Indian Shoot" was announced by an anonymous organization in Wisconsin. The circular described a point system for scoring the shoot: plain Indian, five points; Indian with walleye, ten points; Indian with boat newer than yours, twenty points; Indian using pitchfork, thirty points; Indian tribal lawyer, one hundred points. The white circular mentioned "taking scalps," and the prizes included "six packs of Treaty Beer."

In April 1989, at demonstrations on northern lakes in the state, there were signs that read, "Save a walleye, spear an Indian." Pat Doyle reported for the *Minneapolis Star and Tribune* that a "parade of motorboats" followed a tribal man in a rowboat at midnight on Balsam Lake, Wisconsin. Kenny Pardun was in the rowboat; he held a light in one hand a spear in the other. Someone shouted from a motorboat, "Did you get that light from your ancestors?"

Doyle reported that at Big Butternut Lake there were police in riot helmets to hold back a crowd of about a hundred white protesters, and to protect the rights of tribal people at the boat landing. The crowd shouted at the tribal people in their boats. "Gotta quit handing out those welfare checks so they can't buy a boat," someone shouted. "If we nailed their mailbox shut they'd starve to death." Then a man shouted, "Why don't we go back to our heritage and hunt you guys down?"

Ronald Reagan said, "Maybe we made a mistake in trying to maintain Indian cultures. Maybe we should not have humored them in wanting to stay in that kind of primitive lifestyle." The former president is no trickster, compassionate or otherwise; maybe we should have humored him when he pronounced his unintended ironies. His sense of tribal cultures seems to be based on simulations from western movies. The means to "maintain Indian cultures" were never mistakes; indeed, the bias is in the absence of humor and historical consideration. His voice could be a simulation, the riot and seethe of imperialism in politics and movie scenes. Reagan seemed to be in the movies when he visited Moscow in May 1988, and when he responded to questions about Native American Indians.

The use of the word "Indian" is postmodern, a navigational conception, a colonial invention, a simulation in sound and transcription. Tribal cultures became nominal, diversities were twisted to the core, and oral stories were set in written languages, the translations of discoveries.

Christopher Columbus reasoned that he had reached India, a generous mismeasure, but there were no Indians in India. The origin of the name, according to the *Dictionary of Indian English*, is *sindhu*, river or sea, from Sanskrit. The "name exchanged the initial sibilant for an aspirate" and became Hindu in Persian, a native of India.

Native American Indians are burdened with colonial pantribal names, and with imposed surnames translated from personal tribal nicknames by missionaries and federal agents. More than a hundred million people, and hundreds of distinct tribal cultures, were simulated as Indians; an invented pantribal name, one sound, bears treaties, statutes, and seasons, but no tribal culture, language, religion, or landscape.

The last national census enumerated close to one and a half million tribal people in the United States. The Cherokee are the most populous, followed by the people named the Navajo, Sioux, and Chippewa, the four largest tribes in the country. Some of the least populous tribes are located in New England; however, low populations are not proper measures of tribal interests. The Passamaquoddy and the Penobscot, for example, were awarded more than eighty million dollars in a recent land claims settlement in Maine.

Native American Indians are ever in the news because tribal cultures continue to be dubious measures of civilization and mismeasures of race; tribal shades, names, and poses are collectibles in liberal stories, and the simulated tribes are praised on certain national and

religious holidays. Thanksgiving Day, for instance, imposes an aboriginal retinue and celebrants from the wilderness; however, tribal cultures are not honored on Columbus Day.

"From where the sun now stands, I will fight no more forever," is
attributed to Chief Joseph of the people named the Nez Perce. From the
memorable "surrender speech" to the taxicab driver who "cleaned" a
statue of Chief Seattle, the indigenous cultures of this hemisphere have
become tribal camp, postmodern translations and simulations. The
stories that follow have been selected from recent publications of
books, newspapers, and magazines.

"I realize that there was one area I'd never really exploited: my
lifelong obsession with American Indians," wrote Oleg Cassini, the
costume designer, in *In My Own Fashion: An Autobiography.* "A good
many of my American Indian dresses required intricate beading of a
sort that was not available in Italy. . . . I'd been told Hong Kong was
the place to find such material."

Cassini tried to appease his obsession in an agreement with Peter
MacDonald, then the chairman of the Navajo Tribal Council. The
couturier announced at the National Press Club that he would build, as
a joint venture with the tribal government, a "world-class luxury
resort" on the reservation. The architecture and furnishings of the
tourist resort would "have their base in authentic Navajo designs."
MacDonald said the resort would "reflect the unique culture and
tradition of our people." Moreover, the tribal leader announced: "We
are creating a Navajo Board of Standards for all new tourist facilities on
the reservation to assure that the Navajo name means quality."

Visitors to the Grand Canyon complain that the view is ruined by air
pollution. What some visitors thought might have been smoke from
forest fires turned out to be industrial smog, reported *Time* magazine.
The National Park Service studied weather patterns, the haze, and
determined that the source was the Navajo Generating Station located
on the Navajo Reservation near Page, Arizona. "The plant, burning
24,000 tons of coal daily and releasing an estimated 12 to 13 tons of
sulfur dioxide from its smokestacks every hour, was found responsible." The plant, one of the largest coal fired generators in the nation,
supplies power to Arizona, Nevada, and California. Los Angeles, in a
sense, is air conditioned by coal generated power from the Navajo
Nation. *The New York Times* reported that the Environmental Protection
Agency found "substantial evidence" that the power station was "a
major contributor" to air pollution at the Grand Canyon.

The *Seattle Post-Intelligencer* reported that "Cabbie's scrubbing rubs

Chief Seattle wrong way." A taxicab driver tried to clean the natural patina from the bronze sculpture of the famous tribal orator; he used an acid that damaged the statue. "I tried to do something good and it turned out bad," said the cab driver. "The Indians in the area need to know that the white man cares." Chief Seattle told Isaac Stevens, the governor of Washington Territory, that "when the last red man shall have perished, and the memory of my tribe shall have become a myth among the white men, these shores will swarm with the invisible dead of my tribe. . . . The white man will never be alone."

The *Los Angeles Times* reported in September 1989 that leaders of the Mormon Church "excommunicated the only American Indian ever appointed to the church hierarchy." George Lee, one of more than forty thousand Navajo Mormons, was the first high official "to be erased from membership rolls" in forty-six years. Lee is reported to be the son of a "medicine man." He was excommunicated for "apostasy and other conduct unbecoming a member of the church." Indians are mentioned in the Book of Mormon.

The *Independent*, a newspaper published in Gallup, New Mexico, reported on July 6, 1989, that Russell Means had been arrested by "Navajo police officers . . . as he attempted to make a citizen's arrest of the Bureau of Indian Affairs area director" James Stevens at the tribal government center in Window Rock. Means was held overnight in the Crownpoint "jail on assault and battery charges." He accused the area director of "interfering in Navajo political matters."

The *Navajo Times* reported that "Means had held a press conference the week before in which he said he would place Stevens under citizen's arrest. . . . Means got him in a headlock." Stevens is a San Carlos Apache; Means is Dakota and is married to a Navajo.

The *Albuquerque Journal* indicated that the area director had agreed to meet with the "Pro-Dineh Voters group, a Navajo organization, seeking reinstatement of Chairman Peter MacDonald." The Navajo Supreme Court had affirmed the suspension of MacDonald by the tribal council, following allegations that he "took kickbacks from reservation contractors and personally profited from the tribe's purchase of the Big Boquillas Ranch." Stevens recognized the appointment of an interim tribal chairman. Means opposed that decision and attempted a citizen's arrest.

MacDonald was "stripped of power by his own tribal council" and faces "bribery and corruption charges," Sandy Tolan reported in the *New York Times Magazine* on November 26, 1989. "When MacDonald refused to leave office, he precipitated a five-month crisis in the Navajo government, culminating in a violent confrontation." MacDonald said, "All they want to do is silence people like me who speak out against those who are trying to erode tribal sovereignty."

The Select Committee on Indian Affairs reported that MacDonald "is one example of a tribal chief executive who placed personal enrichment above public service. For years, MacDonald received bogus 'consulting fees,' 'loans' and 'gifts'—and even persuaded the tribe to purchase desert land worth less than $26 million for more than $33 million so that, through a shell company, he could enjoy a secret share of the $7 million markup."

MacDonald was born on a sheep drive near Teec Nos Pos, Arizona. He enlisted in the Marines and became a Navajo Code Talker; later, he graduated from college as an electrical engineer. He returned to the reservation and has been elected to four terms as chairman. Now, he is "likened to a corrupt dictator by many of his own people." Some of his critics contend that he has strayed from the tribal way. "If you cease to live the way of the Navajos, you're going to become less human," Daniel Peaches told Sandy Tolan. "You will have less moral strength."

The *Minnesota Daily* reported in August 1989 that Jim Weaver, an elder member of the Minnesota Chippewa Tribe, would fast until the federal government investigated the White Earth Reservation. Weaver was critical of Darrell Wadena, the elected tribal chairman. "If someone has to die to get this man out," said the elder, "that's what is going to happen." Weaver was serious; he tended his fire. "It's a sacred fire. I keep it going until I either kick the bucket or end the fast." He ended the fast. Wadena told a reporter, "If the news media would just go away and leave it alone, those guys would go home and start eating." White Earth Reservation politics as postmodern, and the poses are ever terminal.

The *Los Angeles Times* reported in September 1989 that the wild rice harvest was ruined in Minnesota. Overnight the tribal cash crop "fell victim to scientific tinkering, big-time agribusiness, Indian complacency and a wave of greed and hype stretching from the farms in the North Woods to the fertile rice paddies of the Sacramento Valley."

Mahnomin, or wild rice, is not a proper rice, but a coarse, indigenous, annual aquatic grass. The wild is nominal, but the wild harvest is protected by state statutes in Minnesota; however, the rice that is a grass has become a postmodern cash crop on idle, not wild, land in California.

Statutes in Minnesota specify that wild rice harvested on public land be done from canoes with push poles and flails to gather the rice. The regulations are based on the traditional harvest practices of woodland tribes. Mahnomin grows best in shallow lakes and rivers; mechanical harvests are forbidden on public waters. The high price of natural wild rice, between five and ten dollars a pound retail, attracted investors. Minnesota legislators responded to the potential capital investments and supported research to develop a commercial grain that would survive mechanical harvesting on private land.

The specialty market for wild rice has provided a source of income on some reservations. Ikwe Marketing, for instance, a group of tribal women on the White Earth Reservation, listed wild rice, native recipes, and handcrafted birchbark baskets in a recent issue of an alternative holiday gift catalog.

The demand for institutional and industrial wild rice has stimulated the commercial development of the market; for example, broken rice was separated and milled for use in pancake flour. Tribal governments invested in commercial paddies, but the most profitable paddies were subsidized by federal agricultural policies. California proved to be a better location to cash in on commercial wild rice than Minnesota.

"Established white rice growers jumped on the bandwagon," reported the *Los Angeles Times*, "To trim a surplus of white rice, many California growers were getting federal set-aside payments to hold some of their land out of production. But idled land still had to be planted with some sort of grass to prevent erosion. And, because wild rice technically was a grass, it started turning up in more and more idled fields. The growers sold the wild rice and kept the government set-aside money to boot."

Syndicated columnist Jack Anderson, in a report about Jamake Highwater, stated that "one of the country's most celebrated Indians has fabricated much of the background that made him famous." Highwater, the author of several books about tribal cultures, wrote a *This Song Remembers*, a collection of portraits published in 1980, that he speaks eleven languages and "entered the university at thirteen."

Anderson revealed that Highwater admitted that he "lied about many details of his life. Asked why someone of such genuine and extraordinary talent felt he had to concoct a spurious background, Highwater said he felt that doors would not have opened for him if he had relied on his talent alone." He claimed advanced degrees from the University of California at Berkeley, and the University of Chicago. "In fact, he admitted he never got any such degrees."

Highwater may have opened doors with his spurious identities, but he stole public attention, and his bent for recognition may have closed doors for honest tribal people who have the moral courage to raise doubts about their own identities. "I am cautious about my success, and about my visibility," he wrote in *This Song Remembers*. "As a tribal person, I've had the rewarding experience of having Native Americans from all tribal backgrounds say, 'What you're doing is good.'" He said he was born in the "early forties" and "raised in northern Montana and southern Alberta, Canada. I'm not enrolled in the Blackfeet tribe, but I spent my first thirteen years among the Blackfeet and Cree people."

Anderson pointed out that Highwater has listed his birthplace as Los Angeles, Canada, South Dakota, Montana, and Normandy, France. "Vine Deloria Jr. and Hank Adams say flatly that Highwater is not an Indian."

In *Shadow Show: An Autobiographical Insinuation*, published in 1986, two years after the column by Jack Anderson, Highwater wrote, "The greatest mystery of my life is my own identity. . . . To escape things that are painful we must reinvent ourselves. Either we reinvent ourselves or we choose not to be anyone at all. We must not feel guilty if we are among those who have managed to survive." He seems to name his identities in others, a culture consumer; his new stories are autoinsinuations, a literature that abandons his dubious connections to tribal cultures.

Highwater wrote in *Shadow Show*, "I begin to think that our borrowed lives are necessities in a world filled with hostility and pain, a confusing world largely devoid of credible social truths."

Ishi, discovered by anthropologists as the last of his tribe, has become the romantic postmodern measure of survivance; he died in a museum at the University of California. His choices were passed over to settlement and civilization; he consented, but he might never have chosen to live and die in a museum.

The Yahi tribal survivor became a popular aboriginal artifact, a voice from the Stone Age. He was a romantic figure in tribal simulations, and was studied with unnatural respect by anthropologists and linguists; however, we must never revise his manners and loneliness as the behavior of a happy slave to science. His tribal identities, and the landscapes he imagined, were translated and transvalued in postmodern education and politics; he lived with one name and an uncommon sinecure, a tenured tribal consultant to enlightened methodologists.

Alfred Kroeber was in New York when Ishi died; he wrote to the curator of the museum, "If there is any talk about the interests of science, say for me that science can go to hell." The distinguished anthropologist anticipated by more than two generations the scientific debate over the reburial of tribal remains.

Ishi was cremated and his remains were placed in a "small black Pueblo jar," the curator wrote. "The funeral was private and no flowers were brought." The inscription reads: *Ishi, the last Yana Indian, 1916.*

Ishi did not choose to live in a museum, but at least his remains were protected by a friend; his bones were not stored in a museum as were the bones of several hundred thousand other tribal people. Some scientists oppose the reburial of tribal remains; others avoid the moral discourse on natural rights and the proposal to establish bone courts to hear and resolve disputes over research interests and reburial.

Douglas Schwartz, president of the School of American Research in Santa Fe, New Mexico, and his associate Jonathan Haas, for instance, have protected their research on tribal remains and their possession of ceremonial artifacts; their research motivation and interests in human remains would be recorded in a bone court.

The distinctions between archaeologists and physical anthropologists are lost in the discourse on reburial. "We archaeologists are bearing the heat for physical anthropologists," Larry Zimmerman told a reporter for the *Chronicle of Higher Education* in September 1989. "We're out there on the front lines at the digs, and they're in the lab not talking to Indians." Zimmerman is a professor at the University of South Dakota. Frank Norick, an anthropologist at the Lowie Museum of Anthropology, University of California, Berkeley, has "gone on record in opposition to such efforts as that of Stanford University to return remains to local tribes."

Thomas White Hawk murdered a jeweler in Vermillion, South Dakota. The nineteen-year-old tribal orphan and college student shot the man in his bedroom, beat him on the head in the kitchen, gathered his blood in a bowl, and then raped his wife several times. The crime was heinous, a vicious and horrific scene in an otherwise pleasant university town on the prairie; the handsome murderer was hiding as a child might do in the closet when the police arrived at the house. White Hawk confessed to the crimes and was sentenced to death in the electric chair.

I read about the crime and the sentence in the *Minneapolis Tribune.* I was in South Dakota a few days later to investigate the crime and organized opposition to capital punishment. I traveled around the state for more than six months to gather information on White Hawk and his family. Three thousand copies of my essay on the case, which is published here, were mailed at no charge to individuals and institutions around the world. I reviewed the court hearings and attended the trial of William Stands, who was with White Hawk at the time of the crime.

Joseph Satten, the psychiatrist from the Menninger Clinic, reported that White Hawk suffered from psychotic episodes and lapsed into "transient" dreams. "His Indian background would tend to make him place a high value on stoicism, emotional impassivity, withdrawal, aloofness, and the denial of dependence on others. In addition, the tendency of some in the dominant culture to devaluate Indians and the Indian culture would tend to accentuate his feelings of loneliness and suspicion." Satten, in the end, supported my narrative description of "cultural schizophrenia."

The governor commuted the death sentence, but the parole board recommended that no further commutations be made in the future. Without the possibility of parole, White Hawk faces a natural death sentence in the state penitentiary. Many people in the state believe that is more than he deserves for his crimes.

I visited White Hawk at the penitentiary in June 1987 and again in 1993. I had not seen him for twenty years; he never told me how he felt about my critical essay on the murder, his motivation, and the sentence. He said he would not have changed a word. White Hawk wrote to his lawyer Douglas Hall, "I have done some heavy thinking and I have been unable to come up with any feasible method for altering Gerald Vizenor's journal to suit our purposes now. . . . Vizenor's work was superbly written and the only elements which I believe we could alter at all would be the placement of the transcript quotes he used. Otherwise, I would change nothing."

SAND CREEK SURVIVORS

> In the national experience race has al-
> ways been of greater importance than
> class. . . . Racism defined natives as non-
> persons within the settlement culture
> and was in a real sense the enabling ex-
> perience of the rising American empire:
> Indian-hating identified the dark others
> that white settlers were not and must not
> under any circumstances become, and it
> helped them wrest a continent and more
> from the hands of these native caretakers
> of the lands.
>
> Richard Drinnon, *Facing West*

First Lieutenant James Cannon testified at the hearing on the Sand Creek Massacre that the tribal bodies he saw after the attack were scalped and butchered by federal troops, "and in many instances their bodies were mutilated in the most horrible manner. . . . I heard of one instance of a child a few months old being thrown in the feed box of a wagon, and after being carried some distance, left on the ground to perish. I also heard of numerous instances in which men had cut the private parts of females, and stretched them over the saddle bows, and wore them over their hats, while riding in the ranks."

Dane Michael White buckled his wide belt around his thin neck and hanged himself from a shower rod in the Wilkin County Jail in Breckenridge, Minnesota. Dane had been held in jail as a criminal for forty-one days, most of that time alone, in isolation, the victim of dominant white colonial institutions. A tribal child with short hair and wide smile, a survivor from Sand Creek, dead at thirteen. Suicide.

Dane White and the Sand Creek Massacre in Colorado are three generations apart in calendar time, but in dreams and visual tribal memories, these grievous events, and thousands more from the White Earth Reservation to the damp concrete bunkers beneath the interstates in San Francisco, are not separated in linear time. The past can be found on tribal faces in the present. The curse of racism rules the ruinous institutions and federal exclaves where tribal people are contained; where tribal blood is measured on colonial reservations. Dane White became a criminal for being truant from a white school.

Clement Beaulieu, mixedblood writer and college teacher, was on special assignment for the *Minneapolis Tribune* at the Red Lake Reservation. For official purposes he was compiling background information on reservation economic development. His personal reasons, however, were tied to tribal friends and his need to hear some fine stories.

Beaulieu had settled into stories and imaginative memories, like an old reservation mongrel, when he was called to the telephone by Frank Premack, the city editor of the *Minneapolis Tribune,* and ordered to be in Sisseton, South Dakota, by morning for a funeral.

"Premack, your humor is cruel," Beaulieu responded long distance. "Sisseton is more than two hundred miles from here."

"Be there."

"But I've been drinking, I'm tired, and I would have to drive all night, alone," Beaulieu pleaded. "The truth is, the best stories are just starting here, good reservations stories. . . . Who is so damned important that we have to cover a funeral in Sisseton?"

"Dane Michael White."

"Who is he?"

"An Indian suicide."

Silence.

"His father lives in Browns Valley, and his mother was living in Chicago, but she moved back to Sisseton. Dane was held in jail like a fucking criminal for forty-one goddamned days . . . cover the funeral, telephone me from there, I want a front page story."

Premack was one of the toughest journalists, perhaps the meanest at times, but he was also one of the most sensitive editors at the *Min-*

neapolis Tribune. No doubt that he was the most imaginative, the most demanding, and the hardest-working editor. Few writers could keep up with him; he caused revolutions in individual writers and readers. His writers loved him and hated him at the same time. When he was a reporter, he was so critical of malfeasance and so perceptive of nonfeasance in government that when he was promoted to editor, elected officials celebrated the departure of his questions and his reports on city government.

"Have a nice drive."

"Shit. . . ."

Beaulieu drank three cups of coffee and started driving at midnight, south through Bemidji, Park Rapids, while whistling in the dark and listening to radio music from Chicago and Little Rock.

The world comes together all at once, he wrote in his notes, when time is turned loose like an animal in the mind park.

Dane White at Sand Creek. Tribal worlds converged between Detroit Lakes and Fergus Falls. Beaulieu thrust his head out the window into the cold wind. Late November, no snow, the earth was tired. Tribal worlds converged in imagination and individual memories. Ceremonial words seemed to bend down on the shoulder of the road, but no one would wait to listen. Even the earthdivers soared past the last tribal survivors through the dark in dreams.

"Dane White is here, in the background of the banquet table," Father William Keohane said in prayer. His gestures were solemn; in slow and tedious motions, his arms and shoulders turned like the branches on an ornamental fruit tree, turning on the wind toward the large painting of the Last Supper mounted like a fastfood billboard behind the small altar in the narrow church. "Lord, remember this child in your Kingdom."

Beaulieu listened. *Remember this child,* turned in his mind over and over like a phrase that never found a place to fit in time. *When is the best time to remember?* Trained to be a dutiful scribe, at least as a reporter, he scratched into his notebook the practiced gentle words of the priest, but he resisted the words, his hand seemed to avoid the words, he hated the words. The sounds burst in his ears and shot down his arm, nothing smooth or soothing, nothing from forgiveness, no calm, no peace from tribal suicide.

How can his words be so soft, so restrained, Beaulieu wrote in his notes. Dane knows no pleasure in the words of the white world; he was trapped and executed in a white institution . . . and now the apologists mutilate this child with funeral words, in the same place in the tribal heart where tribal children were tossed on bayonets and women were dismembered by savage white soldiers. . . . The white apologists repress the revolutions in the heart. . . . Lord, remember what the soldiers and the white world have done to the caretakers of this land.

Clement Beaulieu stepped into a telephone booth to call Frank Premack, his editor. The door was broken, the small space smelled of urine and cigarette smoke. The wind snarled through the cracks in the booth.

"Sisseton is tired."

"I want photographs," said Premack.

"No camera."

"Buy a cheap one at the drugstore, somewhere, and airfreight the film to me this afternoon. . . . We can process it before the last edition. This is front page; send me several shots from the grave."

"Have you ever been out here?"

"Yes, I lived in Aberdeen."

"Well, then you know too well."

"Know what?"

"Cold wind and no fresh fruit."

"Repression, repression can best be measured in the world by the availability of fresh fruit and vegetables," said the editor. "Give me a minute to write that down."

"I am tired."

"We all are, forget it."

"No, these prairie prisons exhaust me."

"Forget the women."

"I was not thinking about women."

"Forget your ideals."

"No, it is the heart that suffers out here."

Saint Catherine's Indian Mission Church hunkered like a trained circus animal in the center of little unpainted houses too close together in double rows, each tied to concrete ribbons. The Indian Mission was dressed in gentle colors, pastel blue and pink, visual denials of violence and internal revolutions. The sidewalk and steps had been washed and swept clean for the funeral. Tribal people arrived in bright red and blue cars, dressed in dark church clothes, men in doubleknit suits and blue shoes, and women dressed in white shoes and print dresses. The cold wind whipped their dresses, shivers ran down their bare arms to the mission door. The prairie wind pushed at the door, holding it closed. A tribal spiritual wind.

Inside the chapel the wind had taken up with the sweet smell of flowers. The metal coffin was closed, locked, institutional isolation, the neck bruises hidden from view, locked from memories. The wooden benches were hard; the service was proper, dull, and repressed in pale colors. Pink and blue sacred auras abounded on the walls, painted with exaggerated bows, white saints who must have soared with the settlers.

We should pull these words down, beat them on the altars until the truth is revealed, beat the sweet phrases from the institutions that have disguised the horrors of racism . . . drive the word pains and agonies from the heart into the cold. . . . We are the victims of these words used to cover the political violence and white horrors in the memories of the tribes.

Hear these primal screams, the tribes scream with the trees and rivers, from diseases, the massacres and mutilations of the heart . . . racist isolation and the repression of the heart in white schools and institutions. . . . Break down the white word walls and dance free from isolation . . . dance in the sun

The procession to the grave was slow and tedious, a mechanical ritual of fifteen automobiles. Even the raw earth, the real earth from beneath the frost line, was covered with an unnatural green carpet, brighter than the prairie burial site. Funerals are for the living, but the tribes were buried in the heart, silent, alone, repressed. Those at the grave seemed to be the last survivors of white racism.

The tribal procession wobbled over the stubble in the cold wind . . . circling the bodies from memories at Sand Creek and Marias River and Wounded Knee we bear the new tribal dead in metal tubs locked to keep death a secret and locked to keep the earth from our bones that reach back to the earth . . . back to our tribal graves.

Hands in white gloves reached to cover an occasional smile, but the eyes, dark tribal eyes, smiled wide over the hidden lips and uneven teeth in the line. There was an innocence and a sense that the innocent were the new victims.

The Blackfeet were sleeping in their village on the Marias River. It was January, cold and dark. The commanding officers ordered the soldiers to "aim to kill, to spare none of the enemy. . . . A terrible scene ensued." This report was published in *Survey of Conditions of Indians in the United States*, and reprinted in *Of Utmost Good Faith* by Vine Deloria.

"Bears Head, frantically waving a paper which bore testimony to his good character and friendliness to the white man, ran toward the command on the bluff, shouting to them to cease firing, entreating them to save the women and children; down he also went with several bullet holes in his body. Of the more than four hundred souls in camp at that time, very few escaped. And when it was over, when the last wounded woman and child had been put out of misery, the soldiers piled the corpses on overturned lodges, firewood, and household property and set fire to it all. . . . Several years afterward I was on the ground. Everywhere scattered about in the long grass and brush, just where the wolves and foxes had left them, gleamed the skulls and bones of those who had been so ruthlessly slaughtered. . . ."

According to G. B. Grinnell, "innocent persons were butchered on this day of shame, ninety of them women, fifty-five babies . . . no punishment of any kind was given the monsters who did it."

American Horse, a survivor at Wounded Knee, testified that "right near the flag of truce a mother was shot down with her infant; the child not knowing its mother was dead was still nursing, and that was especially a very sad sight. The women as they were fleeing with their babies on their backs were killed together, shot right through and women who were heavy with child were also killed. . . .

"Little boys who were not wounded came out of their places of refuge, and as soon as they came in sight a number of soldiers surrounded them and butchered them there."

At the end, when the metal coffin was lowered into the sacred prairie, the six pallbearers, relatives and tribal friends, removed their honoring ribbons from their new suits and dropped them into the grave in silence.

Dane Michael White was buried in an isolated grave, but he must not be forgotten. He must soar in memories with millions of tribal people from the past, their faces in the sun, their smiles in the aspen, their death and our memories a revolution in the heart. We are dancing in the sun . . . we are the pallbearers and the ghost dancers.

"This is Premack."
"Who is taking dictation?"

"Keep it short," said the editor who typed with two fingers and ground his teeth between spoken words. "The second coming is worth no more than a page and a half."

Clement Beaulieu was standing in the telephone booth with the broken door. The prairie wind whipped through the narrow space. He opened his notebook and dictated his story about the funeral.

"First paragraph: Traditional white colonial racists banished tribal cultures and isolated the survivors. . . ."

"Save it for the archives," said Premack.

"What *is* the news?"

"Start dictating," said Premack, grinding his teeth.

"November 21, 1968, dateline Sisseton.

"Catholic funeral services for Dane Michael White were held here Wednesday in English and in the Dakota language at St. Catherine's Indian Mission Church. New paragraph.

"Following the service, attended by seventy-five people, all but six of whom were Dakota Indians, Dane was buried in St. Peter's Catholic Cemetery. New paragraph.

"Born in Sisseton thirteen years ago, he took his own life Sunday in the Wilkin County Jail, Breckenridge, Minnesota, where he had been held since October 7, 1968, awaiting a juvenile court hearing. New paragraph.

"The services and burial for the young Dakota Indian were attended by his father, Cyrus White, Browns Valley, Minnesota; his mother, Burdell Armell, Chicago, Illinois; his maternal and paternal grandparents; his older brother, Timothy; three younger sisters, and many of his school friends. . . . Two hymns were sung in the Dakota language. . . ."

Dane White lost his balance with the more complicated burdens than the separation between tribal words and white institutions, dreams and social manners; he stumbled through the memories, expectations, and contradictions of two families.

Death has been praised for resolving differences in families; death dissolves some pretensions, but suicide never leaves institutions or families blameless.

Dane White was stranded between cultures and between two families. His parents were divorced, and both remarried. Separate families and separate parents attended separate functions following the requiem mass and burial.

Cyrus White, his father, lived in Browns Valley. Burdell Armell, his mother, moved to Chicago, Illinois, leaving the children with their father.

Marian Starr, his maternal grandmother, lived in Long Hollow, seven miles west of Sisseton, and it was there, in the old house near an abandoned church on the well-worn rim of the town, that Dane White seemed to be the most comfortable. It was there in the peaceful nurturance of his tribal grandmother that police officers often found the truant grandchild and returned him to his father and stepmother across the state border.

Cyrus, who was born near Enemy Swim Lake, north of Waubay, South Dakota, worked in Montana as an auto mechanic before he married his second wife, a divorcee with five children, and settled in Browns Valley. Eleven children, ten from two previous marriages and a new infant, shared the manicured space in a neat and clean rented frame house. The father of the families conducted his business with visitors and relatives in the kitchen over the large marbled formica table. The windows were dressed with mail-order curtains, pinched clean and even over the white sills.

"Dane liked it out here," said Marian Starr, "he was happy, laughing, joking around with the other boys." The grandmother sat in a large wooden chair, the padding exposed at the seams, near the space heater, and smiled with her memories. Small stiff trousers, worn by her grandchildren, wagged in slow motion on the clothesline stretched across the room over the stove. The floor was covered with linoleum, cracked, too short to fit the space. Two of the three wooden chairs in the room, turned toward the stove, were backless. Behind the stove there was a cardboard box filled with pieces of plaster, pieces of the puzzle that had dropped from the ceiling lath during the night. Grandmother Starr was too poor to travel and reminisce the past with her childhood friends on the reservation, but she conducted her memories, and the earth dreams around her, with nurturance and humor. Her grandchildren were at ease in the old house, a place where the world made some sense with no pretensions.

Dane White was locked in the Wilkin County Jail in Brekenridge on October 7, 1968. The day before, Herb Mundt, Roberts County Sheriff from South Dakota, found Dane with his tribal grandmother in Long Hollow and held him overnight as a truant fugitive. Arliss Schmitz, Traverse County Sheriff in Minnesota, took Dane from Sisseton to Breckenridge, where, charged with truancy and running away from the home of his father to the home of his grandmother, he was held for forty-one days without a juvenile court hearing.

Beaulieu interviewed both sheriffs and investigated school and juvenile court records in an effort to discover who was responsible for the decision to isolate a child in jail. A foster home placement may not have been satisfactory, but his choice to live with his maternal grandmother had been denied. The one place where he was loved was denied; instead he was jailed.

Five hearings were scheduled and postponed. Dane was in jail a month when the court appointed an attorney, Donald Pederson, to represent the child. The attorney was familiar with court procedures.

"I wanted a foster placement immediately to get the boy out of jail," said the attorney. "I had been told that placing Dane with his grandmother, Marion Starr, had already been decided." There is no record that the court-appointed attorney visited his client or grandmother; rather, he postponed the next scheduled hearing to prepare for the case.

Dane could have been placed in the Pierre Indian Boarding School in South Dakota. School administrators indicated that there was space, but juvenile court officials could not decide on a date to discuss the matter.

Meanwhile, Dane White was alone in a civilized world with little more in a white institution than his tribal dreams. He lettered the word "love" on the back of his belt and wrote "born to lose" on his tennis shoes.

I looked down upon the earth and saw a flame which looked to be a man. . . . I heard all around voices of moaning and woe, Black Elk told John Neihardt in an interview. *It was sad on earth. I felt uneasy and I trembled . . . the man transformed into a gopher and it stood up on its hind legs and turned around. Then this gopher transformed into a herb. This was the most powerful herb. . . . It could be used in war and could destroy a nation.*

"Cyrus came in here and said he wanted me to pick him up," Mundt announced, with his feet racked one over the other on his square desk. He was a person of verbal and visual force, expressing few uncertainties on the prairie between the pale marketplace economics and the defeated tribes.

"I asked Sheriff Mundt to pick him up and give him a good scare," said Cyrus White, leaning on his bare elbows over the kitchen table. "Dane was never in school," he explained, "the kids teased him, calling him dumb and stupid. . . . Sheriff Schmitz said he wanted to take Dane to Breckenridge and decided from there what to do with him."

Minnesota Attorney General Douglas Head ordered an investigation of the suicide. According to the official report Dane Michael White was of average intelligence and seemed to have an interest in drawing.

"Dane saw no one on any regular basis," the report concludes, "other than the Wilkin County Sheriff and his wife, who delivered meals to the boy's cell."

Dane shared a cell block with two other boys for four days, but the rest of the time he was alone, in isolation. Dane showed the two boys how he could hang himself, his suicide game, from a shower curtain rod in his cell.

"Dane was visited by members of his family twice, once for less than an hour by his father and once by his stepmother for about half an hour," the official report continues.

"Without a more exhaustive study of how juveniles are treated in the . . . area, it is impossible to say conclusively that this excessively long jailing was because Dane was an Indian.

"However, the fact of his being Indian cannot be dismissed as immaterial. . . . Dane himself never complained and never indicated that he was other than content in jail, except to the boys who shared his cellblock.

"Dane never initiated conversation, but always had a smile for the sheriff and his wife. It was not unlikely that Dane was acting out how he had been taught, as an Indian, to act in front of white persons in authority.

"From our investigation we received the impression that some persons assumed that the jail was superior to Dane's own home. . . . Dane's appearance of contentment undoubtedly promoted some indifference to his continued incarceration."

"This is Premack."

"Premack, listen," said Beaulieu from the telephone booth at the corner, "three stories in four days, I think I'll come back to the office and write about politicians and their apologies for violence and suicide."

"Who postponed the juvenile court hearings?"

"The judge."

"Why?"

"He was on a hunting trip."

"A hunting trip?"

"Big game hunting in the mountains."

"The bastards," said Premack.

"The white man smacks his law and order on the land, possesses the earth until it can hardly breathe, and then he goes hunting in the mountains while the tribes die in his institutions, in cold isolated cells," said Beaulieu, looking down the main street and kicking the side of the telephone booth with his left foot. "Listen, the state investigators for the Attorney General are down here now, and the word is out not to talk to reporters. The politicians want the story for their uses now, everything is useful to a politician. . . . Someone will apologize and look good when he promises that this will never happen again.

"Shit, I can no longer tell who is more violent, politicians or federal troops. More investigations and reports to reduce all the problems to words and conversations with constituents. . . . Politicians are still keeping the world safe with words rather than guns for white settlers."

"Then, what are you doing?"

"Newspaper side shows in the word wars."

"All the more fun. . . ."

"Come the revolution," said Beaulieu.

"Come the next election, remember democracies?"

"The whole damn country is a wild west show."

"Drive with care."

Senator Walter Mondale from Minnesota, acting chairman, after the assassination of Senator Robert Kennedy, of the subcommittee on Indian Education, attributed the suicide of Dane White and other young tribal people to an "identity crisis" resulting from educational experiences "depicting the Indian as a pagan savage. . . .

"Indians find themselves alienated from their own culture. . . . The problems are particularly pronounced in boarding schools where children are separated from parents and community and sometimes discouraged from even visiting their parents," said Mondale, clear and practiced, in a telephone conversation.

Senator Mondale said that one witness at the subcommittee hearings testified that in one jail near the Navajo Reservation, "in a single year three Indian youths hanged themselves from the same water pipe in the same cell."

Senator Robert Kennedy, who formed and was chairman of the subcommittee, "had spent some time with one of the youths who hanged himself, and I was told that the experience had a lasting impact on Senator Kennedy."

Dane Michael White was a survivor from Sand Creek, Baker Massacre at Marias River, Wounded Knee, and hundreds of racial contests on the prairie, and in words he was abandoned at all the cruel crossroads in the white world. Dane was a victim of colonial domination, manipulation, and cultural invalidation, isolation in a white world of peaceful pretensions.

Colonel John Chivington returned to "his old home in Ohio and settled on a small farm. . . . A few years later his house was burned," wrote Jacob Piatt Dunn in *Massacres of the Mountains; A History of the Indian Wars of the Far West*. Chivington was nominated as a candidate for representative to the legislature, but he "withdrew from the race." About the same time, while he was involved in a bitter disagreement over Indians with Quakers in the Society of Friends, he was pleased to be invited to address a meeting of old settlers in Colorado.

"What says the dust of the two hundred and eight men, women, and children, ranchers, emigrants, herders, and soldiers," said Chivington to an enthusiastic audience of settlers, "who lost their lives at the hands of these Indians? Peaceable? Now we are peaceably disposed, but decline giving such testimonials of our peaceful proclivities, and I say here as I said in my own town, in the Quaker county of Clinton, State of Ohio, one night last week, *I stand by Sand Creek.*"

"The treatment of women, by any Indians, is usually bad, but by the plains Indians especially so," wrote Dunn, who was sympathetic to Chivington.

Dunn wrote sensational stories about the experience of white women who were captured by the tribes. "When a woman is captured by a war-party she is the common property of all of them, each night, till they reach their village, when she becomes the special property of her individual captor, who may sell or gamble her away when he likes. . . . She is also beaten, mutilated, or even killed, for resistance. . . ."

Dunn quoted from an article in the *Rocky Mountain News* on the meeting of the settlers and Colonel Chivington. His *speech was received with an applause from every pioneer which indicated that they, to a man, heartily approved the course of the colonel twenty years ago, in the famous affair in which many of them took part, and the man who applied the scalpel to the ulcer . . . in those critical times, was beyond a doubt the hero of the hour.*

"This is the simple truth," wrote Dunn. "Colorado stands by Sand Creek, and Colonel Chivington soon afterwards brought his family to the Queen City of the Plains, where his remaining days may be passed in peace.

"What an eventful history! And how, through it all, his sturdy manhood has been manifest in every action. Through all the denunciation of that Indian fight, he has never wavered or trembled. *Others have dodged and apologized and crawled, but Chivington never.*"

Dane Michael White was a survivor waiting to dance in the sun, waiting for the ghost dance and the new world, even in words, and he was a victim who turned his revolution inward to his own end. He died in isolation, sacrificed in a white institution, separated from the mountains and the prairie wind he knew on his walks alone, but he is not now separated from our memories and the memories of the tribal "caretakers of the lands."

TERMINAL CREEDS

All societies, however, stable, face recurrent crises and tensions. The shaman is a kind of social safety valve who dramatizes the disequilibrium and employs techniques to reduce it, not the least of which is the dramatization itself. Like all imaginative acts, the shamanistic seance and ritual make the unknown visible and palpable, transforming anxiety into something manageable by giving it form—a name, a shape, and a way of acting as a consequence of this embodiment.

Eleanor Wilner, *Gathering the Winds*

"American Indians lack a word to denote what we call religion," wrote Åke Hultkrantz in *The Religions of the American Indians.* "Of course, nothing else is to be expected in environments where religious attitudes and values permeate cultural life in its entirety and are not isolated from other cultural manifestations."

Tribal cultures did, however, denote in their languages the separation between what is traditional or sacred and what could be considered secular or profane. Tribal cultures reveal supernatural events and remember the past in oral traditional stories. The tellers of these stories were the verbal artists of the time, those who imagined in their visual memories sacred and secular events. The stories that have been recorded, translated, and printed as scripture, however, have altered tribal religious experiences. Published stories have become the standardized versions, the secular work of methodological academics; the artistic imagination has been polarized in print, and the relationships between the tellers of stories and the listeners, the visual references to the natural world, are lost in translation. The formal descriptions of tribal events by outsiders, such as missionaries, explorers, and anthropologists, reveal more about the cultural values of the observer than the imaginative power of spiritual tribal people.

Shamans and the Clerks

Paul Beaulieu, who served the government as an interpreter and who was one of the first settlers at the White Earth Reservation, told about his "experiences with a *jessakkid*," a shaman or healer, in 1858 at Leech Lake. Beaulieu, a Catholic mixedblood, had little faith in the power of tribal shamans. Reports of the "wonderful performances" of the shaman, wrote Walter James Hoffman in his report, "The Mide wiwin; or 'Grand medicine Society' of the Ojibwa," published by the United States Bureau of American Ethnology, "had reached the agency, and as Beaulieu had no faith in jugglers, he offered to wager $100, a large sum, then and there, against goods of equal value, that the juggler could not perform satisfactorily one of the tricks of his repertoire. . . ." The shaman erected a lodge for the occasion. "The framework of vertical poles, inclined to the center, was filled in with interlaced twigs covered with blankets and birchbark from the ground to the top, leaving an upper orifice of about a foot in diameter for the ingress and egress of spirits and the objects to be mentioned, but not large enough for the passage of a man's body. At one side of the lower wrapping a flap was left for the entrance of the *jessakkid*.

"A committee of twelve was selected to see that no communication was possible between the *jessakkid* and confederates. These were reliable people, one of them the Episcopal clergyman of the reservation. The spectators were several hundred in number, but they stood off, not being allowed to approach.

"The *jessakkid* then removed his clothing, until nothing remained but the breechcloth. Beaulieu took a rope," which he selected for the purpose, Hoffman writes, "and first tied and knotted one end about the juggler's ankles; his knees were then securely tied together, next the wrists, after which the arms were passed over the knees and a billet of wood passed through under the knees, thus securing and keeping the arms down motionless. The rope was then passed around his neck, again and again, each time tied and knotted, so as to bring the face down upon the knees." A flat black stone from a river, the sacred spirit stone of the shaman, "was left lying upon his thighs.

"The *jessakkid* was then carried to the lodge and placed inside upon a mat on the ground, and the flap covering was restored so as to completely hide him from view.

"Immediately loud, thumping noises were heard, and the framework began to sway from side to side with great violence; whereupon the clergyman remarked that this was the work of the Evil One and 'it was no place for him,' so he left and did not see the end. After a few minutes of violent movements and swayings of the lodge accompanied by loud inarticulate noises, the motions gradually ceased when the voice of the juggler was heard, telling Beaulieu to go to the house of a friend, near by, and get the rope.

"Now, Beaulieu, suspecting some joke was to be played upon him, directed the committee to be very careful not to permit any one to approach while he went for the rope, which he found at the place indicated, still tied exactly as he had placed it about the neck and extremities of the *jessakkid*. He immediately returned, laid it down before the spectators, and requested of the *jessakkid* to be allowed to look at him, which was granted, but with the understanding that Beaulieu was not to touch him.

"When the covering was pulled aside, the *jessakkid* sat within the lodge, contentedly smoking his pipe, with no other object in sight than the black stone *manidoo*," or manitou, a spiritual stone. Beaulieu paid his wager of one hundred dollars.

"An exhibition of similar presented powers, also for a wager, was announced a short time after, at Yellow Medicine, Minnesota, to be given in the presence of a number of Army people, but at the threat of the Grand Medicine Man of the Leech Lake bands, who probably objected to interference with his lucrative monopoly, the event did not take place and bets were declared off."

Shamanism and tribal spiritual events were often explained in economic terms, the dominant metaphors of the dominant culture. Others have interpreted tribal religious events from secure carrels in libraries. Christopher Vecsey, for example, wrote in his dissertation, "Traditional Ojibwa Religion and its Historical Changes," that the "Ojibwas have lost their trust in their aboriginal" *manidoog,* or manitou, the spirits, "and in themselves. . . . They have changed many of their religious rituals and today hold very few shaking tent ceremonies . . . their traditional religion no longer exists. . . . They stand between their collapsed traditional religion and Christianity, embracing neither." Vecsey seems to perceive tribal religions as museum artifacts.

William Warren, the mixedblood tribal historian, is more serious in his observations of religious events. In *History of the Ojibway Nation,* he wrote that certain rites have been a secret to the whites. Some tribal healers believe that death would come to those who revealed sacred rituals. "Missionaries, travellers, and transient sojourners amongst the Ojibways, who have witnessed the performance of the grand Me-da-we ceremonies," he wrote with reference to the Midewiwin, "have represented and published that it is composed of foolish and unmeaning ceremonies. The writer begs leave to say that these superficial observers labor under a great mistake. The Indian has equal right . . . to say, on viewing the rites of the Catholic and other churches, that they consist of unmeaning and nonsensical ceremonies. There is much yet to be learned from the wild and apparently simple son of the forest, and the most which remains to be learned is to be derived from their religious beliefs."

Fear of shamanic power and the unknown on the part of white people, and the fear of sorcerers and protection of the sacred on the part of tribal healers, has increased the spiritual separation between white observers and tribal cultures. The distance between these world views is vast; those who venture an explanation rather than a mere description of the spiritual separation seem to reach a critical corner in narrative deductions where tribal cultures come to an end in words. Harold Hickerson, for example, wrote that "Chippewa culture is a shambles, so much have the people everywhere had to accommodate to the new conditions imposed by their relations" with the white world. Nowhere, he asserted in *The Chippewa and Their Neighbors: A Study in Ethnohistory,* does the tribe depend upon goods of their own fashioning; much of the traditional material culture has been lost or "replaced and enriched by the introduction of mass-produced commodities from outside."

The Burial of John Ka Ka Geesick

The distance between tribal cultures and the white world is experienced in more than social science methodologies. One instance of cultural strain and unresolved fear of tribal spiritual rites was witnessed at the funeral of John Ka Ka Geesick, a shaman who died at the age of 124 in Warroad, Minnesota. The shaman and healer was born in 1844 and lived most of his life as a trapper and woodsman on a small land allotment on Muskeg Bay at Lake of the Woods.

The white citizens knew the old shaman from the streets; he walked into town for his supplies, for which he paid cash. John Ka Ka Geesick was known to tourists because he had posed for a photograph from which postcards were printed and sold. He was invented and colonized in the photograph, pictured in a blanket and a turkey feather headdress. On the streets of the town he wore common clothes. The feathered visage encouraged the romantic expectations of tourists. He was a town treasure, in a sense, an image from the tribal past, but when he died the mortician dressed him in a blue suit, with a white shirt and necktie. He was not buried in buckskin; he was decorated in a padded coffin, while the citizens of the town planned a ceremonial public funeral in the Warroad School Gymnasium.

Ka Ka Geesick was a man of visions and dreams; his music and world view connected him to a tribal place on the earth. He was secure at the center of his imagination and memories; in a sense, he was in a spiritual balance, blessed to live so long. The world around him, however, invented his culture and advertised his images on picture postcards. The mock headdress, and the standard burial practices, were new forms of colonization. The eldest of the tribe was possessed in photographs and public services to his grave.

Ka Ka Geesick, his legal name, is derived from *gaagige giizhig*, which means *forever* and *day*, or everlasting day, a phonetic transcription from the oral tradition of the Anishinaabeg.

Tribal people were not invited to plan the public celebration in the town. Several tribal families, however, summoned a shaman for traditional burial ceremonies. The white mortician was nervous; he was not accustomed to so much touching of the body. Later, when the coffin was closed, the mortician seemed relieved; he seemed to sigh when the coffin was lowered into the cold grave.

Daniel Raincloud, a healer and shaman from Ponemah on the Red Lake Reservation, conducted the tribal burial ceremonies. White people were invited, but none attended the traditional tribal observance. The white citizens of the town waited at a distance, separated from the tribal event by the double doors of the gymnasium. Outside, white people peered through the cracks in the doors.

"What does he have in that bundle?" a white man asked as he stepped back from the door. The shaman carried a medicine bundle.

"I really never thought there were any medicine men left," said a white woman to the others near the crack in the door.

Inside, Raincloud shook a small rattle; the sound seemed to settle the angular and uncomfortable space at the end of the gymnasium. The tribal men around the coffin sang an honoring song, and then the shaman spoke in a sacred language to *gaagige giizhig*, a path in words and music to the spirit world. Then he placed a pair of red cotton gloves and some tobacco in the coffin while the traditional elders in the circle opened a bundle that contained small finger sandwiches for the burial feast. Packages of cigarettes were opened. Raincloud pointed in the six directions, and then he passed the sandwiches to those present. The coffin was closed and turned several times on the pedestal to free the spirit of *gaagige giizhig*. They smoked cigarettes, shared the tobacco in a sacred time and place with the old shaman before he moved to the spirit world.

When the tribal burial ceremonies ended, the doors of the gymnasium were opened and the space which had been settled with the sound of a rattle was now trembling with the sound of an organ. Christian hymns replaced tribal music, and a white evangelist delivered a passionate eulogy about a man he had never seen inside his church.

John Ka Ka Geesick was buried next to his brother Na May Puk in the Highland Park Cemetery. Several tribal elders stood around the grave in the fresh snow, their feet close to the coal fires that had thawed the earth. The gravediggers waited at a distance, eager to fill the hole before the fresh soil froze.

Cora Katherine Sheppo

Shamanism is an uncommon religious experience that is not limited in time, place, or culture. The shaman is a person who dissolves time, establishes an ecstatic relationship with the spirit world, and learns to speak the languages of animals, birds, and plants. The shaman is a soul or spirit doctor who heals through ecstasies and contact with spirits and unusual forces in the world; the cause of most diseases is understood to be an imbalance in the individual and the world. Shamans, and other healers who have been identified as "medicine men" in the white world, seek to balance the forces in the world through ecstatic experiences: music, herbs, dreams and visions, and ceremonial dances.

There are two souls in the traditional woodland tribal world view: One is a "free soul" that travels in shadows and dreams, and the second soul is centered in the heart, the place of consciousness and emotional experiences. The "free soul" can be separated and lost.

Åke Hultkrantz pointed out that the "notion that a human being may be struck by enchantment or sorcery is quite common," in tribal cultures, and as "a rule the agent of diseases is a supernatural factor, and among the most widespread causes given for disease we may note enchantment, transgression of a taboo, intrusion of foreign objects or beings, and soul loss." The shaman who has experienced symbolic death, and who can dissolve familiar time and visit the dead, has the spiritual power to heal a person who suffers from soul loss. The tribal diagnosis of soul loss, Hultkrantz explained, "presupposes that the sick man's soul, generally the free soul, of its own free will or by force has left the body. At times it may have wandered off into the natural surroundings; at other times it may have been carried away by malevolent spirits, especially the dead. In such cases it is up to the shaman to send his own soul or less often, one of his guardian spirits, to retrieve the runaway soul. . . . Shamanic tales from various places describe how the shamans battle for life and death with the inhabitants of the other world, and how they are pursued by the dead on the return journey. . . ."

Cora Katherine Sheppo told the court psychiatrist that she smothered her grandchild because he had been "spawned by the devil." She said she heard a voice speak to her grandchild when she pushed a pillow down over his face. Bubas would not die, she explained with tears and fear in her eyes; he seemed to be given strength from evil forces. "It was like he could breathe right through the pillows."

Cora Sheppo wrapped her grandchild in a Pendleton blanket with an "Indian" design and delivered him dead to the Minneapolis Children's Hospital a few blocks from her apartment. When the medical doctor uncovered the child he found two ceremonial willow sticks in his chest.

Bubas, his affectionate nickname, was baptized Tenetkoce Yahola. The child, on the afternoon of his death, was dressed in blue cotton overalls which were pulled down to the diaper at his waist. His left foot was bare, the hightop white shoe turned to the wrong side. A small bustle, with two eagle feathers, a ceremonial wooden tomahawk, a white plastic crucifix, and other religious icons were beside him on the colorful wool blanket. Tenetkoce, a tribal name, was born March 21, 1979, in Clairmore, Oklahoma. Twenty months later he was dead; and on November 4, 1980, his grandmother was arrested and charged with murder. Two months later, following a court-ordered psychiatric evaluation, Cora Sheppo waived her right to a jury trial and was found not guilty by reason of mental illness; she was committed to a state mental hospital.

Carl Malmquist, a psychiatric consultant to the district court, interviewed Cora Sheppo for several hours while she was detained in jail, and concluded in his diagnosis that the defendant suffered from a "schizophrenic disorder, paranoid type," which, according to definitions in a psychiatric lexicon, means that a person has "disturbances of thought, mood, and behavior . . . alterations of concept formation that may lead to misinterpretation of reality . . . " with the "presence of grandiose *delusions,* often associated with *hallucinations.*" Cora, a mixedblood, who was forty-two years old at the time of her arrest for murder, had lived at Lac du Flambeau, Wisconsin, as a child, and later in Chicago. She has relatives who live in Kansas and Oklahoma. Cora has three children: two sons, Michael and Lauren, and a daughter, Patricia, who is the mother of Tenetkoce Yahola.

Malmquist reported to the court that Cora Sheppo "has bizarre delusions and thoughts of being controlled by external forces of the devil, and evil powers outside her. There is a feeling of her being split in terms of an external force being in control of her actions, and on that basis, her feeling is that this other-worldly force is responsible for what she felt compelled to do . . . she was required to rescue her grandson from a greater evil by killing him."

Malmquist made it clear in his evaluation that he had "no qualifications or background pertaining to Indian religious practices. I am not acquainted with any contemporary religious ceremonies which require infant sacrifice. . . ."

Julian Silverman has studied acute schizophrenic behavior and shamanic inspiration. He found no significant differences between acute schizophrenics and shamans that "define their abnormal experiences." The differences are found in the "degree of cultural acceptance of a unique resolution of a basic life crisis." In his article, "Shamans and Acute Schizophrenia," Silverman concluded that the "essential difference between the psychosocial environments of the schizophrenic and the shaman lies in the pervasiveness of the anxiety that complicates each of their lives. The emotional supports and the modes of collective solutions of the basic problems of existence available to the shaman," he writes, "greatly alleviate the strain of an otherwise excruciatingly painful existence. Such supports are all too often completely unavailable to the schizophrenic in our culture."

Cora told her daughter and the psychiatrist about the time she was drunk and drove her car off the road at high speed, a suicide attempt. Malmquist reported to the court that "it was after her attempted suicide when she also began to feel that perhaps at one time she had already died. She had an experience of feeling that she was in a tunnel and that someone had put their hands on her shoulders. She stopped and opened her eyes and in front of her was her boyfriend who had died." Loren Valliere, the man she loved, was killed in an auto accident three years earlier. "She recalled hearing him tell her to be good but at the same time, she experienced this as 'death warnings.' She felt it was an invite to rejoin him through death." Valliere and her grandson were born on the same day and month, which she thought was a spiritual connection.

Cora Sheppo was not a shaman, she was not a healer, but her experiences several months before she smothered her grandson have been diagnosed as schizophrenia and seem to be similar to those experiences associated with traditional tribal shamans. She confronted evil forces, she heard voices out of familiar time, and she told the psychiatrist that she had experienced a feeling of death, but her pain and anxieties were not supported in the dominant culture as sacred travel. Perhaps her needs for tribal connections and a sense of spiritual rebirth were manipulated by false healers and certain tribal people with political ambitions, but with incomplete, and sometimes dangerous, visions. The shaman dissolves time and expresses the inspirations of death and rebirth with cultural acceptance; and as a healer the shaman is capable of ecstatic travel in search of lost souls. Cora Sheppo needed a shaman to rescue her soul and save her grandchild.

Michael Harner wrote in *The Ways of the Shaman* that shamanism "is a great mental and emotional adventure, one in which the patient as well as the shaman-healer are involved. Through his heroic journey and efforts, the shaman helps his patients transcends their normal, ordinary definition of reality, including the definition of themselves as ill. The shaman shows his patients that they are not emotionally and spiritually alone in their struggles against illness and death. The shaman shares his special powers and convinces his patients, on a deep level of consciousness, that another human is willing to offer up his own self to help them. The shaman's self-sacrifice calls forth a com-

mensurate emotional commitment from his patients, a sense of obligation to struggle alongside the shaman to save one's self. Caring and
curing go hand in hand."

Patricia Sheppo told William Rouleau, an investigator for the local
county attorney, that her mother had participated in peyote ceremonies but that she had not become serious about tribal spiritual events
until she took part in The Longest Walk, a protest march across the
nation to focus attention on tribal issues. She participated in purification ceremonies in a sweat lodge and she forbore the use of alcohol and
drugs. Cora told the psychiatrist that she had been baptized and
confirmed a Roman Catholic, but, the psychiatrist reported to the court,
"she now liked to think of her religion as being that of a 'traditional
Indian religion.' I asked her what that involved, and she stated they are
always obedient to the Creator, and people have it written into them in
terms of how they are supposed to be. 'We know there's one thing
above all and that's not to criticize. I fall far short from my tendencies
to do bad things like go to taverns and play pool, but I don't drink, lie
or gossip. I would never do anything to dishonor my Lord and Savior.
Morning Star is the son of God. He is Jesus, the light and shining star.
The reservation which I left had very little of the traditional Indian
things left. Nothing has been passed on. All that's left is drinking and I
used to do it, too. All else is forgotten when they drink.'

"It was at that point that I asked," Malmquist reported to the court,
". . . whether she could tell me more about what some of these experiences might have been and if they were connected with the death of
Bubas. She replied, 'He was the spawn of the devil and no one and
nothing will ever change my mind.' She looked directly at me in stating
this, had a look of fixed determination in her eyes, voice and face as she
stated it. It had the tone of being put to me as though asking me to
challenge it since she would never change her mind." Cora said she
realized this on the day her grandson died. "It was not that she had not
been having various thoughts about the devil and evil mixed in with
the 'powers' before that, but rather that until that day, she had felt that
Bubas could be protected by prayer. On that morning she took him out
'into a field' which was apparently a playground near their house.
While at the playground, she prayed with him, asking the Creator for
strength and to save him from the evil one. She would not tell me what
the specific signs were over time that had made her suspect that Bubas
had been 'spawned by the devil,' but she told me she had handled her
suspicions by 'putting them out of my mind by prayer.' She repeated
her conviction that Bubas was spawned by the devil several times. 'I

knew it. I didn't have to be convinced. No one can convince me otherwise.'

"After playing with Bubas in the playground," Malmquist continued in his report to the court, "it dawned on her what she had to do. She put this in terms of going back to her home and taking Bubas upstairs. 'I'd rather have my grandson dead than possessed by the devil. Before that day, I suspected he was spawned by the devil but I put it aside. That day it came out of nowhere. I knew it. I couldn't doubt it. My only regret was that he was my grandson. I would have had to do it to anyone when directed. I don't go around killing little kids.'

"When I asked her why it happened at that particular time, she was not able to tell me, but could only emphasize, as she did many times, that it was overpowering to her and she had not felt able to resist the forces that were making her do it . . . the act was actually under the control of these powers, but it was also done for Bubas. 'All I know is that I was bound and determined to fight for him. He was my grandson and I was doing this for him. When I got into my apartment, I realized right away what I had to do. I couldn't stop until it was done. I wanted to make him sleep as painless as possible. He was going to grow up to be the ultimate power of evil. Only the Creator would have been able to stop him.' She then elaborated her belief that the Creator had picked her to do this job. . . ."

Nelson Sheppo, father of Cora, who lived at Lac du Flambeau, Wisconsin, when he was interviewed, revealed that his daughter had also attended Sun Dance ceremonies. He said that the "Indian religion is something else that a lot of them don't understand, and she don't understand . . . see the Indian religion is strictly believing in the Almighty God. The Holy Spirit they call it. Manitou they call it," or *manidoo.*

"Do you know what that means?"

"Manitou, that's who it is, the Great Spirit. That's God Almighty. See, the Indian never knew Jesus Christ when He was born. They often wondered why that star, bright star. . . . They didn't know what it meant, until the white man come, see. That's what I tell about, like I go on narrating in schools all over the country and I talk about that, see. The Indian didn't know who Jesus Christ was until the white man come."

"You said that she didn't understand the Indian religion?"

"Well . . . to tell the truth she don't understand the drum religion. See, that's the Indian religion, and that's strict. . . . The Indian chief always got up and they said we always ask the Great Spirit to bless us, keep us, that we should be thankful that he gave us everything on this earth that we eat, wild game, wild potatoes, wild turnips, wild celery, all that, everything that's on this earth, that's who gave it to us, the Great Spirit. . . . A lot of professors always say that the Indian went on this hill to talk to the trees maybe, to talk to the rocks, but that's untrue. He goes up there and asks the Great Spirit for blessings. Then, when they used to do that, see."

"Cora didn't understand that . . . ?"

"No, she never . . . I tried to tell her."

Patricia Sheppo told the investigator that she dreamed about the death of her child two weeks before he died. She said she dreamed that he was playing on a slide in a park when "he just died, ya know, and there was nothing I could do about it. . . . I thought the warning was for me to straighten up, ya know, and start spending a lot more time with him . . . and so I started straightening up and then two weeks after that. . . ."

Patricia said that she met the father of her child on The Longest Walk, and that she too became more active in tribal spiritual events. When the investigator asked her if she or her mother had ever come in contact with "bad medicine," she replied that she was not sure. Later, however, she described several unusual events that troubled her enough to remember them. At the Black Hills Alliance, a survival gathering which was held four years ago in South Dakota, Patricia told the investigator about a meeting where the women formed a circle and joined hands. "And then, I don't know, there was a few chants that they were singing, *we are witches, we are women, and there is no beginning, there is no end* . . . that's the way their songs started. And then they were humming, like hummmmm for a real long time, ya know. . . ."

"Is that typical among Indian ladies?"

"No. . . . It was really different, ya know, and I was really, ya know, I thought, what are they doing, ya know, cause I had never . . . I felt really bad because I felt like I had failed trying to get to them about having some self-respect, and right after I got done telling them that, a lot of women started taking off their shirts and walking around braless and stuff, so I just thought wow, ya know, it just kinda blew my mind. . . ."

"What did your mother say about those women?"

"She told me they were witches," she responded.

Earlier in the summer, Patricia said, "a lot of strange things" happened around her apartment where she lived with her son, her mother, and two younger brothers. "Ya know, this really weird black cat started hanging around the house . . . and I didn't like that at all." Once, while she was on a bus, she found a sheet of paper with her name on it, and "it just totally freaked me out because of all the strange things" that had happened. Cora told her to burn the paper.

"What did your mother think it was?"

"My mom thought it was some people trying to get at me, ya know," she told the investigator. "Like the cult or something trying to get me. . . . I am a really strong person, ya know, as far as willpower is concerned. . . . I really couldn't understand why they would be wanting to get at me, ya know."

Patricia and the father of her child were concerned about the adverse influences of a cult; a friend and tribal counselor was invited to search their apartment for possible causes of "bad medicine." The counselor said in an interview with an official investigator for the county that he purified himself with sage before he entered the apartment. "We were looking for a red jacket. . . . One of the methods in bad medicine is the exchange of some kind of clothes. . . . We had located the red jacket and in the pocket of that jacket we also found dried fish from the smoked fish that was placed in their freezer. . . . Cora had told Patty not to eat that fish at all," because it was "being used against them. . . ." The counselor said he also found a "willow wreath that was wrapped like it was some kind of a crown." He also found a pouch filled with a substance similar to tobacco but not a known hallucinogenic plant, and a small painted stick which was believed to be used in adverse medicine practices. "At that point we were instructed to burn these objects by the medicine man so that these objects would not influence any more people. . . ."

Cora told the tribal counselor a month after she had smothered her grandchild that there was something in the apartment. Before the incident, the counselor reported, "she was feeling something in that house. . . . She was hoping that Patty would come home immediately to help her through this thing. She told me that she was feeling somewhat better when she went outside. She went back into the house and I asked her which room in the house . . . did you feel this thing happen. . . . Where did it happen? She told me in the living room. At that point, I told her that there was medicine that was near that living room and in fact we had found different medicines in different rooms. . . . I believe she told me she placed the child on the floor. . . . she said she had tried to stab the baby in the stomach . . . but she said she hit something that sounded like a metal plate. . . . I believe she said she tried to choke this thing, this being with her hands, but when she got her hands around the being's neck the being started getting larger. That its neck muscles started bulging and she felt or saw that this thing was expanding in nature. Pulsating, so as to speak. . . . She was leading up to the point where she used the Sun Dance stakes. . . . [She said] I was using these sacred objects to drive out and kill that spirit, that devil, that being. And she said that is when it died, when I used the Sun Dance stakes. She said these Sun Dance stakes were sacred, they are powerful. I got those from the Sun Dance, they're powerful. She said people, a lot of people won't understand that. . . ."

Patricia was at college that afternoon when she was told her child was in the hospital. She remembered her dream two weeks earlier about his death as she hurried to be at his side. "I just *screamed*, and I seen my mom and I asked her what happened? 'What happened to my baby?' and she said, 'Pat, I don't know.' I said, 'I want to see him, I want to see my baby,' and so I went into this room, the emergency room, and then I seen him laying there, with the sticks in him, and I didn't know what to do. God, all I'd do was hold him and tell him how much I loved him, you know, and, and I said the words *I love you so much*, and I couldn't understand why, why it happened. . . ."

SHADOWS AT LA POINTE

> I believe that all narration, even that of a
> very ordinary event, is an extension of
> the stories told by the great myths that
> explain how this world came into being
> and how our condition has come to be
> as we know it today. I think that an in-
> terest in narration is part of our mode of
> being in the world. . . . And man will
> never be able to do without listening to
> stories.
>
> Mircea Eliade, *Ordeal by Labyrinth*

This morning the lake is clear and calm.

Last night a cold wind washed slivers of ice clear over the beach, the end of a winter to remember. Now, the pale green becomes blue on the horizon. Spring opens in the birch, a meadow moves in the wind. The trees thicken down to the water, an invitation to follow the sun over the old fur trade post to a new world of adventures.

We are late for school.

The slivers of ice that marked the first cattails melt. The sun is warmer on our cheeks. We turn from side to side, new wild flowers. In the distance a thin banner of smoke rises from the first steamer of the season.

We wait on the beach near the dock.
The sand is smooth and cold under our fingers.
MARGARET CADOTTE
ANGELICK FRONSWA

In large block letters we print our names down to the cold water rim, our last names hold back the flood. We are certain that the people who come here on the steamer to visit this island will notice our names and remember that we were here first and late for school. We will be remembered in the future because we boarded the first steamer that followed the sun in our dreams. Someone will tell stories that we were the first mixedbloods on the island, a new people on the earth, and that our names would last forever because we learned how to read and write in a mission school.

Last week when we were late for school, we heard the old men tell stories about the hard winters on the island in the past, a sure message that one more winter had ended. We sat near the old woodstove in the American Fur Company store, painted bright red outside, and listened to the men catch their words in their wrinkled hands. We listened to stories about hard times, adventures on the trail, white men in the bush, and disasters on the lake. The fur trade had changed from the old days remembered in the stories when there were more animals. The market and the animals moved to a new place on the earth; the animals in tribal dreams were weakened by white politics, diseases, competition, and new fashions, but there are hundreds of barrels of fish and corn stored from the last season to feed a population of more than six hundred people. The men in the fur business, the missionaries and their wives, about fifteen people on the island, were white. The rest were tribal people, and more than half were mixedblood families.

We remembered the stories:

Eliza Morrison, mixedblood wife of the hunter and trader John Morrison, was born in November 1837 at La Pointe on Madeline Island. "As I remember," she wrote in an autobiographical letter, "there used to be thirty seven houses on the flats, all of them made of round logs roofed with cedar bark.

"My uncle built a house alongside of ours. For a period of thirty years he was one of those who traded with the Chippewas off to the north and west. They used to get goods from the Company to go out and establish their posts during the winter. They would be gone eight months from home each year and would return quite late in the spring. They used dogs, when they had them. My uncle told me that the Indians would not sell dogs, but they would hire them out to those who were trading with the Indians. The dogs were very large. I used to see some of them brought in. They were yellow, had long hair, and looked like wolves.

"When I was a girl the Chippewas used to come to La Point to be paid off by the government. To my knowledge the largest payment made was eighteen dollars a head. Thousands of Indians came to the island at one time for pay. I used to be very afraid of them. Our folks used to keep us from school while payments were made."

Later, she and her husband moved to Spider Lake near Iron River, Wisconsin, deep in the woodland. She wrote about the hard winters and construction of the first railroad in the area. "My husband feared that we would have to go without bread before spring. . . ." Her husband and eldest son had to leave to find food. "I made up my mind that if they were not back by the time our provisions were consumed I would first kill the chickens to keep my children from starving. . . . When I thought about those hard times my grandmother had, I wondered what would happen to my children and me should my husband and boy fail to get through to Ashland. . . . We had only enough grub for two more meals, small ones at that," when they returned with provisions.

"When the snow got too deep for hunting, my husband began tanning deerskins to have them ready to sell. We both took time to teach our boys to read. We had some friends who would send us books.

"I would say it is hard for me to write a history of my forest life in English. My husband and I would talk to one another in Chippewa, but to our children we spoke in English as much as we could. My husband had a chance to go to school to learn to read and write. He can write in English and in Chippewa if necessary, and he can also talk French when it comes to that. . . . Thirty years ago, about two out of every ten Indians could speak English. Now three-fourths of them can speak English," she remembers from the turn of the century, when she first wrote about her experiences, "but when I see their complexion I feel like using my native language to talk with them. They are pretty well civilized, but there are some who still follow the medicine dance, the pen names, and other old habits.

"The Indians in this vicinity are selling the timber off their allotments. This enables them to live in good houses. Not one family lives in a wigwam anymore. There is a big sawmill here where they can buy lumber. Some have large gardens and sell vegetables to the whites. They hunt in the fall and gather wild rice. And it is a great place for hunting ducks in the spring and in the fall.

"I have nothing more to write. I might say that I have almost consumed the history of my life. Well, I believe this is the end of my story." Eliza died at age eighty-three.

Provident people were seldom without food on the island, we were told time and time again in school. The old tribal mixedbloods remembered that gospel, the one about being civilized, in their slowest stories at the fire. The men turned one to the other, like ceremonial birds around the stove, and winked, pulled at their ears, winked more, smiled some, and then looked down in silence at the stove. The stove seemed human, a listener: the fire cracked on, a wind-checked side of white pine inside, while the old men waited for the first steamer of the season to reach the dock.

We listened to more stories:

One man pulled at his beard and told about the little people on the island. He crouched forward in his chair and measured with his slender hands, floor to nose, "those little fellows were no more than three feet, not one of them could see over the packs they carried with a tumpline across their foreheads.

"These little people were covered with tattoos, one mark for all the fur posts between Montreal and Fort Pierre, and they drank dark rum mixed with wine on the trail," the old man said as he leaned back in his chair and aimed his long finger past his ear, behind him, toward the east. The visitors followed the direction of his finger. "Back there, clear across the widest angle of the lake you can smell those little pork eaters coming upwind a week ahead in a rain storm . . . the smell of pork moves quicker than the eye of a crow."

A stout mixedblood under a wide fur hat told about the time when government agents from the East sent saddles to the woodland, because they thought that all tribal people must ride horses. "A thumb rider in a wild east show shipped us a dozen saddles, so as, no doubt, we could catch rabbits from above.

"One of the missionaries found two horses and tried to teach us to ride," said the old trapper. He never changed his focus from the base of the stove as he spoke. He seemed to growl when he spoke, between phrases, even single words at times, he ground his front teeth together. "The best we could do was cut four holes in a canoe and teach the horses to paddle."

Then a wizened old mixedblood with a smart smile, like a mongrel on a trap line, clapped his hands, pulled up his sleeves to reveal dozens of tattoos dedicated to his wives. "And then some," he added, and all the old men laughed around the stove in the American Fur Company store. When he turned down his sleeves his face turned sallow. He looked into the fire and told about the time he was mentioned in a printed book.

"Thomas Loraine McKenney came through these parts on his tour to the lakes," the mixedblood said as he leaned forward in his chair, the hard wooden chair creaked. The old men and visitors were silent. The fire snapped. "We called the place Michael's Island then, and this McKenney was a demanding fellow with swift eyes and a nervous hand, he must have come from a place where people salute too much. . . . Anyway, he wrote about an old fisherman on the island, sixty-nine years of age, and active as a boy," the old man remembered. He reached into his inside shirt pocket and removed a folded sheet of paper, a page from a book. "Here is what he wrote," the old man said as he began to read. The visitors who had arrived that morning on the steamer shifted their feet on the rough wooden floor, impressed that the old mixedblood could read, and fine print at that.

"His pulse beats only twenty-five strokes in a minute. On his legs, and arms, and breast are tattooed the marks of superiority in his profession, which had been that of a voyageur, and it seems he excelled in carrying packages across the portages, both on account of their weight and the celerity of his movement. . . . On questioning him as to his former life, he said with a slap of the hands, 'he had been the greatest man in the Northwest.'"

"That man," said the old mixedblood as he folded with care the book page and returned it to his pocket, "is me, the greatest man in the Northwest." He opened his shirt and there beneath the thin strands of white hair on his chest, like a sleet storm, was a faded sunset scene on a lake with two crude loons and a canoe.

The third old mixedblood at the American Fur Company store that morning told true stories about the tall people who came from the East. The tall people, he explained to the visitors, never trusted the little people because some little people pretended to be tall people, mocked the tall people in their dances. Tall people never pretend to be little, no matter how far their fortunes fall. Tall people are white, educated, they march and give orders, sweat in dark clothes, and hold pet birds in house cages. The little people are mixedbloods who wear bright colors, dance and dream out of time, trick their friends, animals and birds, in good humor.

"Henry Rowe Schoolcraft was a tall person," the old mixedblood revealed. "He was more than eight feet tall in the cold, even when he slouched. The little people, the pork eaters, had to stand on a trunk or a fence rail to speak in similar space. Schoolcraft was a geologist, a government agent, treaty commissioner, who explored the sacred copper regions of the tribes with Lewis Cass, the territory governor of Michigan.

"Schoolcraft believes he found the sacred copper back on the Ontonogan River but he was mistaken. The shamans planted a chunk of mined copper there; the explorer thought that he had discovered more than the next white man, which made him taller. With the copper find he sprouted an additional inch back East, an inch less in the tribe. He remained the same height when he tried to change the name of this place to Virginia Island. Madeline, the mixedblood wife of Michel Cadotte, remained the favorite name, the place name on the maps.

"He also asked tribal people, even a few mixedbloods, where to find the source of the Mississippi River. He asked his way and then revealed his discoveries back East. He lost three inches there, gained one back in humor, but he took on six more inches back East for the river find. He was a giant then, and it was time to find a mixedblood wife from the wilderness. He did just that, in the daughter of John Johnson, the fur trader from La Pointe. Johnson, who was Irish, married the daughter of Waubojeeg, or Chief White Fisher.

"Schoolcraft gained back a few inches with his marriage, but lost more than a foot when he became an expert on the 'red race' and when he invented the 'Algic tribes,' as he called us out here. This copper hunter learned all he knew about tribal people from his mixedblood relatives, but he gives them no credit for his discoveries.

"When Schoolcraft was the United States Indian agent at Mackinac he came to the island for another visit. We saw him down at the dock, eight to nine feet tall, white people all stood on stools and stilts to shake his enormous hand, as if his hand was a healing animal from a strange place.

"When the tall man died," said the old man in a loud voice to hold the ears of the visitors, "the tribe made a grave house for him about four feet long and put it out behind the mission in the weeds, but back East, we were told, the tall man was buried in a ten foot coffin. . . . Some tell that his coffin is two feet longer since his death, and still growing. . . . The grave house out here has become a bird nest, and even smaller."

The visitors soon departed from the store, ears filled, to conduct their business with the traders, the coopers, and the brownstone cutters, before the steamer departed from the island. Later, the visitors learned that they left the store too soon and missed the best stories about tall people by the old mixedblood with the tattoos. While he told his stories he did a striptease around the stove, exposed all his tattoos but three.

"The second time we heard that tall man with the nervous hands, Thomas Loraine McKenney, that talk and walk man, was out at the American Fur Company post at Fond du Lac," said the mixedblood as he danced in slow motions around the fire. "McKenney was twelve feet tall there, three feet taller than he was when he discovered and wrote about me on the island, twelve feet tall no less; we knew this because the soldiers packed him there flat in a *canot du nord* with room enough for a brass band. Flags and his wild red hair, red as the outside of this store, waved from shore to shore.

"When a man speaks from three sides of his mouth at once, a special number in the government service," said the mixedblood as he danced, "you know he is twelve feet tall and from the East because the little people are three feet tall and it took two of them, one on top of the other, to even shake his hand.

"That twelve foot red said from one side of his mouth that we were his equals, from another side he told us we were children, and from the third side of his mouth he said we were savages. No telling how a mixedblood would be parted in his mouth.

"We never forgot the old red threat and what he said and wrote about the tribes," said the little mixedblood who had removed his coat and shirt to reveal a second time the scenic tattoo on his chest.

McKenney and Governor Lewis Cass, who was much taller than the red one, told us that we were "the worst clad and the most wretched body of Indians" that he ever met with. . . . He said we were "wandering savages who inhabit the sterile and unhospitable shores of the northern lakes . . . the most miserable and degraded of the native tribes. . . . They have little ambition and few ideas . . . ," which was what we wanted the tall people in the government to think about us because when the tall ones admire a tribe, the people become pets and lose their land, their shadows, and their humor.

"We laughed and laughed and danced and dreamed about the tall ones in white water, too tall to fit in their canoes," chanted the old mixedblood as he danced. He did not remove his trousers, but he did fold up the legs to reveal several tattoos in honor of his wives and children and fur post encounters with the tall people. "The canoes turn and the tall logs shoot the rapids, turn wide, dam the rivers, and stop the white water . . . for a time."

"The tall red one spoke to us at Fond du Lac, his words rolled like logs in white water, he demanded that we produce the murderers of four white people," said the mixedblood who stopped his dance and stood erect about four feet tall near the stove. "So we did that, we named four tribal people, and hundreds more who had been murdered by white soldiers and settlers . . . we danced in the dark and named the dead until morning.

"McKenney was not pleased with us, and as he spoke he got smaller and smaller, his lips rolled at a great distance when he told us that 'this is not a thing to pass away like a cloud,' so we named more dead and danced for all those who died at the hands of the tall people. 'If they are not surrendered then,' the tall red one continued, *'destruction will fall on your women and children.* Your father will put out his strong arm. Go, and think of it. Nothing will satisfy us but this.'

"We danced until he disappeared in the distance, a small animal on the run, too small to notice, then in a swarm of transparent flies he vanished," the old mixedblood concluded as he resumed his dance around the stove. Animals and dream figures, faces from the little people in his past, sagged and shivered on the calves of his thin legs.

Richard Drinnon, in *Facing West: The Metaphysics of Indian-Hating and Empire-Building*, wrote about the arrival of Colonel Thomas McKenney, who was "tall and had a military carriage and a shock of red hair," and the other white commissioners at the American Fur Company post at Fond du Lac on July 28, 1826: The expedition, a squadron of barges and canoes which contained a detachment of soldiers, a company band, and staff assistants, "stretched out over a quarter mile, all in order, and 'all with flags flying, and martial music,'" according to the memoirs of the commissioner. "Ashore the troops drilled each morning and were inspected by General Cass and Colonel McKenney, with the latter in his militia uniform. . . ."

McKenney, with more on his mind than land and treaties, demanded that the tribe "produce the alleged murderers of four whites. 'It is a serious matter,' he declared, and unless they obeyed 'you will be visited with your great father's heaviest displeasure. No trader shall visit you—not a pound of tobacco, nor a yard of cloth, shall go into your country. This is not a thing to pass away like a cloud.' Spokesmen for the band under suspicion replied it was difficult to speak for their absent tribesmen."

The man who threatened the tribe, Drinnon wrote, "is perhaps better described as high-handed rather than high-minded. . . . McKenney confidently expected the destruction of tribal cultures. . . . He severed the family connections of his 'little Indians,' used mission schools to batter tribal relations, and by stripping away native languages sought to cut off all ties between generations." McKenney, who was celebrated by some as a champion of tribal reform, was appointed as the head of the new Bureau of Indian Affairs, which was then under the War Department.

We were late for school:
Abigail Spooner was our teacher at the first mission school on Madeline Island. She had a voice that hurt on a spring afternoon, but she worked ever so hard to teach us how to read and write. We were mixedbloods, halfbreeds, neither here nor there to some. Abba, as she was known to friends and families on the island, promised that we could establish in the wilderness a new civilization with books. We had some books, not many, and an occasional magazine passed from house to house, which we shelved in a special place in the corner of the schoolroom. The other books on the island were owned by Lyman Marcus Warren and Truman Warren. The brothers were married to Mary and Charlotte Cadotte, the mixedblood daughters of Michel Cadotte, who was an educated man and was once the factor at the fur post. These families, educated in the east with the tall people, were important; we did not ask to borrow their books to make *our* civilization.

Abba said, "if not now, then at the right time in heaven, the last and perfect civilization for those who believe and are righteous." We believed her then, but most of the time we found real evidence of the civilized world down at the store and at the American Fur Company dock when the steamers arrived with mail, supplies, and visitors.

"The girls with bead pantalets, porcupine moccasins, new blue broadcloth shawls, plaited hair and clean faces looked almost good enough to kiss," noted Charles Penny, who had accompanied the geologist Douglass Houghton on an expedition in search of copper. He visited the island and admired the mixedblood and tribal women of all ages.

Sherman Hall, the superintendent of the school at La Pointe, wrote a letter to a government agent that the teachers have continued their "labors as usual, endeavoring to instruct all who were willing to receive instruction from us, in the duties and doctrines of the Christian religion, and in letters. . . .

"The school during the year has numbered sixty-five different scholars, forty-three males, and twenty-two females. It has been kept in operation regularly during the year, except the usual vacations. . . . The proficiency of the scholars who have been regular attendants is very satisfactory. The branches taught have been spelling, reading, writing, arithmetic, geography and composition. The scholars are taught in the Ojibwa and English languages. The schools are open and free to all who choose to avail themselves of their privileges, no charge being made for books or other expenses. During the past year the Ojibwa and English spelling book, mentioned in my last report as being nearly ready for use, has been introduced into the schools, and used, it is believed, with good effect."

Sherman Hall was a Presbyterian who dedicated his time to the conversion of the tribes, even the mixedbloods. He arrived on the island with his wife and a tribal woman who was once married to a fur trader. Reverend Hall started the mission and the school, and the tribal woman served as his interpreter.

This was not as simple as it might appear, because most of the mixedblood families and the children in the school, like us, were Roman Catholic. This seemed to trouble Reverend Sherman more than the tribal ceremonial dances on the island. He was, at times, critical of Catholics, and once or twice we were released from school to receive our religious instruction. He complained in a letter to his father, who lived back East, that the boatmen and laborers in the fur trade, who were, for the most part, Canadian French and Catholic, "may be as wicked as they choose; the priest can pardon all their sins when they go to Mackinac next year. He will do it, if they pay him a few shillings. I have more fears that the Catholics will cause us difficulties, than the Indians will."

Reverend Hall and his wife were separated from their culture and families in the East. The two of them seemed to be lost, without shadows, with no humor to throw at the weather. Their isolation turned into a dedication to convert the tribes. Sometimes, we whispered, it was the missionaries who needed to be saved. We lived in a world of comedies, thunderstorms, chances like a flight of passenger pigeons over the lake, and surprises, dreams about whales in a fish barrel. Some of our friends think it is strange to find pale, weak and shadowless, individual church heroes, in the middle of old woodland families. The biblical stories were fun to tell, the old men turned them over in the oral tradition. The moral lessons that end in words end in comedies. These missionaries were never loons, never bears, their wives and mothers were never killdeers on the shoreline. We were animals and birds, even when we were converted, and that was the difference between culture and civilization. We once spoke the language of animals, the missionaries were caught in wordwinds.

Reverend Hall, of course, was proud of his religion but he was disappointed with the tribes. We could all tell when he was displeased with us because two small muscles would twitch on his face. He liked us, he spoke our names from time to time when he visited the schoolroom, and he even called us scholars in his reports. He said our names were in his reports and that we would be known in the government. We knew he cared more for us and other mixedblood families at La Pointe than he did for the tribal families on Chequamegon Point and the Bad River Reservation. He reported to a government agent that the mission school there was "discontinued for want of scholars. . . . We regret to see so little interest taken by these Indians in the subject of education. Most of them attach little or no importance to having their children instructed. I have been informed that many of the head men have expressed a desire to have their school money divided among them, as their other annuities are, that they might expend it in the same way. . . .

"In some respects these Indians are improving. Many of them are adopting partial habits of civilization. This is more and more apparent every year in their mode of dress, in their efforts to procure houses to live in, and in their enlarging their gardens and small fields. Many are much more industrious than formerly, and are much less disposed to depend on the same precarious modes of obtaining the means of subsistence, which almost universally prevailed among them formerly. These changes are most apparent among the younger portion of them.

"If the right kind of influences are brought to bear upon them, and they can be shielded from the degrading and destroying evils of intoxicating drink, I do not see why they may not eventually become a civilized and happy people. This however must be the work of time, and will require much perseverance on the part of those who are disposed to live among them for the purpose of teaching them letters, the arts, and the Christian religion."

M A R G A R E T   C A
A N G E L I C K   F R O
The narrow waves from the wake of the streamer washed over the last few letters of our names printed in the sand. We collect names and words, some are secrets, but we take much more time to remember the clothes that visitors wear, their hats and shoes and coats. The trunks on the dock, unloaded from the steamer, capture our attention for hours.

We imagine the contents of the arriving trunks, and we dream we are on an adventure to the cities inside the departing trunks.

When Reverend Hall and his wife first arrived, the content of their trunks and boxes became the talk of the island, but the secrets lasted for a few minutes at the most because they owned little more than their simple clothes. The Warren families gave them some furniture, a washbowl and stand, chairs, tables, and a bedstead, for their little house. "It is not the deprivation of the conveniences of life," he wrote to his friends back east, "that makes us feel more sensibly that we are in a heathen land. It is the want of society. There are not more than three or four, besides our own family, with whom we can communicate in our native tongue at this place."

Madeline Island is our tribal home, the place where the earth began, the place that first came back from the flood. Naanabozho, the trickster, was born here, on this island; the old men told us he was the first little person in the world. He stole fire from across the lake. We are little people. This is our place on the earth, this place is in our bodies, in our words, and in our dreams. Our new names, there in the sand, hold back the next flood, but nothing holds back the tall people who come from the East. Naanabozho must have stolen fire from them; now the tall white people are here and they want the whole earth back as punishment.

Even so, we love to watch white visitors and the dark trunks that come on the steamer from the East, and to listen to the stories at the American Fur Company store across from the dock.

Abba Spooner will think we are late because we were making maple sugar, or something, or we could tell her that we were with the priest for religious instruction.

The Catholic church is located behind the American Fur Company store and warehouses. A high stockade fence surrounds a fruit and vegetable garden and separates the sacred from the secular commercial world of the tall people. The priest lives near the church in a small house built of hewn logs because frame houses are much too expensive to build on the island. The cemetery is next to the church.

A visitor to the island told about how the little people buried the dead in grave houses. "On the whole, it can be truly said that they have more regard for the dead than many whites have. The pagans used to bury various articles used by the deceased during life, also place tobacco or sugar on the grave, or in the drawer made for that purpose in the little house built over the grave. But these customs are falling into disuse more and more. A peculiar feeling or sadness and pity seizes one in passing a pagan grave-yard. . . ."

White children, sons of the missionaries, would raid the grave houses at night and steal the food, a confection with cooked wild rice and maple sugar, the little people placed there.

Right Reverend Frederic Baraga, an Austrian sent by the Leopoldine Society in Vienna, was not welcomed by the lonesome ministers on the island. The first mission resisted encroachment and hoped that Henry Rowe Schoolcraft, the government agent, would refuse the priest a "license of residence." Schoolcraft did not respond; the priest moved to the island and built a church in less than two weeks. During the summer, as if his time there was limited, Father Baraga had baptized more than a hundred mixedbloods and tribal people.

Reverend Sherman Hall wrote to the secretary of the American Board of Commissioners for Foreign Missions in Boston—the little people were considered foreign—that "the Catholics were not prejudiced against the mission school. The priest stationed here encourages their attendance."

Father Francis Pierz, who had established missions at several fur trade posts in the woodland, visited the island that summer. He admired the garden behind the fur post and, of course, the new church and mission. His neck and back caused him pain as he walked. No one seemed to notice, so eager were they to present their accomplishments in the wilderness. He blessed the children when he passed them and complimented those who worked on the island. Later, in a letter he described his experiences with more candor. "A large trading company has a branch store on this island and it is therefore the rendezvous of many Indians and French-Canadians, all of whom lived like pagans before Father Baraga's arrival.

"At first this pious missionary had to contend with many difficulties and hardships, but with his customary, persevering energy and apostolic zeal he soon formed out of these rude, wild barbarians a very large Christian congregation, which continues to grow daily through new conversions. To his great joy he has completed his beautiful new church and a suitable priest's house with the money he brought with him from Europe. . . .

"As regards my own personal experience, having had many opportunities during my three years' stay among the Indians of several places to watch them, pagans as well as Christians, I can justly assert that they are, as a rule, phlegmatic, good-natured, exceedingly patient and docile, and well disposed to lead a good life. Even in their wild, aboriginal state, when they are removed from bad, scandalous people, they do not live at all wickedly and viciously. They listen eagerly to the priest who comes to them, readily embrace the faith, and allow themselves to be soon transformed into good, steadfast Christians.

"But where the poor Indians have been scandalized by the great vices of white Christians, or have been spoiled by intoxicating liquor, and have been seduced by the enemies of religion and prejudiced against our holy faith, they naturally become far harder to convert and civilize. . . ."

Father Baraga was a little man with enormous conversion plans for the tribe. His dark brown hair bounced in long curls as he walked. He was firm, careful in his speech, and when he was out walking on the road, his short legs moved quicker than a shore bird. He was determined to save souls and he warned the teachers at the mission school that "if they meddle with religion I would order all the Catholic children to leave their schools; and I am watching strictly this observance."

The little priest was troubled by tribal manners and woodland culture. He abhorred the wilderness in their lives, and describes cruelties that he relates to savagism. He praised the little people who followed the cross and disapproved of those tribal people who gathered on the island for government payments. The priest even cursed the tribal dances that healed the soul, restored tribal shadows near tall people, and earned a meal. The missionaries rebuked the presentation of bare flesh, rhythmic body movements, and imaginative face paint. Church strictures soon became government policies. The tribes were not permitted to gather to dance.

Julia Spears, the daughter of Lyman Marcus Warren, would have none of this bad talk from the missionaries about tribal dances. She remembered a more peaceful island than did the missionaries. Julia was also known by her tribal nickname Conians, which means "little money" in translation.

Several thousand tribal people came to Madeline Island from various places around the lake to receive government payments according to agreements in treaties. "That year the Indians received ten dollars a head," Julia Spears wrote, "and each family got a very large bundle of goods. . . . They had rations issued out to them during payment. . . . The day before they would start for their homes they had a custom of going to all the stores and houses and dancing for about one hour, expecting food to be given to them. . . . They went around in different parties of about twenty-five or thirty. A party came to our house at the old fort. We were prepared for them. The day before, we cooked a lot of bread, a lot of boiled salt pork and cookies to give them. They came dancing and hooting. They were naked with breechclothes, their bodies painted with black, red, yellow, vermillion, with all kinds of stripes and figures.

"They were a fierce looking crowd. They were all good dancers. After they were through they sat down on the grass and smoked. We gave them their *wapoo* and they were well pleased. They thanked us and shook hands with us as they left." The word *wapoo*, or *wabo*, from the oral tradition, at the end of some words in *anashinaabemowin* denotes fluid or liquid, as in the word *mashkikiwabo*, a liquid medicine, or *ishkotewabo*, "firewater," or an alcoholic drink, according to *A Dictionary of the Otchipwe Language* by Right Reverend Bishop Baraga who was a missionary on the island at this time more than a century ago. Nichols and Nyholm transcribe the word for liquor as *ishkodewaaboo* in *Ojibwewi-Ikidowinan*.

We waited on the dock near the steamboat until no one was watching and then we climbed into two huge brown trunks with bright brass corners. The sun leaped through thin cracks and seams on the curved truck cover, enough light inside to read our secret maps, the ones we charted with places from all the stories we had heard in the store: all the mixedblood routes and portage places between land and lakes and fur posts.

We were silent, alone, breathless, counting our rapid heart beats past the island view, past the distant shores of the lake and over the picture mountains to the cities in the East. We smelled smoke and imagined a circus show with actors and clowns, but instead it was the trader and his dock hands, the ones with the little pighead pipes, smoking their strong tobacco.

We traveled to Fond du Lac.

We listened.

Shingabaossin, an orator of the Crane family from Sault St. Marie, was the first to speak to the tribal leaders and to the tall white men, Lewis Cass and Thomas McKenney, who were treaty commissioners; and Henry Rowe Schoolcraft, the government agent, and others at Fond du

Lac where hundreds of tribal people came together late in the summer to talk about mixedbloods and minerals.

The tribal orator told about other meetings, and agreed that land should be provided for mixedbloods, and then his voice seemed to disappear on the wind when he said that, "our fathers have come here to embrace their children. Listen to what they say. It will be good for you.

"If you have any copper on your lands," said Shingabaossin in a distant voice as he looked over the commissioners to the western horizon where thunderclouds were blooming, "I advise you to sell it. It is of no advantage to us. They can convert it into articles for our use. If any one of you has any knowledge on this subject, I ask you to bring it to light. . . ."

William Whipple Warren, the mixedblood historian, wrote that Shingabaossin did not mean what was attributed to him in translation. When the orator referred to minerals it was "meant more to tickle the ears of the commissioners and to obtain their favor, than as an earnest appeal to his people, for the old chieftain was too much imbued with the superstition prevalent amongst the Indians, which prevents them from discovering their knowledge of minerals and copper boulders to the whites."

Tribal leaders, nevertheless, signed a treaty there that provided in part that the "Chippewa tribe grant to the government of the United States the right to search for, and carry away, any metals or minerals from any part of their country. . . ." The leaders must have believed in the spiritual power of secrets, the unspoken in the oral tradition, because what is held in secrets cannot be discovered and removed. Copper was located in sacred places, the metal had not been used in the secular production of material possessions. The elders signed an agreement on paper, through a translator, but did not tell the white men where the copper could be found.

Pezeekee spoke that morning to the white men who sat behind tables, dressed in dark clothes. The elder from La Pointe placed his right hand over his left forearm and looked toward Henry Connor, the government interpreter, and watched him write down in translation the words he heard. Pezeekee remembered the wind in the bullrushes and turned his words with care. "The name of a speaker has come down to me from my fathers," he said to the commissioners.

"I will not lie.

"That sun that looks upon me, and these, you red children around me, are witnesses. . . . Our women and children are very poor. You have heard it. It need not have been said. You see it. . . . I lend those who have put me here, my mouth. . . .

"This was given to us by our forefathers," he said as he spread a map on the table before the commissioners and interpreters. "There are few now here who were then living." He directed the tall men at the table to notice certain places on the map, tribal communities, memories in space. Then he looked up from the map and over the heads of the tall men. He spoke to them but did not look into their faces. Small clouds seemed to speak through the white pine on the horizon. "You have deserted *your* country," he told the commissioners, looking past their faces. "Where your fathers lived, and your mothers first saw the sun, there you are not. I am alone, am the solitary one remaining on our own ground. . . .

"I am no chief," Pezeekee said and then paused to listen. "I am put here as a speaker. The gift has descended to me. . . . It will be long before I open my mouth to you again. Listen, therefore, to what I say. I live in one place, I do not move about. I live on an open path, where many walk. The traders know me. None can say I ever looked in his cabin or his canoe. My hands are free from the touch of what does not belong to me. . . ."

Pezeekee recovered his map and there was silence.

Then an old man who did not reveal his tribal name told the commissioners that he did not sell the sacred earth for a peace medal and a flag from the government agents. He was troubled, his voice wavered as he spoke: "You told me to sit still and hold down my head, and if I heard bad birds singing, to bend it still lower.

"My friends held down their heads when I approached. When I turned, bad words went out of their mouths against me. I could not sit still. I left the cabin, and went out alone into the wild woods," the old man said as he looked down from time to time at the weeds. "There have I remained, till I heard of your coming. I am here now, to take you by the hand. . . ."

The commissioners were silent.

Obarguwack moved toward the commissioners at the table. She was in her seventies. Her bones were old, and it took her twice the time to walk and talk than it did when she was younger. She said that she was blessed with her age, to live so long was not a curse, she reminded the commissioners as they watched her slow movements. The wrinkles on her face all seemed to converge at her mouth, and when she spoke, and paused to compose her thoughts, the wrinkles moved from her mouth

like ripples expanding from the place a stone skipped on calm water.
She told the commissioners seated at the table under the trees that she
was representing her husband. "His eyes are shut, but his mouth and
ears are still open," she said and then paused a second time to move a
few more steps closer to the table. "He has long wished to see the
Americans. He hopes now to find something in his cabin.

"He has held you by the hand," she told the tall white men. "He
still holds you by the hand. He is poor. His blanket is old and worn out,
like the one you see." She paused again and moved a few steps closer
to the commissioners behind the table to show them the worn blanket
she mentioned. "But he now thinks he sees a better one."

The commissioners waited in silence for a few minutes until the old
woman moved back from the table and then the meeting was ad-
journed until the next day when a treaty would be prepared for
signatures. The commissioners listened, but what the government
wanted had been decided in advance The experiences of tribal people
were translated from the oral tradition, but there was little more than
condescension in the manners of the commissioners. The simple needs
of the tribes, blankets, a place of peace on the earth, medical assistance,
were no match under the trees in the word wars to locate and possess
minerals and natural resources.

James Otis Lewis drew pictures of the tribal people who spoke and
while the treaty was being read in translation by a government inter
preter. The flags in his pictures were all taller than the trees behind the
table. Colonel Thomas McKenney bumped his knee on the corner of
the table as he sat down, prepared to make histories on paper. He
looked toward the eastern horizon, in the opposite direction of the
tribal people there, with a mark of pain in his face while he listened
and waited. Then he looked toward the artist, finding more to consider
in a face on paper than in tribal events in the oral tradition. He brushed
his thick hair back from his forehead, white strands in the red. Even his
hand in his own hair seemed unnatural that afternoon at Fond du Lac.

We remember article four of the treaty:

*It being deemed important that the half-breeds, scattered through this
extensive country, should be stimulated to exertion and improvement by the
possession of permanent property and fixed residences, the Chippewa tribe, in
consideration of the affection they bear to these persons, and of the interest
which they feel in their welfare, grant to each of the persons described . . . six
hundred and forty acres of land. . . .*

"The objects of the commissioners were easily attained," wrote
William Whipple Warren in his *History of the Ojibway Nation*, "but the

Ojibways, who felt a deep love for the offspring of their women who had intermarried with the whites, and cherished them as their own children, insisted on giving them grants of land on the Sault St. Marie River, which they wished our government to recognize and make good.

"These stipulations were annexed by the commissioners to the treaty, but were never ratified by the Senate of the United States. It is merely mentioned here to show the great affection with which the Ojibways regarded their half-breeds, and which they have evinced on every occasion when they have had an opportunity of bettering their condition."

Eighty-five tribal leaders from fifteen different woodland communities signed their marks beneath the signatures of Lewis Cass and Thomas McKenney to a treaty at Fond du Lac in the presence of fourteen white men, two of whom were official commissioners. The tribal leaders, who were awarded peace medals to remember the occasion, were from La Pointe, Rainy Lake, Lac du Flambeau, Ontonagon, Vermilion Lake, River de Corbeau, and other places. The white men were from the East. John Quincy Adams, then president of the United States, signed the treaty, with the exception of the articles that provided for mixedblood people.

We imagined our names on these treaties, we marked these places on our personal dream maps, places the old mixedbloods told about in their stories around the stove at the store. . . . *To each of the children of John Tanner, being of Chippewa descent. . . . To Charlotte Louisa Morrison, wife of Allan Morrison. . . . To Saugemauqua, widow of the late John Baptiste Cadotte, and to her children Louison, Sophia, Archangel, Edward, and Polly, one section each . . . upon the islands and shore of the Saint Mary river wherever good land enough for this purpose can be found. . . .* Our places on the dream maps, our shadows in the stories.

Slivers of sunlight shivered inside the trunks as we were loaded from the dock to the steamboat. Dock men commented on the weight of the possessions of the tall people from the East. Inside the trunks we listened to conversations on the dock and on the deck of the steamboat as people boarded. Comments on the weather, how severe had been the last winter, arrival times at the next ports and fur posts on the lake. We listened and counted our heartbeats, faster and faster across the lake and over the mountains, in a horse-drawn carriage, alone in the parlour of a tall frame house, a mansion with double lace curtains and with windows in the doors. In each trunk we found a parasol, high button boots, fine clothes, hat boxes, and a small chest with precious stones. We imagined the world at the end of the lake where the steamboat stopped for the last time.

The steamboat whistle sounded several times, breathless at the dock, the last invitation to those still on the shore. The sound of the steam whistle was muffled inside the trunks, and each sound was a new port, a new dock, new faces, places on our dream maps. We walked down each dock beneath new parasols, our shadows traveled across the earth.

The steamboat moved from the dock. We could hear conversations on the side of the deck and we could imagine from the dark interior of the trunks all the people on the dock. Our friends from school were there, the old mixedbloods who would tell stories about us in the store, the little priest, all waving to us as we leave the island for the first time. Our names held back the flood at the first place we knew on the earth. We will be remembered forever.

SCREENPLAY

HAROLD OF ORANGE

Sundance 1983

1 *Ext Harold of Orange Coffee House—Sunrise*

Harold Sinseer rumbles down a dirt road on the reservation in his damaged car, assembled from multicolored parts, and stops in front of a row of small commercial buildings. A bald tire rolls up to the screen; a car door squeaks open, and a foot touches the road. Harold has a round brown face and black hair. His cheeks are full and his relaxed stomach behind the wheel folds over his wide beaded belt about two inches. He is dressed in a ribbon shirt and brown leather vest. He gestures with his lips in the tribal manner when he speaks. The sign "Harold of Orange Coffee House" is painted over the front of the building. Another sign, printed on a pine board, "The New School of Socioacupuncture," is suspended in the window of the storefront. Harold wears well-worn moccasins.

HAROLD (to the camera)   Over there, deep in the brush, the Orange River runs through this reservation as fast as it can down to the wild sea . . . We live at the best loop in the river, a natural high rise on the earth . . .

Harold pauses and then he climbs out of his car. He expands his chest and continues speaking to the camera.

HAROLD   We are the Warriors of Orange, tricksters in the new school of sociocupuncture where a little pressure fills the purse . . . We run a clean coffee house, tend to our miniature oranges, and talk about mythic revolutions on the reservation . . .

Harold pauses; he smiles, an ironic gesture, and then he continues talking to the camera.

HAROLD   C'mon in for a pinch of coffee . . .

1A Int View of Harold Through the Coffee House Window

Harold walks to the back of his car, pries open the trunk, removes several bags of plastic cups and dozens of neckties, and then he turns toward the coffee house. Mongrels sit near the front door as he approaches. There is a small sign near the front door: "What This Country Needs is a Good Injun Tuneup." The sign is weathered and curled at the corners.

2 Int Harold of Orange Coffee House—Morning

Screen is filled with a large photographic silhouette of Harold and Fannie posed like the statue of Hiawatha and Minnehaha. Harold walks into the screen, across the silhouette, and the camera follows him around the coffee house. An aluminum coffee urn rests on top of the table or woodstove in the center of the room. Front and rear doors are open. Mongrels move in and out. Light pours in. The walls and ceiling are covered with photographs and radical broadsides. The Warriors of Orange are seated on boxes and chairs, alone and in pairs, drinking coffee and eating fast food. There are two large pots in the corner, an orange tree in one, and a coffee shrub in the other. Several warriors wear hats, one a painter hat. One warrior is reading the *Wall Street Journal*. Snow shoes are stacked in the corner of the room.

PLUMERO   My god, here he is on mythic time . . .

HAROLD   You got the first part right.

PLUMERO   Where to this mornin, chief?

HAROLD   To the Bily Foundation with our pinch beans . . .

NEW CROWS   Not the old pinch bean scheme?

HAROLD   Nothing but the best, hand picked in the traditional way . . .

Harold unloads the cups and neckties on the table next to the wood-stove. The cups bear the pinch bean coffee label. Son Bear sees the neckties and removes his earphones. Powwow music can be heard through the earphones around his neck.

NEW CROWS   Who'd believe in pinch beans?

LUMERO   The same people who fell for miniature oranges.

SON BEAR   Potted oranges?

Plumero picks an orange from the tree in the pot and throws it to Son Bear. Several warriors turn and laugh.

HAROLD   Our orchard grows in tax free bonds . . .

SON BEAR   Orange bonds?

HAROLD   The source of your allowance.

NEW CROWS   From these trees?

New Crows points toward the potted orange tree in the corner.

PLUMERO   We ordered eight crates from an organic farmer in the southwest . . .

HAROLD   Eight? Thought it was fifteen?

PLUMERO   Too expensive, eight's enough for the foundation directors . . .

Harold pours a cup of coffee into his special orange mug and then he walks backwards around the table as he speaks in a dramatic tone of voice. He picks an orange from the miniature tree.

HAROLD   Now, with miniature oranges in hand, we return with a proposal to open coffee houses on reservations around the world . . .

Plumero reaches into a large bin and pulls out a handful of coffee beans.

PLUMERO   And from these pinch beans comes our mythic revolution . . .

Plumero throws the coffee beans into the air.

SON BEAR   What revolution?

HAROLD   Where there are coffee houses there are tricksters and revolutions . . .

NEW CROWS   Coffee never made no warrior . . .

PLUMERO   Maybe not, but there's more tricksters in Berkeley than Beejimee . . .

HAROLD   Bemidji, Bemidji!

PLUMERO   There too.

Harold sorts through the neckties on the table. Coffee beans crunch under foot. Son Bear points at the neckties.

SON BEAR   What're these for?

HAROLD   The uniform for our foundation pinch bean show . . .

NEW CROWS   Nothin doin . . . Not around my neck.

SON BEAR   The whiteman got white from neckties, stopped the blood to his brains . . .

PLUMERO   You got nothin to loose . . .

NEW CROWS   He cut short more than that . . .

Harold holds up several neckties and admires them with a smile.

SON BEAR   Man, ties'll turn us white . . .

PLUMERO   Those white designer shorts you got never cut short your blood supply.

SON BEAR   But mixedbloods run a higher risk . . .

The warriors laugh, and tease the neckties on the table. One warrior finds a bow tie in the pile, he examines it.

HAROLD   Come on, choose a necktie . . . Loose knots for the mixedbloods.

NEW CROWS   We never did this for the orange money.

HAROLD   The stakes are much higher this time around . . . No one can resist a skin in a necktie.

Harold takes the bow tie from the warrior near the table; he clips it on and continues talking.

HAROLD   When we show up in neckties that foundation pack won't remember nothin we tell them but the truth . . .

PLUMERO   What was that again?

HAROLD   Nothin but the truth . . .

Harold throws neckties to the other warriors.

HAROLD   (continued)   Wear these neckties with pride, the pride of a trickster . . .

Son Bear refuses a necktie; others scorn the selection. Powwow music can be heard from the earphones around his neck. Son Bear picks up the two oranges on the table, picks a third from the miniature tree and juggles them.

SON BEAR   We are Warriors of Orange, not white heads . . .

Plumero catches one orange: Harold tucks a necktie in Son Bear's back pocket. The warriors hoot and trill.

PLUMERO   So, where's the meetin?

HAROLD   Board room at the Bily Foundation . . .

PLUMERO   *Bored* room for sure . . .

HAROLD   This time they want something personal . . .

PLUMERO   Like a name ceremony.

HAROLD   Something serious . . .

PLUMERO   Like a ghost dance.

A school bus rattles to a stop in front of the storefront. "The Warriors of Orange" is painted on the side over a cameo portrait of a whiteman, a brand label for miniature oranges. Bus horn honks.

HAROLD   Something active . . .

PLUMERO   Like a softball game in the park.

HAROLD   Right . . .

2A Int Breakfast Meeting at the Board Room—Morning

Kingsley Newton cuts a sliver of strawberry and pushes it back on his fork. Breakfast meeting. Fannie Mason attends the first meeting of the executive committee of the board of directors. She is eager to please. Marion Quiet and Andrew Burch are seated opposite Fannie and Kingsley. One place is vacant, set for Ted Velt who is late for the meeting. Kingsley is mannered, elite, formal, a romantic about tribal cultures. He is dressed in light colored clothing. The other directors are dressed in dark business suits. Fannie wears casual, expensive clothing. Kingsley cuts a strawberry as Fannie speaks. Strawberry on the screen.

FANNIE   D. H. Lawrence wrote that "The most unfree souls go west, and shout of freedom . . . Men are freest when they are most unconscious of freedom . . .

MARION   Like American Indians?

FANNIE   Yes . . .

MARION   Have you lived with them?

FANNIE   Not on a reservation . . . You see, my real interest in Indians was stimulated in college . . .

Andrew leans forward, over his plate, to speak to Fannie.

ANDREW   As you must know, my father was in the timber business . . . We shared numerous adventures with some of the finest native woodsmen . . .

FANNIE   Yes, I have studied the . . .

MARION   Pulp cutters?

FANNIE   The exploitation . . . The, ahh, corporate development of resources on the reservation.

Kingsley attempts to direct the conversation.

KINGSLEY   Fannie studied American Indian folklore . . .

FANNIE   Literature, which is a much larger subject than folklore.

MARION   Do Indians have a written language?

FANNIE   No, they have *oral* traditions.

KINGSLEY   Which reminds me . . . Harold of Orange will make his special presentation to the board this afternoon . . .

MARION   That little orange man?

Marion laughs too hard; she does not notice the silence of the other directors.

ANDREW   Have we not already approved his proposal?

KINGSLEY   Yes, informally as the executive committee.

MARION   Does he know?

KINGSLEY   No . . . Even if he did he would still insist on an oral presentation . . .

MARION   The oral tradition seems so natural to him.

FANNIE   Harold of Orange? Is that his name?

KINGSLEY   Fannie has not yet read his unusual proposal . . .

Marion leans forward to speak to Fannie.

MARION   Harold Sinseer . . .

Marion laughs too hard. Fannie blinks several times when she hears the name. She turns her head from side to side, a nervous tic. She remembers an affair, one night in the park, with Harold ten years earlier.

MARION   Sinseer, if you can believe that as a surname.

Ted Velt, the other member of the executive committee, seems to leap into the board room. His is a small man, breathless, with a forceful personality.

TED   Better late than sorry . . . The scissors were too dull at the ribbon cutting . . .

KINGSLEY   Nice of you to show . . .

Ted is seated, he folds his hands over his plate, breaks into a wide smile, and looks from face to face around the table. Kingsley leans toward Fannie to speak.

KINGSLEY   Watch out for Ted Velt, he made his fortune on tricks and games.

Ted extends his hand across the table to Fannie.

TED   Call me Veltie . . .

FANNIE   Call me Fannie, Veltie . . .

Fannie shakes his hand. Still holding her hand Ted turns his wrist to show his digital watch. He points to his watch with his other hand, across the table.

TED   Watch this . . .

Ted pushes a button on his watch, still holding onto Fannie's hand, and a tune, the theme music from the Lone Ranger, fills the board room.

3 Int The Warriors of Orange Bus—Morning

The warriors are seated on the bus as they chant the lines of a poem. The bus is running. Harold enters last and when he takes his seat the warriors begin their chant.

PLUMERO   Oranges and darkness . . .

NEW CROWS   Oranges and light . . .

SON BEAR   Orangewood and promises . . .

NEW CROWS   Oranges and delight . . .

PLUMERO   Orange warriors . . .

SON BEAR   Oranges for Christ . . .

NEW CROWS   Oranges in magical flight . . .

PLUMERO   We are orange tricksters . . .

HAROLD   And Lawrence is white

The bus lurches forward; voices change from surreal to conversational.

SON BEAR   Lawrence of Arabia?

HAROLD   No, Lawrence of New Mexico . . . David Herbert Lawrence of the red and the white . . .

NEW CROWS   Did you tell him about the oranges?

HAROLD   No, but I told him he was right.

PLUMERO   White about what?

HAROLD   How he loves to hate the dark and how we love to hate the white . . .

3A Ext Bus Moving Down a Dirt Road—Morning

The bus rumbles down a dirt road as the warriors continue their conversation. The question by Son Bear, the answer by Harold, and the song "Our women are poisoned part white ho ho ho ho. . . ." are heard as the bus passes. Guitar music with the song. The song voice over carries into the next scene where Harold and Fannie are intimate in the board room. Guitar music continues to next scene.

SON BEAR   Did Lawrence of New Mexico wear a necktie?

HAROLD   He wore it so tight he faded in the bright light . . .

WARRIORS SONG   Our women are poisoned part white ho ho ho ho peeled part white ho ho ho ho buried deep down where the dead turn around . . .

4 *Int Carpeted Board Room at the*
Foundation—Afternoon

Harold and Fannie are seen in an intimate, private, embrace. Camera
circles close. Fannie remembers; the past is revealed on her face as she
begins to resist the passion of the moment. The resistance is slow,
develops in silence, in subtle facial gestures. She turns away, avoids his
eyes, his lips; we see her face as Harold speaks to her.

HAROLD   Tell me you not still sore.

FANNIE   *No,* I mean yes . . . Forget it. You are ten years too late . . .
    Forget it.

Fannie breaks from his embrace. The board room is decorated with
original works of art by tribal artists; placed for the occasion.

HAROLD   Have you forgotten the oral tradition?

FANNIE   Yes, *and* the interruptions.

Fannie turns from Harold and moves around the table as she speaks,
placing materials on the table for the board meeting. Harold follows
her as he speaks.

HAROLD   The shaman called me back to the reservation.

FANNIE   You told me your grandmother had died.

HAROLD   Well, she did . . .

FANNIE   She died four times that year, right?

Harold follows Fannie around the table.

HAROLD   Hey, Fannie, bend a little, turn with the stories . . . You
    know me, short on apologies.

FANNIE   Do you have a grandmother?

HAROLD   We buried our relatives in college to avoid exams . . . We survived, didn't we?

FANNIE   On fake funerals and borrowed money.

Harold is distracted, nervous. He expands his chest. Fannie touches his arm, affection with a purpose. She smiles, tilts her head, gestures of dominance.

FANNIE   Remember that thousand you borrowed from me?

HAROLD   What thousand?

FANNIE   That thousand you said you needed to buy your grandmother for the fourth time . . .

Harold looks around the room, he is anxious, cornered in his own game. When he turns back to Fannie he is more aggressive.

HAROLD   Listen, we need your money . . . I mean, we need your support for this pinch bean proposal . . . Can we count on you for that much?

Fannie looks down in silence. She turns her ring.

HAROLD   Come on, this proposal is not for me alone.

Fannie looks up and smiles.

FANNIE   Of course not, your proposal is for the traditional elders on the reservation who cannot speak for themselves . . .

HAROLD   You know the old foundation game, we get the money and the foundation gets the good name . . .

FANNIE   No I don't know that . . .

Harold is more dramatic; he raises his voice in poetic anger.

HAROLD   The Warriors of Orange are not victims to please the white man . . . We never cheat people, we are not corrupt politicians with medicine bundles stuffed with false promises . . . We are imaginative survivors, we cross the world in the middle of the block . . .

FANNIE   Save the rest for the foundation directors . . . Listen to me now.

Harold gestures with his lips, he exhales and smiles,

HAROLD   My ears are to the daffodils.

Fannie is more aggressive, at the edge of anger.

FANNIE   You owe me one-thousand dollars.

HAROLD   The check is in the mail . . .

FANNIE   No, no, this afternoon, return my money this afternoon before the directors make their final decision on your proposal . . .

Kingsley Newton enters the board room. He pulls the drapes open and then walks toward Fannie and Harold. The room is filled with light, white. Foundation directors and warriors also enter the room. The warriors are carrying crates of miniature oranges. The directors admire the new tribal art on the walls. Harold notices an affectionate gesture between Fannie and Kingsley. Harold thrusts his chest forward, smiles, and moves close to Fannie's ear to speak.

HAROLD   This afternoon, then, on my grandmother's grave . . .

4A Carpeted Board Room at the Foundation—Afternoon

Kingsley stands in front of a podium. The directors are seated around the conference table. Harold stands next to Kingsley. Fannie is seated near the front of the table. The warriors stand in the back of the board room. Kingsley spreads his arms as he speaks.

KINGSLEY   Now it is my pleasure to present Harold Sinseer, one proud American Indian from the Watteau Point Reservation in beautiful northern Minnesota . . . Some of you know him as Harold of Orange because we funded his last proposal to cultivate an orchard of miniature oranges . . . In a secret place to avoid pests and competition . . . And this afternoon we will have our first taste of the oranges.

Ted Velt arrives late, he bursts through the door into the board room. He notices the crates of oranges, points at them, comments on the portrait on the label, and then greets the warriors, slaps them on the back, and moves to his seat at the table. The warriors are uncomfortable with his attention. Velt takes his seat, stacks his hands on the table and smiles to each director. His watch fills the screen while Kingsley continues his introduction.

TED   Oranges overnight? How about that . . . Hey chief, good to see a little color here for a change . . .

KINGSLEY   Harold has challenged us in the private foundation field to meet his proposal in places around the cities, a removal, as it were, from the carpets . . .

MARION   Not removed too far . . .

ANDREW   Not too long, I trust . . .

KINGSLEY   Where we will experience something serious and ceremonial . . .

Three warriors move forward to the front of the board room and stand with their arms folded, stoical postures. Kingsley is nervous.

KINGSLEY   But first, allow me to introduce his workers, warriors, from the orange orchards . . .

Kingsley makes a sign to each of the warriors.

KINGSLEY   We welcome you one and all, and we celebrate your desire to better yourselves in a miniature orchard of your own on the reservation . . .

Kingsley pauses and then gestures to Harold.

KINGSLEY   My friend, Harold Sinseer . . .

Harold rises to the podium. Guitar music. Harold speaks like an evangelist. He leans forward and turns his head as he speaks.

HAROLD   Once we climbed into church basements to better ourselves with heavy hearts and empty pocketbook speeches . . . The money was good then, but the guilt has changed and so have we . . . So here we are dressed in neckties with oranges and pinch beans . . .

MARION   Mister Sinseer, we have heard so much about your oral traditions . . .

Fannie clears her throat and turns the rings on her fingers.

HAROLD   Listen, first we told you about miniuture oranges and now with two hundred thousand dollars we will serve you pinch bean coffee with the oral tradition . . .

Several warriors loosen their neckties and examine the art on the walls.

MARION   Miniature oranges, and now pinch beans, what ever will be next?

HAROLD   Truffles and cashews . . .

MARION   Truffles? Can you be serious?

HAROLD   Red Lake truffles . . .

Harold pauses in silence. The foundation directors laugh, in short and practiced bursts. Harold clears his throat.

HAROLD   Grand Portage cashews . . . Not to mention White Earth caviar . . .

Harold steps forward to the conference table; he speaks in a secretive tone of voice. The directors lean forward to listen. Fannie examines her fingernails.

HAROLD   Now follow me down the great white road to the orange bus for the first *red* pinch . . .

5 Int Orange Bus on the Road in the City—Afternoon

The bus moves through the city, down Franklyn Avenue, on the way to the first stop, the Naming Ceremony. The foundation directors are not comfortable, seated next to the warriors, but their manners compel them to speak and to raise questions about culture and the weather. Points of view out the window include several scenes of tribal people. Son Bear has his earphones on, he moves in his seat to the beat of powwow music. Harold stands, moves from seat to seat.

MARION   How many Indians live on *your* reservation?

PLUMERO   Seventeen hundred and thirty-nine . . .

Plumero loosens his necktie and flashes a thin smile. Marion turns to comment on the view out the window.

ANDREW   I have considered the origin theories of the American Indians . . . Some are *quite* interesting. I find the Bering Strait migration theory to be the most credible . . . How about you then, what are your thoughts on the subject?

NEW CROWS   Which way, east or west?

ANDREW   Which *way*? What do you mean?

NEW CROWS   Which way across the Bering Strait, *then*?

ANDREW   Yes, I see . . . Well, I hadn't really thought about it that way. Which way do *you* think?

NEW CROWS   From here to there, we emerged from the flood here, the first people, unless you think we are related to the panda bear.

ANDREW   Oh, not at all, not at all . . . Actually, what you say makes a great deal of sense, but the problem I seem to have, you see, is that there is so little evidence to support your idea . . .

NEW CROWS   Jesus Christ was an American Indian . . .

ANDREW   Was he now, who would have guessed?

Andrew examines his fingernails and then looks out the window of the bus. New Crows watches him and smiles. Point of view outside the moving bus: scene of tribal people. Harold takes a seat next to Kingsley. Fannie is at the front of the bus, seated alone.

KINGSLEY   Your warriors certainly are knowledgeable. The directors seem quite impressed . . .

HAROLD   The Warriors of Orange are trained in the art of socioacupuncture . . . We imagine the world and cut our words from the centerfolds of histories . . .

KINGSLEY   Is that a tribal tradition?

Harold cocks his head to the side, smiles, he appears pensive.

HAROLD   We are wild word hunters, tricksters on the run . . .

KINGSLEY   We are impressed . . . You seem to know so much about so many things, from orange trees to linguistics . . .

HAROLD   Not to mention pinch beans . . .

KINGSLEY   Yes, of course . . . I have asked our new associate Fannie Mason to pay particular attention to your oral proposal . . .

Harold turns to the camera and smiles. Cut to Kingsley.

HAROLD   I have a problem which I hesitate to share with you at this time, but you are an understanding person . . .

KINGSLEY   *Yes,* please continue . . .

HAROLD   Well, the problem is money . . . We have none and we wondered if the foundation could advance us about a thousand dollars to cover our expenses for this presentation . . .

KINGSLEY   It would be highly irregular to advance money on your proposal which the full board has not yet approved . . .

HAROLD   We are hard pressed for cash or else I wouldn't think about asking . . .

KINGSLEY   Of course, we will forget that you asked.

Harold moves forward on the bus to direct the driver to the first stop for the Naming Ceremony. Warriors and directors continue talking. Kingsley brushes his suit coat sleeves and tightens his necktie. Son Bear lowers his earphones around his neck, the powwow music can still be heard.

TED   I was reading about American Indian populations in the National Geographic magazine . . .

SON BEAR   Where, in the doctor's office?

TED   We have a subscription . . . The article mentions the revisions of the population estimates of American Indians at the time of Columbus . . .

SON BEAR   Who? Who was that?

TED   Christopher Columbus, when he discovered the New World . . . Well, actually an island . . . How many Indians were there then, here I mean, on this continent?

SON BEAR   None.

TED   None? What do you mean *none*?

SON BEAR   None, not one. Columbus never discovered anything, and when he never did he invented us as Indians because we never heard the word before he dropped by by accident . . .

TED   Of course, I see what you mean . . . Well, let me phrase the question in a different way then. How many tribal people were there here then, ahh, before Columbus invented Indians?

Ted smiles, pleased with his question. He looks out the bus window. Point of view, scene of tribal people. Voice of Son Bear is over the point of view scene. Tradition at a bus stop.

SON BEAR   Forty-nine million, seven hundred twenty-three thousand, one hundred and ninety-six on this continent, including what is now Mexico . . .

TED   Really, that many then?

6 Ext Fry Bread Cart in a Parking Lot—Afternoon

The Warriors of Orange bus rumbles to a stop in a parking lot at Franklyn Circle. The warriors, directors, and others, gather around a large cart on wheels.

THE LAST STAND

Oral Traditional Food

FRY BREAD AND COOL AIDE

THE EDIBLE MENU

miniature orange marmalade
pinch bean espresso
mild moose burgers
totem crackers
COMMODITIES FOR THE RESERVATION BLUES

The directors and warriors gather around The Last Stand where they are each served a piece of fry bread with miniature orange marmalade. The warriors take deep soul bites; but the directors are hesitant, they nibble at their fry bread. The directors are polite and carry their fry bread to the next scene.

HAROLD   This is a special name feast prepared by the Warriors of Orange in honor of all the founders and foundations in the New World . . .

PLUMERO   And a few fakes and fools . . .

Loud music. An audience of white and tribal shoppers, with their bags and carts, gather around the bus, and the fry bread cart. Plumero bears a cigar box with a cigar store Indian on the label. New Crows carries a fist full of orange chicken feathers.

HAROLD   Kingsley Newton . . . The urban spirits have directed me in a dream to select your new name from the cigar box.

Harold closes his eyes as he reaches into the box. Kingsley is nervous. He looks around and tightens his tie.

KINGSLEY   Are you serious?

HAROLD   Who could be serious about anything in a parking lot at a shopping center . . . use your imagination.

KINGSLEY   By all means . . .

HAROLD   Your new name speaks to me from the cigar store Indian box . . .

Harold reaches into the box and selects a property card from a Monopoly game. Loud music. More people gather, move closer.

HAROLD   Your new name is . . . Baltic, your urban dream name is Baltic . . . Congratulations, bear your name with pride . . .

Harold hands the Monopoly card to Kingsley. The warriors hoot and trill; the audience cheers and applauds. Baltic unbuttons his suit coat and swallows a nervous smile. The keeper of The Last Stand hands him another piece of fry bread. He has fry bread in both hands. He nibbles at both. Plumero moves close to Kingsley, whispers in his ear.

PLUMERO   Fry bread is white on the inside, you know.

Kingsley examines both pieces of fry bread, looks up and smiles.

HAROLD   Who will be our next contestant . . . Who will seek a fortune as a founder with a new name? Step forward into an urban dream . . .

Marion is volunteered by the other directors. She is applauded and she applauds herself as she steps forward, but her smile does not relieve her tension. Marion stands next to Plumero.

MARION   Should the oral tradition be a public affair?

PLUMERO   Close your eyes when the shaman calls your name . . .

MARION   Never . . .

HAROLD   The great urban shaman who directs all the interstates has given me your name in a dream . . . Where is the card . . .

Harold closes his eyes and selects a card from the box.

MARION   This better be good . . .

HAROLD   Your name is . . . Connecticut . . .

The audience applauds and the warriors hoot and trill.

HAROLD   Now, one more dream name for the lady over there with the sweet daffodil . . .

The audience looks around. Fannie tries to avoid attention, but her gestures attract attention. She shakes her head and avoids the event. Harold slides his hand into the cigar box, a sensuous gesture. Ted's watch sounds the theme of the Lone Ranger.

HAROLD   My fingers are searching the box, I have a name, the name is *chance, chance* . . . But wait, the name card reads: "Good for one thousand dollars."

The audience applauds and the warriors hoot and trill. Harold hands the card to Fannie, she returns it, puts it in his pocket. Strangers from the audience step forward to receive an urban dream name but the warriors close the box. The remaining feathers are presented to the audience.

HAROLD   The box is closed for the afternoon, all the proud cigar store Indians have retired in the west . . .

*7 Int Orange Bus Moving Down Summit
Avenue—Afternoon*

Bus moves down Summit Avenue. Points of view on the affluent white world. Focus on a personal license plate that reads: "Indian" or "Savage." Harold is sitting next to Andrew. Fannie is behind them, she overhears their conversation.

ANDREW   One is still not certain how your pinch bean trees survive the winter?

HAROLD   Coffee shrubs . . .

ANDREW   Shrubs then . . . Are the beans frost resistant?

Andrew is distracted when Harold points out the window of the bus at a white couple with a white child who wears a feather headdress and carries a rubber tomahawk.

HAROLD   Were you in the war?

ANDREW   The great war?

HAROLD   Yes, the great wars . . . Do you remember those little packets of instant coffee?

ANDREW   Not with pleasure, to be sure . . .

HAROLD   We supplied the great war with the first instant coffee from woodland beans . . . Our tribal children gathered the beans in winter and then we pinched them for the war . . .

ANDREW   Indeed, your stories seem convincing enough, but will we have the pleasure of meeting the live shrubs?

Harold looks out the window of the bus. Point of view, an attractive blonde is washing her car.

HAROLD   That depends on how you see the oral tradition.

ANDREW   I see, well then, please explain.

Harold removes a large red felt-tip pen from his pocket, holds open his left hand, and draws two crude shrubs on the palm of his hand to illustrate his explanation. Fannie leans forward between them, sees the drawings, hears the explanation, and then rolls her eyes and falls back into her seat.

HAROLD   A logical positivist would demand cold clear data to be sure, while a mythic trickster in the oral tradition, on the other hand, would be satisfied with a handful of beans . . . Either way, as you can see, there are still two shrubs . . .

Harold reaches into his pocket and offers Andrew a handful of coffee beans. The director is nonplussed, he holds out both of his hands to receive the beans. Andrew examines the beans; the tries to pinch them, as Harold continues talking.

HAROLD   Remember those code talkers who spoke tribal languages to confuse the enemies?

Harold watches Andrew pinching the beans. Harold takes one bean from his hand and pinches it as he continues to talk. The bean becomes powder. Andrew is amazed.

HAROLD   Well, we maintained an elaborate pinch bean exchange in military units throughout the great war . . .

ANDREW   How did you do that?

HAROLD   That, sir, is a tribal secret . . .

Fannie leans forward and tries to pinch a bean. Andrew continues pinching beans without success. Harold moves back to sit with Kingsley.

HAROLD   Are you still interested in that reservation tour you once asked me about?

KINGSLEY   Yes, that would be interesting . . .

HAROLD   I could make arrangements to hunt wild rice, whatever interests you the most . . . But of course I would need some money in advance to cover the expenses . . . you understand.

KINGSLEY   Of course, let me get back to you on that.

HAROLD   I could make arrangements today . . .

KINGSLEY   I should check my schedule first.

Point of view outside the bus: sunbathers on a balcony.

8 Int Anthropology Department Artifact Cases—
Afternoon

Scene begins with a photographic slide of the ghost dance. Harold steps into the slide, the ghost dance figures are projected on his face and body; he appears to be in the dance. Harold stands in light on an artifact case in an anthropology department. Plumero operates the slide projector. The warriors and directors are gathered near the case. Harold speaks in a deep dramatic tone of voice. Sound of a rattle.

HAROLD   The earth will rise to cover these sacred bones in the ghost dance vision . . . Time will run behind and white people will soon disappear . . .

MARION   What about the mixedbloods?

HAROLD   Mixedbloods will be buried as deep as their white blood . . . The more the deeper . . . Fullbloods will levitate in a sacred dance at the treelines . . .

Several anthropologists, dressed in western attire, string ties, turquoise, are alarmed that the artifacts might be sized by militants. Harold points toward the nervous group of professors. Sound of a rattle. Slide change, death scene from Wounded Knee.

HAROLD   Those anthropologists over there will be buried upside down with their toes exposed like mushrooms . . .

PLUMERO   Poison mushrooms . . .

Ted is nervous; he checks his watch and wrinkles his face.

TED   Get on with the pitch, I mean pinch.

HAROLD   The rivers are dead near the universities, the fish are poisoned, even the carp yawn near shore . . . Birds are stalled in flight . . . Interstates uproot our families . . .

PLUMERO   And we hold the secrets of survival in a tribal pinch bean . . .

Harold seems surprised. His mood changes, he is less serious, he smiles and becomes an evangelist. Slide change, Wild West Show broadside.

HAROLD   Resurrection on a pinch bean.

Two university police officers push through the crowd, followed by a student newspaper reporter. The foundation directors move back to avoid trouble. The anthropologists are relieved. Flash photographs. Harold smiles and steps down from the cases.

POLICE OFFICER   Is this an authorized assemble?

HAROLD   Yes, sir, from the president himself . . .

POLICE OFFICER   Which president?

HAROLD   The university president . . . The Warriors of Orange, he said, are always welcome to examine these tribal artifacts . . .

The students cheer and applaud the warriors.

FANNIE   Sir, perhaps I could explain . . . You see, he is presenting his proposal for . . .

The students boooo and hisssss.

POLICE OFFICER   Who are you?

FANNIE   Fannie Mason, and this is Harold Sinseer . . .

POLICE OFFICER   Sincere?

HAROLD   Sinseer, yes, my name is on this letter . . .

Harold unfolds a letter from a small square and hands it to the police officer. The police officer examines the letter, he turns it upside down, sideways, then smiles. Sound of rattles.

POLICE OFFICER   Sincerely, is that it there?

The police officer points to the bottom of the letter.

HAROLD   Sinseer on the top, sincerely on the bottom, sir . . .

The students, even the anthropologists, laugh.

POLICE OFFICER   Right . . . Are you an Indian?

HAROLD   Right . . . Are you an Irish?

The students appreciate the humorous confrontation.

POLICE OFFICER   Right . . . Could you examine these artifacts while standing on the floor?

HAROLD   I was dancing how high the earth come the ghost dance vision.

POLICE OFFICER   The ghost dance?

HAROLD   When all this disappears . . .

POLICE OFFICER   Right . . . Keep your feet on the floor.

The students applaud while the police officer refolds the letter into a small square; he looks around and then returns the letter to Harold. Sound of a rattle. The anthropologists are embarrassed, the foundation directors are relieved. Slide change to a photograph of Paul Newman in *Buffalo Bill and the Indians.*

NEWS REPORTER   What did you say about the ghost dance?

HAROLD   I said that the river is dead below the brain trust . . .

NEWS REPORTER   What brain trust?

HAROLD   The university faculties . . .

NEWS REPORTER   Are you serious?

HAROLD   Come the ghost dance vision the brain trust will become the brain drain . . .

NEWS REPORTER   That I can believe, but is this a protest against the anthropology department?

HAROLD   The cultures that anthropologists invent never complain about anything . . .

NEWS REPORTER   What are you doing here then?

HAROLD   We are pinching a foundation for grants to establish coffee houses on reservations . . .

NEWS REPORTER   Coffee houses?

HAROLD   Coffee houses foster revolutions.

NEWS REPORTER   I see . . . here's my card, let me know when the revolution is served . . . Make mine with cream.

Harold smiles and then folds the card into a small square. He turns toward the students and continues his stories. His voice is more dramatic.

HAROLD   We come to the cities from our tribal past and pace around our parts here like lost and lonesome animals . . .

Harold continues talking while Kingsley and a foundation director discuss the merits of his proposal. The two are standing at the end of the cases. Guitar music. Slide changes to a portrait of Buffalo Bill Cody. (See next section for Harold's speech.)

ANDREW   Kingsley, tell me, is he serious?

KINGSLEY   Harold insists that he is a trickster . . .

ANDREW   A confidence man?

Harold is telling stories in the background while Kingsley and a foundation director are discussing the merits of his proposal:

HAROLD   In the beginning there were words and pinch beans and when the first flood came the great trickster saved a few beans to create a new earth . . . Then the trickster was word driven from the land the second time, but he saved the secret of the pinch beans and now we come to a foundation with a plan to create coffee houses on reservations . . .

The great spirit created the frost tolerant pinch beans and gave them to the trickster for the tribes . . . The pinch shrubs flower late in the spring and then red berries appear in the summer . . . Late in winter under a whole moon the berries are harvested in birch bark containers . . . The secret is that there is no processing . . .

KINGSLEY   No, a tribal trickster is not the same . . . He is rather sincere, even innocent, artless at times . . . He believes that he can stop time and change the world through imagination.

Andrew is nonplussed, he pulls his ear and frowns.

ANDREW   With a foundation grant of course . . .

KINGSLEY   Of course . . . Who could change the world without a foundation grant?

Kingsley and Andrew smile, they share the same secret.

ANDREW   Quite right, for a proponent of the oral tradition that letter from the president was a smart move.

KINGSLEY   He seems to have a word or a letter for all occasions . . .

The class bell rings and most of the student leave. Slide change, scene of Harold bearing Fannie in his arms, like the pose of the statue of Hiawatha and Minnehaha.

9 Ext Statue of Hiawatha and Minnehaha—Afternoon

The statue is on the screen as the bus approaches and stops. The warriors leave the bus dressed in "Anglo" shirts, the name of their softball team; the directors leave the bus with "Indian" shirts, the name of their team. Fannie and Harold walk toward the field together, he carries the bats and gloves, she carries the softball. Kingsley, who is the umpire, does not wear a team shirt. The directors have removed their suit coats and loosened their ties. Kingsley remains formal, suit coat buttoned. Harold and Fannie are heard speaking, voice over from a distance as they walk away from the statue.

HAROLD   Is it true that Indians are great lovers?

FANNIE   Sometimes, when you catch one with his mouth closed in an "Anglo" shirt . . .

10 Ext Softball Diamond—Afternoon

The "Indians" and the "Anglos" are huddled in separate teams. Harold in a huddle with the warriors who are the "Anglos."

HAROLD   Listen gang, we are the "Anglos" and we're here to win and win big . . . Play by the rules if you must, but rape and plunder to win the game . . . When the "Indians" talk about the earth and their sacred ceremonies, steal a base, win the game like we stole their land, with a smile . . . Score, score, score, in the name of god, win, and send those "Indians" back to the reservation as victims, where the slow grass grows . . . We'll mine the resources later.

PLUMERO   But if you should lose, you can't count on a job with the Bureau of Indian Affairs to get even . . .

Harold pulls off his "Anglos" shirt and walks over to the "Indians" team huddle. The directors are stoical.

HAROLD   We are in the cities now and we must never forget what the missionaries said our elders said around the fires . . .

TED   Lead me to the foundations?

HAROLD   That was much earlier, we dropped the first grant proposal with the pilgrims . . . The elders said we should never enter the game to win but to dream . . . We are made in dreams and the white man is the one who must win . . . When we help him win we are free and soon the white man will want to be like us, and when that happens we can leave him, once and for all times, a winner, on the reservations he made for us . . .

MARION   Who invented that game?

HAROLD   Boy Scouts and anthropologists.

ANDREW   The Order of the Arrow, you will be pleased to know, still whistles in the dark.

HAROLD   Competition is not our curse, but we are the best tricksters in town to let the white man win with pride . . .

TED   Trick the white devils to win? . . . That defies all reason.

Harold puts on his "Anglos" shirt and returns to his team which is first at bat. Fannie is the pitcher for the "Indians" and Harold, who is the first at the plate for his team, is the pitcher for the "Anglos." Harold dances at the plate. The first ball rolls across the plate, ball one. The second rolls behind him, ball two.

HAROLD   Throw the ball, this is not a treaty conference . . .

Ball three rolls over the plate.

HAROLD   C'mon, just *one* high enough to hit and you can be my Indian guide forever . . .

Fannie pitches a fast ball, strike one; strike two. Then she rolls the fourth ball over the plate and Harold walks to first base. Ted is an "Indian" at first base. Harold talks to Ted.

HAROLD   This is my first visit to a real reservation . . . Where is your bingo hall?

TED   Behind the smoke shop, honkie . . .

Harold steals to second base. Harold talks to Andrew on second base.

HAROLD   My great grandmother was an Indian princess once . . .

ANDREW   Cherokee, no doubt . . . Listen, my grandmother was a
French Duchess . . .

Harold steals to third base. Harold talks with Marion on third base; he
removes a moccasin and hands it to Marion.

HAROLD   An old Indian guide gave these moccasins to my grandfather . . . I was wondering if you could tell me what tribe made
them . . .

Marion, of the "Indians" team, sniffs the toe of the moccasin; she
ponders the smell, and then sniffs it again.

MARION   Yes, these were worn by an old gambler who lived three
miles north of Bad Medicine Lake . . .

HAROLD   What tribe is that?

MARION   Mixedblood Nacirema . . .

Harold seems to move from base to base, inning to inning, in magical
flight. He appears and disappears in fast cuts of the game. Fannie
comes to bat; Harold teases her with a fast ball, strike one, but she hits
the second pitch out of the park. Harold dances on the mound.

HAROLD   White people always want to be better Indians than the
Indians . . . The missionaries never translated the meaning of a
"home run."

MARION   We blame everything on the Bureau of Indian Affairs . . .
Even when we win.

The players ad lib from base to base; the "Indians" win the game.

11 Int Carpeted Board Room at the Bily
Foundation—Afternoon

The directors and warriors return to the board room, exhausted, for the conclusion of the proposal; all are seated around the conference table still wearing their team shirts from the softball game.

KINGSLEY   Thank you for remaining to the end of this most unusual oral traditional ball game . . .

MARION   The pretend Indians won again . . .

PLUMERO   So did the pretend "Anglos."

TED   Most unusual, most unusual, but I do have one last question before we adjourn . . .

HAROLD   Your questions are my very answers.

Kingsley frowns. Ted twists his face as he speaks.

TED   The Warriors of Orange, all of you, have been perfect gentlemen . . . Calm and mannered throughout, which makes my question all the more difficult to construct without appearing . . .

HAROLD   Without sounding like a racist?

Harold removes his "Anglos" shirt and throws it on the table.

TED   Exactly . . . You understand then?

HAROLD   Perhaps we could help you find the first *un*racist words . . . Does your question have anything to do with our proposal?

TED   Not at all . . . Pinch beans will give us all a good name.

Ted waves his arms wide. Harold smiles and then gestures with his lips to the warriors.

HAROLD   Savagism, the question must be about savagism and civilization.

TED   Well, yes, in the broadest sense of the word.

PLUMERO   How broad can a savage be?

HAROLD   Would you like to meet a beautiful tribal woman?

TED   No . . . Well, of course, but not in an improper manner . . .

PLUMERO   How about a hunting guide?

TED   No, that's not it at all, but that would be interesting now that you mention it . . .

PLUMERO   Sweat lodge ceremonies . . . Purification?

TED   No, not that either . . . Well, what I mean is that I am too sensitive to the heat . . .

PLUMERO   A shaman, an herbal healing then?

Ted is more relaxed, he takes pleasure in being the center of attention; the pursuit of the question.

TED   What does a shaman do?

Harold and Plumero and the other warriors become more aggressive. Plumero pulls his "Anglos" shirt off and throws it on the table.

PLUMERO   Leather and beadwork?

The warriors are restless, they rise and move around the room; they remove their "Anglos" shirts and stop from time to time to stare at the directors. Ted clears his throat.

TED   No, not beadwork . . . My wife bought too much, dozens of beautiful objects for practically nothing from an old Indian woman who was in the hospital . . . What I mean is that my wife was a volunteer and she took care of this woman . . . No, not beads this time.

Ted thrusts his head back like a bird. He pinches his lips with his two

fingers and then expands his chest as he buttons his suit coat. He clears
his throat. The warriors circle his chair. Sound of a rattle. Plumero
raises his voice and bangs the table with his fist.

PLUMERO   *Indian alcoholism . . .*

Kingsley stiffens and looks over to Fannie. Fannie rolls her head and
looks at the ceiling. Ted is pleased, the warriors have discovered his
question.

TED   That's it! Yes, thank you, yes, my question is about Indian
drinking, but it bothered me to say the word . . .

Ted examines his watch.

HAROLD   The old firewater thesis, of course, we should have
known . . .

Kingsley is uncomfortable and interrupts the conversation.

KINGSLEY   What he means to say, is that he has worked with American Indians who have had serious drinking problems and he appre-
ciates how sensitive the subject can be . . . Even in the best of times,
we all have had some problem with spirits . . .

HAROLD   The "Indians" seemed sober to me during the ball
game . . .

PLUMERO   Even the "Anglos" . . .

The board room is silent. The warriors and directors all look off in
different directions.

TED   That's what I mean . . . That's exactly what I wanted to ask you
about . . . You are all so sober, and you should be *proud* that you
are . . .

The warriors turn on their heels. Harold interrupts the director with a
harsh tone of voice. Ted still enjoys the attention.

HAROLD   What *is* your question?

TED   My question is, ahh, how did all of you overcome the need and temptation to use alcohol? You are so sober, a credit to your race . . .

Fannie and Kingsley cover their eyes with their hands. Faces are frozen in time and place. Harold begins to smile. He claps his hands.

HAROLD   Pinch beans, pinch beans my friend are the cure . . .

The warriors hoot and trill. Ted seems confused.

TED   Pinch beans?

HAROLD   Pinch beans are the perfect booze blocker, the beans block the temptation to take alcohol from evil white men . . . Our proposal to establish coffee houses will lead to a sober, as well as a mythic, revolution . . .

TED   Fantastic, indeed this is fantastic, you've got my vote for sure . . .

KINGSLEY   And not a minute too soon, I hasten to add . . .

HAROLD   Let me explain how our pinch beans will . . .

Kingsley stands and interrupts Harold; he raises his voice.

KINGSLEY   Harold, we congratulate you and your warriors on a fine presentation . . . something personal and ceremonial . . .

ANDREW   Ever so memorable . . .

HAROLD   Pinch seven beans once a day into warm water while looking at a tree and your delusions of progress and domination will dissolve . . .

The directors smile and applaud. The warriors have removed their "Anglos" shirts, but the directors still wear their "Indians" shirts. Harold moves closer to Kingsley at the end of the table.

HAROLD   Listen, I have been avoiding the real reason I need the thousand dollars . . . I did not want to trouble you with my personal problems.

KINGSLEY   Please, trust me . . .

HAROLD   My traditional grandmother died last week . . .

KINGSLEY   Harold, I am so sorry . . .

HAROLD   She lived a full and wonderful life, she cared for me during the hard times on the reservation, and now, well, we don't have the money to bury her . . . She is at home now laid out in the kitchen waiting to enter the spirit world . . . Do you suppose you could borrow me one thousand dollars to bury her?

KINGSLEY   Borrow? Oh, yes, of course . . . Harold, you should have come to me sooner . . .

Kingsley writes a check and hands it to Harold.

HAROLD   Thank you, you are most generous . . . Please keep this to yourself because I am embarrassed to ask my friends for money . . .

KINGSLEY   My lips are sealed . . . Could I attend the funeral?

HAROLD   Ahh, this is a traditional burial . . . But we will invite you up to the reservation in about a week.

Harold crosses the board room; he looks back to be sure he is not being watched, and then endorses the check. He looks around again, sees that Kingsley is involved in a conversation, and then hands the check to Fannie.

HAROLD   At last, we are even . . .

Fannie examines the check, rolls her head, looks toward Kingsley, and then to Harold. She crumples the check in her fist.

12 *Ext Orange Bus Moving Past on the Interstate—Late Afternoon*

Harold and the warriors smile and wave from the windows of the bus as it passes in slow motion on the interstate. Harold speaks, voice over as the bus passes, in a poetic tone of voice. Guitar and sound of rattle.

HAROLD   We are the Warriors of Orange and we move in mythic time . . . We are elusive birds in borrowed nests, animals at the treelines in late winter . . . We are thunderclouds on the run . . . We are tricksters in the best humor, we leave no culture stains from separations, nothing so cruel as civilization and loneliness . . .

The bus disappears in the distance.

13 *Ext Harold of Orange Coffee House—Sunset*

The Harold of Orange Coffee House at sunset. The bus stops in front of the building. The warriors stumble out and walk into the building. The lights are turned on in the coffee house, and the sign is illuminated. Harold is the last to leave the bus. Near the bus, with the coffee house in the background, he speaks to the camera for the last time.

HAROLD   (to the camera)   This is where the revolution starts, on a gravel road in the brush . . . At a reservation coffee house in the softwoods . . . Remember, you were here with some of the best trickster founders of this new earth . . .

Harold smiles and turns from the camera. He walks toward the coffee house. In the last shot Harold is seen through the front window of the coffee house with other warriors. Harold and the warriors burst into wild laughter and the scene fades.

End

BIBLIOGRAPHY

SELECTED BIBLIOGRAPHY OF
WORKS BY GERALD VIZENOR

Books

Manifest Manners: Postindian Warriors of Survivance. Wesleyan University Press, University Press of New England, 1994.

Dead Voices: Natural Agonies in the New World, a novel. University of Oklahoma Press, 1992.

Parolefrecce, translation of *Wordarrows* by Maria Vittoria D'Amico. Italian edition in the literature series "Indianamericana." Edited by Laura Coltelli. University of Pisa, 1992.

The Heirs of Columbus, a novel. Wesleyan University Press, University Press of New England, 1991; paperbound edition 1992.

Landfill Meditation, collection of short stories. Wesleyan University Press, University Press of New England, 1991.

Interior Landscapes: Autobiographical Myths and Metaphors. University of Minnesota Press, 1990.

Crossbloods: Bone Courts, Bingo, and Other Reports, a collection of essays. University of Minnesota Press, Minneapolis, 1990. This new edition includes several revised essays on the American Indian Movement that first appeared in a *Minneapolis Tribune* editorial series, and *Tribal Scenes and Ceremonies,* Nodin Press, 1976.

Griever: An American Monkey King in China, a novel. Fiction Collective Award, 1986, American Book Award, 1988, second edition published by the University of Minnesota Press, 1990.

Bearheart: The Heirship Chronicles, a novel, new revised edition. University of Minnesota Press, 1990. *Darkness in Saint Louis Bearheart,* first edition, Truck Press, 1978.

Narrative Chance, Postmodern Discourse on Native American Literatures. University of New Mexico Press, 1989. Edited with an introduction and an essay on "Trickster Discourse." Second edition, University of Oklahoma Press, 1993.

The Trickster of Liberty: Tribal Heirs to a Wild Baronage, a novel. University of Minnesota Press, 1988.

Touchwood: A collection of Ojibwe Prose, edited with an introduction and two stories. New Rivers Press, Saint Paul, 1987.

Matsushima: Pine Islands, collected haiku poems. Nodin Press, 1984.

The People Named the Chippewa: Narrative Histories. University of Minnesota Press, 1983; second printing, 1987.

Earthdivers: Tribal Narratives on Mixed Descent. University of Minnesota Press, 1983.

Summer in the Spring: Ojibwe Lyric Poems and Tribal Stories, edited songs and stories. Nodin Press, 1981. New revised edition, *Summer in The Spring: Anishinaabe Lyric Poems and Stories.* University of Oklahoma Press, 1993.

Wordarrows: Indians and Whites in the New Fur Trade. University of Minnesota Press, 1978; second printing, 1989.

The Everlasting Sky: New Voices from the People Named the Chippewa. Macmillan, 1972.

Thomas James White Hawk, investigative narrative on the trial, capital punishment, and commutation of the death sentence of Thomas James White Hawk. Four Winds Press, 1968.

Beaulieu and Vizenor Families: Genealogies. Printed privately, Minneapolis, 1983. Genealogical charts, photographs, articles, and bibliography.

Escorts to White Earth, 1868–1968, 100 Year Reservation, edited. Four Winds Press, 1968.

Empty Swings, original haiku. Nodin Press, 1967.

Raising the Moon Vines, original haiku. Callimachus Press, 1964.

Seventeen Chirps, original haiku. Nodin Press, 1964. Reprinted 1968.

Slight Abrasions: A Dialogue in Haiku, with Jerome Downes. Nodin Press, 1966.

Essays and Other Publications

"The Tragic Wisdom of Salamanders," an essay, in *Sacred Trusts: Essays on Stewardship and Responsibility,* edited by Michael Katakis. Mercury House, 1993.

"Gambling on Sovereignty," editorial essay on tribal casinos, *The Japan Times Weekly,* Tokyo, Japan, August 1993. Same essay published in *American Indian Quarterly,* Summer 1992.

"Naming of Ishi Court," in *Notes From Native California,* Summer 1993.

"Our Land: Anishinaabe," haiku poems by Gerald Vizenor, photographs by Bjorn Sletto. *Native Peoples Magazine,* Spring 1993.

"Many Point Camp," an autobiographical essay, in *Inheriting the Land*, edited by Mark Vinz and Thom Tammaro. University of Minnesota Press, 1993.

"Ishi Bares His Chest: Tribal Simulations and Survivance," a critical essay, in *Partial Recall: Photographs of Native North Americans*, edited by Lucy Lippard. New Press, 1992.

"Wortlichtspiele," scenes from *Harold of Orange*, the screenplay, translated into German, *Chelsea Hotel*, a magazine for the arts, Eggingen, Germany, Volume 2, 1992.

"Sturmpuppen," the chapter "Storm Puppets," from *The Heirs of Columbus*, translated into German, *Chelsea Hotel*, a magazine for the arts, Eggingen, Germany, Volume 1, 1992.

"Native American Indian Literature: Critical Metaphors of the Ghost Dance," lead essay in *World Literature Today*, Spring 1992.

"The Moccasin Games," original radio script, translated into German, Sender Feiers Berlin, 1992. Broadcast on many radio stations in Germany.

"Bound Feet" and "Holosexual Clown," from *Griever: An American Monkey King in China*, published in *The Before Columbus Foundation Fiction Anthology*. W. W. Norton, 1992.

"Moccasin Games," revised short story, in *Without Discovery*, edited by Ray Gonzalez. Broken Moon Press, 1991.

"The Baron of Patronia" and "China Browne," stories in *Talking Leaves: Contemporary American Short Stories*, edited by Craig Lesley, Laurel Paperback, Dell, 1991.

"Bone Courts: The Natural Rights of Tribal Remains," revised and expanded essay on reburial in *The Interrupted Life*. The Museum of Contemporary Art, New York, 1991.

"Luminous Thighs," short story in *The Lightning Within*, edited by Alan Velie. University of Oklahoma Press, 1991.

"The Last Lecture," short story in *American Indian Literature*, an anthology edited by Alan Velie. University of Oklahoma Press, 1991.

"Café Réserve ou les origins du café instanté," translated by Manuel Van Thienen, "Reservation Cafe: The Origins of American Indian Instant Coffee" in *Sur le dos de la Tortue*, revue bilingue de litérature amerindienne, 1991.

"The Stone Trickster," *Northeast Indian Quarterly*, Fall 1991.

"Confrontation or Negotiation," an essay on the American Indian Movement in *Native American Testimony*, edited by Peter Nabokov. Viking Penguin, 1991.

"The Heirs of Columbus," selected stories in *Fictional International*, Fall 1991. Reprinted as *Looking Glass*, a collection of stories, edited by Clifford Trafzer. San Diego State University Press.

"Socioacupuncture: Mythic Reversals and the Striptease in Four Scenes," an imaginative essay in *Out There: Maginalization and Contemporary Cultures*. MIT Press, The New Museum of Contemporary Art, New York, 1990.

Reprinted from *The American Indian and Problems of History,* edited by Calvin Martin. Oxford University Press, 1987.

"An Introduction to Haiku," sixteen poems and and a critical introduction in *Neeuropa,* Summer, Spring, 1991, 1992.

"Four Skin," short story in *Tamaqua,* Winter 1991.

"Almost a Whole Trickster," a short story in *A Gathering of Flowers,* edited by Joyce Carol Thomas. Harper and Row, 1990.

"Almost Browne: The Twice Told Trickster," PEN Syndicated Fiction Project, 1990. Newspaper and radio distribution, and publication in *American Short Fiction.* University of Texas Press.

"Moccasin Games," short story, *Caliban 9,* Spring 1990.

"Postmodern Discourse on Native American Literature," *Halcyon,* A Journal of the Humanities, Volume 12, 1990, Nevada Humanities Commission.

"Native American Dissolve," *Oshkaabewis Native Journal,* Volume 1, Number 1, 1990, Bemidji State University, Minnesota.

Interview in *Winged Words: American Indian Writers Speak,* edited by Laura Coltelli. University of Nebraska Press, 1990.

"Gerald Vizenor: The Trickster Heirs of Columbus," an interview by Laura Coltelli, University of Pisa, in *Native American Literature,* Forum 2, 3, 1990, 1991, Pisa, Italy.

"Water Striders," collection of original haiku poems. Porter Broadside Series, Moving Parts Press, Santa Cruz, California, limited edition, 1989.

"The Pink Flamingos," short story in *Caliban 7,* Winter 1989.

"Bad Breath," a short story in *An Illuminated History of the Future,* edited by Curtis White. Illinois State University and Fiction Collective Two, Norman, and Boulder, 1989.

L'arbe à paroles: 14 poètes amérindiens contemporains, choisis et traduits par Manuel Van Thienen, seven poems in translation. Identités Wallonie, automne 89, Bruxelles, Belgique.

"Feral Lasers," short story in *Caliban 6,* Fall 1989.

"Trickster Discourse," an essay on criticism in *Wicazo Sa Review,* a Journal of Indian Studies, University of Washington, Cheney, Spring 1989.

"Narrative Chance," an essay reprinted in *Before Columbus Review,* a quarterly review of multicultural literature, Winter 1989.

Five poems in *Harper's Anthology of 20th Century Native American Poetry,* edited by Duane Niatum. Harper & Row, 1988.

"Almost Browne," a short story in *Indian Youth of America,* Sioux City, Iowa, Winter 1988.

"Bound Feet," in *Fiction International.* San Diego University Press, 1987.

"Wampum to Pictures of Presidents," in *From Different Shores: Perspectives on Race and Ethnicity in America,* edited by Ronald Takaki. Oxford University Press, 1987.

"Crows Written on the Poplars: Autocritical Autobiographies," in *I Tell You Now: Autobiographical Essays by Native American Writers,* edited by Arnold Krupat. University of Nebraska Press, 1987.

"Follow the Trickroutes: An Interview with Gerald Vizenor," *Survival This Way: Interviews with American Indian Poets,* edited by Joeseph Bruchac. University of Arizona Press, 1987.

"Episodes in Mythic Verism: Monsignor Missalwait's Interstate," in *The New Native American Novel.* University of New Mexico Press, Albuquerque, 1986.

"Reservation Cafe: The Origin of American Instant Coffee," short story in *Earth Power Coming,* edited by Simon Ortiz. Navajo Community College Press, 1983.

Bearheart, selections in *Stand in Good Relations to the Earth,* and several poems in *American Indian Poets,* translated and edited by Alexandre Vaschenko. Raduga, Moscow, 1983.

"Four Haiku Poems," translated into German, *Geflusterte Pfeile.* Von Loeper Verlag, Karlsruhe, Germany, 1982.

"I Know What You Mean, Erdupps MacChurbbs," autobiographical stories in *Growing Up in Minnesota: Ten Writers Remember Their Childhoods,* edited by Chester Anderson. University of Minnesota Press, 1976.

"Brixton: A New Circus of Proud People," editorial essay, *Minneapolis Tribune,* January 31, 1982.

"Indian Alcoholics Are Individuals, not White Mice," editorial essay, *Minneapolis Tribune,* April 23, 1982.

"Buffalo Bill. An Emblem of Ersatz History," editorial essay, *Minneapolis Tribune,* November 29, 1981.

"Indian Manikins with Few References," editorial essay, *Minneapolis Tribune,* September 5, 1981.

"Dennis Banks: What Sort of Hero?" editorial essay, *Minneapolis Tribune,* July 22, 1978.

"White Hawk and the Prairie Fun Dancers," narrative in *University of Minnesota Alumni Magazine,* two parts, October and November, 1978.

"Indian Education and Senator Mondale at Rough Rock," feature article, *Twin Citian Magazine,* May 1969. Reprinted in the *Congressional Record,* August 1969.

"Why Must Thomas White Hawk Die?" feature article, *Twin Citian Magazine,* June 1968.

"Job Corps Center at Lydick Lake," feature article, *Twin Citian Magazine,* August 1966. Reprinted in the *Congressional Record,* September 1966.

Book Reviews

Review of *On the Translation of Native American Literatures,* edited by Brian Swann, *World Literature Today,* Spring 1993.

"Christopher Columbus: Lost Havens in the Ruins of Representation," review essay, thirteen new books on Columbus, *American Indian Quarterly,* Fall 1992.

Review of *PrairyErth* by William Least Heat-Moon, *San Francisco Chronicle,*

Sunday, October 6, 1991. Expanded review in *World Literature Today*, 1992.

Review of *Mean Spirit* by Linda Hogan, *World Literature Today*, Winter 1991.

Interpretive review of *Tripmaster Monkey* by Maxine Hong Kongston, *American Book Review*, January 1990.

Review of *The Fast Men* by Tom McNab, *Los Angeles Times Book Review*, May 1988, and *American Indian Quarterly*, 1990.

Review of *Tripmaster Monkey* by Maxine Hong Kingston, *Los Angeles Times Book Review*, front page review, April 23, 1989.

Review of *The Fencepost Chronicles* by W. P. Kinsella, *Los Angeles Times Book Review*, December 20, 1987.

Acknowledgements continued from page iv

published in *Genre*, The University of Oklahoma. "The Tragic Wisdom of Salamanders" is reprinted from *Sacred Trust*, edited by Michael Katakis, Mercury House. "Reversal of Fortunes" was first published in *Caliban*. "Crossbloods" is the introduction to *Crossbloods: Bone Courts, Bingo, and Other Reports*. Copyright © 1976 and 1990 by Gerald Vizenor. University of Minnesota Press. "Sand Creek Survivors" is reprinted from *Earthdivers: Tribal Narratives on Mixed Descent*. Copyright © 1981 by Gerald Vizenor. University of Minnesota Press. "Terminal Creeds" and "Shadows at La Pointe" are reprinted from *The People Named the Chippewa*. Copyright © 1984 by Gerald Vizenor. University of Minnesota Press.

The screen play *Harold of Orange* won the Film-in-the-Cities national screenwriting competition, in connection with the Robert Redford Film Institute, in 1983. The film *Harold of Orange* was released in 1984.

UNIVERSITY PRESS OF NEW ENGLAND publishes books under its own imprint and is the publisher for Brandeis University Press, Brown University Press, University of Connecticut, Dartmouth College, Middlebury College Press, University of New Hampshire, University of Rhode Island, Tufts University, University of Vermont, Wesleyan University Press, and Salzburg Seminar.

GERALD VIZENOR is Professor of Native American Literature at the University of California, Berkeley. His recent books are *Manifest Manners* (1994), *Dead Voices* (1992), *The Heirs of Columbus* (1991), *Landfill Meditation: Crossblood Stories* (1991), *Crossbloods: Bone Courts, Bingo, and Other Reports* (1990), and *Interior Landscapes* (1990). His *Griever: An American Monkey King in China* won the 1990 American Book Award. He is the series editor of American Indian Literature and Critical Studies, University of Oklahoma Press.

A. ROBERT LEE is Reader in American Literature at the University of Kent at Canterbury, England, and has taught at the University of California, Berkeley, and other American universities. His publications include eleven volumes in the Vision Critical Series, Everyman editions of Melville, *A Permanent Etcetera: Cross-Cultural Perspectives on Postwar America*, and a wide range of essays on ethnic American literature.

Library of Congress Cataloging-in-Publication Data

Vizenor, Gerald Robert, 1934–
    Shadow distance : a Gerald Vizenor reader / Gerald Vizenor.
    p. cm.
    Includes bibliographical references.
    ISBN 0–8195–5277–1 (cloth). — ISBN 0–8195–6281–5 (pa)
    I. Title.
PS3572.I9A6   1994
813'.54—dc20   94–15403
∞